CREAM OF THE CROP

"Pronzini has quietly established a reputation as a master of the modern mystery."
—*Publishers Weekly*

"Pronzini's energy seems undiminished and his cool intelligence as appealing as ever."
—*Kirkus Reviews*

"Filled with mayhem and murder."
—Amazon reader

"A skilled writer working at the top of his ability."
—*Denver Post*

"Pronzini is a magnificent entertainer of the first rank."
—Ed Gorman

"Pronzini never disappoints."
—*GoodReads*

"Buy him, read him, and relax."
—*Los Angeles Times*

CREAM OF THE CROP: BEST MYSTERY & SUSPENSE STORIES OF BILL PRONZINI

Stark House Press • Eureka California

REAM OF THE CROP: BEST MYSTERY & SUSPENSE STORIES OF BILL PRONZINI

Published by Stark House Press
1315 H Street
Eureka, CA 95501, USA
griffinskye3@sbcglobal.net
www.starkhousepress.com

CREAM OF THE CROP
Copyright © 2024 by Bill Pronzini. (See Acknowledgements for original copyright information.)

Published by arrangement with the author. All rights reserved under International and Pan-American Copyright Conventions.

ISBN: 979-8-88601-099-2

Cover and text design by Mark Shepard, shepgraphics.com

PUBLISHER'S NOTE
This is a work of fiction. Names, characters, places and incidents are either the products of the author's imagination or used fictionally, and any resemblance to actual persons, living or dead, events or locales, is entirely coincidental.

Without limiting the rights under copyright reserved above, no part of this publication may be reproduced, stored, or introduced into a retrieval system or transmitted in any form or by any means (electronic, mechanical, photocopying, recording or otherwise) without the prior written permission of both the copyright owner and the above publisher of the book.

First Stark House Press Edition: August 2024

ACKNOWLEDGMENTS

"Opportunity," "Smuggler's Island," "Thin Air". Copyright © 1967, 1977. 1979, 2001 by Bill Pronzini. First published in *Alfred Hitchcock's Mystery Magazine.*

"Proof of Guilt," "Sweet Fever," "Under the Skin," "Strangers in the Fog," "A Craving for Originality," "Liar's Dice," "Out of the Depths," "Home is the Place Where," "Gunpowder Alley," "The Cemetery Man," "Hooch," "Snap," "Goodbye, Ms. Damico," "Who You Been Grapplin' With?". Copyright © 1973, 1976, 1977, 1978, 1979, 1992, 1994, 1995, 2013, 2014, 2015, 2019, 2023 by Bill Pronzini. First published in *Ellery Queen's Mystery Magazine.*

"Stacked Deck." Copyright © 1987 by Bill Pronzini. First published in *New Black Mask.*

"Possibilities." Copyright © 2006 by Bill Pronzini. First published in *The Strand Magazine.*

"Cat's-Paw." Copyright © 1983 by Bill Pronzini. First published in a Waves Press limited edition.

"Skeleton Rattle Your Mouldy Leg." Copyright © 1984 by Bill Pronzini. First published in *The Eyes Have It.*

"Incident in a Neighborhood Tavern." Copyright © 1988 by Bill Pronzini. First published in *An Eye for Justice.*

"Stakeout." Copyright © 1990 by Bill Pronzini. First published in *Justice for Hire.*

"Souls Burning." Copyright © 1991 by Bill Pronzini. First published in *New Crimes 3.*

"La Bellezza delle Bellezze." Copyright © 1991 by Bill Pronzini. First published in *Invitation to Murder.*

"The Big Bite." Copyright © 2000 by Bill Pronzini. First published in *The Shamus Game.*

Preface 9

Standalones
   Opportunity (1967) 13
   Proof of Guilt (1973) 24
   Sweet Fever (1976) 33
   Smuggler's Island (1977) 38
   Under the Skin (1977) 53
   Strangers in the Fog (1978) 58
   A Craving for Originality (1979) 66
   Stacked Deck (1987) 75
   Liar's Dice (1992) 95
   Out of the Depths (1994) 102
   Possibilities (2006) 117
   The Cemetery Man (2013) 131
   Hooch (2014) 139
   Snap (2015) 147
   Goodbye, Ms. Damico (2023) 162

Carpenter & Quincannon
   Gunpowder Alley (2012) 173

Nameless Detective
   Thin Air (1979) 197
   Cat's-Paw (1983) 214
   Skeleton Rattle Your Mouldy Leg (1984) 233
   Incident in a Neighborhood Tavern (1988) 256
   Stakeout (1990) 263
   Souls Burning (1991) 274
   La Bellezza delle Bellezze (1991) 281
   Home is the Place Where (1995) 305
   The Big Bite (2000) 313
   Who You Been Grapplin' With? (2014) 326

PREFACE

Choosing the stories for inclusion in this volume was a relatively easy task. All the selections are personal favorites for one reason or another. They are the most accomplished and original stories I was capable of producing at the time each was written, and the older ones have stood the test of time well.

This is purely a subjective opinion, of course. If an individual familiar (or unfamiliar) with my work were to undertake the unenviable job of reading or rereading the upwards of 300 mystery and suspense stories I've published over the past half-century, their final choices would surely be somewhat different. But I probably wouldn't agree with at least some of them. Who better knows an author's work, after all, than the author himself?

The selections here span a broad range of topics, themes, settings, and types of crime fiction (detective, impossible crime, dark suspense, etc.). Some are grim, some upbeat, some wryly humorous; no two are alike. The one unifying factor in all 26 is that they're character-driven. People good and bad, who they are and what makes them act and react the way they do, are the core ingredient of any successful piece of fiction.

The standalone stories cover the entire length of my career. "Opportunity" was my first story of any quality and my first sale to *Alfred Hitchcock's Mystery Magazine*; "Goodbye, Ms. Damico," the most recent of more than 60 appearances in *Ellery Queen's Mystery Magazine*, was published last year. Several have been honored by peers: "Strangers in the Fog" received a Best Short Story nomination from the Mystery Writers of America, and others were included in "best of the year" anthologies. "Proof of Guilt" (incidentally my first sale to EQMM) was adapted for an episode of the British TV series *Tales of the Unexpected*. "Liar's Dice" was the basis for a 1995 made-for-U.S. TV film.

Carpenter & Quincannon, an 1890s detective duo, are the protagonists of nine novels, five in collaboration with my wife Marcia Muller, and numerous stories. "Gunpowder Alley" is the cream of the shorts featuring them. It, too, was a "best of the year" anthology selection.

The Nameless Detective entries require a bit of commentary. The character was "born" in a short story in 1968; the first novel to feature him, *The Snatch,* was published three years later. The series lasted far longer than I could have hoped it would, an aggregate of 41 novels, three collections, and several uncollected stories published from 1968 to 2017. He was nameless not by choice but because I couldn't think of a name that suited him, the primary reason being that in essence he's my alter ego – we have the same likes and dislikes, the same opinions, biases, vulnerabilities – and it would have been like renaming myself. I finally admitted to this in print in the later books by having other characters refer to him as Bill.

At the outset of his career he was a pulp magazine-collecting lone wolf detective, with a one-man agency and a cop friend named Eberhardt. As the series progressed I sought to keep it fresh by incorporating a variety of changes in his personal and professional life. I had Eberhardt leave police work and become his partner for a time. Gave him a love interest: Kerry Wade, the daughter of two pulp writers, whom he ultimately marries. Disposed of Eberhardt for characterological reasons and replaced him with a young assistant, Tamara Corbin, hired for her computer skills, who eventually becomes his new partner. There are other changes as well, but the aforementioned are noteworthy because of the chronology of the ten stories collected here.

These ten, published between 1979 and 2014, are the high points among the two dozen or so of Nameless's short cases. As with some of the standalones, they've also had their share of accolades. "Cat's-Paw" was the recipient of a Private Eye Writers Best Short Story Shamus Award. "Incident in a Neighborhood Tavern" was another MWA Best Short Story nominee. Five were "best of the year" selections.

Writing each of these 26 "entertainments," as Graham Greene labeled his crime fiction, gave me a good deal of pleasure. May reading (or rereading) them provide some of the same pleasure.

Petaluma, CA
October 2023

STANDALONES

OPPORTUNITY

Coretti and I went to check the thing out.

The call had come in to the captain of detectives at eight thirty-five from an occasionally reliable department informant named Scully. We were logging reports in the squad room when the word came down. It had been a quiet night, like you can get in early winter, the sound of the wind and a thin rain snapping at the windows, and none of us relished the thought of leaving the warmth of the squad room. So we matched coins with the two other teams of inspectors on the four-to-midnight swing to see who would take the squeal. Coretti and I lost.

It didn't sound like much, but then you never know. A parlor collector for a string of bookie joints in Southern California had vanished with a substantial amount of weekend receipts. Scully didn't know how much, but since the betting had been unusually heavy at Caliente on Saturday his guess was six figures. Scully's tip, uncorroborated and filtering north on the grapevine, was that this Feldstein had beat it to San Francisco and gone into hiding in a tenement hotel near Hunters Point. The captain thought we ought to run a check.

Coretti and I rode the elevator down to the garage in the basement of the Hall of Justice and signed a check-out slip for an unmarked sedan. We drove out into the frigid, drizzling San Francisco night. The hotel Scully had named was off Third Street, in an area that was primarily industrial. At least it wouldn't be a long ride.

Neither of us had much to say. We'd been partners a long time and we didn't need a lot of conversation. The heater in the sedan made labored whirring sounds and threw nothing but cold air against our feet.

Coretti picked up Third at Townsend, followed it out over China Basin. I lit a cigarette as we passed over the bridge, and as soon as I exhaled smoke the pain in my stomach almost doubled me over on the seat. I jammed my hand under my breastbone and held it there, waiting for the sharpness of the seizure to subside so I could breathe again.

"Arne," Coretti said, "you all right?"

I fumbled out the bottle of prescription painkiller, swallowed some of it. It was strong stuff and it worked quickly. Pretty soon I said, "Yeah. Okay now."

"The ulcer again?"

"What else," I said.

"You take that medicine like it was candy. Doesn't seem to be helping much."

"It's mostly for the pain. Doc says I've got to have an operation. He's afraid the thing will rupture."

"So when you going in, Arne?"

"I'm not."

He gave me a sharp look. "Why not? Man, a perforated ulcer can kill you."

"I can't afford an operation right now. I'm up to my ass in bills. You've got a family, Bob. You know how it is."

"Yeah, I know how it is."

"Maybe next summer," I said. "The car loan'll be paid off then."

"Does the captain know how bad the ulcer is?"

"No, and don't you tell him. I haven't even told my wife yet."

"You can't keep it a secret, Arne," Coretti said. "Some of the boys are beginning to notice these spasms you get. Captain's bound to find out. It'd be a lot easier if you told him yourself."

"You know as well as I do what it means if I tell him—disability. I can barely live on what I make now, Bob. How can I live on disability pay?"

"Just the same, you can't keep on this way. You look worn out. If you won't go in for the operation, why not take some time off at least? You've got sick leave coming."

"Maybe you're right. I could use a rest."

"Sure I'm right," Coretti said. "And if I were you, I'd do some serious thinking about that operation. Talk it over with Gerry, too."

"Some R&R is all I need for now. I'll tell Gerry when the time comes."

"When you can't put the operation off any longer, you mean."

"Let's just drop the subject, okay? I don't feel like talking anymore right now."

It had begun to rain in earnest now. Coretti put the wipers on high. The bitter cold wind blowing in across the Bay whipped sheets of water across the windshield, and you could hear it howling at the windows of the sedan. I sat with my legs straight out in front of me to ease the gnawing in my stomach. I wished I were home in bed with Gerry's warm little body against my back.

Coretti made a left-hand turn, drove two blocks, made another turn. The hotel stood between a storage warehouse for an interstate truck line and an iron foundry, midway on the block. It was a three-story wooden affair, well over half a century old—a shambling reminder of another era. A narrow alley separated it from the iron foundry on the right.

We left the sedan's semi-warmth and hurried inside. The rain was like ice on the back of my neck. The lobby stank of age—must and disinfectant, the smell of death wrapped in formaldehyde. It was small, dark, sparsely furnished; no elevator, just a staircase leading to the upper floors. A desk paralleled the wall on the right. No one was behind it.

"Nice place," Coretti said, glancing around. "Homey, you know?"

From behind a closed door next to the desk came the sounds of a TV, the volume turned up high. We went over there and I knocked and pretty soon a rheumy-looking old character in a T-shirt and baggy trousers held up by three-inch-wide suspenders peered out at us.

"You the night clerk?" I asked him.

"Yep. Night clerk, night manager, handyman." He peered harder. "You fellas looking for a room? If you are, I got to tell you we—"

"Police," I said. We showed him our shields. "Inspectors Kelstrom and Coretti. We're here about one of your tenants."

"That so? Which one?"

"The man's name is Feldstein, but I doubt he'd be using it."

"Feldstein?" The old man shook his head. "Nope, no one here by that name. Only a few of the rooms occupied now. We're closing up month after next. Building's being torn down."

"Is that right?"

"Yep. Don't know what I'm gonna do then. Retire, maybe, if I can find a place to live on my lousy pension." Noise erupted from the TV behind him. He cocked an ear, listened until the noise subsided. "I been watching the fights," he said. "Heavyweight match tonight. Not much of a scrap, though. They don't put on a show like they used to. You fellas fight fans?"

"No," I said. I wished I had some coffee, and to hell with what the doctor had said. It was damn cold in this rat trap. "These few tenants of yours. Any of them new, here just a couple of days?"

"Matter of fact, there is one fella. Day clerk didn't want to rent to him, on account of us closing up pretty soon, but he paid extra. Wish it'd been me on duty got that little bonus." He sighed. "Name's Collins. I only seen him once. Stays in his room, mostly."

"What does he look like?"

"Little guy, kind of skinny. Has a mole or something on his left cheek."

Coretti and I exchanged a glance. The description matched Feldstein's.

"He in his room now?" Coretti asked.

"Far as I know."

"What's his room number?"

"Three-o-six." The old man did some more peering. "There ain't going to be any trouble, is there?"

"Let's hope not," I said. "You just stay in your room and watch the rest of the fights."

"Sure. Sure thing, Inspector."

We left him and took the stairs up to the third floor. The hallway was lit only by a pale bulb on the wall at the far end. No sounds came from behind any of the closed doors we passed. When we reached 306, I stood against the wall on one side of the door and Coretti did the same on the other. Then I reached out and rapped sharply on the panel.

Inside, there was a faint creaking of bedsprings, then nothing but silence. I knocked again. Nothing. I felt the tiny hairs on my neck lift and my stomach started to ache. The cold, stale air seemed suddenly charged with tension.

We had our service revolvers drawn when a wary voice said from inside, "Who is it?"

"Night clerk," I said.

I thought it was a passable imitation of the old man's voice, but it wasn't. The slugs came fast, three of them, ripping jagged splinters from the wood and gouging plaster from the opposite wall. The reports seemed to echo for a couple of seconds. Then it was quiet again.

Coretti and I hugged the wall, waiting. After a little time I heard a faint scraping sound, another that I had no trouble identifying. Feldstein was trying to get out the window.

I stepped back to get leverage, moved over in front of the door and slammed my foot against the wood just above the knob. The lock ripped loose and the door banged against the inner wall. I went in low and to the left, Coretti right behind me. Feldstein was at the window, one leg over the sill, a pasteboard suitcase in one hand and a snubnosed revolver in the other. I threw myself to the floor as he fired, spoiling the shot I had at him. The bullet missed both of us. Coretti squeezed off in return, dodging, but he missed, too. In the next second Feldstein was out through the window and on the fire escape, a dim shadow in the rain.

I pulled up onto my knees, snapped a quick shot that shattered the window glass. Another miss. I heard the fugitive's heavy shoes pounding down the fire escape as I gained my feet. Coretti had gotten tangled up in a chair, I saw then. I yelled at him, "Downstairs, Bob! Cut him off in the alley!"

I ran to the window and got my head out. Not a smart move because Feldstein was directly below, with a clear upward slant. His first slug tore a hole in the window frame a few inches above my head, the second screamed off the railing in front of me and sprayed my face with iron filings.

Feldstein didn't wait to try a third shot. I could hear him running again. Cursing myself for a fool, the pain like a hot iron in my gut, I heaved myself through the window and crouched on the slats. He was at the second floor level now, scrambling down the rain-slick steps. I steadied my weapon and fired low, trying for his legs. That shot missed wide, but the next took him in the hip or thigh. I saw him buckle. He lost his grip on the suitcase and his arms flailed as he staggered sideways. He banged hard into the railing. The bar caught him just below the waist and pitched him over. I heard him scream once, just once, then the thud of his body slamming the alley floor below.

I straightened slowly, wiping sweat and rain off my face. Coretti was coming up the alley, running. I looked to see if anyone was behind him, roused by the gunfire, but there was no one.

The fire escape was one of the old-fashioned types that ended flush with the pavement. That made it easy for me to get down there in a hurry. Coretti was bent over Feldstein by then. I started toward him, and all of a sudden I couldn't seem to get any air into my lungs. A tongue of fire licked down from my stomach to my groin. I dropped to one knee, my head hanging down, fighting to breathe.

"Arne, you hit?" Coretti was beside me now, one hand on my shoulder.

"No. Ulcer . . . medicine . . ."

He found the bottle in my coat pocket, uncapped it, got some of the painkiller into me. It seemed to take a long time for it to work. When the hurt finally subsided and I could get my breath, he helped me to my feet.

"You okay now?"

"Better. Just give me a minute."

"Maybe I ought to call the paramedics . . ."

"No. I'm okay I tell you." The pain was almost completely gone. I sucked in some of the damp air, looking over to where

Feldstein lay. "What about him?"

"Dead. Broken neck."

"We've got to radio in."

"Better get the suitcase first. Can you climb back up the stairs?"

I said I could, but I leaned on Coretti on the way up. I was pretty shaky, all right. At the second floor level, the pasteboard suitcase lay against the wire mesh of the railing. Coretti picked it up. When we reached the third floor and climbed back into Feldstein's room, I was oozing sweat.

Coretti laid the suitcase on the bed. I said, "Open it up, let's have a look." He nodded, flipped the catches, lifted the lid.

The suitcase was jammed full of money—fifties and hundreds in thick bundles. Plain wrappers with numbers written on them in pencil bound each stack. We stood there looking down at them, neither of us saying anything. The stench of cordite still lingered in the air.

I could feel tension rebuilding. Outside, the rain hammered in a steady cadence on the fire escape. The wind coming through the shattered window felt icy. In the hallway somebody coughed, somebody else said something in a low nervous voice. Other tenants. But they were hanging back, too scared to look in here. Coretti went over and yelled at them to get back in their rooms, then closed the door.

When he returned to the bed he said softly, "How much you think is in there, Arne?"

"I don't know."

Coretti began to take the bundles out of the suitcase, putting them on the bed. I didn't try to stop him. "If the numbers on those wrappers are right," he said when he was done, "there's a hundred and twelve thousand here. A hundred and twelve thousand dollars, Arne." His voice had a funny sound to it.

My throat was dry. I hadn't thought about the money before. A routine assignment, stolen cash, a thief in hiding—it happens every day, it's just a part of the job. But now, looking down at the bundles on the bed, the money took on weight, substance. It filled my thoughts. I kept staring at it, transfixed by it, more money than I would ever see again in my lifetime, and I was thinking what it would be like to have that much cash, half that much, enough to pay off the bulk of my debts, enough for the operation, enough so Gerry and I could start living decently.

It could be ours, it could be ours so damned easy. No one would ever know, we could tell them we didn't find any money here, it was dirty money anyway. It could be ours, one hundred and twelve thousand dollars, fifty-six thousand apiece . . .

My stomach throbbed again. I could hear my heart pounding. I was still sweating, sweating like a pig in this cold room.

"Arne?" Coretti's voice was almost a whisper.

I swallowed against the dryness in my throat. I didn't say anything.

"You're thinking it, too, aren't you."

"Yeah," I said, "I'm thinking it, too."

"We could do it, Arne."

"I don't know. Maybe, but . . . I don't know."

"We could do it," Coretti said again.

"In fifteen years I've never taken a penny. Never even fixed a parking ticket."

"Neither have I. But this isn't a piece of small-time graft, this is a hundred and twelve thousand dollars. A chance like this comes once in a lifetime. Just once."

"I know that, dammit."

He licked his lips. "Well?"

The windblown rain was coming down harder now. I could feel the chill wetness against my face. "It's a hell of a big risk. You know what'd happen if we got caught."

"Sure I know. But I say it's worth it. I say we won't get caught."

"If we claim there wasn't any money, the captain'll be suspicious."

"Let him be. What could he prove?"

"The day clerk probably saw the suitcase when Feldstein checked in."

"So we leave the suitcase. We can carry all the money in our pockets, under our coats."

"There'd still be an investigation."

"What could he *prove*, Arne?"

"As soon as we started spending the money they'd know."

"A little at a time," Coretti said. "That's what we do, parcel it out a little at a time. It's gambling money, there's no way the bills can be traced."

"Christ, Bob, you've been a cop as long as I have. It's the little things that trip you up, the unforeseen things. You know that as well as I do."

Coretti tongued his lips again.

"We'd go to prison," I said. "Think about your family. What becomes of them if that happens?"

"I am thinking about my family. I'm thinking about all the

things I want my wife and kids to have that I can't give them. That's all I'm thinking about right now."

I kept looking at the money, and thinking, the way Coretti was, about the piled-up bills and the secondhand furniture and car and the second-rate clothing and all the doing without and the burning, throbbing thing that was eating a hole in the pit of my stomach. But at the same time I was thinking about the fifteen years I'd been a straight arrow, an honest cop, and the convictions a man has, the pattern of life he sets for himself, and what would happen if he were to sacrifice everything he believed in for one big gamble, one grab for the brass ring. Even if we got away with it, I knew that it would prey on my conscience, eat a hole in me bigger than the one in my gut and eventually destroy me.

I closed my eyes, and I saw Gerry's face, Gerry's proud smile, and I took a deep breath and opened my eyes and I said to Coretti, "No. I can't do it, I won't do it."

"Arne—"

"No, Bob. No."

Quickly, savagely, I began stuffing the bundles of cash back into the suitcase. Coretti grabbed my arm, but I shook it off and kept on refilling the case. When I was done I snapped the catch shut and hefted it and turned to face him.

"I'm going downstairs and report in," I said. "And I'm going to tell them about the money, every dollar of it. That's the way it's going to be, Bob. That's the way it *has* to be."

He didn't say anything. His eyes locked with mine.

"You going to try to stop me?" I said.

A few seconds passed before he said, "No," and stepped aside.

I went out into the hall and down the stairs, feeling the weight of the suitcase in my hand and against my leg, and I didn't look back. The old man was waiting in the lobby, his eyes big and scared behind his glasses. He rattled questions at me, but I shoved past him and went out to the sedan. I locked the suitcase in the trunk, then called the Hall and told them what had happened.

Afterward I sat waiting with the wheezing heater on high. I'd been there five minutes when Coretti showed. He walked slowly to the passenger side and got in without looking at me. Both of us just sat there. The silence was as deep as it had been in the room upstairs.

He broke it by asking, "Did you report in?"

"Yeah."

Silence again. Then he said, "God help me, I almost shot you up there. When you were putting the money back in the suitcase. I almost pulled my weapon and shot you in the back."

I had nothing to say. What can you say to a thing like that?

"Don't you understand?" Coretti said. "I almost murdered you. You've been my friend and my partner for ten years and I almost blew you away."

"But you didn't," I said finally.

"But I almost did."

"Money like that . . . it can do funny things to a man. Think how we'd be, what we might do, if we'd taken it."

"Maybe you're right. I still think we could've gotten away with it. Now we'll never know. But it scared the hell out of me, what I almost did up there. I thought I knew myself, but now . . ." He shook his head.

"You think it was an easy decision for me, Bob?"

"I know it wasn't. Don't you think I know that?"

"The best thing for both of us is to try to forget it ever happened."

"I don't know if I can," Coretti said.

My hand wasn't steady as I reached into the pocket of my shirt for a cigarette. The pack was crushed and wet. I crumpled it, threw it into the back seat. Wordlessly Coretti extended his pack to me. I took one, and our eyes met again, briefly, then we both looked away.

I lit the cigarette and inhaled deeply, feeling the smoke curl into my lungs. I stared out at the empty street and the falling rain, taking slow drags—and there was a savage tearing sensation under my breastbone, a fiery pain so intense I cried out. Then I couldn't breathe, couldn't move. My vision blurred. The last thing I saw was Coretti reaching out to me. And the last thing I heard was the high, keening wail of sirens slicing through the wet, black night.

I woke up in the hospital. Full of dope, hooked up to machines and an IV. I didn't feel any pain, but my middle was a mass of bandages. A nurse came in, looked at me, went away again. Then my doctor was there. He asked me how I was feeling. I told him groggy and then asked him, "What happened?"

"Exactly what I warned you might happen," he said. "Your ulcer perforated. You're a very lucky man, Mr. Kelstrom. You almost died on the operating table."

"Yeah," I said. "Lucky."

"If you'd listened to me when I first told you you needed an operation, this would not have happened. As it is . . . well, barring complications you should be all right in time."

"In time. What's that mean? How long am I going to be in here?"

"A few weeks. After that, two or three months convalescence at home."

"Weeks? Months?"

"Recovery from a perforated ulcer is a slow process, Mr. Kelstrom."

"I've got a wife and kid. How can I support my family if I'm flat on my back?"

"I'm sorry," the doctor said, "but you really have no one to blame but yourself."

He went away and the nurse came back and gave me some more dope that knocked me out. When I woke up again, Gerry was there holding my hand.

"Oh, Arne," she said, "we almost lost you. Why didn't you tell me how bad the ulcer was? Why didn't you have the operation right away?"

"We couldn't afford it. All the damn bills . . ."

"We could've managed. We'll manage as it is, but . . ." She broke off and looked away. Then she put on a smile and said, "We'll be all right. Don't worry, everything's going to be fine."

I didn't say anything. This time I was the one who looked away.

Later, Coretti and the captain came in. They stood awkwardly, Coretti not making eye contact with me. The whole time he was there he looked at a spot on the wall above my head. The captain said some things about what a good cop I was, how he was putting Coretti and me up for departmental citations. He said I'd get full disability while I was recuperating. He said that if it turned out I couldn't work the field anymore, he'd see to it I had a desk job for as long as I wanted it. He didn't mention the money, but he didn't need to. We all knew that it would be unclaimed and eventually wind up going to the state.

Coretti didn't say a word until they were ready to leave. Then he said to the wall, "Good luck, Arne. Take care of yourself." That was all. After they were gone, I wondered if he'd be back to see me. I didn't think he would. I didn't think I'd be seeing much of him at all anymore.

I lay there and thought about the money. One hundred and twelve thousand dollars divided in two, fifty-six thousand dollars—the one big opportunity that I'd turned my back on. I thought about the fifteen years I'd been an honest, by-the-book cop, and all the bribes and payoffs, all the chances I'd had for some quick and easy cash that would have made my life and Gerry's life easier, all those other opportunities I'd let slip away because of convictions that you couldn't eat and couldn't pay the bills with.

We'll manage, Gerry had said. *Don't worry, everything's going to be fine.*

Well, I wasn't worrying. Not anymore. And everything was going to be fine. Because now I knew with a brand new conviction what I was going to do when I returned to duty.

I knew just exactly what I was going to do.

PROOF OF GUILT

I've been a city cop for thirty-two years now, and during that time I've heard of and been involved in some of the weirdest, most audacious crimes imaginable—on and off public record. But as far as I'm concerned, the murder of an attorney named Adam Chillingham is the damnedest case in my experience, if not in the entire annals of crime.

You think I'm exaggerating? Well, listen to the way it was.

My partner Jack Sherrard and I were in the Detective Squad Room one morning last summer when this call came in from a man named Charles Hearn. He said he was Adam Chillingham's law clerk, and that his employer had just been shot to death; he also said he had the killer trapped in the lawyer's private office.

It seemed like a fairly routine case at that point. Sherrard and I drove out to the Dawes Building, a skyscraper in a new business development on the city's south side, and rode the elevator up to Chillingham's suite of offices on the sixteenth floor. Hearn and a woman named Clarisse Tower, who told us she had been the dead man's secretary, were waiting in the anteroom with two uniformed patrolmen who had arrived minutes earlier.

According to Hearn, a man named George Dillon had made a ten-thirty appointment with Chillingham, had kept it punctually, and had been escorted by the attorney into the private office at that exact time. At ten-forty Hearn thought he heard a muffled explosion from inside the office, but he couldn't be sure because the walls were partially soundproofed.

Hearn got up from his desk in the anteroom and knocked on the door and there was no response; then he tried the knob and found that the door was locked from the inside, Miss Tower confirmed all this, although she said she hadn't heard any sound; her desk was farther away from the office door than was Hearn's.

A couple of minutes later the door had opened and George Dillon had looked out and calmly said that Chillingham had been murdered. He had not tried to leave the office after the announcement; instead, he'd seated himself in a chair near the desk and lighted a cigarette. Hearn satisfied himself that his employer was dead, made a hasty exit, but had the presence of mind to lock the door from the outside by the simple expediency of transferring the key from the inside to the outside—thus sealing Dillon in the office with the body. After which Hearn put in his call to Headquarters.

So Sherrard and I drew our guns, unlocked the door, and burst into the private office. This George Dillon was sitting in the chair across the desk, very casual, both his hands up in plain sight. He gave us a relieved look and said he was glad the police had arrived so quickly.

I went over and looked at the body, which was sprawled on the floor behind the desk; a pair of French windows were open in the wall just beyond, letting in a warm summer breeze. Chillingham had been shot once in the right side of the neck, with what appeared by the size of the wound to have been a small-caliber bullet; there was no exit wound, and there were no powder burns.

I straightened up, glanced around the office, and saw that the only door was the one that we had just come through. There was no balcony or ledge outside the open windows—just a sheer drop of sixteen stories to a parklike, well-landscaped lawn that stretched away for several hundred yards. The nearest building was a hundred yards distant, angled well to the right. Its roof was about on a level with Chillingham's office, it being a lower structure than the Dawes Building; not much of the roof was visible unless you peered out and around.

Sherrard and I then questioned George Dillon—and he claimed he hadn't killed Chillingham. He said the attorney had been standing at the open windows, leaning out a little, and that all of a sudden he had cried out and fallen down with the bullet in his neck. Dillon said he'd taken a look out the windows, hadn't seen anything, checked that Chillingham was dead, then unlocked the door and summoned Hearn and Miss Tower.

When the coroner and the lab crew finally got there, and the doc had made his preliminary examination, I asked him about the wound. He confirmed my earlier guess—a small-caliber bullet, probably a .22 or .25. He couldn't be absolutely sure, of course, until he took out the slug at the post-mortem.

I talked things over with Sherrard and we both agreed that it was pretty much improbable for somebody with a .22 or .25 caliber weapon to have shot Chillingham from the roof of the nearest building; a small caliber like that just doesn't have a range of a hundred yards and the angle was almost too sharp. There was nowhere else the shot could have come from—except from inside the office. And that left us with George Dillon, whose story was obviously false and who just as obviously had killed the attorney while the two of them were locked inside this office.

You'd think it was pretty cut-and-dried then, wouldn't you? You'd think all we had to do was arrest Dillon and charge him with homicide, and our job was finished. Right?

Wrong.

Because we couldn't find the gun.

Remember, now, Dillon had been locked in that office—except for the minute or two it took Hearn to examine the body and slip out and relock the door—from the time Chillingham died until the time we came in. And both Hearn and Miss Tower swore that Dillon hadn't stepped outside the office during that minute or two. We'd already searched Dillon and he had nothing on him. We searched the office—I mean, we *searched* that office—and there was no gun there.

We sent officers over to the roof of the nearest building and down onto the landscaped lawn; they went over every square inch of ground and rooftop, and they didn't find anything. Dillon hadn't thrown the gun out the open windows then, and there was no place on the face of the sheer wall of the building where a gun could have been hidden.

So where was the murder weapon? What had Dillon done with it? Unless we found that out, we had no evidence against him that would stand up in a court of law; his word that he *hadn't* killed Chillingham, despite the circumstantial evidence of the locked room, was as good as money in the bank. It was up to us to prove him guilty, not up to him to prove himself innocent. You see the problem?

We took him into a large book-filled room that was part of the Chillingham suite—what Hearn called the "archives"—and sat him down in a chair and began to question him extensively. He was a big husky guy with blondish hair and these perfectly guileless eyes; he just sat there and looked at us and answered in a polite voice, maintaining right along that he hadn't killed the lawyer.

We made him tell his story of what had happened in the office a dozen times, and he explained it the same way each time—no variations. Chillingham had locked the door after they entered, and then they sat down and talked over some business. Pretty soon Chillingham complained that it was stuffy in the room, got up, and opened the French windows; the next thing Dillon knew, he said, the attorney collapsed with the bullet in him. He hadn't heard any shot, he said; Hearn must be mistaken about a muffled explosion.

I said finally, "All right, Dillon, suppose you tell us why you came to see Chillingham. What was this business you discussed?"

"He was my father's lawyer," Dillon said, "and the executor of my father's estate. He was also a thief. He stole three hundred and fifty thousand dollars of my father's money."

Sherrard and I stared at him. Jack said, "That gives you one hell of a motive for murder, if it's true."

"It's true," Dillon said flatly. "And yes, I suppose it does give me a strong motive for killing him. I admit I hated the man, I hated him passionately."

"You admit that, do you?"

"Why not? I have nothing to hide."

"What did you expect to gain by coming here to see Chillingham?" I asked. "Assuming you didn't come here to kill him."

"I wanted to tell him I knew what he'd done, and that I was going to expose him for the thief he was."

"You tell him that?"

"I was leading up to it when he was shot."

"Suppose you go into a little more detail about this alleged theft from your father's estate."

"All right." Dillon lit a cigarette. "My father was a hard-nosed businessman, a self-made type who acquired a considerable fortune in textiles; as far as he was concerned, all of life revolved around money. But I've never seen it that way; I've always been something of a free spirit and to hell with negotiable assets. Inevitably, my father and I had a falling-out about fifteen years ago, when I was twenty-three, and I left home with the idea of seeing some of the big wide world—which is exactly what I did.

"I traveled from one end of this country to the other, working at different jobs, and then I went to South America for a while. Some of the wanderlust finally began to wear off, and I decided to come back to this city and settle down—maybe even patch things up with my father. I arrived several days ago and learned then that he had been dead for more than two years."

"You had no contact with your father during the fifteen years you were drifting around?"

"None whatsoever. I told you, we had a falling-out. And we'd never been close to begin with."

Sherrard asked, "So what made you suspect Chillingham had stolen money from your father's estate?"

"I am the only surviving member of the Dillon family; there

are no other relatives, not even a distant cousin. I knew my father wouldn't have left me a cent, not after all these years, and I didn't particularly care; but I *was* curious to find out to whom he had willed his estate."

"And what did you find out?"

"Well, I happen to know that my father had three favorite charities," Dillon said. "Before I left, he used to tell me that if I didn't 'shape-up,' as he put it, he would leave every cent of his money to those three institutions."

"He didn't, is that it?"

"Not exactly. According to the will, he left two hundred thousand dollars to each of two of them—the Cancer Society and the Children's Hospital. He also, according to the will, left three hundred and fifty thousand dollars to the Association for Medical Research."

"All right," Sherrard said, "so what does that have to do with Chillingham?"

"Everything," Dillon told him. "My father died of a heart attack—he'd had a heart condition for many years. Not severe, but he fully expected to die as a result of it one day. And so he did. And because of this heart condition, his third favorite charity—the one he felt the most strongly about—was the Heart Fund."

"Go on," I said, frowning.

Dillon put out his cigarette and gave me a humorless smile. "I looked into the Association for Medical Research and I did quite a thorough bit of checking. It doesn't exist; there *isn't* any Association for Medical Research. And the only person who could have invented it is or was my father's lawyer and executor, Adam Chillingham."

Sherrard and I thought that over and came to the same conclusion. I said, "So even though you never got along with your father, and you don't care about money for yourself, you decided to expose Chillingham."

"That's right. My father worked hard all his life to build his fortune, and admirably enough, he decided to give it to charity at his death. I believe in worthwhile causes, I believe in the work being done by the Heart Fund, and it sent me into a rage to realize they had been cheated out of a substantial fortune that could have gone toward valuable research."

"A murderous rage?" Sherrard asked softly.

Dillon showed us his humorless smile again. "I didn't kill Adam Chillingham," he said. "But you'll have to admit, he deserved killing—and that the world is better off without the likes of him."

I might have admitted that to myself, if Dillon's accusations were valid, but I didn't admit it to Dillon. I'm a cop, and my job is to uphold the law; murder is murder, whatever the reasons for it, and it can't be gotten away with.

Sherrard and I hammered at Dillon a while longer, but we couldn't shake him at all. I left Jack to continue the field questioning and took a couple of men and re-searched Chillingham's private office. No gun. I went up onto the roof of the nearest building and searched that personally. No gun. I took my men down into the lawn area and supervised another minute search. No gun.

I went back to Chillingham's suite and talked to Charles Hearn and Miss Tower again, and they had nothing to add to what they'd already told us; Hearn was "almost positive" he had heard a muffled explosion inside the office, but from the legal point of view, that was the same as not having heard anything at all.

We took Dillon down to Headquarters finally, because we knew damned well he had killed Adam Chillingham, and advised him of his rights and printed him and booked him on suspicion. He asked for counsel, and we called a public defender for him, and then we grilled him again in earnest. It got us nowhere.

The F.B.I. and state check we ran on his fingerprints got us nowhere either; he wasn't wanted, he had never been arrested, he had never even been printed before. Unless something turned up soon in the way of evidence—specifically, the missing murder weapon—we knew we couldn't hold him very long.

The next day I received the lab report and the coroner's report, and the ballistics report on the bullet taken from Chillingham's neck—.22 caliber, all right. The lab's and coroner's findings combined to tell me something I'd already guessed: the wound and the calculated angle of trajectory of the bullet did not entirely rule out the remote possibility that Chillingham had been shot from the roof of the nearest building. The ballistics report, however, told me something I hadn't guessed—something that surprised me a little.

The bullet had no rifling marks.

Sherrard blinked at this when I related the information to him.

"No rifling marks?" he said. "Hell, that means the slug wasn't fired from a gun at all, at least not a lawfully manufactured one. A homemade weapon, you think, Walt?"

"That's how it figures," I agreed. "A kind of zipgun probably. Anybody can make one; all you need is a length of tubing or the like and a bullet and a grip of some sort and a detonating cap."

"But there was no zipgun, either, in or around Chillingham's office. We'd have found it if there was."

I worried my lower lip meditatively. "Well, you can make one of those zips from a dozen or more small component parts, you know; even the tubing could be soft aluminum, the kind you can break apart with your hands. When you're done using it, you can knock it down again into its components. Dillon had enough time to have done that, before opening the locked door."

"Sure," Sherrard said. "But then what? We *still* didn't find anything—not a single thing—that could have been used as part of a homemade zip."

I suggested we go back and make another search, and so we drove once more to the Dawes Building. We re-combed Chillingham's private office—we'd had a police seal on it to make sure nothing could be disturbed—and we re-combed the surrounding area. We didn't find so much as an iron filing. Then we went to the city jail and had another talk with George Dillon.

When I told him our zipgun theory, I thought I saw a light flicker in his eyes; but it was the briefest of reactions, and I couldn't be sure. We told him it was highly unlikely a zipgun using a .22-caliber bullet could kill anybody from a distance of a hundred yards, and he said he couldn't help that, *he* didn't know anything about such a weapon. Further questioning got us nowhere.

And the following day we were forced to release him, with a warning not to leave the city.

But Sherrard and I continued to work doggedly on the case; it was one of those cases that preys on your mind constantly, keeps you from sleeping well at night, because you know there has to be an answer and you just can't figure out what it is. We ran checks into Chillingham's records and found that he had made some large private investments a year ago, right after the Dillon will had been probated. And as George Dillon had claimed, there was no Association for Medical Research; it was a dummy charity, apparently set up by Chillingham for the explicit purpose of stealing old man Dillon's $350,000. But there was no definite proof of this, not enough to have convicted Chillingham of theft in a court of law; he'd covered himself pretty neatly.

As an intelligent man, George Dillon had no doubt realized

that a public exposure of Chillingham would have resulted in nothing more than adverse publicity and the slim possibility of disbarment—hardly sufficient punishment in Dillon's eyes. So he had decided on what to him was a morally justifiable homicide. From the law's point of view, however, it was nonetheless Murder One.

But the law still had no idea what he'd done with the weapon, and therefore, as in the case of Chillingham's theft, the law had no proof of guilt.

As I said, though, we had our teeth into this one and we weren't about to let go. So we paid another call on Dillon, this time at the hotel where he was staying, and asked him some questions about his background. There was nothing more immediate we could investigate, and we thought that maybe there was an angle in his past that would give us a clue toward solving the riddle.

He told us, readily enough, some of what he'd done during the fifteen years since he'd left home, and it was a typical drifter's life: lobster packer in Maine, ranch hand in Montana, oil worker in Texas, road construction in South America. But there was a gap of about four years that he sort of skimmed over without saying anything specific. I jumped on that and asked him some direct questions, but he wouldn't talk about it.

His reluctance made Sherrard and me more than a little curious; we both had that cop's feeling it was important, that maybe it was the key we needed to unlock the mystery. We took the mug shots we'd made of Dillon and sent them out, along with a request for information as to his whereabouts during the four blank years, to various law-enforcement agencies in Florida—where he'd admitted to being just prior to the gap, working as a deckhand on a Key West charter-fishing boat.

Time dragged on, and nothing turned up, and we were reluctantly forced by sheer volume of other work to abandon the Chillingham case; officially, it was now buried in the Unsolved File. Then, three months later, we had a wire from the Chief of Police of a town not far from Fort Lauderdale. It said they had tentatively identified George Dillon from the pictures we'd sent and were forwarding by airmail special delivery something that might conceivably prove the nature of Dillon's activities during at least part of the specified period.

Sherrard and I fidgeted around waiting for the special delivery to arrive, and when it finally came I happened to be the only one of us in the squad room. I tore the envelope open, and what was inside was a multicolored and well-aged poster, with a picture of a man who was undeniably George Dillon depicted on it. I looked at the picture and read what was written on the poster at least a dozen times.

It told me a lot of things all right, that poster did. It told me exactly what Dillon had done with the homemade zipgun he had used to kill Adam Chillingham—an answer that was at once fantastic and yet so simple you'd never ever consider it. And it told me there wasn't a damned thing we could do about it now, that we couldn't touch him, that George Dillon actually had committed a perfect murder.

I was brooding over this when Jack Sherrard returned to the squad room. He said, "Why so glum, Walt?"

"The special delivery from Florida finally showed up," I said, and watched instant excitement animate his face. Then I saw most of it fade while I told him what I'd been brooding about, finishing with, "We simply can't arrest him now, Jack. There's no evidence, it doesn't exist any more; we can't prove a thing. And maybe it's just as well in one respect, since I kind of liked Dillon and would have hated to see him convicted for killing a crook like Chillingham. Anyway, we'll be able to sleep nights now."

"Damn it, Walt, will you tell me what you're talking about!"

"All right. Remember when we got the ballistics report and we talked over how easy it would be for Dillon to have made a zipgun? And how he could make the whole thing out of a dozen or so small component parts, so that afterward he could break it down again into those small parts?"

"Sure, sure. But I still don't care if Dillon used a hundred components, we didn't find a single one of them. Not one. So what, if that's part of the answer, did he do with them? There's not even a connecting bathroom where he could have flushed them down. What did he do with the damned zipgun?"

I sighed and slid the poster—the old carnival side-show poster—around on my desk so he could see Dillon's picture and read the words printed below it: STEAK AND POTATOES AND APPLE PIE IS OUR DISH; NUTS, BOLTS, PIECES OF WOOD, BITS OF METAL IS HIS! YOU HAVE TO SEE IT TO BELIEVE IT: THE AMAZING MR. GEORGE, THE MAN WITH THE CAST-IRON STOMACH.

Sherrard's head jerked up and he stared at me open-mouthed.

"That's right," I said wearily. "He *ate* it."

SWEET FEVER

Quarter before midnight, like on every evening except the Sabbath or when it's storming or when my rheumatism gets to paining too bad, me and Billy Bob went down to the Chigger Mountain railroad tunnel to wait for the night freight from St. Louis. This here was a fine summer evening, with a big old fat yellow moon hung above the pines on Hankers Ridge and mockingbirds and cicadas and toads making a soft ruckus. Nights like this, I have me a good feeling, hopeful, and I know Billy Bob does too.

They's a bog hollow on the near side of the tunnel opening, and beside it a woody slope, not too steep. Halfway down the slope is a big catalpa tree, and that was where we always set, side by side with our backs up against the trunk.

So we come on down to there, me hobbling some with my cane and Billy Bob holding onto my arm. That moon was so bright you could see the melons lying in Ferdie Johnson's patch over on the left, and the rail tracks had a sleek oiled look coming out of the tunnel mouth and leading off toward the Sabreville yards a mile up the line. On the far side of the tracks, the woods and the rundown shacks that used to be a hobo jungle before the county sheriff closed it off thirty years back had them a silvery cast, like they was all coated in winter frost.

We set down under the catalpa tree and I leaned my head back to catch my wind. Billy Bob said, "Granpa, you feeling right?"

"Fine, boy."

"Rheumatism ain't started paining you?"

"Not a bit."

He give me a grin. "Got a little surprise for you."

"The hell you do."

"Fresh plug of blackstrap," he said. He come out of his pocket with it. "Mr. Cotter got him in a shipment just today down at his store."

I was some pleased. But I said, "Now you hadn't ought to go spending your money on me, Billy Bob."

"Got nobody else I'd rather spend it on."

I took the plug and unwrapped it and had me a chew. Old man like me ain't got many pleasures left, but fresh blackstrap's one; good corn's another. Billy Bob gets us all the corn we need from Ben Logan's boys. They got a pretty good sized still up on Hankers Ridge, and their corn is the best in this part of the hills. Not that either of us is a drinking man, now. A little touch after supper and on special days is all. I never did hold with drinking too much, or doing anything too much, and I taught Billy Bob the same.

He's a good boy. Man couldn't ask for a better grandson. But I raised him that way—in my own image, you might say—after both my own son Rufus and Billy Bob's ma got taken from us in 1947. I reckon I done a right job of it, and I couldn't be less proud of him than I was of his pa, or love him no less, either.

Well, we set there and I worked on the chew of blackstrap and had a spit every now and then, and neither of us said much. Pretty soon the first whistle come, way off on the other side of Chigger Mountain. Billy Bob cocked his head and said, "She's right on schedule."

"Mostly is," I said, "this time of year."

That sad lonesome hungry ache started up in me again—what my daddy used to call the "sweet fever." He was a railroad man, and I grew up around trains and spent a goodly part of my early years at the roundhouse in the Sabreville yards. Once, when I was ten, he let me take the throttle of the big 2-8-0 Mogul steam locomotive on his highballing run to Eulalia, and I can't recollect no more finer experience in my whole life. Later on I worked as a callboy, and then as a fireman on a 2-10-4, and put in some time as a yard tender engineer, and I expect I'd have gone on in railroading if it hadn't been for the Depression and getting myself married and having Rufus. My daddy's short-line company folded up in 1931, and half a dozen others too, and wasn't no work for either of us in Sabreville or Eulalia or anywheres else on the iron. That squeezed the will right out of him, and he took to ailing, and I had to accept a job on Mr. John Barnett's truck farm to support him and the rest of my family. Was my intention to go back into railroading, but the Depression dragged on, and my daddy died, and a year later my wife Amanda took sick and passed on, and by the time the war come it was just too late.

But Rufus got him the sweet fever too, and took a switchman's job in the Sabreville yards, and worked there right up until the night he died. Billy Bob was only three then; his own sweet fever comes most purely from me and what I taught him. Ain't no doubt trains been a major part of all our lives, good and bad, and ain't no doubt neither they get into a man's blood and maybe change him, too, in one way and another. I reckon they do.

The whistle come again, closer now, and I judged the St. Louis freight was just about to enter the tunnel on the other side of the mountain. You could hear the big wheels singing on the track, and if you listened close you could just about hear the banging of couplings and the hiss of air brakes as the engineer throttled down for the curve. The tunnel don't run straight through Chigger Mountain; she comes in from the north and angles to the east, so that a big freight like the St. Louis got to cut back to quarter speed coming through.

When she entered the tunnel, the tracks down below seemed to shimmy, and you could feel the vibration clear up where we was sitting under the catalpa tree. Billy Bob stood himself up and peered down toward the black tunnel mouth like a bird dog on a point. The whistle come again, and once more, from inside the tunnel, sounding hollow and miseried now. Every time I heard it like that, I thought of a body trapped and hurting and crying out for help that wouldn't come in the empty hours of the night. I swallowed and shifted the cud of blackstrap and worked up a spit to keep my mouth from drying. The sweet fever feeling was strong in my stomach.

The blackness around the tunnel opening commenced to lighten, and got brighter and brighter until the long white glow from the locomotive's headlamp spilled out onto the tracks beyond. Then she come through into my sight, her light shining like a giant's eye, and the engineer give another tug on the whistle, and the sound of her was a clattering rumble as loud to my ears as a mountain rock-slide. But she wasn't moving fast, just kind of easing along, pulling herself out of that tunnel like a night crawler out of a mound of earth.

The locomotive clacked on past, and me and Billy Bob watched her string slide along in front of us. Flats, boxcars, three tankers in a row, more flats loaded down with pine logs big around as a privy, a refrigerator car, five coal gondolas, another link of boxcars. Fifty in the string already, I thought. She won't be dragging more than sixty, sixty-five....

Billy Bob said suddenly, "Granpa, look yonder!"

He had his arm up, pointing. My eyes ain't so good no more, and it took me a couple of seconds to follow his point, over on our left and down at the door of the third boxcar in the last link. It was sliding open, and clear in the moonlight I saw a man's head come out, then his shoulders.

"It's a floater, Granpa," Billy Bob said, excited. "He's gonna jump. Look at him holding there—he's gonna jump."

I spit into the grass. "Help me up, boy."

He got a hand under my arm and lifted me up and held me until I was steady on my cane. Down there at the door of the boxcar, the floater was looking both ways along the string of cars and down at the ground beside the tracks. That ground was soft loam, and the train was going slow enough that there wasn't much chance he would hurt himself jumping off. He come to that same idea, and as soon as he did he flung himself off the car with his arms spread out and his hair and coattails flying in the slipstream. I saw him land solid and go down and roll over once. Then he knelt there, shaking his head a little, looking around.

Well, he was the first floater we'd seen in seven months. The yard crews seal up the cars nowadays, and they ain't many ride the rails anyhow, even down in our part of the country. But every now and then a floater wants to ride bad enough to break a seal, or hides himself in a gondola or on a loaded flat. Kids, oldtime hoboes, wanted men. They's still a few.

And some of 'em get off right down where this one had, because they know the St. Louis freight stops in Sabreville and they's yardmen there that check the string, or because they see the rundown shacks of the old hobo jungle or Ferdie Johnson's melon patch. Man rides a freight long enough, no provisions, he gets mighty hungry; the sight of a melon patch like Ferdie's is plenty enough to make him jump off.

"Billy Bob," I said.

"Yes, Granpa. You wait easy now."

He went off along the slope, running. I watched the floater, and he come up on his feet and got himself into a clump of bushes alongside the tracks to wait for the caboose to pass so's he wouldn't be seen. Pretty soon the last of the cars left the tunnel, and then the caboose with a signalman holding a red-eye lantern out on the platform. When she was down the tracks and just about beyond my sight, the floater showed himself again and had him another look around. Then, sure enough, he made straight for the melon patch.

Once he got into it I couldn't see him, because he was in close to the woods at the edge of the slope. I couldn't see Billy Bob neither. The whistle sounded one final time, mournful, as the lights of the caboose disappeared, and a chill come to my neck and set there like a cold dead hand. I closed my eyes and listened to the last singing of the wheels fade away.

It weren't long before I heard footfalls on the slope coming near, then the angry sound of a stranger's voice, but I kept my eyes shut until they walked up close and Billy Bob said,

"Granpa." When I opened 'em the floater was standing three feet in front of me, white face shining in the moonlight—scared face, angry face, evil face.

"What the hell is this?" he said. "What you want with me?"

"Give me your gun, Billy Bob," I said.

He did it, and I held her tight and lifted the barrel. The ache in my stomach was so strong my knees felt weak and I could scarcely breathe. But my hand was steady.

The floater's eyes come wide open and he backed off a step. "Hey," he said, "hey, you can't—"

I shot him twice.

He fell over and rolled some and come up on his back. They wasn't no doubt he was dead, so I give the gun back to Billy Bob and he put it away in his belt. "All right, boy," I said.

Billy Bob nodded and went over and hoisted the dead floater onto his shoulder. I watched him trudge off toward the bog hollow, and in my mind I could hear the train whistle as she'd sounded from inside the tunnel. I thought again, as I had so many times, that it was the way my boy Rufus and Billy Bob's ma must have sounded that night in 1947, when the two floaters from the hobo jungle broke into their home and raped her and shot Rufus to death. She lived just long enough to tell us about the floaters, but they was never caught. So it was up to me, and then up to me and Billy Bob when he come of age.

Well, it ain't like it once was, and that saddens me. But they's still a few that ride the rails, still a few take it into their heads to jump off down there when the St. Louis freight slows coming through the Chigger Mountain tunnel.

Oh my yes, they'll *always* be a few for me and Billy Bob and the sweet fever inside us both.

SMUGGLER'S ISLAND

The first I heard that somebody had bought Smuggler's Island was late on a cold, foggy morning in May. Handy Manners and Davey and I had just brought the *Jennie Too* into the Camaroon Bay wharf, loaded with the day's limit in salmon—silvers mostly, with a few big kings—and Handy had gone inside the processing shed at Bay Fisheries to call for the tally clerk and the portable scales. I was helping Davey hoist up the hatch covers, and I was thinking that he handled himself fine on the boat and what a shame it'd be if he decided eventually that he didn't want to go into commercial fishing as his livelihood. A man likes to see his only son take up his chosen profession. But Davey was always talking about traveling around Europe, seeing some of the world, maybe finding a career he liked better than fishing. Well, he was only nineteen. Decisions don't come quick or easy at that age.

Anyhow, we were working on the hatch covers when I heard somebody call my name. I glanced up, and Pa and Abner Frawley were coming toward us from down-wharf, where the cafe was. I was a little surprised to see Pa out on a day like this; he usually stayed home with Jennie when it was overcast and windy because the fog and cold air aggravated his lumbago.

The two of them came up and stopped, Pa puffing on one of his home-carved meerschaum pipes. They were both seventy-two and long-retired—Abner from a manager's job at the cannery a mile up the coast, Pa from running the general store in the village—and they'd been cronies for at least half their lives. But that was where all resemblance between them ended. Abner was short and round and white-haired, and always had a smile and a joke for everybody. Pa, on the other hand, was tall and thin and dour; if he'd smiled any more than four times in the forty-seven years since I was born I can't remember it. Abner had come up from San Francisco during the Depression, but Pa was a second-generation native of Camaroon Bay, his father having emigrated from Ireland during the short-lived potato boom in the early 1900s. He was a good man and a decent father, which was why I'd given him a room in our house when Ma died six years ago, but I'd never felt close to him.

He said to me, "Looks like a good catch, Verne."

"Pretty good," I said. "How come you're out in this weather?"

"Abner's idea. He dragged me out of the house."

I looked at Abner. His eyes were bright, the way they always got when he had a choice bit of news or gossip to tell. He said, "Fella from Los Angeles went and bought Smuggler's Island. Can you beat that?"

"Bought it?" I said. "You mean outright?"

"Yep. Paid the county a hundred thousand cash."

"How'd you hear about it?"

"Jack Kewin, over to the real estate office."

"Who's the fellow who bought it?"

"Name's Roger Vauclain," Abner said. "Jack don't know any more about him. Did the buying through an agent."

Davey said, "Wonder what he wants with it?"

"Maybe he's got ideas of hunting treasure," Abner said and winked at him. "Maybe he heard about what's hidden in those caves."

Pa gave him a look. "Old fool," he said.

Davey grinned, and I smiled a little and turned to look to where Smuggler's Island sat wreathed in fog half a mile straight out across the choppy harbor. It wasn't much to look at, from a distance or up close. Just one big oblong chunk of eroded rock about an acre and a half in size, surrounded by a lot of little islets. It had a few stunted trees and shrubs, and a long headland where gulls built their nests, and a sheltered cove on the lee shore where you could put in a small boat. That was about all there was to it—except for those caves Abner had spoken of.

They were located near the lee cove and you could only get into them at low tide. Some said caves honeycombed the whole underbelly of the island, but those of us who'd ignored warnings from our parents as kids and gone exploring in them knew that this wasn't so. There were three caves and two of them had branches that led deep into the rock, but all of the tunnels were dead ends.

This business of treasure being hidden in one of those caves was just so much nonsense, of course—sort of a local legend that nobody took seriously. What the treasure was supposed to be was two million dollars in greenbacks that had been hidden by a rackets courier during Prohibition, when he'd been chased to the island by a team of Revenue agents. There was also supposed to be fifty cases of high-grade moonshine secreted there.

The bootlegging part of it had a good deal of truth though. This section of the northern California coast was a hotbed of illegal liquor traffic in the days of the Volstead Act, and the scene of several confrontations between smugglers and Revenue agents; half a dozen men on both sides had been killed, or had turned up missing and presumed dead. The way the bootleggers worked was to bring ships down from Canada outfitted as distilleries—big stills in their holds, bottling equipment, labels for a dozen different kinds of Canadian whiskey—and anchor them twenty-five miles offshore. Then local fishermen and imported hirelings would go out in their boats and carry the liquor to places along the shore, where trucks would be waiting to pick it up and transport it down to San Francisco or east into Nevada. Smuggler's Island was supposed to have been a short-term storage point for whiskey that couldn't be trucked out right away, which may or may not have been a true fact. At any rate, that was how the island got its name.

Just as I turned back to Pa and Abner, Handy came out of the processing shed with the tally clerk and the scales. He was a big, thick-necked man, Handy, with red hair and a temper to match; he was also one of the best mates around and knew as much about salmon trolling and diesel engines as anybody in Camaroon Bay. He'd been working for me eight years, but he wouldn't be much longer. He was saving up to buy a boat of his own and only needed another thousand or so to swing the down payment.

Abner told him right away about this Roger Vauclain buying Smuggler's Island. Handy grunted and said, "Anybody that'd want those rocks out there has to have rocks in his head."

"Who do you imagine he is?" Davey asked.

"One of those damn-fool rich people probably," Pa said. "Buy something for no good reason except that it's there and they want it."

"But why Smuggler's Island in particular?"

"Got a fancy name, that's why. Now he can say to his friends, why look here, I own a place up north called Smuggler's Island, supposed to have treasure hidden on it."

I said, "Well, whoever he is and whyever he bought it, we'll find out eventually. Right now we've got a catch to unload."

"Sure is a puzzler though, ain't it, Verne?" Abner said.

"It is that," I admitted. "It's a puzzler, all right."

If you live in a small town or village, you know how it is when something happens that has no immediate explanation. Rumors start flying, based on few or no facts, and every time one of them is retold to somebody else it gets exaggerated. Nothing much goes on in a place like Camaroon Bay anyhow—conversation is pretty much limited to the weather and the actions of tourists and how the salmon are running or how the crabs seem to be thinning out a little more every year. So this Roger Vauclain buying Smuggler's Island got a lot more lip service paid to it than it would have someplace else.

Jack Kewin didn't find out much about Vauclain, just that he was some kind of wealthy resident of southern California. But that was enough for the speculations and the rumors to build on. During the next week I heard from different people that Vauclain was a real-estate speculator who was going to construct a small private club on the island; that he was a retired bootlegger who'd worked the coast during Prohibition and had bought the island for nostalgic reasons; that he was a front man for a movie company that was going to film a big spectacular in Camaroon Bay and blow up the island in the final scene. None of these rumors made much sense, but that didn't stop people from spreading them and half-believing in them.

Then, one night while we were eating supper Abner came knocking at the front door of our house on the hill above the village. Davey went and let him in, and he sat down at the table next to Pa. One look at him was enough to tell us that he'd come with news.

"Just been talking to Lloyd Simms," he said as Jennie poured him a cup of coffee. "Who do you reckon just made a reservation at the Camaroon Inn?"

"Who?" I asked.

"Roger Vauclain himself. Lloyd talked to him on the phone less than an hour ago, says he sounded pretty hard-nosed. Booked a single room for a week, be here on Thursday."

"Only a single room?" Jennie said. "Why, I'm disappointed, Abner. I expected he'd be traveling with an entourage." She's a practical woman and when it comes to things she considers nonsense, like all the hoopla over Vauclain and Smuggler's Island, her sense of humor sharpens into sarcasm.

"Might be others coming up later," Abner said seriously.

Davey said, "Week's a long time for a rich man to spend in a place like Camaroon Bay. I wonder what he figures to do all that time?"

"Tend to his island, probably," I said.

"Tend to it?" Pa said. "Tend to what? You can walk over the whole thing in two hours."

"Well, there's always the caves, Pa."

He snorted. "Grown man'd have to be a fool to go wandering in those caves. Tide comes in while he's inside, he'll drown for sure."

"What time's he due in on Thursday?" Davey asked Abner.

"Around noon, Lloyd says. Reckon we'll find out then what he's planning to do with the island."

"Not planning to do anything with it, I tell you," Pa said. "Just wants to own it."

"We'll see," Abner said. "We'll see."

Thursday was clear and warm, and it should have been a good day for salmon; but maybe the run had started to peter out, because it took us until almost noon to make the limit. It was after two o'clock before we got the catch unloaded and weighed in at Bay Fisheries. Davey had some errands to run and Handy had logged enough extra time, so I took the *Jennie Too* over to the commercial slips myself and stayed aboard her to hose down the decks. When I was through with that I set about replacing the port outrigger line because it had started to weaken and we'd been having trouble with it.

I was doing that when a tall man came down the ramp from the quay and stood just off the bow, watching me. I didn't pay much attention to him; tourists stop by to rubberneck now and then, and if you encourage them they sometimes hang around so you can't get any work done. But then this fellow slapped a hand against his leg, as if he were annoyed, and called out in a loud voice, "Hey, you there. Fisherman."

I looked at him then, frowning. I'd heard that tone before: sharp, full of self-granted authority. Some city people are like that; to them, anybody who lives in a rural village is a low-class hick. I didn't like it and I let him see that in my face. "You talking to me?"

"Who else would I be talking to?"

I didn't say anything. He was in his forties, smooth looking, and dressed in white ducks and a crisp blue windbreaker. If nothing else, his eyes were enough to make you dislike him immediately; they were hard and unfriendly and said that he was used to getting his own way.

He said, "Where can I rent a boat?"

"What kind of boat? To go sport fishing?"

"No, not to go sport fishing. A small cruiser."

"There ain't any cruisers for rent here."

He made a disgusted sound, as if he'd expected that. "A big outboard then," he said. "Something seaworthy."

"It's not a good idea to take a small boat out of the harbor," I said. "The ocean along here is pretty rough—"

"I don't want advice," he said. "I want a boat big enough to get me out to Smuggler's Island and back. Now who do I see about it?"

"Smuggler's Island?" I looked at him more closely. "Your name happen to be Roger Vauclain, by any chance?"

"That's right. You heard about me buying the island, I suppose. Along with everybody else in this place."

"News gets around," I said mildly.

"About that boat," he said.

"Talk to Ed Hawkins at Bay Marine on the wharf. He'll find something for you."

Vauclain gave me a curt nod and started to turn away.

I said, "Mind if I ask *you* a question now?"

He turned back. "What is it?"

"People don't go buying islands very often," I said, "particularly one like Smuggler's. I'd be interested to know your plans for it."

"You and every other damned person in Camaroon Bay."

I held my temper. "I was just asking. You don't have to give me an answer."

He was silent for a moment. Then he said, "What the hell, it's no secret. I've always wanted to live on an island, and that one out there is the only one around I can afford."

I stared at him. "You mean you're going to *build* on it?"

"That surprises you, does it?"

"It does," I said. "There's nothing on Smuggler's Island but rocks and a few trees and a couple of thousand nesting gulls. It's fogbound most of the time, and even when it's not the wind blows at thirty knots or better."

"I like fog and wind and ocean," Vauclain said. "I like isolation. I don't like people much. That satisfy you?"

I shrugged. "To each his own."

"Exactly," he said, and went away up the ramp.

I worked on the *Jennie Too* another hour, then I went over to the Wharf Cafe for a cup of coffee and a piece of pie. When I came inside I saw Pa, Abner, and Handy sitting at one of the copper-topped tables. I walked over to them.

They already knew that Vauclain had arrived in Camaroon Bay. Handy was saying, "Hell, he's about as friendly as a shark. I was over to Ed Hawkins's place shooting the breeze when he came in and demanded Ed get him a boat. Threw his weight around for fifteen minutes until Ed agreed to rent him his own Chris-Craft. Then he paid for the rental in cash, slammed two fifties on Ed's desk like they were singles and Ed was a beggar."

I sat down. "He's an eccentric, all right," I said. "I talked to him for a few minutes myself about an hour ago."

"Eccentric?" Abner said, and snorted. "That's just a name they give to people who never learned manners or good sense."

Pa said to me. "He tell you what he's fixing to do with Smuggler's Island, Verne?"

"He did, yep."

"Told Abner too, over to the Inn." Pa shook his head, glowering, and lighted a pipe. "Craziest damned thing I ever heard. Build a house on that mess of rock, live out there. Crazy, that's all."

"That's a fact," Handy said. "I'd give him more credit if he was planning to hunt for that bootlegger's treasure."

"Well, I'm sure not going to relish having him for a neighbor," Abner said. "Don't guess anybody else will either."

None of us disagreed with that. A man likes to be able to get along with his neighbors, rich or poor. Getting along with Vauclain, it seemed, was going to be a chore for everybody.

In the next couple of days Vauclain didn't do much to improve his standing with the residents of Camaroon Bay. He snapped at merchants and waitresses, ignored anybody who tried to strike up a conversation with him, and complained twice to Lloyd Simms about the service at the Inn. The only good thing about him, most people were saying, was that he spent the better part of his days on Smuggler's Island—doing what, nobody knew exactly—and his nights locked in his room. Might have been he was drawing up plans there for the house he intended to build on the island.

Rumor now had it that Vauclain was an architect, one of those independents who'd built up a reputation, like Frank Lloyd Wright in the old days, and who only worked for private individuals and companies. This was probably true since it originated with Jack Kewin; he'd spent a little time with Vauclain and wasn't one to spread unfounded gossip. According to Jack, Vauclain had learned that the island was for sale more than six months ago and had been up twice before by helicopter from San Francisco to get an aerial view of it.

That was the way things stood on Sunday morning when Jennie and I left for church at 10:00. Afterward we had lunch at a place up the coast, and then, because the weather was cool but still clear, we went for a drive through the redwood country. It was almost 5:00 when we got back home.

Pa was in bed—his lumbago was bothering him, he said—

and Davey was gone somewhere. I went into our bedroom to change out of my suit. While I was in there the telephone rang, and Jennie called out that it was for me.

When I picked up the receiver Lloyd Simms's voice said, "Sorry to bother you, Verne, but if you're not busy I need a favor."

"I'm not busy, Lloyd. What is it?"

"Well, it's Roger Vauclain. He went out to the island this morning like usual, and he was supposed to be back at three to take a telephone call. Told me to make sure I was around then, the call was important—you know the way he talks. The call came in right on schedule, but Vauclain didn't. He's still not back, and the party calling him has been ringing me up every half hour, demanding I get hold of him. Something about a bid that has to be delivered first thing tomorrow morning."

"You want me to go out to the island, Lloyd?"

"If you wouldn't mind," he said. "I don't much care about Vauclain, the way he's been acting, but this caller is driving me up a wall. And it could be something's the matter with Vauclain's boat; can't get it started or something. Seems kind of funny he didn't come back when he said he would."

I hesitated. I didn't much want to take the time to go out to Smuggler's Island, but then if there was a chance Vauclain was in trouble I couldn't very well refuse to help.

"All right," I said. "I'll see what I can do."

We rang off, and I explained to Jennie where I was going and why. Then I drove down to the basin where the pleasure-boat slips were and took the tarp off Davey's sixteen-foot Sportliner inboard. I'd bought it for him on his sixteenth birthday, when I figured he was old enough to handle a small boat of his own, but I used it as much as he did. We're not so well off that we can afford to keep more than one pleasure craft.

The engine started right up for a change—usually you have to choke it several times on cool days—and I took her out of the slips and into the harbor. The sun was hidden by overcast now and the wind was up, building small whitecaps, running fogbanks in from the ocean but shredding them before they reached the shore. I followed the south jetty out past the breakwater and into open sea. The water was choppier there, the color of gunmetal, and the wind was pretty cold; I pulled the collar of my jacket up and put on my gloves to keep my hands from numbing on the wheel.

When I neared the island I swung around to the north shore and into the lee cove. Ed Hawkins's Chris-Craft was tied up there, all right, bow and stern lines made fast to outcroppings on a long, natural stone dock. I took the Sportliner in behind it, climbed out onto the bare rock, and made her fast. On my right, waves broke over and into the mouths of three caves, hissing long fans of spray. Gulls wheeled screeching above the headland; farther in, scrub oak and cypress danced like bobbers in the wind. It all made you feel as though you were standing on the edge of the world.

There was no sign of Vauclain anywhere at the cove, so I went up through a tangle of artichoke plants toward the center of the island. The area there was rocky but mostly flat, dotted with undergrowth and patches of sandy earth. I stopped beside a gnarled cypress and scanned from left to right. Nothing but emptiness. Then I walked out toward the headland, hunched over against the pull of the wind. But 1 didn't find him there either.

A sudden thought came to me as I started back and the hairs prickled on my neck. What if he'd gone into the caves and been trapped there when the tide began to flood? If that was what had happened, it was too late for me to do anything—but I started to run anyway, my eyes on the ground so I wouldn't trip over a bush or a rock.

I was almost back to the cove, coming at a different angle than before, when I saw him.

It was so unexpected that I pulled up short and almost lost my footing on loose rock. The pit of my stomach went hollow. He was lying on his back in a bed of artichokes, one arm flung out and the other wrapped across his chest. There was blood under his arm, and blood spread across the front of his windbreaker. One long look was all I needed to tell me he'd been shot and that he was dead.

Shock and an eerie sense of unreality kept me standing there another few seconds. My thoughts were jumbled; you don't think too clearly when you stumble on a dead man, a murdered man. And it was murder, I knew that well enough. There was no gun anywhere near the body, and no way it could have been an accident.

Then I turned, shivering, and ran down to the cove and took the Sportliner away from there at full throttle to call for the county sheriff.

Vauclain's death was the biggest event that had happened in Camaroon Bay in forty years, and Sunday night and Monday nobody talked about anything else. As soon as word got around that I was the one who'd discovered the body, the doorbell and the telephone didn't stop ringing—friends and neighbors, newspaper people, investigators. The only place I had any peace was on the *Jennie Too* Monday morning, and not much there because Davey and Handy wouldn't let the subject alone while we fished.

By late that afternoon the authorities had questioned just about everyone in the area. It didn't appear they'd found out anything though. Vauclain had been alone when he'd left for the island early Sunday; Abner had been down at the slips then and swore to the fact. A couple of tourists had rented boats from Ed Hawkins during the day, since the weather was pretty good, and a lot of locals were out in the harbor on pleasure craft. But whoever it was who had gone to Smuggler's Island after Vauclain, he hadn't been noticed.

As to a motive for the shooting, there were all sorts of wild speculations. Vauclain had wronged somebody in Los Angeles and that person had followed him here to take revenge. He'd treated a local citizen badly enough to trigger a murderous rage. He'd got in bad with organized crime and a contract had been put out on him. And the most farfetched theory of all: He'd actually uncovered some sort of treasure on Smuggler's Island and somebody'd learned about it and killed him for it. But the simple truth was, nobody had any idea why Vauclain was murdered. If the sheriff's department had found any clues on the island or anywhere else, they weren't talking—but they weren't making any arrests either.

There was a lot of excitement, all right. Only underneath it all people were nervous and a little scared. A killer seemed to be loose in Camaroon Bay, and if he'd murdered once, who was to say he wouldn't do it again? A mystery is all well and good when it's happening someplace else, but when it's right on your doorstep you can't help but feel threatened and apprehensive.

I'd had about all the pestering I could stand by four o'clock, so I got into the car and drove up the coast to Shelter Cove. That gave me an hour's worth of freedom. But no sooner did I get back to Camaroon Bay, with the intention of going home and locking myself in my basement workshop, than a sheriff's cruiser pulled up behind me at a stop sign and its horn started honking. I sighed and pulled over to the curb.

It was Harry Swenson, one of the deputies who'd questioned me the day before, after I'd reported finding Vauclain's body. We knew each other well enough to be on a first-name basis. He said, "Verne, the sheriff asked me to talk to you again, see if there's anything you might have overlooked yesterday. You mind?"

"No, I don't mind," I said tiredly.

We went into the Inn and took a table at the back of the dining room. A couple of people stared at us, and I could see Lloyd Simms hovering around out by the front desk. I wondered how long it would be before I'd stop being the center of attention every time I went someplace in the village.

Over coffee, I repeated everything that had happened Sunday afternoon. Harry checked what I said with the notes he'd taken; then he shook his head and closed the notebook.

"Didn't really expect you to remember anything else," he said, "but we had to make sure. Truth is, Verne, we're up against it on this thing. Damnedest case I ever saw."

"Guess that means you haven't found out anything positive."

"Not much. If we could figure a motive, we might be able to get a handle on it from that. But we just can't find one."

I decided to give voice to one of my own theories. "What about robbery, Harry?" I asked. "Seems I heard Vauclain was carrying a lot of cash with him and throwing it around pretty freely."

"We thought of that first thing," he said. "No good, though. His wallet was on the body, and there was three hundred dollars in it and a couple of blank checks."

I frowned down at my coffee. "I don't like to say this, but you don't suppose it could be one of these thrill killings we're always reading about?"

"Man, I hope not. That's the worst kind of homicide there is."

We were silent for a minute or so. Then I said, "You find anything at all on the island? Any clues?"

He hesitated. "Well," he said finally, "I probably shouldn't discuss it—but then, you're not the sort to break a confidence. We did find one thing near the body. Might not mean anything, but it's not the kind of item you'd expect to come across out there."

"What is it?"

"A cake of white beeswax," he said.

"Beeswax?"

"Right. Small cake of it. Suggest anything to you?"

"No," I said. "No, nothing."

"Not to us either. Aside from that, we haven't got a thing. Like I said, we're up against it. Unless we get a break in the next couple of days, I'm afraid the whole business will end up in the Unsolved file. That's unofficial, now."

"Sure," I said.

Harry finished his coffee. "I'd better get moving," he said. "Thanks for your time, Verne."

I nodded, and he stood up and walked out across the dining room. As soon as he was gone, Lloyd came over and wanted to know what we'd been talking about. But I'd begun to feel oddly nervous all of a sudden, and there was something tickling at the edge of my mind. I cut him off short, saying, "Let me be, will you, Lloyd? Just let me be for a minute."

When he drifted off, looking hurt, I sat there and rotated my cup on the table. Beeswax, I thought. I'd told Harry that it didn't suggest anything to me, and yet it did, vaguely. Beeswax. White beeswax . . .

It came to me then—and along with it a couple of other things, little things. I went cold all over, as if somebody had opened a window and let the wind inside the room. I told myself I was wrong, that it couldn't be. But I wasn't wrong. It made me sick inside, but I wasn't wrong.

I knew who had murdered Roger Vauclain.

When I came into the house I saw him sitting out on the sun deck, just sitting there motionless with his hands flat on his knees, staring out to sea. Or out to where Smuggler's Island sat, shining hard and ugly in the glare of the dying sun.

I didn't go out there right away. First I went into the other rooms to see if anybody else was home, but nobody was. Then, when I couldn't put it off any longer, I got myself ready to face it and walked onto the deck.

He glanced at me as I leaned back against the railing. I hadn't seen much of him since finding the body, or paid much attention to him when I had; but now I saw that his eyes looked different. They didn't blink. They looked at me, they looked past me, but they didn't blink.

"Why'd you do it, Pa?" I said. "Why'd you kill Vauclain?"

I don't know what I expected his reaction to be. But there wasn't any reaction. He wasn't startled, he wasn't frightened, he wasn't anything. He just looked away from me again and sat there like a man who has expected to hear such words for a long time.

I kept waiting for him to say something, to move, to blink his eyes. For one full minute and half of another, he did nothing. Then he sighed, soft and tired, and he said, "I knew somebody'd find out this time." His voice was steady, calm. "I'm sorry it had to be you, Verne."

"So am I."

"How'd you know?"

"You left a cake of white beeswax out there," I said. "Fell out of your pocket when you pulled the gun, I guess. You're just the only person around here who'd be likely to have white beeswax in his pocket, Pa, because you're the only person who hand-carves his own meerschaum pipes. Took me a time to remember that you use wax like that to seal the bowls and give them a luster finish."

He didn't say anything.

"Couple of other things too," I said. "You were in bed yesterday when Jennie and I got home. It was a clear day, no early fog, nothing to aggravate your lumbago. Unless you'd been out someplace where you weren't protected from the wind—someplace like in a boat on open water. Then there was Davey's Sportliner starting right up for me. Almost never does that on cool days unless it's been run recently, and the only person besides Davey and me who has a key is you."

He nodded. "It's usually the little things," he said. "I always figured it'd be some little thing that'd finally do it."

"Pa," I said, "why'd you kill him?"

"He had to go and buy the island. Then he had to decide to build a house on it. I couldn't let him do that. I went out there to talk to him, try to get him to change his mind. Took my revolver along, but only just in case; wasn't intending to use it. Only he wouldn't listen to me. Called me an old fool and worse, and then he give me a shove. He was dead before I knew it, seems like."

"What'd him building a house have to do with you?"

"He'd have brought men and equipment out there, wouldn't he? They'd have dug up everything, wouldn't they? They'd have sure dug up the Revenue man."

I thought he was rambling. "Pa . . ."

"You got a right to know about that too," he said. He blinked then, four times fast. "In 1929 a fella named Frank Eberle and me went to work for the bootleggers. Hauling whiskey. We'd go out maybe once a month in Frank's boat, me acting as shotgun, and we'd bring in a load of 'shine—mostly to Shelter Cove, but sometimes we'd be told to drop it off on Smuggler's for a day or two. It was easy money, and your ma and me needed it, what with you happening along; and what the hell, Frank always said, we were only helping to give the people what they wanted.

"But then one night in 1932 it all went bust. We brought a shipment to the island and just after we started unloading it this man run out of the trees waving a gun and yelling that we were under arrest. A Revenue agent, been lying up there in ambush. Lying alone because he didn't figure to have much trouble, I reckon—and I found out later the government people had bigger fish to fry up to Shelter Cove that night.

"Soon as the agent showed himself, Frank panicked and started to run. Agent put a shot over his head, and before I could think on it I cut loose with the rifle I always carried. I killed him, Verne, I shot that man dead."

He paused, his face twisting with memory. I wanted to say something—but what was there to say?

Pa said, "Frank and me buried him on the island, under a couple of rocks on the center flat. Then we got out of there. I quit the bootleggers right away, but Frank, he kept on with it and got himself killed in a big shoot-out up by Eureka just before Repeal. I knew they were going to get me too someday. Only time kept passing and somehow it never happened, and I almost had myself believing it never would. Then this Vauclain came along. You see now why I couldn't let him build his house?"

"Pa," I said thickly, "it's been forty-five years since all that happened. All anybody'd have dug up was bones. Maybe there's something there to identify the Revenue agent, but there couldn't be anything that'd point to you."

"Yes, there could," he said. "Just like there was something this time—the beeswax and all. There'd have been something, all right, and they'd have come for me."

He stopped talking then, like a machine that had been turned off, and swiveled his head away and just sat staring again. There in the sun, I still felt cold. He believed what he'd just said; he honestly believed it.

I knew now why he'd been so dour and moody for most of my life, why he almost never smiled, why he'd never let me get close to him. And I knew something else too: I wasn't going to tell the sheriff any of this. He was my father and he was seventy-two years old, and I'd see to it that he didn't hurt anybody else. But the main reason was, if I let it happen that they really did come for him he wouldn't last a month. In an awful kind of way the only thing that'd been holding him together all these years was his certainty they would come someday.

Besides, it didn't matter anyway. He hadn't actually got away with anything. He hadn't committed one unpunished murder, or now two unpunished murders, because there is no such thing. There's just no such thing as the perfect crime.

I walked over and took the chair beside him, and together we sat quiet and looked out at Smuggler's Island. Only I didn't see it very well because my eyes were full of tears.

UNDER THE SKIN

In the lobby lounge of the St. Francis Hotel, where he and Tom Olivet had gone for a drink after the A.C.T. dramatic production was over, Walter Carpenter sipped his second Scotch-and-water and thought that he was a pretty lucky man. Good job, happy marriage, kids of whom he could be proud, and a best friend who had a similar temperament, similar attitudes, aspirations, likes and dislikes. Most people went through life claiming lots of casual friends and a few close ones, but seldom did a perfectly compatible relationship develop as it had between Tom and him. He knew brothers who were not nearly as close. Walter smiled. That's just what the two of us are like, he thought. Brothers.

Across the table Tom said, "Why the sudden smile?"

"Oh, just thinking that we're a hell of a team," Walter said.

"Sure," Tom said. "Carpenter and Olivet, the Gold Dust Twins."

Walter laughed. "No, I mean it. Did you ever stop to think how few friends get along as well as we do? I mean, we like to do the same things, go to the same places. The play tonight, for example. I couldn't get Cynthia to go, but as soon as I mentioned it to you, you were all set for it."

"Well, we've known each other for twenty years," Tom said. "Two people spend as much time together as we have, they get to thinking alike and acting alike. I guess we're one head on just about everything, all right."

"A couple of carbon copies," Walter said. "Here's to friendship."

They raised their glasses and drank, and when Walter put his down on the table he noticed the hands on his wristwatch. "Hey," he said. "It's almost eleven-thirty. We'd better hustle if we're going to catch the train. Last one for Daly City leaves at midnight."

"Right," Tom said.

They split the check down the middle, then left the hotel and walked down Powell Street to the Bay Area Rapid Transit station at Market. Ordinarily one of them would have driven in that morning from the Monterey Heights area where they lived two blocks apart, but Tom's car was in the garage for minor repairs, and Walter's wife Cynthia had needed their car for errands. So they had ridden a BART train in, and after work they'd had dinner in a restaurant near Union Square before going on to the play.

Inside the Powell station Walter called Cynthia from a pay phone and told her they were taking the next train out; she said she would pick them up at Glen Park. Then he and Tom rode the escalator down to the train platform. Some twenty people stood or sat there waiting for trains, half a dozen of them drunks and other unsavory-looking types. Subway crime had not been much of a problem since BART, which connected several San Francisco points with a number of East Bay cities, opened two years earlier. Still, there were isolated incidents. Walter began to feel vaguely nervous; it was the first time he had gone anywhere this late by train.

The nervousness eased when a westbound pulled in almost immediately and none of the unsavory-looking types followed them into a nearly empty car. They sat together, Walter next to the window. Once the train had pulled out he could see their reflections in the window glass. Hell, he thought, the two of us even look alike sometimes. Carbon copies, for a fact. Brothers of the spirit.

A young man in workman's garb got off at the 24th and Mission stop, leaving them alone in the car. Walter's ears popped as the train picked up speed for the run to Glen Park. He said, "These new babies really move, don't they?"

"That's for sure," Tom said.

"You ever ride a fast-express passenger train?"

"No," Tom said. "You?"

"No. Say, you know what would be fun?"

"What?"

"Taking a train trip across Canada," Walter said. "They've still got crack passenger expresses up there—they run across the whole of Canada from Vancouver to Montreal."

"Yeah, I've heard about those," Tom said.

"Maybe we could take the families up there and ride one of them next summer," Walter said. "You know, fly to Vancouver and then fly home from Montreal."

"Sounds great to me."

"Think the wives would go for it?"

"I don't see why not."

For a couple of minutes the tunnel lights flashed by in a yellow blur; then the train began to slow and the globes steadied into a widening chain. When they slid out of the tunnel into the Glen Park station, Tom stood up and Walter followed him to the doors. They stepped out. No one was waiting to get on, and the doors hissed closed again almost immediately. The westbound rumbled ahead into the tunnel that led to Daly City.

The platform was empty except for a man in an overcoat and a baseball cap lounging against the tiled wall that sided the escalators; Walter and Tom had been the only passengers to get off. The nearest of the two electronic clock-and-message boards suspended above the platform read 12:02.

The sound of the train faded into silence as they walked toward the escalators, and their steps echoed hollowly. Midnight-empty this way, the fluorescent-lit station had an eerie quality. Walter felt the faint uneasiness return and impulsively quickened his pace.

They were ten yards from the escalators when the man in the overcoat moved away from the wall and came toward them. He had the collar pulled up around his face and his chin tucked down into it; the bill of the baseball cap hid his forehead, so that his features were shadowy. His right hand was inside a coat pocket.

The hair prickled on Walter's neck. He glanced at Tom to keep from staring at the approaching man, but Tom did not seem to have noticed him at all.

Just before they reached the escalators the man in the overcoat stepped across in front of them, blocking their way, and planted his feet. They pulled up short. Tom said, "Hey," and Walter thought in sudden alarm: Oh, my God!

The man took his hand out of his pocket and showed them the long thin blade of a knife. "Wallets," he said flatly. "Hurry it up, don't make me use this."

Walter's breath seemed to clog in his lungs; he tasted the brassiness of fear. There was a moment of tense inactivity, the three of them as motionless as wax statues in a museum exhibit. Then, jerkily, his hand trembling, Walter reached into his jacket pocket and fumbled his wallet out.

But Tom just stood staring, first at the knife and then at the man's shadowed face. He did not seem to be afraid. His lips were pinched instead with anger. "A damned mugger," he said.

Walter said, "Tom, for God's sake!" and extended his wallet. The man grabbed it out of his hand, shoved it into the other slash pocket. He moved the knife slightly in front of Tom.

"Get it out," he said.

"No," Tom said, "I'll be damned if I will."

Walter knew then, instantly, what was going to happen next. Close as the two of them were, he was sensitive to Tom's moods. He opened his mouth to shout at him, tell him not to do it; he tried to make himself grab onto Tom and stop him physically. But the muscles in his body seemed paralyzed.

Then it was too late. Tom struck the man's wrist, knocked it and the knife to one side, and lunged forward.

Walter stood there, unable to move, and watched the mugger sidestep awkwardly, pulling the knife back. The coat collar fell away, the baseball cap flew off as Tom's fist grazed the side of the man's head—and Walter could see the mugger's face clearly: beard-stubbled, jutting chin, flattened nose, wild blazing eyes.

The knife, glinting light from the overhead fluorescents, flashed between the mugger and Tom, and Tom stiffened and made a grunting, gasping noise. Walter looked on in horror as the man stepped back with the knife, blood on the blade now, blood on his hand. Tom turned and clutched at his stomach, eyes glazing, and then his knees buckled and he toppled over and lay still.

He killed him, Walter thought, he killed Tom but he did not feel anything yet. Shock had given the whole thing a terrible dreamlike aspect. The mugger turned toward him, looked at him out of those burning eyes. Walter wanted to run, but there was nowhere to go with the tracks on both sides of the platform, the electrified rails down there, and the mugger blocking the escalators. And he could not make himself move now any more than he had been able to move when he realized Tom intended to fight.

The man in the overcoat took a step toward him, and in that moment, from inside the eastbound tunnel, there was the faint rumble of an approaching train. The suspended message board flashed CONCORD, and the mugger looked up there, looked back at Walter. The eyes burned into him an instant longer, holding him transfixed. Then the man turned sharply, scooped up his baseball cap, and ran up the escalator.

Seconds later he was gone, and the train was there instead, filling the station with a rush of sound that Walter could barely hear for the thunder of his heart.

The policeman was a short thick-set man with a black mustache, and when Walter finished speaking he looked up gravely from his notebook. "And that's everything that happened, Mr. Carpenter?"

"Yes," Walter said, "that's everything."

He was sitting on one of the round tile-and-concrete benches in the center of the platform. He had been sitting there ever since it happened. When the eastbound train had braked to a halt, one of its disembarking passengers had been a BART security officer. One train too late, Walter remembered thinking dully at the time; he's one train too late. The security officer had asked a couple of terse questions, then had draped his coat over Tom and gone upstairs to call the police.

"What can you tell me about the man who did it?" the policeman asked. "Can you give me a description of him?"

Walter's eyes were wet; he took out his handkerchief and wiped them, shielding his face with the cloth, then closing his eyes behind it. When he did that he could see the face of the mugger: the stubbled cheeks, the jutting chin, the flat nose— and the eyes, above all those malignant eyes that had said as clearly as though the man had spoken the words aloud: *I've got your wallet, I know where you live. If you say anything to the cops I'll come after you and give you what I gave your friend.*

Walter shuddered, opened his eyes, lowered the handkerchief, and looked over to where the group of police and laboratory personnel were working around the body. Tom Olivet's body. Tom Olivet, lying there dead.

We were like brothers, Walter thought. We were just like brothers.

"I can't tell you anything about the mugger," he said to the policeman. "I didn't get a good look at him. I can't tell you anything at all."

STRANGERS IN THE FOG

Hannigan had just finished digging the grave, down in the tule marsh where the little saltwater creek flowed toward the Pacific, when the dark shape of a man came out of the fog.

Startled, Hannigan brought the shovel up and cocked it weaponlike at his shoulder. The other man had materialized less than twenty yards away, from the direction of the beach, and had stopped the moment he saw Hannigan. The diffused light from Hannigan's lantern did not quite reach the man; he was a black silhouette against the swirling billows of mist. Beyond him the breakers lashed at the hidden shore in a steady pulse.

Hannigan said, "Who the hell are you?"

The man stood staring down at the roll of canvas near Hannigan's feet, at the hole scooped out of the sandy earth. He seemed to poise himself on the balls of his feet, body turned slightly, as though he might bolt at any second. "I'll ask you the same question," he said, and his voice was tense, low-pitched.

"I happen to live here." Hannigan made a gesture to his left with the shovel, where a suggestion of shimmery light shone high up through the fog. "This is a private beach."

"Private graveyard, too?"

"My dog died earlier this evening. I didn't want to leave him lying around the house."

"Must have been a pretty big dog."

"He was a Great Dane," Hannigan said. He wiped moisture from his face with his free hand. "You want something, or do you just like to take strolls in the fog?"

The man came forward a few steps, warily. Hannigan could see him more clearly then in the pale lantern glow: big, heavy-shouldered, damp hair flattened across his forehead, wearing a plaid lumberman's jacket, brown slacks, and loafers.

"You got a telephone I can use?"

"That would depend on why you need to use it."

"I could give you a story about my car breaking down," the big man said, "but then you'd just wonder what I'm doing down here instead of up on the Coast Highway."

"I'm wondering that anyway."

"It's safe down here, the way I figured it."

"I don't follow," Hannigan said.

"Don't you listen to your radio or TV?"

"Not if I can avoid it."

"So you don't know about the lunatic who escaped from the state asylum at Tescadero."

The back of Hannigan's neck prickled. "No," he said.

"Happened late this afternoon," the big man said. "He killed an attendant at the hospital—stabbed him with a kitchen knife. He was in there for the same kind of thing. Killed three people with a kitchen knife."

Hannigan did not say anything.

The big man said, "They think he may have headed north, because he came from a town up near the Oregon border. But they're not sure. He may have come south instead—and Tescadero is only twelve miles from here."

Hannigan gripped the handle of the shovel more tightly. "You still haven't said what you're doing down here in the fog."

"I came up from San Francisco with a girl for the weekend," the big man said. "Her husband was supposed to be in Los Angeles, on business, only I guess he decided to come home early. When he found her gone he must have figured she'd come up to this summer place they've got and so he drove up without calling first. We had just enough warning for her to throw me out."

"You let this woman throw you out?"

"That's right. Her husband is worth a million or so, and he's generous. You understand?"

"Maybe," Hannigan said. "What's the woman's name?"

"That's my business."

"Then how do I know you're telling me the truth?"

"Why wouldn't I be?"

"You might have reasons for lying."

"Like if I was the escaped lunatic, maybe?"

"Like that."

"If I was, would I have told you about him?"

Again Hannigan was silent.

"For all I know," the big man said, "you could be the lunatic. Hell, you're out here digging a grave in the middle of the night—"

"I told you, my dog died. Besides, would a lunatic dig a grave for somebody he killed? Did he dig one for that attendant you said he stabbed?"

"Okay, neither one of us is the lunatic." The big man paused and ran his hands along the side of his coat. "Look, I've had enough of this damned fog; it's starting to get to me. Can I use your phone or not?"

"Just who is it you want to call?"

"Friend of mine in San Francisco who owes me a favor. He'll drive up and get me. That is, if you wouldn't mind my hanging around your place until he shows up."

Hannigan thought things over and made up his mind. "All right. You stand over there while I finish putting Nick away. Then we'll go up."

The big man nodded and stood without moving. Hannigan knelt, still grasping the shovel, and rolled the canvas-wrapped body carefully into the grave. Then he straightened, began to scoop in sandy earth from the pile to one side. He did all of that without taking his eyes off the other man.

When he was finished he picked up the lantern, then gestured with the shovel, and the big man came around the grave. They went up along the edge of the creek, Hannigan four or five steps to the left. The big man kept his hands up and in close to his chest, and he walked with the tense springy stride of an animal prepared to attack or flee at any sudden movement. His gaze hung on Hannigan's face; Hannigan made it reciprocal.

"You have a name?" Hannigan asked him.

"Doesn't everybody?"

"Very funny. I'm asking your name."

"Art Vickery, if it matters."

"It doesn't, except that I like to know who I'm letting inside my house."

"I like to know whose house I'm going into," Vickery said.

Hannigan told him. After that neither of them had anything more to say.

The creek wound away to the right after fifty yards, into a tangle of scrubbrush, sage, and tule grass; to the left and straight ahead were low rolling sand dunes, and behind them the earth became hard-packed and rose sharply into the bluff on which the house had been built. Hannigan took Vickery onto the worn path between two of the dunes. Fog massed around them in wet gray swirls, shredding as they passed through it, reknitting again at their backs. Even with the lantern, visibility was less than thirty yards in any direction, although as they neared the bluff the house lights threw a progressively brighter illumination against the screen of mist.

They were halfway up the winding path before the house itself loomed into view—a huge redwood-and-glass structure with a wide balcony facing the sea. The path ended at a terraced patio, and there were wooden steps at the far end that led up alongside the house.

When they reached the steps Hannigan gestured for Vickery to go up first. The big man did not argue; but he ascended sideways, looking back down at Hannigan, neither of his hands touching the railing. Hannigan followed by four of the wood runners.

At the top, in front of the house, was a parking area and a small garden. The access road that came in from the Coast Highway and the highway itself were invisible in the misty darkness. The light over the door burned dully, and as Vickery moved toward it Hannigan shut off the lantern and put it and the shovel down against the wall. Then he started after the big man.

He was just about to tell Vickery that the door was unlocked and to go on in when another man came out of the fog.

Hannigan saw him immediately, over on the access road, and stopped with the back of his neck prickling again. This newcomer was about the same size as Vickery, and Hannigan himself; thick through the body, dressed in a rumpled suit but without a tie. He had wildly unkempt hair and an air of either agitation or harried intent. He hesitated briefly when he saw Hannigan and Vickery, then he came toward them holding his right hand against his hip at a spot covered by his suit jacket.

Vickery had seen him by this time and he was up on the balls of his feet again, nervously watchful. The third man halted opposite the door and looked back and forth between Hannigan and Vickery. He said, "One of you the owner of this house?"

"I am," Hannigan said. He gave his name. "Who are you?"

"Lieutenant McLain, Highway Patrol. You been here all evening, Mr. Hannigan?"

"Yes."

"No trouble of any kind?"

"No. Why?"

"We're looking for a man who escaped from the hospital at Tescadero this afternoon," McLain said. "Maybe you've heard about that?"

Hannigan nodded.

"Well, I don't want to alarm you, but we've had word that he may be in this vicinity."

Hannigan wet his lips and glanced at Vickery.

"If you're with the Highway Patrol," Vickery said to McLain, "how come you're not in uniform?"

"I'm in Investigation. Plainclothes."

"Why would you be on foot? And alone? I thought the police

always traveled in pairs."

McLain frowned and studied Vickery for a long moment, penetratingly. His eyes were wide and dark and did not blink much. At length he said, "I'm alone because we've had to spread ourselves thin in order to cover this whole area, and I'm on foot because my damned car came up with a broken fanbelt. I radioed for assistance, and then I came down here because I didn't see any sense in sitting around waiting and doing nothing."

Hannigan remembered Vickery's words on the beach: *I could give you a story about my car breaking down.* He wiped again at the dampness on his face.

Vickery said, "You mind if we see some identification?"

McLain took his hand away from his hip and produced a leather folder from his inside jacket pocket. He held it out so Hannigan and Vickery could read it. "That satisfy you?"

The folder corroborated what McLain had told them about himself; but it did not contain a picture of him. Vickery said nothing.

Hannigan asked, "Have you got a photo of this lunatic?"

"None that will do us any good. He destroyed his file before he escaped from the asylum, and he's been in there sixteen years. The only pictures we could dig up are so old, and he's apparently changed so much, the people at Tescadero tell us there's almost no likeness any more."

"What about a description?"

"Big, dark-haired, regular features, no deformities or identifying narks. That could fit any one of a hundred thousand men or more in Northern California."

"It could fit any of the three of us," Vickery said.

McLain studied him again. "That's right, it could."

"Is there anything else about him?" Hannigan asked. "I mean, could he pretend to be sane and get away with it?"

"The people at the hospital say yes."

"That makes it even worse, doesn't it?"

"You bet it does," McLain said. He rubbed his hands together briskly. "Look, why don't we talk inside? It's pretty cold out here."

Hannigan hesitated. He wondered if McLain had some other reason for wanting to go inside, and when he looked at Vickery it seemed to him the other man was wondering the same thing. But he could see no way to refuse without making trouble.

He said, "No, I guess not. The door's open."

For a moment all three of them stood motionless, McLain

still watching Vickery intently. Vickery had begun to fidget under the scrutiny. Finally, since he was closest to the door, he jerked his head away, opened it, and went in sideways, the same way he had climbed the steps from the patio. McLain kept on waiting, which left Hannigan no choice except to follow Vickery. When they were both inside, McLain entered and shut the door.

The three of them went down the short hallway into the big beam-ceilinged family room. McLain glanced around at the fieldstone fireplace, the good reproductions on the walls, the tasteful modern furnishings. "Nice place," he said. "You live here alone, Mr. Hannigan?"

"No, with my wife."

"Is she here now?"

"She's in Vegas. She likes to gamble and I don't."

"I see."

"Can I get you something? A drink?"

"Thanks, no. Nothing while I'm on duty."

"I wouldn't mind having one," Vickery said. He was still fidgeting because McLain was still watching him and had been the entire time he was talking to Hannigan.

Near the picture window that took up the entire wall facing the ocean was a leather-topped standing bar; Hannigan crossed to it. The drapes were open and wisps of the gray fog outside pressed against the glass like skeletal fingers. He put his back to the window and lifted a bottle of bourbon from one of the shelves inside the bar.

"I didn't get your name," McLain said to Vickery.

"Art Vickery. Look, why do you keep staring at me?"

McLain ignored that. "You a friend of Mr. Hannigan's?"

"No," Hannigan said from the bar. "I just met him tonight, a few minutes ago. He wanted to use my phone."

McLain's eyes glittered slightly. "Is that right?" he said. "Then you don't live around here, Mr. Vickery?"

"No, I don't live around here."

"Your car happened to break down too, is that it?"

"Not exactly."

"What then—exactly?"

"I was with a woman, a married woman, and her husband showed up unexpectedly." There was sweat on Vickery's face now. "You know how that is."

"No," McLain said, "I don't. Who was this woman?"

"Listen, if you're with the Highway Patrol as you say, I don't want to give you a name."

"What do you mean, *if* I'm with the Highway Patrol as I say? I told you I was, didn't I? I showed you my identification, didn't I?"

"Just because you're carrying it doesn't make it yours."

McLain's lips thinned and his eyes did not blink at all now. "You trying to get at something, mister? If so, maybe you'd better just spit it out all at once."

"I'm not trying to get at anything," Vickery said. "There's an unidentified lunatic running around loose in this damned fog."

"So you're not even trustful of a law officer."

"I'm just being careful."

"That's a good way to be," McLain said. "I'm that way myself. Where do you live, Vickery?"

"In San Francisco."

"How were you planning to get home tonight?"

"I'm going to call a friend to come pick me up."

"Another lady friend?"

"No."

"All right. Tell you what. You come with me up to where my car is, and when the tow truck shows up with a new fanbelt I'll drive you down to Bodega. You can make your call from the Patrol station there."

A muscle throbbed in Vickery's temple. He tried to match McLain's stare, but it was only seconds before he averted his eyes.

"What's the matter?" McLain said. "Something you don't like about my suggestion?"

"I can make my call from right here."

"Sure, but then you'd be inconveniencing Mr. Hannigan. You wouldn't want to do that to a total stranger, would you?"

"You're a total stranger," Vickery said. "I'm not going out in that fog with you, not alone and on foot."

"I think maybe you are."

"No. I don't like those eyes of yours, the way you keep staring at me."

"And I don't like the way you're acting, or your story, or the way you look," McLain said. His voice had got very soft, but there was a hardness underneath that made Hannigan— standing immobile now at the bar—feel ripples of cold along his back. "We'll just be going, Vickery. Right now."

Vickery took a step toward him, and Hannigan could not tell if it was involuntary or menacing. Immediately McLain swept the tail of his suit jacket back and slid a gun out of a holster on his hip, centered it on Vickery's chest. The coldness on

Hannigan's back deepened; he found himself holding his breath.

"Outside, mister," McLain said.

Vickery had gone pale and the sweat had begun to run on his face. He shook his head and kept on shaking it as McLain advanced on him, as he himself started to back away. "Don't let him do it," Vickery said desperately. He was talking to Hannigan but looking at the gun. "Don't let him take me out of here!"

Hannigan spread his hands. "There's nothing I can do."

"That's right, Mr. Hannigan," McLain said, "you just let me handle things. Either way it goes with this one, I'll be in touch."

A little dazedly, Hannigan watched McLain prod Vickery into the hall, to the door; heard Vickery shout something. Then they were gone and the door slammed shut behind them.

Hannigan got a handkerchief out of his pocket and mopped his forehead. He poured himself a drink, swallowed it, poured and drank a second. Then he went to the door.

Outside, the night was silent except for the rhythmic hammering of the breakers in the distance. There was no sign of Vickery or McLain. Hannigan picked up the shovel and the lantern from where he had put them at the house wall and made his way down the steps to the patio, down the fogbound path toward the tule marsh.

He thought about the two men as he went. Was Vickery the lunatic? Or could it be McLain? Well, it didn't really matter; all that mattered now was that Vickery might say something to somebody about the grave. Which meant that Hannigan had to dig up the body and bury it again in some other place.

He hadn't intended the marsh to be a permanent burial spot anyway; he would find a better means of disposal later on. Once that task was taken care of, he could relax and make a few definite plans for the future. Money was made to be spent, particularly if you had a lot of it. It was too bad he had never been able to convince Karen of that.

At the gravesite Hannigan set the lantern down and began to unearth the strangled body of his wife.

And that was when the third man, a stranger carrying a long sharp kitchen knife, crept stealthily out of the fog. . .

A CRAVING FOR ORIGINALITY

Charlie Hackman was a professional writer. He wrote popular fiction, any kind from sexless Westerns to sexy Gothics to over-sexed historical romances, whatever the current trends happened to be. He could be counted on to deliver an acceptable manuscript to order in two weeks. He had published 9,000,000 words in a fifteen-year career, under a variety of different names (Allison St. Cyr being the most prominent), and he couldn't tell you the plot of any book he'd written more than six months ago. He was what is euphemistically known in the trade as "a dependable wordsmith," or "a versatile pro," or "a steady producer of commercial commodities."

In other words, he was well-named: Hackman was a hack.

The reason he was a hack was not because he was fast and prolific, or because he contrived popular fiction on demand, or because he wrote for money. It was because he was and did all these things with no ambition and no sense of commitment. It was because he wrote without originality of any kind.

Of course, Hackman had not started out to be a hack; no writer does. But he had discovered early on, after his first two novels were rejected with printed slips by thirty-seven publishers each, that (a) he was not very good, and (b) what talent he did possess was in the form of imitations. When he tried to do imaginative, ironic, meaningful work of his own he failed miserably; but when he imitated the ideas and visions of others, the blurred carbon copies he produced were just literate enough to be publishable.

Truth to tell, this didn't bother him very much. The one thing he had always wanted to be was a professional writer; he had dreamed of nothing else since his discovery of the Hardy Boys and Tarzan books in his pre-teens. So from the time of his first sale he accepted what he was, shrugged, and told himself not to worry about it. What was wrong with being a hack, anyway? The writing business was full of them—and hacks, no less than nonhacks, offered a desirable form of escapist entertainment to the masses; the only difference was, his readership had nondiscriminating tastes. Was his product, after all, any less honorable than what television offered? Was he hurting anybody, corrupting anybody? No. Absolutely not. So what was wrong with being a hack?

For one and a half decades, operating under this cheerful set of rationalizations, Hackman was a complacent man. He wrote from ten to fifteen novels per year, all for minor and exploitative paperback houses, and earned an average annual sum of $35,000. He married an ungraceful woman named Grace and moved into a suburban house on Long Island. He went bowling once a week, played poker once a week, argued conjugal matters with his wife once a week, and took the train into Manhattan to see his agent and editors once a week. Every June he and Grace spent fourteen pleasant days at Lake George in the Adirondacks. Every Christmas Grace's mother came from Pennsylvania and spent fourteen miserable days with them.

He drank a little too much sometimes and worried about lung cancer because he smoked three packs of cigarettes a day. He cheated moderately on his income tax. He coveted one of his neighbors' wives. He read all the current paperback bestsellers, dissected them in his mind, and then reassembled them into similar plots for his own novels. When new acquaintances asked him what he did for a living he said, "I'm a writer," and seldom failed to feel a small glow of pride.

That was the way it was for fifteen years—right up until the morning of his fortieth birthday.

Hackman woke up on that morning, looked at Grace lying beside him, and realized she had put on at least forty pounds since their marriage. He listened to himself wheeze as he lit his first cigarette of the day. He got dressed and walked downstairs to his office, where he read the half page of manuscript still in his typewriter (an occult pirate novel, the latest craze). He went outside and stood on the lawn and looked at his house. Then he sat down on the porch steps and looked at himself.

I'm not just a writer of hack stories, he thought sadly, I'm a liver of a hack life.

Fifteen years of cohabiting with trite fictional characters in hackneyed fictional situations. Fifteen years of cohabiting with an unimaginative wife in a trite suburb in a hackneyed lifestyle in a conventional world. Hackman the hack, doing the same things over and over again; Hackman the hack, grinding out books and days one by one. No uniqueness in any of it, from the typewriter to the bedroom to the Adirondacks.

No originality.

He sat there for a long while, thinking about this. No originality. Funny. It was like waking up to the fact that, after forty years, you've never tasted pineapple, that pineapple was missing from your life. All of a sudden you craved pineapple; you wanted it more than you'd ever wanted anything before.

Pineapple or originality—it was the same principle.

Grace came out eventually and asked him what he was doing. "Thinking that I crave originality," he said, and she said, "Will you settle for eggs and bacon?" Trite dialogue, Hackman thought. Hackneyed humor. He told her he didn't want any breakfast and went into his office.

Originality. Well, even a hack ought to be able to create something fresh and imaginative if he applied himself; even a hack learned a few tricks in fifteen years. How about a short story? Good. He had never written a short story, he would be working in new territory already. Now how about a plot?

He sat at his typewriter. He paced the office. He lay down on the couch. He sat at the typewriter again. Finally the germ of an idea came to him and he nurtured it until it began to develop. Then he began to type.

It took him all day to write the story, which was about five thousand words long. That was his average wordage per day on a novel, but on a novel he never revised so much as a comma. After supper he went back into the office and made pen-and-ink corrections until eleven o'clock. Then he went to bed, declined Grace's reluctant offer of "a birthday present," and dreamed about the story until 6:00 A.M. At which time he got up, retyped the pages, made some more revisions in ink, and retyped the story a third time before he was satisfied. He mailed it that night to his agent.

Three days later the agent called about a new book contract. Hackman asked him, "Did you have a chance to read the short story I sent you?"

"I read it, all right. And sent it straight back to you."

"Sent it back? What's wrong with it?"

"It's old hat," the agent said. "The idea's been done to death."

Hackman went out into the backyard and lay down in the hammock. All right, so maybe he was doomed to hackdom as a writer; maybe he just wasn't capable of *writing* anything original. But that didn't mean he couldn't *do* something original, did it? He had a quick mind, a good grasp of what was going on in the world. He ought to be able to come up with at least one original idea, maybe even an idea that would not only satisfy his craving for originality but change his life, get him out of the stale rut he was in.

He closed his eyes.

He concentrated.

He thought about jogging backward from Long Island to Miami Beach and then applying for an entry in the Guinness

A CRAVING FOR ORIGINALITY

Book of World Records.

Imitative.

He thought about marching naked through Times Square at high noon, waving a standard paperback contract and using a bullhorn to protest man's literary inhumanity to man.

Trite.

He thought about adopting a red-white-and-blue disguise and robbing a bank in each one of the original thirteen states.

Derivative.

He thought about changing his name to Holmes, finding a partner named Watson, and opening a private inquiry agency that specialized in solving the unsolved and insoluble.

Parrotry.

He thought about doing other things legal and illegal, clever and foolish, dangerous and harmless.

Unoriginal. Unoriginal. Unoriginal.

That day passed and several more just like it. Hackman became obsessed with originality—so much so that he found himself unable to write, the first serious block he had had as a professional. It was maddening, but every time he thought of a sentence and started to type it out, something would click in his mind and make him analyze it as original or banal. The verdict was always banal.

He thought about buying a small printing press, manufacturing bogus German Deutsche marks in his basement, and then flying to Munich and passing them at the Oktoberfest.

Counterfeit.

Hackman took to drinking a good deal more than his usual allotment of alcohol in the evenings. His consumption of cigarettes rose to four packs a day and climbing. His originality quotient remained at zero.

He thought about having a treasure map tattooed on his chest, claiming to be the sole survivor of a gang of armored car thieves, and conning all sorts of greedy people out of their life savings.

Trite.

The passing days turned into passing weeks. Hackman still wasn't able to write; he wasn't able to do much of anything except vainly overwork his brain cells. He knew he couldn't function again as a writer or a human being until he did something, *anything* original.

He thought about building a distillery in his garage and becoming Long Island's largest manufacturer and distributor of bootleg whiskey.

Hackneyed.

Grace had begun a daily and voluble series of complaints. Why was he moping around, drinking and smoking so much? Why didn't he go into his office and write his latest piece of trash? What were they going to do for money if he didn't fulfill his contracts? How would they pay the mortgage and the rest of their bills? What was the *matter* with him, anyway? Was he going through some kind of midlife crisis or what?

Hackman thought about strangling her, burying her body under the acacia tree in the backyard—committing the perfect crime.

Stale. Bewhiskered.

Another week disappeared. Hackman was six weeks overdue now on an occult pirate novel and two weeks overdue on a male-action novel; his publishers were upset, his agent was upset; where the hell were the manuscripts? Hackman said he was just polishing up the first one. "Sure you are," the agent said over the phone. "Well, you'd better have it with you when you come in on Friday. I mean that, Charlie. You'd better deliver."

Hackman thought about kidnapping the star of Broadway's top musical extravaganza and holding her for a ransom of $1,000,000 plus a role in her next production.

Old stuff.

He decided that things couldn't go on this way. Unless he came up with an original idea pretty soon, he might just as well shuffle off this mortal coil.

He thought about buying some rat poison and mixing himself an arsenic cocktail.

More old stuff.

Or climbing a utility pole and grabbing hold of a high-tension wire.

Prosaic. Corny.

Or hiring a private plane to fly him over the New Jersey swamps and then jumping out at two thousand feet.

Ho-hum.

Damn! He couldn't seem to go on, he couldn't seem not to go on. So what was he going to do?

He thought about driving over to Pennsylvania, planting certain carefully faked documents inside Grace's mother's house, and turning the old bat in to the F.B.I. as a foreign spy.

Commonplace.

On Friday morning he took his cigarettes (the second of the five packs a day he was now consuming) and his latest hangover down to the train station. There he boarded the express for Manhattan and took a seat in the club car.

He thought about hijacking the train and extorting $20,000,000 from the state of New York.

Imitative.

When the train arrived in Manhattan he trudged the six blocks to his agent's office. In the elevator on the way up an attractive young blonde gave him a friendly smile and said it was a nice day, wasn't it?

Hackman thought about making her his mistress, having a torrid affair, and then running off to Acapulco with her and living in sin in a villa high above the harbor and weaving Mexican serapes by day and drinking tequila by night.

Hackneyed.

The first thing his agent said to him was, "Where's the manuscript, Charlie?" Hackman said it wasn't ready yet, he was having a few personal problems. The agent said, "You think you got problems? What about my problems? You think I can afford to have hack writers missing deadlines and making editors unhappy? That kind of stuff reflects back on me, ruins my reputation. I'm not in this business for my health, so maybe you'd better just find yourself another agent."

Hackman thought about bashing him over the head with a paperweight, disposing of the body, and assuming his identity after first gaining sixty pounds and going through extensive plastic surgery.

Moth-eaten. Threadbare.

Out on the street again, he decided he needed a drink and turned into the first bar he came to. He ordered a triple vodka and sat brooding over it. I've come to the end of my rope, he thought. If there's one original idea in this world, I can't even imagine what it is. For that matter, I can't even imagine a partly original idea, which I'd settle for right now because maybe there isn't anything completely original any more.

"What am I going to do?" he asked the bartender.

"Who cares?" the bartender said. "Stay, go, drink, don't drink—it's all the same to me."

Hackman sighed and got off his stool and swayed out onto East 52nd Street. He turned west and began to walk back toward Grand Central, jostling his way through the midafternoon crowds. Overhead, the sun glared down at him between the buildings like a malevolent eye.

He was nearing Madison Avenue, muttering clichés to himself, when the idea struck him.

It came out of nowhere, full-born in an instant, the way most great ideas (or so he had heard) always do. He came to an abrupt standstill. Then he began to smile. Then he began to laugh. Passersby gave him odd looks and detoured around him, but Hackman didn't care. The idea was all that mattered.

It was inspired.
It was imaginative.
It was meaningful.
It was original.

Oh, not one-hundred-percent original—but that was all right. He had already decided that finding total originality was an impossible goal. This idea was close, though. It was close and it was wonderful and he was going to do it. Of course he was going to do it; after all these weeks of search and frustration, how could he not do it?

Hackman set out walking again. His stride was almost jaunty and he was whistling to himself. Two blocks south he entered a sporting goods store and found what he wanted. The salesman who waited on him asked if he was going camping. "Nope," Hackman said, and winked. "Something much more original than that."

He left the store and hurried down to Madison to a bookshop that specialized in mass-market paperbacks. Inside were several long rows of shelving, each shelf containing different categories of fiction and nonfiction, alphabetically arranged. Hackman stepped into the fiction section, stopped in front of the shelf marked "Historical Romances," and squinted at the titles until he located one of his own pseudonymous works. Then he unwrapped his parcel.

And took out the woodsman's hatchet.
And got a comfortable grip on its handle.
And raised it high over his head.
And—

Whack! Eleven copies of *Love's Tender Fury* by Allison St. Cyr were drawn and quartered.

A male customer yelped; a female customer shrieked. Hackman took no notice. He moved on to the shelf marked "Occult Pirate Adventure," raised the hatchet again, and—

Whack! Nine copies of *The Devil Daughter of Jean Lafitte* by Adam Caine were exorcised and scuttled.

On to "Adult Westerns." And—

Whack! Four copies of *Lust Rides the Outlaw Trail* by Galen McGee bit the dust.

Behind the front counter a chubby little man was jumping up and down, waving his arms. "What are you doing?" he kept shouting at Hackman. "What are you doing?"

"Hackwork!" Hackman shouted back. "I'm a hack writer doing hackwork!"

He stepped smartly to "Gothic Suspense." And—

Whack! Five copies of *Mansion of Dread* by Melissa Ann Farnsworth were reduced to rubble.

On to "Male Action Series," and—

Whack! Ten copies of Max Ruffe's *The Grenade Launcher #23: Blowup at City Hall* exploded into fragments.

Hackman paused to survey the carnage. Then he nodded in satisfaction and turned toward the front door. The bookshop was empty now, but the chubby little man was visible on the sidewalk outside, jumping up and down and semaphoring his arms amid a gathering crowd. Hackman crossed to the door in purposeful strides and threw it open.

People scattered every which way when they saw him come out with the hatchet aloft. But they needn't have feared; he had no interest in people, except as bit players in this little drama. After all, what hack worth the name ever cared a hoot about his audience?

He began to run up 48th Street toward Fifth Avenue, brandishing the hatchet. Nobody tried to stop him, not even when he lopped off the umbrella shading a frankfurter vendor's cart.

"I'm a hack!" he shouted.

And shattered the display window of an exclusive boutique.

"I'm Hackman the hack!" he yelled.

And halved the product and profits of a pretzel vendor.

"I'm Hackman the hack and I'm hacking my way to glory!" he bellowed.

And sliced the antenna off an illegally parked Cadillac limousine.

He was almost to Fifth Avenue by this time. Ahead of him he could see a red signal light holding up crosstown traffic; this block of 48th Street was momentarily empty. Behind him he could hear angry shouts and what sounded like a police whistle. He looked back over his shoulder. Several people were giving pursuit, including the chubby little man from the bookshop; the leader of the pack, a blue uniform with a red face atop it, was less than fifty yards distant.

But the game was not up yet, Hackman thought. There were more bookstores along Fifth; with any luck he could hack his way through two or three before they got him. He decided south was the direction he wanted to go, pulled his head around, and started to sprint across the empty expanse of 48th.

Only the street wasn't empty any longer; the signal on Fifth had changed to green for the eastbound traffic. He ran right out in front of an oncoming car.

He saw it too late to jump clear, and the driver saw him too late to brake or swerve. But before he and the machine joined forces, Hackman had just enough time to realize the full scope of what was happening—and to feel a sudden elation. In fact, he wished with his last wish that he'd thought of this himself. It was the crowning touch, the final fillip, the *coup de grace*; it lent the death of Hackman, unlike the life of Hackman, a genuine originality.

Because the car that did him in was not just a car; it was a New York City taxi cab.

Otherwise known as a hack.

STACKED DECK

1

From where he stood in the shadow of a split-bole Douglas fir, Deighan had a clear view of the cabin down below. Big harvest moon tonight, and only a few streaky clouds scudding past now and then to dim its hard yellow shine. The hard yellow glistened off the surface of Lake Tahoe beyond, softened into a long silverish stripe out toward the middle. The rest of the water shone like polished black metal. All of it was empty as far as he could see, except for the red-and-green running lights of a boat well away to the north, pointed toward the neon shimmer that marked the North Shore gambling casinos.

The cabin was big, made of cut pine logs and redwood shakes. It had a railed redwood deck that overlooked the lake, mostly invisible from where Deighan was. A flat concrete pier jutted out into the moonstruck water, a pair of short wooden floats making a T at its outer end. The boat tied up there was a thirty-foot Chris-Craft with sleeping accommodations for four. Nothing but the finer things for the Shooter.

Deighan watched the cabin. He'd been watching it for three hours now, from this same vantage point. His legs bothered him a little, standing around like this, and his eyes hurt from squinting. Time was, he'd had the night vision of an owl. Not anymore. What he had now, that he hadn't had when he was younger, was patience. He'd learned that in the last three years, along with a lot of other things—patience most of all.

On all sides the cabin was dark, but that was because they'd put the blackout curtains up. The six of them had been inside for better than two hours now, the same five-man nucleus as on every Thursday night except during the winter months, plus the one newcomer. The Shooter went to Hawaii when it started to snow. Or Florida or the Bahamas—someplace warm. Mannlicher and Brandt stayed home in the winter. Deighan didn't know what the others did, and he didn't care.

A match flared in the darkness between the carport, where the Shooter's Caddy Eldorado was slotted, and the parking area back among the trees. That was the lookout—Mannlicher's boy. Some lookout: he smoked a cigarette every five minutes, like clockwork, so you always knew where he was. Deighan watched him smoke this one. When he was done, he threw the butt away in a shower of sparks, and then seemed to remember that he was surrounded by dry timber and went after it and stamped it out with his shoe. Some lookout.

Deighan held his watch up close to his eyes, pushed the little button that lighted its dial. Ten-nineteen. Just about time. The lookout was moving again, down toward the lake. Pretty soon he would walk out on the pier and smoke another cigarette and admire the view for a few minutes. He apparently did that at least twice every Thursday night—that had been his pattern on each of the last two—and he hadn't gone through the ritual yet tonight. He was bored, that was the thing. He'd been at his job a long time and it was always the same; there wasn't anything for him to do except walk around and smoke cigarettes and look at three hundred square miles of lake. Nothing ever happened. In three years nothing had ever happened.

Tonight something was going to happen.

Deighan took the gun out of the clamshell holster at his belt. It was a Smith & Wesson .38 wadcutter, lightweight, compact—a good piece, one of the best he'd ever owned. He held it in his hand, watching as the lookout performed as if on cue—walked to the pier, stopped, then moved out along its flat surface. When the guy had gone halfway, Deighan came out of the shadows and went down the slope at an angle across the driveway, to the rear of the cabin. His shoes made little sliding sounds on the needled ground, but they weren't sounds that carried.

He'd been over this ground three times before, dry runs the last two Thursday nights and once during the day when nobody was around; he knew just where and how to go. The lookout was lighting up again, his back to the cabin, when Deighan reached the rear wall. He eased along it to the spare-bedroom window. The sash went up easily, noiselessly. He could hear them then, in the rec room—voices, ice against glass, the click and rattle of the chips. He got the ski mask from his jacket pocket, slipped it over his head, snugged it down. Then he climbed through the window, put his penlight on just long enough to orient himself, went straight across to the door that led into the rec room.

It didn't make a sound, either, when he opened it. He went in with the revolver extended, elbow locked. Sturgess saw him first. He said, "Jesus Christ!" and his body went as stiff as if he were suffering a stroke. The others turned in their chairs, gawking. The Shooter started up out of his.

Deighan said, fast and hard, "Sit still if you don't want to die. Hands on the table where I can see them—all of you. Do it!"

They weren't stupid; they did what they were told. Deighan

watched them through a thin haze of tobacco smoke. Six men around the hexagonal poker table, hands flat on its green baize, heads lifted or twisted to stare at him. He knew five of them. Mannlicher, the fat owner of the Nevornia Club at Crystal Bay; he had Family ties, even though he was a Prussian, because he'd once done some favors for an east-coast capo. Brandt, Mannlicher's cousin and private enforcer, who doubled as the Nevornia's floor boss. Bellah, the quasi-legitimate real-estate developer and high roller. Sturgess, the bankroll behind the Jackpot Lounge down at South Shore. And the Shooter—hired muscle, hired gun, part-time coke runner, whose real name was Dennis D'Allesandro. The sixth man was the pigeon they'd lured in for this particular game, a lean guy in his fifties with Texas oil money written all over him and his fancy clothes—Donley or Donavan, something like that.

Mannlicher was the bank tonight; the table behind his chair was covered with stacks of dead presidents—fifties and hundreds, mostly. Deighan took out the folded-up flour sack, tossed it on top of the poker chips that littered the baize in front of Mannlicher. "All right. Fill it."

The fat man didn't move. He was no pushover; he was hard, tough, mean. And he didn't like being ripped off. Veins bulged in his neck, throbbed in his temples. The violence in him was close to the surface now, held thinly in check.

"You know who we are?" he said. "Who I am?"

"Fill it."

"You dumb bastard. You'll never live to spend it."

"Fill the sack. *Now*."

Deighan's eyes, more than his gun, made up Mannlicher's mind for him. He picked up the sack, pushed around in his chair, began to savagely feed in the stacks of bills.

"The rest of you," Deighan said, "put your wallets, watches, jewelry on the table. Everything of value. Hurry it up."

The Texan said, "Listen heah—" and Deighan pointed the .38 at his head and said, "One more word, you're a dead man." The Texan made an effort to stare him down, but it was just to save face; after two or three seconds he lowered his gaze and began stripping the rings off his fingers.

The rest of them didn't make any fuss. Bellah was sweating; he kept swiping it out of his eyes, his hands moving in little jerks and twitches. Brandt's eyes were like dull knives, cutting away at Deighan's masked face. D'Allesandro showed no emotion of any kind. That was his trademark; he was your original iceman. They might have called him that, maybe, if he'd been like one of those old-timers who used an ice pick or a blade. As it was, with his preferences, the Shooter was the right name for him.

Mannlicher had the sack full now. The platinum ring on his left hand, with its circle of fat diamonds, made little gleams and glints in the shine from the low-hanging droplight. The idea of losing that bothered him even more than losing his money; he kept running the fingers of his other hand over the stones.

"The ring," Deighan said to him. "Take it off."

"Go to hell."

"Take it off or I'll put a third eye in the middle of your forehead. Your choice."

Mannlicher hesitated, tried to stare him down, didn't have any better luck at it than the Texan. There was a tense moment; then, because he didn't want to die over a piece of jewelry, he yanked the ring off, slammed it down hard in the middle of the table.

Deighan said, "Put it in the sack. The wallets and the rest of the stuff too."

This time Mannlicher didn't hesitate. He did as he'd been told.

"All right," Deighan said. "Now get up and go over by the bar. Lie down on the floor on your belly."

Mannlicher got up slowly, his jaw set and his teeth clenched as if to keep the violence from spewing out like vomit. He lay down on the floor. Deighan gestured at Brandt, said, "You next. Then the rest of you, one at a time."

When they were all on the floor he moved to the table, caught up the sack. "Stay where you are for ten minutes," he told them. "You move before that, or call to the guy outside, I'll blow the place up. I got a grenade in my pocket, the fragmentation kind. Anybody doubt it?"

None of them said anything.

Deighan backed up into the spare bedroom, leaving the door open so he could watch them all the way to the window. He put his head out, saw no sign of the lookout. Still down by the lake somewhere. The whole thing had taken just a few minutes.

He swung out through the window, hurried away in the shadows—but in the opposite direction from the driveway and the road above. On the far side of the cabin there was a path that angled through the pine forest to the north; he found it, followed it at a trot. Enough moonlight penetrated through the branches overhead to let him see where he was going.

He was almost to the lakefront when the commotion started

back there: voices, angry and pulsing in the night, Mannlicher's the loudest of them. They hadn't waited the full ten minutes, but then he hadn't expected them to. It didn't matter. The Shooter's cabin was invisible from here, cut off by a wooded finger of land a hundred yards wide. And they wouldn't be looking for him along the water, anyway. They'd be up on the road, combing that area; they'd figure automatically that his transportation was a car.

The hard yellow-and-black gleam of the lake was just ahead, the rushes and ferns where he'd tied up the rented Beachcraft inboard. He moved across the sandy strip of beach, waded out to his calves, dropped the loaded flour sack into the boat, and then eased the craft free of the rushes before he lifted himself over the gunwale. The engine caught with a quiet rumble the first time he turned the key.

They were still making noise back at the cabin, blundering around like fools, as he eased away into the night.

2

The motel was called the Whispering Pines. It was back off Highway 28 below Crystal Bay, a good half mile from the lake, tucked up in a grove of pines and Douglas fir. Deighan's cabin was the farthest from the office, detached from its nearest neighbor by thirty feet of open ground.

Inside he sat in darkness except for flickering light from the television. The set was an old one; the picture was riddled with snow and kept jumping every few seconds. But he didn't care; he wasn't watching it. Or listening to it: he had the sound turned off. It was on only because he didn't like waiting in the dark.

It had been after midnight when he came in—too late to make the ritual call to Fran, even though he'd felt a compulsion to do so. She went to bed at eleven-thirty; she didn't like the phone to ring after that. How could he blame her? When he was home and she was away at Sheila's or her sister's, he never wanted it to ring that late either.

It was one-ten now. He was tired, but not too tired. The evening was still in his blood, warming him, like liquor or drugs that hadn't quite worn off yet. Mannlicher's face . . . that was an image he'd never forget. The Shooter's, too, and Brandt's, but especially Mannlicher's.

Outside, a car's headlamps made a sweep of light across the curtained window as it swung in through the motel courtyard.

When it stopped nearby and the lights went out, Deighan thought: It's about time.

Footsteps made faint crunching sounds on gravel. Soft knock on the door. Soft voice following: "Prince? You in there?"

"Door's open."

A wedge of moonlight widened across the floor, not quite reaching to where Deighan sat in the lone chair with the .38 wadcutter in his hand. The man who stood silhouetted in the opening made a perfect target—just a damned airhead, any way you looked at him.

"Prince?"

"I'm over here. Come on in, shut the door."

"Why don't you turn on a light?"

"There's a switch by the door."

The man entered, shut the door. There was a click and the ceiling globe came on. Deighan stayed where he was, but reached over with his left hand to turn off the TV.

Bellah stood blinking at him, running his palms along the sides of his expensive cashmere jacket. He said nervously, "For God's sake, put the gun away. What's the idea?"

"I'm the cautious type."

"Well, put it away. I don't like it."

Deighan got to his feet, slid the revolver into his belt holster. "How'd it go?"

"Hairy, damned hairy. Mannlicher was like a madman." Bellah took a handkerchief out of his pocket, wiped his forehead. His angular face was pale, shiny-damp. "I didn't think he'd take it this hard. Christ."

That's the trouble with people like you, Deighan thought. You never think. He pinched a cigarette out of his shirt pocket, lit it with the Zippo Fran had given him fifteen years ago. Fifteen years, and it still worked. Like their marriage, even with all the trouble. How long was it now? Twenty-two years in May? Twenty-three?

Bellah said, "He started screaming at D'Allesandro. I thought he was going to choke him."

"Who? Mannlicher?"

"Yeah. About the window in the spare bedroom."

"What'd D'Allesandro say?"

"He said he always keeps it locked, you must have jimmied it some way that didn't leave any traces. Mannlicher didn't believe him. He thinks D'Allesandro forgot to lock it."

"Nobody got the idea it was an inside job?"

"No."

"Okay then. Relax, Mr. Bellah. You're in the clear."

Bellah wiped his face again. "Where's the money?"

"Other side of the bed. On the floor."

"You count it?"

"No. I figured you'd want to do that."

Bellah went over there, picked up the flour sack, emptied it on the bed. His eyes were bright and hot as he looked at all the loose green. Then he frowned, gnawed at his lower lip, and poked at Mannlicher's diamond ring. "What'd you take this for? Mannlicher is more pissed about the ring than anything else. He said his mother gave it to him. It's worth ten thousand."

"That's why I took it," Deighan said. "Fifteen percent of the cash isn't a hell of a lot."

Bellah stiffened. "I set it all up, didn't I? Why shouldn't I get the lion's share?"

"I'm not arguing, Mr. Bellah. We agreed on a price; OK, that's the way it is. I'm only saying I got a right to a little something extra."

"All right, all right." Bellah was looking at the money again. "Must be at least two hundred thousand," he said. "That Texan, Donley, brought fifty grand alone."

"Plenty in his wallet too, then."

"Yeah."

Deighan smoked and watched Bellah count the loose bills and what was in the wallets and billfolds. There was an expression on the developer's face like a man has when he's fondling a naked woman. Greed, pure and simple. Greed was what drove Lawrence Bellah; money was his best friend, his lover, his god. He didn't have enough ready cash to buy the lakefront property down near Emerald Bay—property he stood to make three or four million on, with a string of condos—and he couldn't raise it fast enough any legitimate way; so he'd arranged to get it by knocking over his own weekly poker game, even if it meant crossing some hard people. He had balls, you had to give him that. He was stupid as hell, and one of these days he was liable to end up in pieces at the bottom of the lake, but he did have balls.

He was also lucky, at least for the time being, because the man he'd picked to do his strong-arm work was Bob Prince. He had no idea the name was a phony, no idea the whole package on Bob Prince was the result of three years of careful manipulation. All he knew was that Prince had a reputation as dependable, easy to work with, not too smart or money-hungry, and that he was willing to do any kind of muscle work. Bellah didn't have an inkling of what he'd really done by hiring Bob Prince. If he kept on being lucky, he never would.

Bellah was sweating by the time he finished adding up the take. "Two hundred and thirty-three thousand and change," he said. "More than we figured on."

"My cut's thirty-five thousand," Deighan said.

"You divide fast." Bellah counted out two stacks, hundreds and fifties, to one side of the flowered bedspread. Then he said, "Count it? Or do you trust me?"

Deighan grinned. He rubbed out his cigarette, went to the bed, and took his time shuffling through the stacks. "On the nose," he said when he was done.

Bellah stuffed the rest of the cash back into the flour sack, leaving the watches and jewelry where they lay. He was still nervous, still sweating; he wasn't going to sleep much tonight, Deighan thought.

"That's it, then," Bellah said. "You going back to Chicago tomorrow?"

"Not right away. Thought I'd do a little gambling first."

"Around here? Christ, Prince. . . ."

"No. Reno, maybe. I might even go down to Vegas."

"Just get away from Tahoe."

"Sure," Deighan said. "First thing in the morning."

Bellah went to the door. He paused there to tuck the flour sack under his jacket; it made him look as if he had a tumor on his left side. "Don't do anything with that jewelry in Nevada. Wait until you get back to Chicago."

"Whatever you say, Mr. Bellah."

"Maybe I'll need you again sometime," Bellah said. "You'll hear from me if I do."

"Any time. Any old time."

When Bellah was gone, Deighan put five thousand dollars into his suitcase and the other thirty thousand into a knapsack he'd bought two days before at a South Shore sporting goods store. Mannlicher's diamond ring went into the knapsack, too, along with the better pieces among the rest of the jewelry. The watches and the other stuff were no good to him; he bundled those up in a hand towel from the bathroom, stuffed the bundle into the pocket of his down jacket. Then he had one more cigarette, set his portable alarm clock for six A. M., double-locked the door, and went to bed on the left side, with the revolver under the pillow near his right hand.

3

In the dawn light the lake was like smoky blue glass, empty except for a few optimistic fishermen anchored close to the eastern shoreline. The morning was cold, autumn-crisp, but there was no wind. The sun was just beginning to rise, painting the sky and its scattered cloud-streaks in pinks and golds. There was old snow on the upper reaches of Mount Tallac, on some of the other Sierra peaks that ringed the lake.

Deighan took the Beachcraft out half a mile before he dropped the bundle of watches and worthless jewelry overboard. Then he cut off at a long diagonal to the north that brought him to within a few hundred yards of the Shooter's cabin. He had his fishing gear out by then, fiddling with the glass rod and tackle—just another angler looking for rainbow, Mackinaw, and cutthroat trout.

There wasn't anybody out and around at the Shooter's place. Deighan glided past at two knots, angled into shore a couple of hundred yards beyond, where there were rushes and some heavy brush and trees overhanging the water. From there he had a pretty good view of the cabin, its front entrance, the Shooter's Caddy parked inside the carport.

It was eight o'clock, and the sun was all the way up, when he switched off the engine and tied up at the bole of a collapsed pine. It was a few minutes past nine-thirty when D'Allesandro came out and walked around to the Caddy. He was alone. No chippies from the casinos this morning, not after what had gone down last night. He might be going to the store for cigarettes, groceries, or to a café somewhere for breakfast. He might be going to see somebody, do some business. The important thing was, how long would he be gone?

Deighan watched him back his Caddy out of the carport, drive it away and out of sight on the road above. He stayed where he was, fishing, waiting. At the end of an hour, when the Shooter still hadn't come back, he started the boat's engine and took his time maneuvering around the wooded finger of land to the north and then into the cove where he'd anchored last night. He nosed the boat into the reeds and ferns, swung overboard, and pushed it farther in, out of sight. Then he caught up the knapsack and set off through the woods to the Shooter's cabin.

He made a slow half circle of the place, keeping to the trees. The carport was still empty. Nothing moved anywhere within the range of his vision. Finally he made his way down to the rear wall, around it and along the side until he reached the front door. He didn't like standing out here for even a little while because there was no cover; but this door was the only one into the house, except for sliding doors to the terrace and a porch on the other side, and you couldn't jimmy sliding doors easily and without leaving marks. The same was true of windows. The Shooter would have made sure they were all secure anyway.

Deighan had one pocket of the knapsack open, the pick gun in his hand, when he reached the door. He'd got the pick gun from a housebreaker named Caldwell, an old-timer who was retired now; he'd also got some other tools and lessons in how to use them on the various kinds of locks. The lock on the Shooter's door was a flush-mounted, five-pin cylinder lock, with a steel lip on the door frame to protect the bolt and strike plate. That meant it was a lock you couldn't loid with a piece of plastic or a shim. It also meant that with a pick gun you could probably have it open in a couple of minutes.

Bending, squinting, he slid the gun into the lock. Set it, working the little knob on top to adjust the spring tension. Then he pulled the trigger—and all the pins bounced free at once and the door opened under his hand.

He slipped inside, nudged the door shut behind him, put the pick gun away inside the knapsack, and drew on a pair of thin plastic gloves. The place smelled of stale tobacco smoke and stale liquor. They hadn't been doing all that much drinking last night; maybe the Shooter had nibbled a few too many after the rest of them finally left. He didn't like losing money and valuables any more than Mannlicher did.

Deighan went through the front room. Somebody'd decorated the place for D'Allesandro: leather furniture, deer and antelope heads on the walls, Indian rugs on the floors, tasteful paintings. Cocaine deals had paid for part of it; contract work, including two hits on greedy Oakland and San Francisco drug dealers, had paid for the rest. But the Shooter was still small-time. He wasn't bright enough to be anything else. Cards and dice and whores-in-training were all he really cared about.

The front room was no good; Deighan prowled quickly through the other rooms. D'Allesandro wasn't the kind to have an office or a den, but there was a big old-fashioned rolltop desk in a room with a TV set and one of those big movie-type screens. None of the desk drawers was locked. Deighan pulled out the biggest one, saw that it was loaded with Danish porn magazines, took the magazines out and set them on the floor.

He opened the knapsack and transferred the thirty thousand dollars into the back of the drawer. He put Mannlicher's ring in there, too, along with the other rings and a couple of gold chains the Texan had been wearing. Then he stuffed the porn magazines in at the front and pushed the drawer shut.

On his way back to the front room he rolled the knapsack tight around the pick gun and stuffed them into his jacket pocket. He opened the door, stepped out. He'd just finished resetting the lock when he heard the car approaching on the road above.

He froze for a second, looking up there. He couldn't see the car because of a screen of trees; but then he heard its automatic transmission gear down as it slowed for the turn into the Shooter's driveway. He pulled the door shut and ran toward the lake, the only direction he could go. Fifty feet away the log-railed terrace began, raised up off the sloping ground on redwood pillars. Deighan caught one of the railings, hauled himself up and half rolled through the gap between them. The sound of the oncoming car was loud in his ears as he landed, off balance, on the deck.

He went to one knee, came up again. The only way to tell if he'd been seen was to stop and look, but that was a fool's move. Instead he ran across the deck, climbed through the railing on the other side, dropped down, and tried to keep from making noise as he plunged into the woods. He stopped moving after thirty yards, where ferns and a deadfall formed a thick concealing wall. From behind it, with the .38 wadcutter in his hand, he watched the house and the deck, catching his breath, waiting.

Nobody came up or out of the deck. Nobody showed himself anywhere. The car's engine had been shut off sometime during his flight; it was quiet now, except for birds and the faint hum of a powerboat out on the lake.

Deighan waited ten minutes. When there was still nothing to see or hear, he transcribed a slow curl through the trees to where he could see the front of the cabin. The Shooter's Caddy was back inside the carport, no sign of haste in the way it had been neatly slotted. The cabin door was shut. The whole area seemed deserted.

But he waited another ten minutes before he was satisfied. Even then, he didn't holster his weapon until he'd made his way around to the cove where the Beachcraft was hidden. And he didn't relax until he was well out on the lake, headed back toward North Shore.

4

The Nevomia was one of North Shore's older clubs, but it had undergone some recent modernizing. Outside, it had been given a glass and gaudy-neon face-lift. Inside, they'd used more glass, some cut crystal, and a wine-red decor that included carpeting, upholstery, and gaming tables.

When Deighan walked in a few minutes before two, the banks of slots and the blackjack tables were getting moderately heavy play. That was because it was Friday; some of the small-time gamblers liked to get a jump on the weekend crowds. The craps and roulette layouts were quiet. The high rollers were like vampires: they couldn't stand the daylight, so they only came out after dark.

Deighan bought a roll of quarters at one of the change booths. There were a couple of dozen rows of slots in the main casino—flashy new ones, mostly, with a few of the old scrolled nickel-plated jobs mixed in for the sake of nostalgia. He stopped at one of the old quarter machines, fed in three dollars' worth. Lemons and oranges. He couldn't even line up two cherries for a three-coin drop. He smiled crookedly to himself, went away from the slots and into the long concourse that connected the main casino with the new, smaller addition at the rear.

There were telephone booths along one side of the concourse. Deighan shut himself inside one of them, put a quarter in the slot, pushed 0 and then the digits of his home number in San Francisco. When the operator came on he said it was a collect call; that was to save himself the trouble of having to feed in a handful of quarters. He let the circuit make exactly five burrs in his ear before he hung up. If Fran was home, she'd know now that he was all right. If she wasn't home, then she'd know it later when he made another five-ring call. He always tried to call at least twice a day, at different times, because sometimes she went out shopping or to a movie or to visit with Sheila and the kids.

It'd be easier if she just answered the phone, talked to him, but she never did when he was away. Never. Sheila or anybody else wanted to get hold of her, they had to call one of the neighbors or come over in person. She didn't want anything to do with him when he was away, didn't want to know what he was doing or even when he'd be back. "Suppose I picked up the phone and it wasn't you?" she'd said. "Suppose it was somebody telling me you were dead? I couldn't stand that." That part of it didn't make sense to him. If he were dead, somebody'd come by and tell it to her face; dead was dead, and what difference did it make how she got the news? But he didn't argue with her. He didn't like to argue with her, and it didn't cost him anything to do it her way.

He slotted the quarter again and called the Shooter's number. Four rings, five, and D'Allesandro's voice said, "Yeah?"

"Mr. Carson?"

"Who?"

"Isn't this Paul Carson?"

"No. You got the wrong number."

"Oh, sorry," Deighan said, and rang off.

Another quarter in the slot. This time the number he punched out was the Nevornia's business line. A woman's voice answered, crisp and professional. He said, "Mr. Mannlicher. Tell him it's urgent."

"Whom shall I say is calling?"

"Never mind that. Just tell him it's about what happened last night."

"Sir, I'm afraid I can't—"

"Tell him last night's poker game, damn it. He'll talk to me."

There was a click and some canned music began to play in his ear. He lit a cigarette. He was on his fourth drag when the canned music quit and the fat man's voice said, "Frank Mannlicher. Who's this?"

"No names. Is it all right to talk on this line?"

"Go ahead, talk."

"I'm the guy who hit your game last night."

Silence for four or five seconds. Then Mannlicher said, "Is that so?" in a flat, wary voice.

"Ski mask, Smith & Wesson .38, grenade in my jacket pocket. The take was better than two hundred thousand. I got your ring—platinum with a circle of diamonds."

Another pause, shorter this time. "So why call me today?"

"How'd you like to get it all back—the money and the ring?"

"How?"

"Go pick it up. I'll tell you where."

"Yeah? Why should you do me a favor?"

"I didn't know who you were last night. I wasn't told. If I had been, I wouldn't of gone through with it. I don't mess with people like you, people with your connections."

"Somebody hired you, that it?"

"That's it."

"Who?"

"D'Allesandro."

"*What?*"

"The Shooter. D'Allesandro."

". . . Bullshit."

"You don't have to believe me. But I'm telling you—he's the one. He didn't tell me who'd be at the game, and now he's trying to screw me on the money. He says there was less than a hundred and fifty thousand in the sack; I know better."

"So now you want to screw him."

"That's right. Besides, I don't like the idea of you pushing to find out who I am, maybe sending somebody to pay me a visit someday. I figure if I give you the Shooter, you'll lose interest in me."

More silence. "Why'd he do it?" Mannlicher said in a different voice—harder, with that edge of violence it had held last night. "Hit the game like that?"

"He needs big money, fast. He's into some kind of scam back east; he wouldn't say what it is."

"Where's the money and the rest of the stuff?"

"At his cabin. We had a drop arranged in the woods; I put the sack there last night, he picked it up this morning when nobody was around. The money's in his desk—the big rolltop. Your ring, too. That's where it was an hour ago, anyhow, when I walked out."

Mannlicher said, "In his desk," as if he were biting the words off something bitter.

"Go out there, see for yourself."

"If you're telling this straight, you got nothing to worry about from me. Maybe I'll fix you up with a reward or something. Where can I get in touch?"

"You can't," Deighan said. "I'm long gone as soon as I hang up this phone."

"I'll make it five thousand. Just tell me where you—"

Deighan broke the connection.

His cigarette had burned down to the filter; he dropped it on the floor, put his shoe on it before he left the booth. On his way out of the casino he paused long enough to push another quarter into the same slot machine he'd played before. More lemons and oranges. This time he didn't smile as he moved away.

5

Narrow and twisty, hemmed in by trees, old Lake Road branched off Highway 28 and took two miles to get all the way to the lake. But it wasn't a dead-end; another road picked it up at the lakefront and looped back out to the highway. There were several nice homes hidden away in the area—it was called Pine Acres—with plenty of space between them. The Shooter's cabin was a mile and a half from the highway, off an even narrower lane called Little Cove Road. The only other cabin within five hundred yards was a summer place that the owners had already closed up for the year.

Deighan drove past the intersection with Little Cove, went two-tenths of a mile, parked on the turnout at that point. There wasn't anybody else around when he got out, nothing to see except trees and little winks of blue that marked the nearness of the lake. If anybody came along they wouldn't pay any attention to the car. For one thing, it was a '75 Ford Galaxy with nothing distinctive about it except the antenna for the GTE mobile phone. It was his—he'd driven it up from San Francisco—but the papers on it said it belonged to Bob Prince. For another thing, Old Lake Road was only a hundred yards or so from the water here, and there was a path through the trees to a strip of rocky beach. Local kids used it in the summer; he'd found that out from Bellah. Kids might have decided to stop here on a sunny autumn day as well. No reason for anybody to think otherwise.

He found the path, went along it a short way to where it crossed a little creek, dry now and so narrow it was nothing more than a natural drainage ditch. He followed the creek to the north, on a course he'd taken three days ago. It led him to a shelflike overhang topped by two chunks of granite outcrop that leaned against each other like a pair of old drunks. Below the shelf, the land fell away sharply to the Shooter's driveway some sixty yards distant. Off to the right, where the incline wasn't so steep and the trees grew in a pack, was the split-bole Douglas fir where he'd stood waiting last night. The trees were fewer and more widely spaced apart between here and the cabin, so that from behind the two outcrops you had a good look at the Shooter's property, Little Cove Road, the concrete pier, and the lake shimmering under the late-afternoon sun.

The Caddy Eldorado was still slotted inside the carport. It was the only car in sight. Deighan knelt behind where the outcrops came together to form a notch, rubbed tension out of his neck and shoulders while he waited.

He didn't have to wait long. Less than ten minutes had passed when the car appeared on Little Cove Road, slowed, turned down the Shooter's driveway. It wasn't Mannlicher's fancy limo; it was a two-year-old Chrysler—Brandt's, maybe. Brandt was driving it: Deighan had a clear view of him through the side window as the Chrysler pulled up and stopped near the cabin's front door. He could also see that the lone passenger was Mannlicher.

Brandt got out, opened the passenger door for the fat man, and the two of them went to the cabin. It took D'Allesandro ten seconds to answer Brandt's knock. There was some talk, not much; then Mannlicher and Brandt went in, and the door shut behind them.

All right, Deighan thought. He'd stacked the deck as well as he could; pretty soon he'd know how the hand—and the game—played out.

Nothing happened for maybe five minutes. Then he thought he heard some muffled sounds down there, loud voices that went on for a while, something that might have been a bang, but the distance was too great for him to be sure that he wasn't imagining them. Another four or five minutes went by. And then the door opened and Brandt came out alone, looked around, called something back inside that Deighan didn't understand. If there was an answer, it wasn't audible. Brandt shut the door, hurried down to the lake, went out onto the pier. The Chris-Craft was still tied up there. Brandt climbed on board, disappeared for thirty seconds or so, reappeared carrying a square of something gray and heavy. Tarpaulin, Deighan saw when Brandt came back up the driveway. Big piece of it—big enough for a shroud.

The Shooter's hand had been folded. That left three of them still in the game.

When Brandt had gone back inside with the tarp, Deighan stood and half ran along the creek and through the trees to where he'd left the Ford. Old Lake Road was deserted, He yanked open the passenger door, leaned in, caught up the mobile phone, and punched out the emergency number for the county sheriff's office. An efficient-sounding male voice answered.

"Something's going on on Little Cove Road," Deighan said, making himself sound excited. "That's in Pine Acres, you know? It's the cabin at the end, down on the lake. I heard shots—people shooting at each other down there. It sounds like a war."

"What's the address?"

"I don't know the address, it's the cabin right on the lake. People *shooting* at each other. You better get right out there."

"Your name, sir?"

"I don't want to get involved. Just hurry, will you?"

Deighan put the receiver down, shut the car door, ran back along the path and along the creek to the shelf. Mannlicher and Brandt were still inside the cabin. He went to one knee again behind the outcrops, drew the .38 wadcutter, held it on his thigh.

It was another two minutes before the door opened down there. Brandt came out, looked around as he had before, went back inside—and then he and Mannlicher both appeared, one at each end of a big, tarp-wrapped bundle. They started to carry it down the driveway toward the lake. Going to put it on the boat, Deighan thought, take it out now or later on, when it's dark. Lake Tahoe was sixteen hundred feet deep in the middle. The bundle wouldn't have been the first somebody'd dumped out there.

He let them get clear of the Chrysler, partway down the drive, before he poked the gun into the notch, sighted, and fired twice. The shots went where he'd intended them to, wide by ten feet and into the roadbed so they kicked up gravel. Mannlicher and Brandt froze for an instant, confused. Deighan fired a third round, putting the slug closer this time, and that one panicked them: they let go of the bundle and began scrambling.

There was no cover anywhere close by; they both ran for the Chrysler. Brandt had a gun in his hand when he reached it, and he dropped down behind the rear deck, trying to locate Deighan's position. Mannlicher kept on scrambling around to the passenger door, pulled it open, pushed himself across the seat inside.

Deighan blew out the Chrysler's near front tire. Sighted, and blew out the rear tire. Brandt threw an answering shot his way, but it wasn't even close. The Chrysler was tilting in Deighan's direction as the tires flattened. Mannlicher pushed himself out of the car, tried to make a run for the cabin door with his arms flailing, his fat jiggling. Deighan put a bullet into the wall beside the door. Mannlicher reversed himself, fell in his frantic haste, crawled back behind the Chrysler.

Reloading the wadcutter, Deighan could hear the sound of cars coming fast up on Little Cove Road. No sirens, but revolving lights made faint bloodred flashes through the trees.

From behind the Chrysler Brandt fired again, wildly.

Beyond him, on the driveway, one corner of the tarp-wrapped bundle had come loose and was flapping in the wind off the lake.

A county sheriff's cruiser, its roof light slashing the air, made the turn off Little Cove onto the driveway. Another one was right behind it. In his panic, Brandt straightened up when he saw them and fired once, blindly, at the first in line.

Deighan was on his feet by then, hurrying away from the outcrops, holstering his weapon. Behind him he heard brakes squeal, another shot, voices yelling, two more shots. All the sounds faded as he neared the turnout and the Ford. By the time he pulled out onto the deserted road, there was nothing to hear but the sound of his engine, the screeching of a jay somewhere nearby.

Brandt had thrown in his hand by now; so had Mannlicher.

This pot belonged to him.

6

Fran was in the backyard, weeding her garden, when he got home late the following afternoon. He called to her from the doorway, and she glanced around and then got up, unsmiling, and came over to him. She was wearing jeans and one of his old shirts and a pair of gardening gloves, and her hair was tied in a long ponytail. Used to be a light, silky brown, her hair; now it was mostly gray. His fault. She was only forty-six. A woman of forty-six shouldn't be so gray.

She said, "So you're back." She didn't sound glad to see him, didn't kiss him or touch him at all. But her eyes were gentle on his face.

"I'm back."

"You all right? You look tired."

"Long drive. I'm fine; it was a good trip."

She didn't say anything. She didn't want to hear about it, not any of it. She just didn't want to know.

"How about you?" he asked. "Everything been okay?"

"Sheila's pregnant again."

"Christ. What's the matter with her? Why don't she get herself fixed? Or get Hank fixed?"

"She likes kids."

"I like kids too, but four's too many at her age. She's only twenty-seven."

"She wants eight."

"She's crazy," Deighan said. "What's she want to bring all

those kids into a world like this for?"

There was an awkward moment. It was always awkward at first when he came back. Then Fran said, "You hungry?"

"You know me. I can always eat." Fact was, he was starved. He hadn't eaten much up in Nevada, never did when he was away. And he hadn't had anything today except an English muffin and some coffee for breakfast in Truckee.

"Come into the kitchen," Fran said. "I'll fix you something."

They went inside. He got a beer out of the refrigerator; she waited and then took out some covered dishes, some vegetables. He wanted to say something to her, talk a little, but he couldn't think of anything. His mind was blank at times like this. He carried his beer into the living room.

The goddamn trophy case was the first thing he saw. He hated that trophy case; but Fran wouldn't get rid of it, no matter what he said. For her it was like some kind of shrine to the dead past. All the mementoes of his years on the force—twenty-two years, from beat patrolman in North Beach all the way up to inspector on the narcotics squad. The certificate he'd won in marksmanship competition at the police academy, the two citations from the mayor for bravery, other crap like that. Bones, that's all they were to him. Pieces of a rotting skeleton. What was the sense in keeping them around, reminding both of them of what he'd been, what he'd lost?

His fault he'd lost it, sure. But it was their fault too, goddamn them. The laws, the lawyers, the judges, the system. No convictions on half of all the arrests he'd ever made—half! Turning the ones like Mannlicher and Brandt and D'Allesandro loose, putting them right back on the street, letting them make their deals and their hits, letting them screw up innocent lives. Sheila's kids, his grandkids—lives like that. How could they blame him for being bitter? How could they blame him for taking too many drinks now and then?

He sat down on the couch, drank some of his beer, lit a cigarette. Ah Christ, he thought, it's not them. You know it wasn't them. It was you, you dumb bastard. They warned you twice about drinking on duty. And you kept on doing it, you were hog-drunk the night you plowed the departmental sedan into that vanload of teenagers. What if one of *those* kids had died? You were lucky, by God. You got off easy.

Sure, he thought. Sure. But he'd been a good cop, damn it, a cop inside and out; it was all he knew how to be. What was he supposed to do after they threw him off the force? Live on his half-pension? Get a job as a part-time security guard? Forty-four years old, no skills, no friends outside the department—what the hell was he supposed to do?

He'd invented Bob Prince, that was what he'd done. He'd gone into business for himself.

Fran didn't understand. "You'll get killed one of these days," she'd said in the beginning. "It's vigilante justice," she'd said. "You think you're Rambo, is that it?" she'd said. She just didn't understand. To him it was the same job he'd always done, the only one he was any good at, only now *he* made up some of the rules. He was no Rambo, one man up against thousands, a mindless killing machine; he hated that kind of phony flag-waving crap. It wasn't real. What he was doing, that was real. It meant something. But a hero? No. Hell, no. He was a sniper, that was all, picking off a weak or a vulnerable enemy here and there, now and then. Snipers weren't heroes, for Christ's sake. Snipers were snipers, just like cops were cops.

He finished his beer and his cigarette, got up, went into Fran's sewing room. The five thousand he'd held out of the poker-game take was in his pocket—money he felt he was entitled to because his expenses ran high sometimes, and they had to eat, they had to live. He put the roll into her sewing cabinet, where he always put whatever money he made as Bob Prince. She'd spend it when she had to, parcel it out, but she'd never mention it to him or anyone else. She'd told Sheila once that he had a sales job, he got paid in cash a lot, that was why he was away from home for such long periods of time.

When he walked back into the kitchen she was at the sink, peeling potatoes. He went over and touched her shoulder, kissed the top of her head. She didn't look at him; stood there stiffly until he moved away from her. But she'd be all right in a day or two. She'd be fine until the next time Bob Prince made the right kind of connection.

He wished it didn't have to be this way. He wished he could roll back the clock three years, do things differently, take the gray out of her hair and the pain out of her eyes. But he couldn't. It was just too late.

You had to play the cards you were dealt, no matter how lousy they were. The only thing that made it tolerable was that sometimes, on certain hands, you could find ways to stack the damn deck.

LIAR'S DICE

"Excuse me. Do you play liar's dice?"

I looked over at the man two stools to my right. He was about my age, early forties; average height, average weight, brown hair, medium complexion—really a pretty nondescript sort except for a pleasant and disarming smile. Expensively dressed in an Armani suit and a silk jacquard tie. Drinking white wine. I had never seen him before. Or had I? There was something familiar about him, as if our paths *had* crossed somewhere or other, once or twice.

Not here in Tony's, though. Tony's is a suburban-mall bar that caters to the shopping trade from the big department and grocery stores surrounding it. I stopped in no more than a couple of times a month, usually when Connie asked me to pick up something at Safeway on my way home from San Francisco, occasionally when I had a Saturday errand to run. I knew the few regulars by sight, and it was never very crowded anyway. There were only four patrons at the moment: the nondescript gent and myself on stools, and a young couple in a booth at the rear.

"I do play, as a matter of fact," I said to the fellow. Fairly well too, though I wasn't about to admit that. Liar's dice and I were old acquaintances.

"Would you care to shake for a drink?"

"Well, my usual limit is one . . ."

"For a chit for your next visit, then."

"All right, why not? I feel lucky tonight."

"Do you? Good. I should warn you, I'm very good at the game."

"I'm not so bad myself."

"No, I mean I'm *very* good. I seldom lose."

It was the kind of remark that would have nettled me if it had been said with even a modicum of conceit. But he wasn't bragging; he was merely stating a fact, mentioning a special skill of which he felt justifiably proud. So instead of annoying me, his comment made me eager to test him.

We introduced ourselves; his name was Jones. Then I called to Tony for the dice cups. He brought them down, winked at me, said, "No gambling now," and went back to the other end of the bar. Strictly speaking, shaking dice for drinks and/or money is illegal in California. But nobody pays much attention to nuisance laws like that, and most bar owners keep dice cups on hand for their customers. The game stimulates business. I know because I've been involved in some spirited liar's dice tournaments in my time.

Like all good games, liar's dice is fairly simple—at least in its rules. Each player has a cup containing five dice, which he shakes out but keeps covered so only he can see what is showing face up. Then each makes a declaration or "call" in turn: one of a kind, two of a kind, three of a kind, and so on. Each call has to be higher than the previous one, and is based on what the player *knows* is in his hand and what he *thinks* is in the other fellow's—the combined total of the ten dice. He can lie or tell the truth, whichever suits him; but the better liar he is, the better his chances of winning. When one player decides the other is either lying or has simply exceeded the laws of probability, he says, "Come up," and then both reveal their hands. If he's right, he wins.

In addition to being a clever liar, you also need a good grasp of mathematical odds and the ability to "read" your opponent's facial expressions, the inflection in his voice, his body language. The same skills an experienced poker player has to have, which is one reason the game is also called liar's poker.

Jones and I each rolled one die to determine who would go first; mine was the highest. Then we shook all five dice in our cups, banged them down on the bar. What I had showing was four treys and a deuce.

"Your call, Mr. Quint."

"One five," I said.

"One six."

"Two deuces."

"Two fives."

"Three treys."

"Three sixes."

I considered calling him up, since I had no sixes and he would need three showing to win. But I didn't know his methods and I couldn't read him at all. I decided to keep playing.

"Four treys."

"Five treys."

"Six treys."

Jones smiled and said, "Come up." And he had just one trey (and no sixes). I'd called six treys and there were only five in our combined hands; he was the winner.

"So much for feeling lucky," I said, and signaled Tony to bring another white wine for Mr. Jones. On impulse I decided a second Manhattan wouldn't hurt and ordered that too.

Jones said, "Shall we play again?"

"Two drinks is definitely my limit."

"For dimes, then? Nickels or pennies, if you prefer."

"Oh, I don't know . . ."

"You're a good player, Mr. Quint, and I don't often find someone who can challenge me. Besides, I have a passion as well as an affinity for liar's dice. Won't you indulge me?"

I didn't see any harm in it. If he'd wanted to play for larger stakes, even a dollar a hand, I might have taken him for a hustler despite his Armani suit and silk tie. But how much could you win or lose playing for a nickel or a dime a hand? So I said, "Your call first this time," and picked up my dice cup.

We played for better than half an hour. And Jones wasn't just good; he was uncanny. Out of nearly twenty-five hands, I won two—*two*. You could chalk up some of the disparity to luck, but not enough to change the fact that his skill was remarkable. Certainly he was the best I'd ever locked horns with. I would have backed him in a tournament anywhere, anytime.

He was a good winner, too: no gloating or chiding. And a good listener, the sort who seems genuinely (if superficially) interested in other people. I'm not often gregarious, especially with strangers, but I found myself opening up to Jones—and this in spite of him beating the pants off me the whole time.

I told him about Connie, how we met and the second honeymoon trip we'd taken to Lake Louise three years ago and what we were planning for our twentieth wedding anniversary in August. I told him about Lisa, who was eighteen and a freshman studying film at UCLA. I told him about Kevin, sixteen now and captain of his high school baseball team, and the five-hit, two home run game he'd had last week. I told him what it was like working as a design engineer for one of the largest engineering firms in the country, the nagging dissatisfaction and the desire to be my own boss someday, when I had enough money saved so I could afford to take the risk. I told him about remodeling our home, the boat I was thinking of buying, the fact that I'd always wanted to try hang-gliding but never had the courage.

Lord knows what else I might have told him if I hadn't noticed the polite but faintly bored expression on his face, as if I were imparting facts he already knew. It made me realize just how much I'd been nattering on, and embarrassed me a bit. I've never liked people who talk incessantly about themselves, as though they're the focal point of the entire universe. I can be a good listener myself; and for all I knew, Jones was a lot more interesting than bland Jeff Quint.

I said, "Well, that's more than enough about me. It's your turn, Jones. Tell me about yourself."

"If you like, Mr. Quint." Still very formal. I'd told him a couple of times to call me Jeff but he wouldn't do it. Now that I thought about it, he hadn't mentioned his own first name.

"What is it you do?"

He laid his dice cup to one side. I was relieved to see that; I'd had enough of losing but I hadn't wanted to be the one to quit. And it was getting late—dark outside already—and Connie would be wondering where I was. A few minutes of listening to the story of his life, I thought, just to be polite, and then—

"To begin with," Jones was saying, "I travel."

"Sales job?"

"No. I travel because I enjoy traveling. And because I can afford it. I have independent means."

"Lucky you. In more ways than one."

"Yes."

"Europe, the South Pacific—all the exotic places?"

"Actually, no. I prefer the U.S."

"Any particular part?"

"Wherever my fancy leads me."

"Hard to imagine anyone's fancy leading him to Bayport," I said. "You have friends or relatives here?"

"No, I have business in Bayport."

"Business? I thought you said you didn't need to work. . . ."

"Independent means, Mr. Quint. That doesn't preclude a purpose, a direction in one's life."

"You do have a profession, then?"

"You might say that. A profession and a hobby combined."

"Lucky you," I said again. "What is it?"

"I kill people," he said.

I thought I'd misheard him. "You . . . what?"

"I kill people."

"Good God. Is that supposed to be a joke?"

"Not at all. I'm quite serious."

"What do you mean, you *kill* people?"

"Just what I said."

"Are you trying to tell me you're . . . some kind of paid assassin?"

"Not at all. I've never killed anyone for money."

"Then why . . . ?"

"Can't you guess?"

"No, I can't guess. I don't want to guess."
"Call it personal satisfaction," he said.
"What people? Who?"
"No one in particular," Jones said. "My selection process is completely random. I'm very good at it too. I've been killing people for... let's see, nine and a half years now. Eighteen victims in thirteen states. And, oh yes, Puerto Rico—one in Puerto Rico. I don't mind saying that I've never even come close to being caught."

I stared at him. My mouth was open; I knew it but I couldn't seem to unlock my jaw. I felt as if reality had suddenly slipped away from me, as if Tony had dropped some sort of mind-altering drug into my second Manhattan and it was just now taking effect. Jones and I were still sitting companionably, on adjacent stools now, he smiling and speaking in the same low, friendly voice. At the other end of the bar Tony was slicing lemons and limes into wedges. Three of the booths were occupied now, with people laughing and enjoying themselves. Everything was just as it had been two minutes ago, except that instead of me telling Jones about being a dissatisfied design engineer, he was calmly telling me he was a serial murderer.

I got my mouth shut finally, just long enough to swallow into a dry throat. Then I said, "You're crazy, Jones. You must be insane."

"Hardly, Mr. Quint. I'm as sane as you are."
"I don't believe you killed eighteen people."
"Nineteen," he said. "Soon to be twenty."
"Twenty? You mean... someone in Bayport?"
"Right here in Bayport."
"You expect me to believe you intend to pick somebody at random and just... murder him in cold blood?"
"Oh no, there's more to it than that. Much more."
"More?" I said blankly.
"I choose a person at random, yes, but carefully. Very carefully. I study my target, follow him as he goes about his daily business, learn everything I can about him down to the minutest detail. Then the cat and mouse begins. I don't murder him right away; that wouldn't give sufficient, ah, satisfaction. I wait... observe... plan. Perhaps, for added spice, I reveal myself to him. I might even be so bold as to tell him to his face that he's my next victim."

My scalp began to crawl.

"Days, weeks... then, when the victim least expects it, a gunshot, a push out of nowhere in front of an oncoming car, a hypodermic filled with digitalin and jabbed into the body on a crowded street, simulating heart failure. There are many ways to kill a man. Did you ever stop to consider just how many different ways there are?"

"You . . . you're not saying—"

"What, Mr. Quint? That I've chosen *you?*"

"Jones, for God's sake!"

"But I have," he said. "You are to be number twenty."

One of my hands jerked upward, struck his arm. Involuntary spasm; I'm not a violent man. He didn't even flinch. I pulled my hand back, saw that it was shaking, and clutched the fingers tight around the beveled edge of the bar.

Jones took a sip of wine. Then he smiled—and winked at me.

"Or then again," he said, "I might be lying."

". . . What?"

"Everything I've just told you might be a lie. I might not have killed nineteen people over the past nine and a half years; I might not have killed anyone, ever."

"I don't . . . I don't know what you—"

"Or I might have told you part of the truth . . . that's another possibility, isn't it? Part fact, part fiction. But in that case, which is which? And to what degree? Am I a deadly threat to you, or am I nothing more than a man in a bar playing a game?"

"Game? What kind of sick—"

"The same one we've been playing all along. Liar's dice."

"Liar's dice?"

"My own special version," he said, "developed and refined through years of practice. The perfect form of the game, if I do say so myself—exciting, unpredictable, filled with intrigue and mortal danger for myself as well as my opponent."

I shook my head. My mind was a seething muddle; I couldn't seem to fully grasp what he was saying.

"I don't know any more than you do at this moment how you'll play your part of the hand, Mr. Quint. That's where the excitement and the danger lies. Will you treat what I've said as you would a bluff? Can you afford to take that risk? Or will you act on the assumption that I've told the monstrous truth, or at least part of it?"

"Damn you . . ." Weak and ineffectual words, even in my own ears.

"And if you do believe me," he said, "what course of action will you take? Attack me before I can harm you, attempt to kill me . . . here and now in this public place, perhaps, in front of witnesses who will swear the attack was unprovoked? Try to follow me when I leave, attack me elsewhere? I might well be armed, and an excellent shot with a handgun. Go to the police . . . with a wild-sounding and unsubstantiated story that they surely wouldn't believe? Hire a detective to track me down? Attempt to track me down yourself? Jones isn't my real name, of course, and I've taken precautions against anyone finding out my true identity. Arm yourself and remain on guard until, if and when, I make a move against you? How long could you live under such intense pressure without making a fatal mistake?"

He paused dramatically. "Or—and this is the most exciting prospect of all, the one I hope you choose—will you mount a clever counterattack, composed of lies and deceptions of your own devising? Can you actually hope to beat me at my own game? Do you dare to try?"

He adjusted the knot in his tie with quick, deft movements, smiling at me in the back-bar mirror—not the same pleasant smile as before. This one had shark's teeth in it. "Whatever you do, I'll know about it soon afterward. I'll be waiting . . . watching . . . and I'll know. And then it will be my turn again."

He slid off his stool, stood poised behind me. I just sat there; it was as if I were paralyzed.

"Your call, Mr. Quint," he said. And he was gone into the night.

OUT OF THE DEPTHS

He came tumbling out of the sea, dark and misshapen, like a being that was not human. A creature from the depths; or a jumbee, the evil spirit of West Indian superstition. Fanciful thoughts, and Shea was not a fanciful woman. But on this strange, wild night nothing seemed real or explicable.

At first, with the moon hidden behind the running scud of clouds, she'd seen him as a blob of flotsam on a breaking wave. The squall earlier had left the sea rough and the swells out toward the reef were high, their crests stripped of spume by the wind. The angry surf threw him onto the strip of beach, dragged him back again; another wave flung him up a little farther. The moon reappeared then, bathing sea and beach and rocks in the kind of frost-white shine you found only in the Caribbean. Not flotsam—something alive. She saw his arms extend, splayed fingers dig into the sand to hold himself against the backward pull of the sea. Saw him raise a smallish head above a massive, deformed torso, then squirm weakly toward the nearest jut of rock. Another wave shoved him the last few feet. He clung to the rock, lying motionless with the surf foaming around him.

Out of the depths, she thought.

The irony made her shiver, draw the collar of her coat more tightly around her neck. She lifted her gaze again to the rocky peninsula farther south. Windflaw Point, where the undertow off its tiny beach was the most treacherous on the island. It had taken her almost an hour to marshal her courage to the point where she was ready—almost ready—to walk out there and into the ocean. *Into* the depths. Now...

Massive clouds sealed off the moon again. In the heavy darkness Shea could just make him out, still lying motionless on the fine coral sand. Unconscious? Dead? I ought to go down there, she thought. But she could not seem to lift herself out of the chair.

After several minutes he moved again: dark shape rising to hands and knees, then trying to stand. Three tries before he was able to keep his legs from collapsing under him. He stood swaying, as if gathering strength; finally staggered onto the path that led up through rocks and sea grape. Toward the house. Toward her.

On another night she would have felt any number of emotions by this time: surprise, bewilderment, curiosity, concern. But not on this night. There was a numbness in her mind, like the numbness in her body from the cold wind. It was as if she were dreaming, sitting there on the open terrace—as if she'd fallen asleep hours ago, before the clouds began to pile up at sunset and the sky turned the color of a blood bruise.

A new storm was making up. Hammering northern this time, from the look of the sky. The wind had shifted, coming out of the northeast now; the clouds were bloated and simmering in that direction and the air had a charged quality. Unless the wind shifted again soon, the rest of the night would be even wilder.

Briefly the clouds released the moon. In its white glare she saw him plodding closer, limping, almost dragging his left leg. A man, of course—just a man. And not deformed: what had made him seem that way was the life jacket fastened around his upper body. She remembered the lights of a freighter or tanker she had seen passing on the horizon just after nightfall, ahead of the squall. Had he gone overboard from that somehow?

He had reached the garden, was making his way past the flamboyant trees and the thick clusters of frangipani. Heading toward the garden door and the kitchen: she'd left the lights on in there and the jalousies open. It was the lights that had drawn him here, like a beacon that could be seen a long distance out to sea.

A good thing she'd left them on or not? She didn't want him here, a cast-up stranger, hurt and needing attention—not on this night, not when she'd been so close to making the walk to Windflaw Point. But neither could she refuse him access or help. John would have, if he'd been drunk and in the wrong mood. Not her. It was not in her nature to be cruel to anyone, except perhaps herself.

Abruptly Shea pushed herself out of the chair. He hadn't seen her sitting in the restless shadows, and he didn't see her now as she moved back across the terrace to the sliding glass doors to her bedroom. Or at least if he did see her, he didn't stop or call out to her. She hurried through the darkened bedroom, down the hall, and into the kitchen. She was halfway to the garden door when he began pounding on it.

She unlocked and opened the door without hesitation. He was propped against the stucco wall, arms hanging and body slumped with exhaustion. Big and youngish, that was her first impression. She couldn't see his face clearly.

"Need some help," he said in a thick, strained voice. "Been in the water . . . washed up on your beach. . . ."

"I know, I saw you from the terrace. Come inside."

"Better get a towel first. Coral ripped a gash in my foot... blood all over your floor."

"All right. I'll have to close the door. The wind...."

"Go ahead."

She shut the door and went to fetch a towel, a blanket, and the first-aid kit. On the way back to the kitchen she turned the heat up several degrees. When she opened up to him again she saw that he'd shed the life jacket. His clothing was minimal: plaid wool shirt, denim trousers, canvas shoes, all nicked and torn by coral. Around his waist was a pouch-type waterproof belt, like a workman's utility belt. One of the pouches bulged slightly.

She gave him the towel, and when he had it wrapped around his left foot he hobbled inside. She took his arm, let him lean on her as she guided him to the kitchen table. His flesh was cold, sea-puckered; the touch of it made her feel a tremor of revulsion. It was like touching the skin of a dead man.

When he sank heavily onto one of the chairs, she dragged another chair over and lifted his injured leg onto it. He stripped off what was left of his shirt, swaddled himself in the blanket. His teeth were chattering.

The coffeemaker drew her; she poured two of the big mugs full. There was always hot coffee ready and waiting, no matter what the hour—she made sure of that. She drank too much coffee, much too much, but it was better than drinking what John usually drank. If she—

"You mind sweetening that?"

She half-turned. "Sugar?"

"Liquor. Rum, if you have it?"

"Jamaican rum." That was what John drank.

"Best there is. Fine."

She took down an open bottle, carried it and the mugs to the table, and watched while he spiked the coffee, drank, then poured more rum and drank again. Color came back into his stubbled cheeks. He used part of the blanket to rough-dry his hair.

He was a little older than she, early thirties, and in good physical condition: broad chest and shoulders, muscle-knotted arms. Sandy hair cropped short, thick sandy brows, a long-chinned face burned dark from exposure to the sun. The face was all right, might have been attractive except for the eyes. They were a bright off-blue color, shielded by lids that seemed perpetually lowered like flags at half-mast, and they didn't blink much. When the eyes lifted to meet and hold hers something in them made her look away.

"I'll see what I can do for your foot."

"Thanks. Hurts like hell."

The towel was already soaking through. Shea unwrapped it carefully, revealing a deep gash across the instep just above the tongue of his shoe. She got the shoe and sock off. More blood welled out of the cut.

"It doesn't look good. You may need a doctor —"

"No," he said, "no doctor."

"It'll take stitches to close properly."

"Just clean and bandage it, okay?"

She spilled iodine onto a gauze pad, swabbed at the gash as gently as she could. The sharp sting made him suck in his breath, but he didn't flinch or utter another sound. She laid a second piece of iodined gauze over the wound and began to wind tape tightly around his foot to hold the skin flaps together.

He said, "My name's Tanner. Harry Tanner."

"Shea Clifford."

"Shea. That short for something?"

"It's a family name."

"Pretty."

"Thank you."

"So are you," he said. "Real pretty with your hair all windblown like that."

She glanced up at him. He was smiling at her. Not a leer, just a weary smile, but it wasn't a good kind of smile. It had a predatory look, like the teeth-baring stretch of a wolf's jowls.

"No offense," he said.

"None taken." She lowered her gaze, watched her hands wind and tear tape. Her mind still felt numb. "What happened to you? Why were you in the water?"

"That damn squall a few hours ago. Came up so fast I didn't have time to get my genoa down. Wave as big as a house knocked poor little *Wanderer* into a full broach. I got thrown clear when she went over or I'd have sunk with her."

"Were you sailing alone?"

"All alone."

"Single-hander? Or just on a weekend lark?"

"Single-hander. You know boats, I see."

"Yes. Fairly well."

"Well, I'm a sea tramp," Tanner said. "Ten years of island-hopping and this is the first time I ever got caught unprepared."

"It happens. What kind of craft was *Wanderer*?"

"Bugeye ketch. Thirty-nine feet."

"Shame to lose a boat like that."

He shrugged. "She was insured."

"How far out were you?"

"Five or six miles. Hell of a long swim in a choppy sea."

"You're lucky the squall passed as quickly as it did."

"Lucky I was wearing my life jacket, too," Tanner said. "And lucky you stay up late with your lights on. If it weren't for the lights I probably wouldn't have made shore at all."

Shea nodded. She tore off the last piece of tape and then began putting the first-aid supplies away in the kit.

Tanner said, "I didn't see any other lights. This house the only one out here?"

"The only one on this side of the bay, yes."

"No close neighbors?"

"Three houses on the east shore, not far away."

"You live here alone?"

"With my husband."

"But he's not here now."

"Not now. He'll be home soon."

"That so? Where is he?"

"In Merrywing, the town on the far side of the island. He went out to dinner with friends."

"While you stayed home."

"I wasn't feeling well earlier."

"Merrywing. Salt Cay?"

"That's right."

"British-owned, isn't it?"

"Yes. You've never been here before?"

"Not my kind of place. Too small, too quiet, too rich. I prefer the livelier islands—St. Thomas, Nassau, Jamaica."

"St. Thomas isn't far from here," Shea said. "Is that where you were heading?"

"More or less. This husband of yours—how big is he?"

". . . Big?"

"Big enough so his clothes would fit me?"

"Oh," she said, "yes. About your size."

"Think he'd mind if you let me have a pair of his pants and a shirt and some underwear? Wet things of mine are giving me a chill."

"No, of course not. I'll get them from his room."

She went to John's bedroom. The smells of his cologne and pipe tobacco were strong in there; they made her faintly nauseous. In haste she dragged a pair of white linen trousers and a pullover off hangers in his closet, turned toward the dresser as she came out. And stopped in midstride.

Tanner stood in the open doorway, leaning against the jamb, his half-lidded eyes fixed on her.

"*His* room," he said. "Right."

"Why did you follow me?"

"Felt like it. So you don't sleep with him."

"Why should that concern you?"

"I'm naturally curious. How come? I mean, how come you and your husband don't share a bed?"

"Our sleeping arrangements are none of your business."

"Probably not. Your idea or his?"

"What?"

"Separate bedrooms. Your idea or his?"

"Mine, if you must know."

"Maybe he snores, huh?"

She didn't say anything.

"How long since you kicked him out of your bed?"

"I didn't kick him out. It wasn't like that."

"Sure it was. I can see it in your face."

"My private affairs—"

"—are none of my business. I know. But I also know the signs of a bad marriage when I see them. A bad marriage and an unhappy woman. Can't tell me you're not unhappy."

"All right," she said.

"So why don't you divorce him? Money?"

"Money has nothing to do with it."

"Money has something to do with everything."

"It isn't money."

"He have something on you?"

"No."

"Then why not just dump him?"

You're not going to divorce me, Shea. Not you, not like the others. I'll see you dead first. I mean it, Shea. You're mine and you'll stay mine until I decide I don't want you anymore. . . .

She said flatly, "I'm not going to talk about my marriage to you. I don't know you."

"We can fix that. I'm an easy guy to know."

She moved ahead to the dresser, found underwear and socks, put them on the bed with the trousers and pullover. "You can change in here," she said, and started for the doorway.

Tanner didn't move.

"I said —"

"I heard you, Shea."

"Mrs. Clifford."

"Clifford," he said. Then he smiled, the same wolfish lip-stretch he'd shown her in the kitchen. "Sure—Clifford. Your husband's name wouldn't be John, would it? John Clifford?"

She was silent.

"I'll bet it is. John Clifford, Clifford Yacht Designs. One of the best marine architects in Miami. Fancy motor sailers and racing yawls."

She still said nothing,

"House in Miami Beach, another on Salt Cay—this house. And you're his latest wife. Which is it, number three or number four?"

Between her teeth she said, "Three."

"He must be what, fifty now? And worth millions. Don't tell me money's not why you married him."

"I won't tell you anything."

But his wealth wasn't why she'd married him. He had been kind and attentive to her at first. And she'd been lonely after the bitter breakup with Neal. John had opened up a whole new, exciting world to her: travel to exotic places, sailing, the company of interesting and famous people. She hadn't loved him, but she had been fond of him; and she'd convinced herself she would learn to love him in time. Instead, when he revealed his dark side to her, she had learned to hate him.

Tanner said, "Didn't one of his other wives divorce him for knocking her around when he was drunk? Seems I remember reading something like that in the Miami papers a few years back. That why you're unhappy, Shea? He knock you around when he's drinking?"

Without answering, Shea pushed past him into the hallway. He didn't try to stop her. In the kitchen again she poured yet another cup of coffee and sat down with it. Even with her coat on and the furnace turned up, she was still cold. The heat from the mug failed to warm her hands.

She knew she ought to be afraid of Harry Tanner. But all she felt inside was deep weariness. An image of Windflaw Point, the tiny beach with its treacherous undertow, flashed across the screen of her mind—and was gone again just as swiftly. Her courage, or maybe her cowardice, was gone too. She was no longer capable of walking out to the point, letting the sea have her. Not tonight and probably not ever again.

She sat listening to the wind clamor outside. It moaned in the twisted branches of the banyan tree; scraped palm fronds against the roof tiles. Through the open window jalousies she could smell ozone mixed with the sweet fragrances of white ginger blooms. The new storm would be here soon in all its fury.

The wind kept her from hearing Tanner reenter the kitchen. She sensed his presence, looked up, and saw him standing there with his eyes on her like probes. He'd put on all of John's clothing and found a pair of Reeboks for his feet. In his left hand he held the waterproof belt that had been strapped around his waist.

"Shirt's a little snug," he said, "but a pretty good fit otherwise. Your husband's got nice taste."

Shea didn't answer.

"In clothing, in houses, and in women."

She sipped her coffee, not looking at him.

Tanner limped around the table and sat down across from her. When he laid the belt next to the bottle of rum, the pouch that bulged made a thunking sound. "Boats too," he said. "I'll bet he keeps his best designs for himself; he's the kind that would. Am I right, Shea?"

"Yes."

"How many boats does he own?"

"Two."

"One's bound to be big. Oceangoing yacht?"

"Seventy-foot custom schooner."

"What's her name?"

"*Moneybags.*"

Tanner laughed. "Some sense of humor."

"If you say so."

"Where does he keep her? Here or Miami?"

"Miami."

"She there now?"

"Yes."

"And the other boat? That one berthed here?"

"The harbor at Merrywing."

"What kind is she?"

"A sloop," Shea said. "*Carib Princess.*"

"How big?"

"Thirty-two feet."

"She been back and forth across the Stream?"

"Several times, in good weather."

"With you at the helm?"

"No."

"You ever take her out by yourself?"

"No. He wouldn't allow it."

"But you can handle her, right? You said you know boats. You can pilot that little sloop without any trouble?"

"Why do you want to know that? Why are you asking so many questions about John's boats?"

"John's boats, John's houses, John's third wife." Tanner laughed again, just a bark this time. The wolfish smile pulled his mouth out of shape. "Are you afraid of me, Shea?"

"No."

"Not even a little?"

"Why? Should I be?"

"What do you think?"

"I'm not afraid of you," she said.

"Then how come you lied to me?"

"Lied? About what?"

"Your husband. Old John Clifford."

"I don't know what you mean."

"You said he'd be home soon. But he won't be. He's not in town with friends, he's not even on the island."

She stared silently at the steam rising from her cup. Her fingers felt cramped, as if she might be losing circulation in them.

"Well, Shea? That's the truth, isn't it."

"Yes. That's the truth."

"Where is he? Miami?"

She nodded.

"Went there on business and left you all by your lonesome."

"It isn't the first time."

"Might be the last, though." Tanner reached for the rum bottle, poured some of the dark liquid into his mug, drank, and then smacked his lips. "You want a shot of this?"

"No."

"Loosen you up a little."

"I don't need loosening up."

"You might after I tell you the truth about Harry Tanner."

"Does that mean you lied to me too?"

"I'm afraid so. But you 'fessed up and now it's my turn."

In the blackness outside the wind gusted sharply, banging a loose shutter somewhere at the front of the house. Rain began to pelt down with open-faucet suddenness.

"Listen to that," Tanner said. "Sounds like we're in for a big blow, this time."

"What did you lie about?"

"Well, let's see. For starters, about how I came to be in the water tonight. My bugeye ketch didn't sink in the squall. No, *Wanderer's* tied up at a dock in Charlotte Amalie."

She sat stiffly, waiting.

"Boat I was on didn't sink either," Tanner said. "At least as far as I know it didn't. I jumped overboard. Not long after the squall hit us."

There was still nothing for her to say.

"If I hadn't gone overboard, the two guys I was with would've shot me dead. They tried to shoot me in the water but the ketch was pitching like crazy and they couldn't see me in the dark and the rain. I guess they figured I'd drown even with a life jacket on. Or the sharks or barracuda would get me."

Still nothing.

"We had a disagreement over money. That's what most things come down to these days—money. They thought I cheated them out of twenty thousand dollars down in Jamaica, and they were right, I did. They both put guns on me before I could do anything and I thought I was a dead man. The squall saved my bacon. Big swell almost broached us, knocked us all off our feet. I managed to scramble up the companionway and go over the side before they recovered."

The hard beat of the rain stopped as suddenly as it had begun. Momentary lull: the full brunt of the storm was minutes away yet.

"I'm not a single-hander," he said, "not a sea tramp. That's another thing I lied about. Ask me what it is I really am, Shea. Ask me how I make my living."

"I don't have to ask."

"No? Think you know?"

"Smuggling. You're a smuggler."

"That's right. Smart lady."

"Drugs; I suppose."

"Drugs, weapons, liquor, the wretched poor yearning to breathe free without benefit of a green card. You name it, I've handled it. Hell, smuggling's a tradition in these waters. Men have been doing it for three hundred years, since the days of the Spanish Main." He laughed. "A modern freebooter, that's what I am. Tanner the Pirate. Yo ho ho and a bottle of rum."

"Why are you telling me all this?"

"Why not? Don't you find it interesting?"

"No."

"Okay, I'll give it to you straight. I've got a problem—a big problem. I jumped off that ketch tonight with one thing besides the clothes on my back, and it wasn't money." He pulled the waterproof belt to him, unsnapped the pouch that bulged, and showed her what was inside. "Just this."

Her gaze registered the weapon—automatic, large caliber,

lightweight frame—and slid away. She was not surprised; she had known there was a gun in the pouch when it made the thunking sound.

Tanner set it on the table within easy reach. "My two partners got my share of a hundred thousand from the Jamaica run. I might be able to get it back from them and I might not; they're a couple of hard cases and I'm not sure it's worth the risk. But I can't do anything until I quit this island. And I can't leave the usual ways because my money and my passport are both on that damn ketch. You see my dilemma, Shea?"

"I see it."

"Sure you do. You're a smart lady, like I said. What else do you see? The solution?"

She shook her head.

"Well, I've got a dandy." The predatory grin again. "You know, this really is turning into my lucky night. I couldn't have washed up in a better spot if I'd planned it. John Clifford's house, John Clifford's smart and pretty wife. And not far away, John Clifford's little sloop, the *Carib Princess*."

The rain came again, wind-driven with enough force to rattle the windows. Spray blew in through the screens behind the open jalousies. Shea made no move to get up and close the glass. Tanner didn't even seem to notice the moisture.

"Here's what we're going to do," he said. "At dawn we'll drive in to the harbor. You do have a car here? Sure you do; he wouldn't leave you isolated without wheels. Once we get there we go on-board the sloop and you take her out. If anybody you know sees us and says anything, you tell them I'm a friend or relative and John said it was okay for us to go for a sail without him."

She asked dully, "Then what?"

"Once we're out to sea? I'm not going to kill you and dump your body overboard, if that's worrying you. The only thing that's going to happen is we sail the *Carib Princess* across the Stream to Florida. A little place I know on the west coast up near Pavilion Key where you can sneak a boat in at night and keep her hidden for as long as you need to."

"And then?"

"Then I call your husband and we do some business. How much do you think he'll pay to get his wife and his sloop back safe and sound? Five hundred thousand? As much as a million?"

"My God," she said. "You're crazy."

"Like a fox."

"You couldn't get away with it. You *can't*."

"I figure I can. You think he won't pay because the marriage is on the rocks? You're wrong, Shea. He'll pay, all right. He's the kind that can't stand losing anything that belongs to him, wife or boat, and sure as hell not both at once. Plus he's had enough bad publicity; ignoring a ransom demand would hurt his image and his business and I'll make damned sure he knows it."

She shook her head again, a limp, rag-doll wobbling, as if it were coming loose from the stem of her neck.

"Don't look so miserable," Tanner said cheerfully. "I'm not such a bad guy when you get to know me, and there'll be plenty of time for us to get acquainted. And when old John pays off, I'll leave you with the sloop and you can sail her back to Miami. Okay? Give you my word on that."

He was lying: his word was worthless. He'd told her his name, the name of his ketch and where it was berthed; he wouldn't leave her alive to identify him. Not on the Florida coast. Not even here.

Automatically Shea picked up her mug, tilted it to her mouth. Dregs. Empty. She pushed back her chair, crossed to the counter, and poured the mug full again. Tanner sat relaxed, smiling, pleased with himself. The rising steam from the coffee formed a screen between them, so that she saw him as blurred, distorted. Not quite human, the way he had first seemed to her when he came out of the sea earlier.

Jumbee, she thought. Smiling evil.

The gale outside flung sheets of water at the house. The loose shutter chattered like a jackhammer until the wind slackened again.

Tanner said, "Going to be a long wet night." He made a noisy yawning sound. "Where do you sleep, Shea?" The question sent a spasm through her body.

"Your bedroom—where is it?"

Oh God. "Why?"

"I told you, it's going to be a long night. And I'm tired and my foot hurts and I want to lie down. But I don't want to lie down alone. We might as well start getting to know each other the best way there is."

No, she thought. No, no, no.

"Well, Shea? Lead the way."

No, she thought again. But her legs worked as if with a will of their own, carried her back to the table. Tanner sat forward as she drew abreast of him, started to lift himself out of the chair.

She pivoted and threw the mug of hot coffee into his face.

She hadn't planned to do it, acted without thinking; it was almost as much of a surprise to her as it was to him. He yelled and pawed at his eyes, his body jerking so violently that both he and the chair toppled over sideways. Shea swept the automatic off the table and backed away with it extended at arm's length.

Tanner kicked the chair away and scrambled unsteadily to his feet. Bright red splotches stained his cheeks where the coffee had scalded him; his eyes were murderous. He took a step toward her, stopped when he realized she was pointing his own weapon at him. She watched him struggle to regain control of himself and the situation.

"You shouldn't have done that, Shea."

"Stay where you are."

"That gun isn't loaded."

"It's loaded. I know guns too."

"You won't shoot me." He took another step.

"I will. Don't come any closer."

"No you won't. You're not the type. I can pull the trigger on a person real easy. Have, more than once." Another step. "But not you. You don't have what it takes."

"Please don't make me shoot you. Please, please don't."

"See? You won't do it because you can't."

"Please."

"You won't shoot me, Shea."

On another night, any other night, he would have been right. But on this night—

He lunged at her.

And she shot him.

The impact of the high-caliber bullet brought him up short, as if he had walked into an invisible wall. A look of astonishment spread over his face. He took one last convulsive step before his hands came up to clutch at his chest and his knees buckled.

Shea didn't see him fall; she turned away. And the hue and the cry of the storm kept her from hearing him hit the floor. When she looked again, after several seconds, he lay face down and unmoving on the tiles. She did not have to go any closer to tell that he was dead.

There was a hollow queasiness in her stomach. Otherwise she felt nothing. She turned again, and there was a blank space of time, and then she found herself sitting on one of the chairs in the living room. She would have wept then but she had no tears. She had cried herself dry on the terrace.

After a while she became aware that she still gripped Tanner's automatic. She set it down on an end table; hesitated, then picked it up again. The numbness was finally leaving her mind, a swift release that brought her thoughts into sharpening focus. When the wind and rain lulled again she stood, walked slowly down the hall to her bedroom. She steeled herself as she opened the door and turned on the lights.

From where he lay sprawled across the bed, John's sightless eyes stared up at her. The stain of blood on his bare chest, drying now, gleamed darkly in the lamp glow.

Wild night, mad night.

She hadn't been through hell just once, she'd been through it twice. First in here and then in the kitchen.

But she hadn't shot John. She hadn't. He'd come home at nine, already drunk, and tried to make love to her, and when she denied him he'd slapped her, kept slapping her. After three long hellish years she couldn't take it anymore, not anymore. She'd managed to get the revolver out of her nightstand drawer . . . not to shoot him, just as a threat to make him leave her alone. But he'd lunged at her, in almost the same way Tanner had, and they'd struggled, and the gun had gone off. And John Clifford was dead.

She had started to call the police. Hadn't because she knew they would not believe it was an accident. John was well liked and highly respected on Salt Cay; his public image was untarnished and no one, not even his close friends, believed his second wife's divorce claim or that he could ever mistreat anyone. She had never really been accepted here—some of the cattier rich women thought she was a gold digger—and she had no friends of her own in whom she could confide. John had seen to that. There were no marks on her body to prove it, either; he'd always been very careful not to leave marks.

The island police would surely have claimed she'd killed him in cold blood. She'd have been arrested and tried and convicted and put in a prison much worse than the one in which she had lived the past three years. The prospect of that was unbearable. It was what had driven her out onto the terrace, to sit and think about the undertow at Windflaw Point. The sea, in those moments, had seemed her only way out.

Now there was another way.

Her revolver lay on the floor where it had fallen. John had given it to her when they were first married, because he was away so much; and he had taught her how to use it. It was one of three handguns he'd bought illegally in Miami.

Shea bent to pick it up. With a corner of the bedsheet she wiped the grip carefully, then did the same to Tanner's automatic. That gun too, she was certain, would not be registered anywhere.

Wearily she put the automatic in John's hand, closing his fingers around it. Then she retreated to the kitchen and knelt to place the revolver in Tanner's hand. The first-aid kit was still on the table; she would use it once more, when she finished talking to the chief constable in Merrywing.

We tried to help Tanner, John and I, she would tell him. And he repaid our kindness by attempting to rob us at gunpoint. John told him we kept money in our bedroom; he took the gun out of the nightstand before I could stop him. They shot each other. John died instantly, but Tanner didn't believe his wound was as serious as it was. He made me bandage it and then kept me in the kitchen, threatening to kill me too. I managed to catch him off guard and throw coffee in his face. When he tried to come after me the strain aggravated his wound and he collapsed and died.

If this were Miami, or one of the larger Caribbean islands, she could not hope to get away with such a story. But here the native constabulary was unsophisticated and inexperienced because there was so little crime on Salt Cay. They were much more likely to overlook the fact that John had been shot two and a half hours before Harry Tanner. Much more likely, too, to credit a double homicide involving a stranger, particularly when they investigated Tanner's background, than the accidental shooting of a respected resident who had been abusing his wife. Yes, she might just get away with it. If there was any justice left for her in this world, she would—and one day she'd leave Salt Cay a free woman again.

Out of the depths, she thought as she picked up the phone. Out of the depths. . . .

POSSIBILITIES

I had been in the backyard no more than two minutes when Roger Telford's bald head popped up above the boundary fence. It was hardly a surprise. Very little that goes on in my neighborhood escapes notice by Telford and his wife Aileen. To merely call them nosy neighbors would be to do them an injustice. They are the quintessential, prototypical poster children for nosy neighbors—sly, sneaky, suspicious, intrusive, rude, and annoying in the extreme.

"I thought I heard snuffling and growling noises over there," he said. "Don't tell me Suzanne has let you buy a dog."

"All right," I said, "I won't."

"*Is* that mutt yours?"

"He's not a mutt. He's a Rottweiler mix. He belongs to the Lindemans, next block over."

"Well, it's a good thing he doesn't belong to you. Aileen and I don't like dogs, especially big dogs. Messy. Always digging things up. Bark all the damn time."

"George doesn't bark much."

"George? How do you know his name?"

"It's on his collar tag."

"Well, it's a stupid name for a mutt. What's he doing in your yard?"

"Visiting," I said. "There's a loose board in our back fence that I haven't gotten around to fixing yet."

"What's that he's chewing on?"

"Well, it looks like a bone . . . yes, by golly, that's what it is all right. A bone."

"Damn big one. I don't think I've ever seen a bone quite like that. He carry it in with him?"

"No. I gave it to him."

"*You* did? Where'd you get a bone like that?"

"Out of our freezer."

His face wrinkled into an expression resembling a contemplative basset hound's. Telford likes to believe he is a deep thinker. His wife likes to believe she is too. They labor under this self-deception because they're both writers of a sort. He concocts texts on how to fix this or that around the house and she writes cookbooks, her magnum opus being *The Sublime Purple Vegetable: Eggplant Delicacies from Around the World*. They both work at home, giving them ample opportunity to pursue their alternate joint career of meddling in other people's business.

"Is that where all those packages came from, too?" he asked at length.

"What packages?"

"Jammed into your trash can this morning."

"Roger, I'm surprised at you. You usually employ more subtle means of snooping than pawing through garbage cans."

"It wasn't me doing the pawing," he said indignantly. "It was one of those other damn neighborhood mutts. Caught it dragging one of the packages out when I rolled my own can out for pick up. I chased it off and put the package back into your can. That's when I happened to notice all the others."

"Very good," I said. "Very inventive. You ought to give fiction writing a try."

"It happens to be the truth. So why did you throw out all that good meat?"

"It wasn't good. Not anymore. Venison, mostly, that one of my coworkers gave us last year."

"What was wrong with it?"

"Freezer burn," I said.

"What?"

"It's a phenomenon that takes place when you leave things in the freezer too long. Surely you've come across references to it while researching those books you write."

"I know what freezer burn is. But the packages I saw were mostly thawed."

"Well, of course they were. I took them out of the freezer and put them into the trash can last night. All except the bone for George. Freezer burn doesn't bother him."

Telford did his basset hound impression again. To avoid watching him at his mental labors, I looked up at the sky. It was a nice evening, clear but a little too crisp to sit out on the porch and read. I sighed. Autumn was almost here. The leaves on the maple tree were already starting to turn.

"What was all that noise coming from your place last night?" Telford demanded. He never asks; he always demands. "You don't make noise like that cleaning out a freezer. Late, too—went on until after eleven. Sounded like power tools."

"It was," I said. "I was working in the basement."

"Doing what?"

"Completing a project."

"What kind of project?"

"A private kind."

"Big secret," Telford said peevishly. "You had the shades

closed over the basement windows. Matter of fact, you've had most of your curtains and shades drawn the past couple of days."

"Must have been frustrating for you, not being able to look in with your binoculars."

"You think I'd spy on you with binoculars?"

"I know you would. I've seen you doing it."

He made a noise in his throat not unlike the one George had made when I had given him the bone. "Damn late to be using power tools," he said. "Kept Aileen and me awake. Must've kept Suzanne awake, too."

"I doubt it."

"Oh? Why not?"

"She wasn't here."

"What do you mean, she wasn't here?"

George seemed to have grown as bored with the conversation as I had. He'd been lying on the grass with the bone propped between his forepaws, gnawing on it. Now he stood up, took a firmer grip with his teeth, shook himself, and trotted off toward the back fence.

"Well, Howard?"

"Well what?"

"What'd you mean, Suzanne wasn't here last night?"

"Just what I said. She's not here today, either. That's why George was allowed to visit and why I felt free to give him the bone, in case you're wondering."

"Where is she? Where'd she go?"

"Away," I said.

"Away? When? Where?"

"Two days ago. On a trip."

"The hell you say. I was home all day Sunday. Aileen and I were both home, and we didn't see either of you leave."

"I know you try to keep tabs on everything that goes on over here, Roger, but now and then you do miss something. Now if you don't mind, I have things to do in the house."

He called something after me, but I closed my ears to it. Silence and privacy, in my neighborhood and on my property, are rare and precious states to be retreated into with all dispatch whenever possible.

I was in Suzanne's bedroom closet, taking articles of her clothing off hangers and folding them into Teflon bags, when the telephone rang. Aileen Telford, predictably enough.

"Howard," she said in her nasal voice, "where's Suzanne?"

"Suzanne is away. As Roger has no doubt told you by now."

"Well, I need to talk to her. A question for my new book of parsnip recipes. Where did she go?"

"She's visiting."

"Visiting who? Where?"

"Her sister, if you must know. She's been ill."

"Suzanne is ill?"

I sighed. "Not Suzanne. Her sister."

"I didn't know Suzanne had a sister. She never mentioned her to me."

"She seldom speaks of her. They've never been close."

"Then why did she go visit her?"

"I just explained why. Her sister is ill. Family duty."

"When will she be back?"

"I don't know. It might be a while. A long while."

There was a deep-thinking pause before Aileen said, "Where does her sister live?"

"Duluth. That's in Minnesota."

"I know where Duluth is. What's her sister's name and phone number?"

"I can't tell you that."

"What? Why can't you?"

"Suzanne doesn't want to be disturbed. She doesn't want her sister disturbed. You calling her up would qualify as a disturbance."

Another pause. At length she said in sepulchral tones, "Howard, I don't mind saying that Roger and I are a little concerned."

"About Suzanne's sister?"

"About Suzanne."

"Why should you be concerned about Suzanne?"

"All sorts of funny things seem to have been going on over there the past few days. That's why."

"You think so? Define funny."

"You know what I mean. You can't blame us for wondering—"

"Can't I?" I said, and hung up on her.

When I came out through the front door with another cardboard carton, Telford was standing at the base of the porch steps. More accurately, he was hopping at the base of the steps from one foot to the other as if he had to go to the bathroom. I had witnessed this behavior many times before. Coupled with the gaudy yellow sweatsuit he was wearing, it meant that he was about to head off on his morning jog-and-snoop around the neighborhood.

"What's all this, Howard?" He waved a hand at my car in the driveway, the back seat and trunk of which I had already filled with other cartons and plastic bags. "You're not moving out, are you?"

"And deprive you of a prime surveillance object? No such luck."

"What's in all those boxes and bags?"

"What do you suppose is in them?"

"Looks like it might be clothing and stuff."

"Brilliant deduction," I said. "Clothing and stuff is what it is."

"What're you planning to do with it?"

"What I usually do with rummage. Take it to Goodwill."

"Rummage, eh? Seems like a lot."

"It is a lot. Obviously."

I carried the last carton to the car and put it on the passenger seat. Telford followed, still hopping.

"Mostly your stuff?" he asked then.

"No. As a matter of fact, it's mostly Suzanne's."

That produced a frown. "How come?"

"How come what?"

"How come it's mostly her things you're getting rid of?"

"She doesn't have any use for them any longer."

"What does that mean?"

"It means she no longer has any use for them."

"Why doesn't she?"

"You'll have to ask her when she gets home."

"I'm asking you."

"You'll be leaving frustrated, then. My answer is that it's none of your business."

Telford showed up again that afternoon, shortly after I returned home. I'd left Howard J. Bennett & Associates, Income Tax Specialists—i.e., one hardworking CPA and two junior partners—early to do some shopping. I was unloading the trunk of the car, with the garage door still open, when all of a sudden there he was breathing down my neck. Quick and silent, like a sneaky ghost.

"What's that you've got there?" he said. "Is that paint?"

"Your ratiocinative powers are amazing. Did you deduce the contents from the words 'White Latex Paint' on the can, or was it some other clue?"

"What're you going to paint?"

"My workshop, if you must know."

"Didn't look like it needed painting, the last time I saw it."

"Well, it does now. There are marks on two of the walls."

"Marks?"

"You know—nicks, scrapes, stains."

His eyes narrowed. "What kind of stains?"

"Now what kind of stains would there be on workroom walls?"

"You tell me."

"Splatters of wood sealant, varnish, that sort of thing. You can't do woodworking without splattering now and then."

"Splattering," he repeated, as if it were a nasty word.

I took the other item I'd purchased out of the trunk and closed the lid.

"What's that?" Telford said.

"Well, now, let's see. It's shaped like a bowling bag, it's the size of a bowling bag, and it even resembles a bowling bag. Could it be a bowling bag?"

"You don't bowl."

"How do you know I don't?"

"You've never said anything about it. And I've never seen you with any bowling equipment before."

"I used to bowl regularly before I met Suzanne. She thinks it's a silly game."

"So do I. Where are your ball and shoes?"

"I haven't bought those yet."

"Then how come you bought a bag?"

"I liked the looks of this one."

"Seems ordinary to me. How come you decided to start bowling again?"

"For the exercise."

"In spite of what Suzanne thinks, is that it?"

"She doesn't have a say in the matter."

"Why doesn't she?"

"Because she doesn't," I said.

At a few minutes past midnight, I switched off the living room lights and went to peer around a corner of the side window curtain. The Telford house, as much of it as I could see looming above the boundary fence, was completely dark.

I gathered up the parcel I'd prepared, made my way through the kitchen to the utility porch, and let myself out into the backyard. The night was clear. There was no moon, but the stars were bright enough to enable me to navigate. I crossed to the gardening shed, removed a spade, and carried it into the rose garden. In the shadows between two of the larger bushes—a pure white damascena and an orange Floribunda, two of Suzanne's favorites—I dug a hole in the soft earth, fairly deep, and buried the parcel. Then I replaced the spade and hurried back to the house.

I wasn't absolutely sure, but when I glanced at the Telford house I thought I detected movement behind the open window to their upstairs bedroom.

The next day was Telford-free, miraculously enough, until six o'clock. I was out front then, watering the lawn, when Aileen appeared, out for her daily constitutional. Roger had his morning jog-and-snoop around the neighborhood, she had her evening walk-and-snoop. You had to admire their methods, the well-coordinated way in which they covered their territory, marching off at different times of the day in different directions to bother people, like a crack stealth commando team.

She came my way in her quick, choppy gait and stopped on the sidewalk a few feet from where I stood. If her husband resembled a basset hound, Aileen's breed was fox terrier—small and wiry with angular features and a long, quivery nose that always seemed moist and shiny, perfect for poking into places it didn't belong.

"Well, Howard," she said, "I don't suppose you've heard from Suzanne."

"But I have. She called last night."

"Did she? And how is her sister's health?"

"Improving."

"So then she'll be coming home soon."

"Possibly not," I said.

The long nose twitched. "Why not, if she isn't needed in Duluth?"

"She may be staying on there just the same."

"For how long?"

"Indefinitely."

"What's that? She's never coming back?"

"Indefinitely doesn't mean never, Aileen."

"Why would she stay in Duluth?"

"She likes it there. More than she likes me, I'm sorry to say."

"Are you trying to tell me she's left you?"

"I'm not trying to tell you anything."

Another twitch. A scowl. "I don't believe Suzanne would give up her home, everything she owns, on a sudden whim. That's not like her."

"I didn't say it was sudden."

"I still don't believe it."

"You don't know her as well as you think you do. Or me, either."

"Well, in your case, that's for sure."

She turned and strode off, muttering, "I knew it. I knew it!" just loud enough for me to hear.

I finished watering, then sat on the porch steps to bask in the evening quiet. I hadn't been there five minutes when the other Telford came marching up my front walk. Direct assault mission, it turned out—an unusual tactic for him.

"Up late again last night, weren't you, Bennett?" he said without preamble.

"So it's Bennett instead of Howard now, is it?"

"*Very* late. Long after midnight."

"If I was," I said, "you and Aileen must've been, too. Just a couple of night owls."

"What were you up to, digging in your rose garden so damn late?"

I raised an eyebrow. "Binoculars weren't enough for you, is that it? Now you've gone high tech and bought an infrared scope for better night spying?"

"You didn't answer my question."

"No, and I'm not going to. What I do on my own property day or night is no one's business but my own."

He sputtered noisily, like a faulty gas-powered lawn-mower. "You won't get away with it, Bennett."

"Get away with what?"

"We'll see to that, one way or another. We'll get to the bottom of this."

"Will you?" I smiled at him. "I like puzzles myself. Great time-passers."

"Puzzles?"

"Sifting through all the many possibilities, looking for pieces that fit together to form the true picture. Very stimulating, mentally."

"I don't know what you're talking about."

"No," I said, "of course you don't."

"More rummage for Goodwill?"

Morning. My open garage. And the Telford fox terrier at it again.

"That's right, Aileen," I said. "More rummage for Goodwill."

"All of it Suzanne's, I suppose."

"You can suppose anything you like."

"Getting rid of everything of hers. Because you claim she's not coming back."

"I made no such claim."

"I don't believe she went to Duluth. I'll bet she doesn't even have a sister."

"A bet you'd lose. She did and she does."

"So you say."

"And what do you say, Aileen?"

She jabbed an accusatory finger at me. "I say she never left. I say you did something to her."

"Such as what?"

"Something unspeakable. You won't get away with it."

"Roger implied the same thing last night."

I placed the last of the Teflon sacks in the trunk of the car. That left only the bowling bag. Aileen seemed to notice it for the first time. Her nose twitched and her teeth snapped together.

"That bag," she said. "What have you got in there?"

"It's a bowling bag. So there must be a bowling ball inside."

"You told Roger you didn't own a ball."

"Did I? He must have misunderstood."

I picked up the bag by its handles, hefting it.

Aileen gasped and drew back. "That stain on the side. It looks . . . *wet*."

I said, "You're imagining things," and swung the bag inside the trunk.

Another gasp, louder.

"Now what's the matter?"

"It didn't thump when you put it down. It . . . it . . ."

"It what?"

"*Squished*."

"Bowling balls don't squish, Aileen."

"I know what I heard!" She was backing away now, her hands up as if to ward off an attack. Her face had assumed the color of the flesh of her favorite sublime vegetable. Her eyes literally bulged.

"Now what could I have in a bowling bag," I said, "that would make a squishing sound?"

She said something that sounded like "Gaahh!" and fled.

The doorbell rang at seven that evening. Two men in business suits stood on the porch outside, one dark and heavyset, the other fair and loose-coupled. The dark one said, "Mr. Howard Bennett?"

"Yes? What can I do for you?"

"Police officers." They held up badges in leather cases. "My name is Pilofsky. This is Detective Jenkins. We'd like a few words with you, if you don't mind."

"Not at all," I said, "though I can't imagine why."

"All right if we come inside?"

I led them into the living room. Jenkins said, "We'll get right to the point, Mr. Bennett. We've had a report of suspicious activity concerning you and your wife."

"Ah," I said. "Now I understand. The Telfords. I should have known they would call you."

"Why is that?"

"They're the people for whom the phrase 'neighbors from hell' was coined. Sneaks and snoops of the worst sort, and melodramatic to boot. They've been insufferable since Suzanne was called away unexpectedly several days ago."

"Where is your wife, Mr. Bennett?" Pilofsky asked.

"Visiting her bedridden sister in Duluth. I told the Telfords that more than once."

"Is she coming back?"

"Of course. As soon as her sister's condition improves."

"Mrs. Telford claims you told her your wife was leaving you and staying in Duluth permanently."

"Then she misunderstood me. Just as both of them have persisted in misunderstanding a series of perfectly innocent incidents."

"Suppose you give us your version of those incidents."

I obliged at some length. Jenkins took notes.

Pilofsky said, "You didn't address the issue of the 'wet and squishy' bowling bag."

"Oh, that. Aileen Telford has a hyperactive imagination—she's a writer, you know. The bag wasn't wet. It was merely stained. And there was nothing in it except an old bowling ball of mine. She heard what she wanted to hear when I set it down."

"Where are the bag and ball now?"

"They went to Goodwill with the other rummage," I lied. Actually I had pitched the bag into an industrial dumpster not far from my office when no one was looking.

Both of them nodded and Jenkins made another note.

"So you see," I said, "it's all just a tempest in a teapot."

"So it would seem," Pilofsky said.

"Be all right if we had a look around?" Jenkins asked. "It's your privilege to say no, naturally. We don't have a search warrant." The implication here, of course, was that they could just go get one if they felt it necessary.

"More than all right," I said. "Be my guests. I have nothing to hide."

I conducted them through the house, top to bottom. They were polite and respectful, but quite thorough in their probings. They exhibited particular interest in my newly painted workshop and the rest of the basement, examining my tools and even looking inside the big Amana freezer. Naturally they found nothing incriminating. There was nothing for them to find.

From the basement I took them outside, where I unearthed the hideous ceramic bird sculpture I had buried in the rose garden. "I did it on a whim," I said. "I've always hated that sculpture, and with Suzanne away . . . well, I just couldn't stand to look at it any longer."

"Why bury it?" Pilofsky asked. "Why not just chuck it in the trash?"

I said sheepishly, "To be frank, I was covering my backside. I thought that if Suzanne noticed the sculpture was missing and became upset, I could always dig it up and pretend it had been misplaced." I sighed. "Now that I have dug it up, I suppose I might as well put it back where it belongs. It was a foolish notion to begin with."

Before they left, Jenkins asked for the name, address, and phone number of Suzanne's sister in Duluth. I provided the information, saying, "Please don't call her there unless it's absolutely necessary. I'm sure you understand."

"We just need it for our report, Mr. Bennett."

"Then you're satisfied that this has all been a misunderstanding?"

"Not to mention a waste of the taxpayers' time and money."

"I suppose it's too much to hope that the Telfords will be satisfied too."

"If we are," Pilofsky said meaningfully, "they'd better be."

Neither member of the Snoop Couple bothered me the next day or the morning of the one following. I saw neither hide nor hair of either of them, in fact. But that only meant that they had changed their tactics from overt to covert. They wouldn't be satisfied, no matter what the police had said to them, until they saw Suzanne, hale and hearty, with their own eyes.

Which is why, on the following morning, I drove off whistling.

The three P.M. flight from Duluth was on time. Suzanne was waiting with her bag when I pulled up to the curb at Arrivals, scowling at her watch even though I wasn't even a minute late.

On the way out of the airport I said, "It's good to have you home, dear."

"Horse apples," she said. Her favorite epithet, and one I've always loathed. "You were probably wishing I'd stayed away a lot longer."

"That's not true."

"Of course it's true. Well, you may get your wish. If my sister's condition doesn't improve over the next week or so, I'll probably have to go back there again."

"I'm sorry to hear that," I said.

"Horse apples. Don't try to deny you've liked living alone. All that freedom to stick your nose in a book and neglect your chores."

"I've never neglected my chores."

"Not when I'm around to prod you into doing them. I don't suppose you did everything on the list I gave you?"

"Ah, but I did."

"Finished building the new table for my sewing room?"

"In one evening."

"Took everything on my rummage list to Goodwill?"

"Yes, dear. Plus some odds and ends from the basement."

"Painted that ugly workshop of yours?"

"All four walls."

"Cleaned out the pantry and the freezer?"

"And the refrigerator. A good thing I did, too. There was a honeydew melon hidden in back that we bought weeks ago and forgot about."

"It must've been rotten."

"It was," I said. "Squishy, in fact."

"Mmm," she said. "Did you do anything else besides loaf?"

"Oh, I had some fun with the Telfords."

"Fun? With those busybodies?"

"We played a game."

"What kind of game?"

"Actually, it was one they made up. I never would have thought of it myself. But I learned the rules quickly and even invented a few of my own."

"Mmm. Who won?"

"I did."

"How nice for you," she said, and let the subject drop. She never has had any interest in my small triumphs.

When we arrived home, I made a point of parking prominently in the middle of the driveway and helping Suzanne out of the car. The Telfords had been sitting on their porch. They both scrambled to their feet when they saw her, their necks craning, looking like a pair of ungainly, agitated geese. I waved at them cheerfully. They ducked into their house without even waving back.

After I finished the dinner dishes, I sat on the front porch to watch dusk settle over the neighborhood. The evening was warmish and dusk is my favorite part of the day—quiet, peaceful, a contemplative time. Lights showed in the Telford house, but there was no sign of either Roger or Aileen. For the first time in as long as I could remember, all their window curtains were drawn and none of them were fluttering at the corners. It would be a good long while, if ever, I thought, before they resumed their spying on the Bennett household. After years of abuse, the prospect of protracted peace and privacy was a heady one.

The screen door banged after awhile and Suzanne came out to plop down next to me. "Why are you grinning?" she demanded.

"Was I grinning? I didn't realize it."

"What were you thinking about?"

"Oh, this and that. Possibilities."

"I don't understand you, Howard. Sometimes I wonder what possessed me to marry you in the first place."

Before I could frame a response, George, the Lindemans' Rottweiler mix, came trotting around the corner of the house. Suzanne let out a little screech that caused the dog to stop and flatten slightly with his ears back.

"Howard!"

"Don't worry," I said. "He's harmless."

"Harmless? An ugly brute like that? How did he get into our yard?"

"There's a loose board in the back fence—"

"Loose board? Why haven't you fixed it? What's the matter with you? A beast like that, running loose. There's no telling what kind of damage he'll do. Get rid of him this instant!"

I got up and went down the porch steps. George's tail began to wag. He came over and licked my hand.

"And don't come back until you've fixed that board. Do you hear me?"

"Yes, dear. You don't need to shout."

"Horse apples," she said. She went back inside and slammed the door behind her.

I said, "Come on, George," and led the dog around back and across the yard. He didn't want to leave. He stood looking up at me with round, eager eyes, his tongue lolling. I leaned down and patted his head.

"I don't have anything for you tonight, boy," I told him. "But I might have something in the foreseeable future. You never know. Life is full of possibilities."

Then I shooed him out and went to get my tools so I could pretend to fix the loose board in the fence.

THE CEMETERY MAN

The first time I saw the Cemetery Man, as I came to call him, I knew he wasn't the usual kind of visitor we have at Shady Oaks. Most folks who come to visit the resting places of loved ones and friends follow one or more of the grid of interior roads so as to get as close to the gravesites as they can. This fellow parked his black sedan—a rental, I found out later—just inside the main entrance gates, opposite the administration building, and walked from there. He wasn't dressed right for the warm Indian summer weather, either, in a long black overcoat. And he didn't seem to know where he wanted to go.

Shady Oaks stretches over more than fifteen hillside acres just outside the Los Alegres city limits. The Catholic and Jewish cemeteries are east of the administration building, the larger, wider nondenominational and historic sections west of it. There are a couple of dozen blacktop roads that crisscross the grounds; the ten that lead uphill vertically are known to employees as Up Roads, the seven that run horizontally as Crossroads, and each one is numbered. On the west side the gravesite and outdoor crypt sections between the roads are lettered from A through Z, with A being the lowest near the entrance gates and Z far up on the brow of the hill. I'm explaining all this to give you an idea of what Shady Oaks is like and so you'll know what I mean when I say I was working on #1 Crossroad above A Section the first time I saw the Cemetery Man.

What I was doing there was cleaning up leaves and twigs and branches that had blown down in a recent windstorm. It was a weekday afternoon in October and the grounds were mostly deserted. The work was easy enough and I was taking my time, so I noticed him as soon as he drove in and parked. He stood for a minute or so to look around, then headed on foot into A Section.

He was nobody I'd ever seen before. Close to seventy, somewhat frail-looking even at a distance, yet his back was straight and there was purpose in the way he moved. When he reached the first row of the A Section gravesites, he paused long enough at each to peer at the markers before moving on to the next. Looking for a particular plot, I thought, but not the way somebody does when he's forgotten the exact location of one he's visited before. As if he had no idea where the one he wanted was located.

He didn't find it in A Section. While I raked and piled and bagged, I watched him cross #2 Up Road farther west and search through the B Section rows. The one he was looking for wasn't there, either. He went uphill next, into F Section above where I was on #1 Crossroad.

Well, I'm what they call a people person. I know a good many of the visitors who come to Shady Oaks, on account of I've lived in the Los Alegres area all my life, and I enjoy passing the time of day with folks and offering a helping hand whenever I can. I admit to being a curious fellow, too—some might say nosy, not that that bothers me. Curiosity may have killed the cat, but it never did me any harm.

So I tossed the last bag of debris into the back of my pickup and walked up to where the Cemetery Man was moving among the F Section plots. When he reached the near end of a row, I went up to him and smiled and said, "Afternoon. Having trouble finding a plot?"

He turned toward me, and I have to say I felt a little shock when I saw him up close. His cheeks and forehead were crosshatched with deep-cut lines; two that curved down around his mouth looked as if they might have been framed and dug out with a pair of calipers. His eyes were deep-sunk, the pupils shiny-dark with what I'd seen too many times not to recognize as grief and sorrow. The word that came to me when I looked into that face for the first time was "ravaged."

He said in a thin, raspy voice, "I'll find it eventually."

"Maybe I can help. Jim Foley's my name. Head groundskeeper at Shady Oaks for twenty-two years and counting. I don't claim to know the names and locations of everyone at rest here, but I do know quite a few. Who is it you're searching for?"

He hesitated so long I thought he was going to turn away without answering.

Then he said, "Peter J. Anderson," but I had the feeling he gave the name reluctantly.

"Anderson, Peter Anderson." The name didn't ring any bells, not then. "Quite a few Andersons here, as you'd imagine. When did he pass on?"

"Twelve years ago. August eleventh, Two Thousand Two."

"Member of a large family?"

"I don't know."

"Oh? You're not a relative, then?"

"No."

"Friend of the deceased, or of a family member?"

"No."

I thought it was funny that he'd be hunting for a stranger's grave, but I didn't say so. I said, "Are you sure he's interred at Shady Oaks?"

"Yes. I'm sure."

"Well, you know, the quickest way to find out his resting place is to check with Mrs. O'Brien in the administration office. Each plot has a number that can be cross-referenced by name and date—"

"That won't be necessary. I'll find it on my own. I have time."

"This is a pretty big cemetery," I said, "more than two thousand plots and crypts in this part alone—"

"I have time," he said again.

I thought that was queer, too. But I said, "Yes, sir. Suit yourself. One thing you might want to know: No need to go looking in the sections up on the brow of the hill. That's the oldest part of Shady Oaks, where most of our founding families are buried; some of the graves date all the way back to Gold Rush days. No new burials up there in more than fifty years."

"Thank you," he said, and then he did turn away. And went right on with his search.

It was about time for me to take my afternoon break, but the Cemetery Man was such an odd old duck I didn't want to leave off keeping an eye on him. I went down and got into my pickup and drove on up to #2 Crossroad, where I had a clear view of him while I did some more raking and bagging.

He must have covered about a third of F Section before I saw him stop and stay stopped in front of a gravesite in the shadow of a big live oak. His body stiffened—I could tell that even from a distance—and he stood there staring at the plot for a minute or so without moving. Then he bowed his head, as if he might be praying, and stood like that for a longer time, must've been at least five minutes.

Afterward I watched him walk along #1 Crossroad to where his rental car was parked, and I thought, Well, that's that. But it wasn't. He didn't get in and drive off as I expected him to. Instead he opened the trunk, took out what looked to be a large bouquet of flowers, and headed straight back to F Section.

When he came uphill toward the grave he'd found, I could make out that the flowers were carnations and two or three kinds of lilies—all of them white and all artificial. Each gravesite has metal cups sunk into the ground for flowers and such; the Cemetery Man arranged his bouquet in the one there, stood again for a little time with his head bowed. Then he returned to his car again and this time he did drive on out.

Well, that curiosity of mine got the best of me. Once I was sure he wasn't coming back, I went to the plot under the big live oak. And when I looked at the headstone above the bunch of artificial flowers, I got my second little surprise of the day.

EVELYN BROWN
1983-2004
Earth Has No Sorrow That
Heaven Cannot Heal

Why had the old fellow asked for the grave of a man named Peter J. Anderson and then put flowers on a woman's named Evelyn Brown? The Anderson name might have been a falsehood, I supposed, and he'd been looking for Brown all along, but that didn't make sense, either. The only possibility I could think of that did make sense was that there was some sort of family connection between the Andersons and the Browns.

It was puzzling, all right, but in a minor sort of way. I had too much work to do to fuss about it. And I figured I'd never know one way or another because I'd never see him again.

Wrong. He was back again next day.

He must've come in sometime in the morning, but it wasn't until around one o'clock that I saw his car parked in the same spot inside the gates, then him a little while later. My assistants and I had a burial to prepare for in the Catholic Cemetery, and some other work to attend to in the northeast quadrant after that, and I took time to eat my brown-bag lunch before I headed over onto the west side. I was on #3 Crossroad, on my way to fix a leaking hose bib on #4 Up Road, when I spotted him.

There's a long curving row of crypts in a grove of pepper trees on that part of #3 Crossroad, where folks who don't believe in ground burial inter the ashes of loved ones who have been cremated. That was where the Cemetery Man was, peering at the nameplates on the crypts. He didn't pay any attention to me as I rolled slowly by. I almost stopped, but my sense of what's right and proper in dealing with visitors trumped my curiosity and kept me from doing it.

I put new washers in the leaking hose bib, moved a fallen tree limb that was partially blocking #4 Up Road. The Cemetery Man had finished examining the crypts, I saw when I drove back past, and was now up in J Section. Standing before one of the plots just off #3 Up Road—standing the way he had in front of Evelyn Brown's grave, stiff and still with his head bowed. Evidently he'd found what he was looking for today. After the switch yesterday, I couldn't help wondering if it was Peter J. Anderson's resting place or somebody else's.

I drove up to #4 Crossroad, turned in there, and stopped. By then the Cemetery Man was moving again, down to #2 Crossroad—heading for his car. Same thing as yesterday, then: he took another bunch of artificial flowers from the trunk, brought them back to the new grave he'd found in J Section, arranged them in front of the headstone there, and stood for another minute or so with his head bowed. The bouquet looked to be identical to the one he'd put on Evelyn Brown's grave—white carnations, white lilies.

Ten minutes later, he was back in his black sedan and gone.

Didn't take me long after he passed through the gates to go have a look at the marker on the J Section plot. Peter J. Anderson. 1977-2002.

Well, that should have satisfied me. The Cemetery Man had come hunting for two graves, not just one, found them both, paid his respects and left flowers—end of story. Except that I had a feeling it wasn't. And it still didn't explain why he'd given me Peter J. Anderson's name and not Evelyn Brown's, or why he'd been so bent on locating their graves without help.

I drove to the administration building and asked Kay O'Brien, who has worked at Shady Oaks almost as long as I have, to look up the records on both plots. She didn't ask me why I wanted the information. If I have too much curiosity, she doesn't have any at all.

There was no connection between the Brown and Anderson plots, or at least none in the records. I'd been thinking that maybe the same person might be paying annual maintenance fees for both, but that wasn't the case. One of the surviving members of the Brown family paid for upkeep on their plot; nobody paid for upkeep on the Anderson grave. That's often the case with deceased individuals who come from poor families or have no families at all. We try to do a minimal amount of upkeep on those anyway, gratis, but there's too much other work and barely enough public funding to maintain the roads and pay my and my crew's salaries.

The only thing Evelyn Brown and Peter J. Anderson seemed to have in common was that they'd both died young, in their twenties, about fifteen months apart. Something about that stirred in the back of my mind, but it was vague and my memory's not as sharp it used to be. I couldn't quite dredge it out.

I told myself to forget it, it was really none of my business, and in any event the Cemetery Man was now gone for good. But I wasn't a bit surprised when he showed up again the following day.

I was just pulling out of the maintenance yard above the administration building, heading out on my morning rounds, when his black sedan rolled in through the gates and stopped in the same place as before. He was still wearing that black overcoat even though it was even warmer today. He walked up to #4 Crossroad, then over into M Section.

Picking up where he'd left off the day before. Still looking.

Well, now I really had the wind up, as the British say. I had to fight down a couple of impulses, one to go poking around inside his car—he hadn't locked it—to see if I could find out who he was, the other to chase after him and ask him point blank what he was up to. I had my job to consider, after all, and one sure way to lose it would be to hassle a visitor without good cause.

But I couldn't just ignore him, either, and go on about my work as if he wasn't there. So I hung around the general area, doing little make-work projects while I watched him conduct the same sort of methodical search as on the previous two days.

He went from M Section up to Q and down to N. The noon hour came and went; I didn't bother to eat my lunch, which shows you how intent I was on the Cemetery Man. At one-thirty he was in R Section, which is mostly lawn on a gently rolling plateau, the grave markers nearly all plaques and small slabs that he had to stoop to read. And that was where he found the third grave.

I was standing alongside the pickup, fiddling with the tools inside the open side compartment, when he stopped and stared, then straightened and stood stiff-backed and bowed his head—exactly as he had at the Brown and Anderson sites. He stayed at this grave even longer than the others before he went off to his car. The ritual with the bouquet of flowers would be the same as before, I thought. And it was.

When he finished and walked away again, I hurried down to that third grave in R Section and leaned over to read what was etched on the already-tarnished bronze plaque.

SARAH JANE NOWITZKY
1985-2004
"Death is Only a Shadow
Across the Path to Heaven"

All sorts of bells went off in my head then. Even with a bad memory you don't forget a name like Sarah Jane Nowitzky. Or what happened to her. And once you remember that, you can't help but remember the connection between her and Evelyn Brown and Peter J. Anderson.

The Cemetery Man had almost reached the main drive. I ran for my pickup, got it turned around, and went barreling down that way. He had the door to the black sedan open when I got there. I braked nose up to the car's front bumper and jumped out and faced him square.

"Mister," I said, "I saw you put those flowers on Sarah Jane Nowitzky's grave."

All he said was, "Yes, I was aware of you watching me."

"Evelyn Brown's and Peter Anderson's, too. You know what those three people have in common besides being young when they died? I sure do."

He knew, all right. "They were all murdered," he said, "between Two Thousand Two and Two Thousand Four. Each in a terrible way."

"That's right, and the murders were never solved. And now here you come ten years after the last one, looking for their graves and putting flowers on 'em. I think you better tell me why."

"Or else you'll go to the police."

"Straight to the police."

"That's the right thing to do, Mr. Foley. I'll even go with you if you like."

It wasn't what I'd expected him to say, and it took some of the wind out of me.

"You will?"

He nodded and then looked past me into the middle distance. "Evelyn Brown, Peter Anderson, Sarah Jane Nowitsky," he said after a few seconds, in a voice not much louder than a whisper. "The only three in this area, thank God."

"What do you mean, the only three in this area?"

"I don't suppose it matters if I tell you. It won't be long until it all comes out." The Cemetery Man pulled his coat collar up to his chin, as if he were feeling a sudden chill. "There were thirty-four others over nearly thirty years. Not only in California—in eleven other states across the country."

I guess I gawked at him. "Thirty-seven murders?"

"Twenty-six women and eleven men, most under the age of thirty. All killed by the same man, an itinerant carpenter named George Lampton who died of lung cancer three weeks ago. During his lifetime he was never identified, never punished for his crimes."

"But then . . . how do you know he's the one?"

"There was a diary among his effects. Names, dates, places. Methods. Each of his crimes recorded in explicit detail. A scrapbook, too—newspaper clippings, burial notices."

"My God!"

"The FBI has them now," the Cemetery Man said. "They'll release the story to the media only after they've completed a thorough investigation. I should have enough time."

"Enough time for what?"

"To locate most if not all of the graves of his thirty-seven victims, pray for each of them, tell them how sorry I am."

"But why? Why would you want to do that?"

"I have to," he said, and tears glistened now on his ravaged face. "George Lampton was my son."

HOOCH

The three of us were in the cab of the chicken rancher's truck, heading to Bringle's Cove on the Sonoma County coast to pick up a whiskey shipment from Canada. The second truck, the bigger Graham, was five minutes or so behind us. It was five in the morning and there was hardly any traffic, but you never want to run trucks close together so it looks like a caravan, no matter what the hour. Angelo was driving and the kid, Bennie Sago, was in the middle between us. He had his Thompson gun tight between his knees, his skinny fingers sliding back and forth over the butt. My chopper was propped against the door, Angelo's up behind the seat. The payoff money was in a sack underneath. Nobody touched that but me.

The kid was antsy as hell. Not scared, far as I could tell, just excited. This was his first run with Angelo and me. Twenty-three, twenty-four, face like a beagle, straggly mustache, hair slicked down flat with pomade. Too cocky, too mouthy for my liking, but I had to put up with him for the time being. He'd been working for Renzo four or five months now, hired on as a favor to a gee Renzo knew in the Central Valley, and the jobs he'd done so far were up to snuff. When Renzo told you to partner with somebody, you didn't argue.

"Three hundred cases coming in, right, Joey?" this Bennie said for the second or third time.

"I already told you."

"Some twelve-year old Scotch, too," Angelo said. "Twenty cases."

"Twelve-year-old? Sure be swell to get a couple of bottles of that."

"Don't even think about swiping any," I said, "you know what's good for you."

"Hey, Joey, I was only kidding," the kid said. He gave a nervous little laugh. "I'd never do nothing like that."

"Damn well better not."

He was quiet for half a mile. Then he said, "You think we'll have any trouble?"

"No."

"I don't mean with the Coast Guard or the Feds. Fix is in up at Point Arena, right? Draw them all up to Mendocino County while we make the pick-up down here. But what about hijackers?"

"What about them?" Angelo said.

"Never know when they'll show. On land or on the ocean."

"No trouble with hijackers in over a year."

"Could still happen, though."

"Not this run. Don't wet your pants worrying about it."

"I'm not worrying." The kid's fingers kept sliding over the Thompson, fondling it like you would a woman. "Just thinking what it'd be like to see some action."

"You wouldn't like it."

"I don't know, maybe I would."

"You just think you would. Get into a shootout, you'd wet your pants for sure."

"Not me. Uh-uh, not me."

"You ever fire that Thompson at a man?" I said.

"No. Just target practice so far. But it wouldn't bother me none. I'm ready, willing, and able."

"Sure you are. All hot to trot."

Bennie was quiet for a while, until we cut off Highway One just south of Bodega Bay. It was getting close to dawn by then. Dark night, no moon, sky full of running clouds, fogbank out on the horizon—a good night for Cap Doolin's speedboat to leave Bodega Bay and slip into Bringle's Cove without being spotted.

"Say, Joey," the kid said then, "you ever read *Little Caesar*?" Out of the blue, just like that.

"Little what?"

"*Little Caesar*. You know, the book by W.R. Burnett."

"No. Never heard of it."

"It's the real goods, all about this Chicago gang-boss named Rico Bandello. Only problem with it is, he gets bumped off in the end."

"Then why the hell bother to read it?"

"Because it's the real goods, like I said. *The Maltese Falcon*, that's another one with the real goods. You ever read that one?"

"No."

"But you heard of the guy wrote it, Dashiell Hammett?"

"No."

"Never heard of Hammett? Ah, come on."

"You calling me a liar?"

"No, no. I'm just surprised, that's all. He's a local bird. Lives in San Francisco, hangs out at John's Grill on Ellis Street. I almost met him there once about a year ago, right after *The Maltese Falcon* got published as a book. It was a serial in *Black Mask* before that."

"So what?"

"He wrote some other books, too," the kid said. "*Red Harvest.*

The Dain Curse. Short stories, too. I read 'em all. He's some writer, that Hammett. Even better than Burnett."

"Yeah?" Angelo said. "What's he write about?"

"Knockovers, mob wars, cheating dames, you name it. And private dicks—Sam Spade, the Continental Op. Real tough gees. He used to be a private dick himself, so he knows all about how they operate."

"Sure he does," I said. "Then how come he quit being one?"

"So he could write. That's what he always wanted to do. You really ought to read one of his books, Joey."

"I got no time to read books."

"His stories in *Black Mask*, then. You know *Black Mask*, right?"

"No."

"What's *Black Mask*?" Angelo said.

"It's a pulp magazine. You never heard of it?"

"No."

"You guys ought to read it," the kid said. "Hammett's stories ain't the only swell ones. Raoul Whitfield, Frederick Nebel, Carroll John Daly—they deliver the goods too."

"Yeah? What do those birds write about?"

"Same like Hammett."

"You do a lot of reading, huh, Bennie?" Angelo said.

"Oh, sure. A lot."

"Bad for your eyes."

"Hah. You sound like my old lady."

We were less than a mile now from the side road that led to Bringle's Cove. There was still no traffic. Bringle's was the best delivery spot along this section of the coast. Off the beaten track, natural jetty, no hidden offshore rocks or kelp beds to foul up a boat's engine, no place for Feds or hijackers to set up in ambush. We'd been using the cove off and on since '27 and never had any trouble.

"I do a lot of writing, too," the kid said. "One of these days I'm gonna write some stories for *Black Mask*. Right now I'm writing a book."

"A book, huh?" Angelo said.

"Yeah. I been working on it ever since I come up permanent from the valley."

"What kind of book?"

"A fiction book, a novel like *Little Caesar* and *The Maltese Falcon*, only better. Real tough, tougher than Burnett and Hammett."

"What's it about, this book of yours?"

"The liquor business. Write what you know, that's what they tell you."

Angelo didn't say anything. I said, "That mean you're writing about us, the operation?"

"Well, yeah, sort of."

"Renzo, me, Angelo, you?"

"We're all in it, sure, but not under our real names, not so's we'd be recognized. I mean, I'm giving the real inside dope on how the racket works out here, but it's all disguised, fictionalized. Nothing the cops or Feds could use, you don't have to worry none about that."

"What happens to us in this book of yours?"

"Nothing. That's the beauty of it, see? None of us gets caught or shot up like Rico Bandello." The kid squirmed some more and then laughed. "We outfox the cops and the Feds, same as we're doing in real life, and get away clean in the end. Pretty nifty, huh?"

"Yeah," I said. "Nifty."

"I call it *Hooch*. Couldn't ask for a better title. *Hooch*."

We jounced over the side road into Bringle's Cove. It was a few minutes before dawn, still mostly dark, just enough daylight so you could tell the beach, the cliffside caves, the jetty were all empty except for squawking seagulls. Angelo drove into the biggest of the caves where we always left the trucks. The three of us got out with the choppers and me with the money sack and stood around waiting. The kid was still antsy. Once he said, "Man, I can't wait to get out there and make the pickup. Action or no action." I told him to shut his mouth and for once he shut it.

The big Graham, its canvas sides rolled halfway up so you could see the produce boxes stacked inside, rattled in about five minutes later. Three-man crew on it too. Six soldiers and six machine guns were all we'd need even if we ran into hijackers. That had only happened once on any of my runs, and what that bunch got out of it was two dead and a shot-up boat. It wasn't anything to sweat about.

Cap Doolin showed up right on time, with just enough dawn in the sky so he could drift in without running lights. His boat was a forty-foot cruiser with twin diesels, squat-hulled and clean-decked, flush from stem to stern except for a small glassed-in pilot's hood. She could outrun any Coast Guard cutter and had proved it more than once. Doolin eased her in close to the end of the jetty, just long enough for the six of us to climb on board. Then we headed out, running wide open once we got far enough offshore.

There was a wind and the water was choppy. Spray rattled like birdshot against the pilot house windows. Nobody said anything, not even the kid. He had his sea legs and he seemed to be handling himself all right, with his lip still buttoned.

It was full light when we neared the big Canadian rumrunner, anchored in the fogbank outside the twelve-mile limit. You couldn't see her clear until we got close, and even then she looked like a ghost ship in the fog. The kid stood gawking at her through the windscreen. "Hey," he said then, "hey, she's one big mother, ain't she."

She was that. Hundred and ten feet, narrow-gutted, low-hulled, painted battleship gray from her waterline to the trucks of her stubby masts. Like a long, lean whale.

"How much liquor can she carry?"

"Sixty tons loaded full," Doolin said.

"Sixty! Man!"

Doolin slid us alongside, up against the heavy rope fenders hanging from the ship's bulwark. The six of us were all on deck by then, spreading out to watch and wait. Crewmen with machine guns were stationed on the rumrunner's deck too. But it was all just everybody being careful. We'd done plenty of business with this bunch before.

I went over to the rail and tossed the money sack up to the Canadian captain. He knew all the cash would be there so he never bothered to count it anymore, just went ahead and ordered his crew to strip the hatch covers off the cargo hold. Doolin and his men did the same on the speedboat. I kept one eye on the kid while this was going on. Still up to snuff, but still keyed up too, his eyes jumping this way and that. The way he held his chopper, his finger skipping back and forth across the trigger, you could tell he was hoping somebody would start something.

The rumrunner's electric power winch started to whir. The first fifty cases, already loaded into the rope net sling, came up fast out of her hold. The winchman swung them over on the flexible steel cable, lowered them quick through the cruiser's open hatch. Everybody had the transfer down pat. It didn't take more than an hour to load and unload all six slings.

"Smooth as silk," the kid said when Doolin had us underway again. "But I still kind of wish we'd run into hijackers. Make a swell chapter for my book."

"You and your goddamn book," Angelo said.

We made short work of the Bringle's Cove transfer too. Two

hundred cases went onto the Graham, hidden by the produce crates. We took the other hundred in the chicken truck, including the twenty of twelve-year-old Scotch that somebody up here in the county had ordered special. The Graham headed northeast to Santa Rosa to make its delivery, we drove south to Constantine's chicken ranch outside Petaluma. Constantine would handle local distribution from there.

In Angelo's flivver, on the way to the Sausalito ferry, the kid started chattering again about the book he was writing. *Hooch* this, *Hooch* that. And some more about how all of us were in it under made-up names.

It was early evening by the time I got to the Bay Area Distributors warehouse, on the Embarcadero down by Islais Creek. Renzo's operation was big, the biggest in San Francisco and the North Bay. More than four hundred on his payroll, contracts with haulers and distributors and homegrown suppliers of cheap jackass brandy and dago red. He ran it all from here, but he had another storage warehouse in South S.F. and a third up in Santa Rosa. All of them were packed with barrels of wine, crates of the jackass brandy, bonded Canadian Club and the best Scotch and Irish whiskey. Just about any liquor anybody could want, even some fancy cordials from France and Italy.

None of the warehouses had ever been raided. The fix was in with the city coppers and the county sheriffs here and up north. A few of the Feds, too. Not everybody's got his price but plenty enough do. We'd had a little trouble with a couple of rival gangs trying to muscle in, but we handled them the way we handled the hijackers. Everything was running smooth now, smooth as silk like the kid said. But you still had to be careful. Real careful. You couldn't afford to take chances.

Stairs at the far wall led up to Renzo's office. I could smell the wine in there as I climbed up. Most of it was good, pre-Prohibition Burgundy from Sonoma and Napa counties, but there was plenty of the cheap stuff too. You couldn't smell it from outside. The walls were thick concrete with wood facing. The warehouse was like a fortress.

Renzo's office was blue with the smoke from the Toscanelli stogies he smoked. Why he liked those stinking black tule roots I couldn't figure. You had to drag hard just to get smoke from one end to the other and even then you couldn't get enough to inhale.

"Hey, Joey," he said. "How'd it go up the coast?"

"Like usual. Clean operation."

"Good, good. So how come you don't look happy?"

"I think maybe we got a problem."

"Yeah? What kind of problem?"

I told him what kind.

He fired up another Toscanelli while he thought it over. Then he said, "Yeah. Yeah, I see what you mean. Probably nothing to get worked up about, but we can't afford to take chances."

"Just what I was thinking. You want me to handle it?"

"You're my right hand, Joey. I wouldn't trust nobody else."

The next night I called up Angelo and had him come get me in his flivver. He didn't say much when I told him what we were going to do. Good boy, Angelo. Reliable. Did what he was told and didn't ask questions.

We picked up Bennie Sago at his apartment on Fell Street. He said when he climbed in, "So what's happening tonight? Another coast run?"

"No," I said. "We got some business down in Brisbane."

"What kind of business?"

"You'll find out when we get there."

We headed south out of the city. "How's that book of yours coming?" I asked him.

"Real good. I'm telling you, Joey, *Hooch* is gonna be better than *Little Caesar, Red Harvest,* all the rest. It'll sell like hotcakes, then get made into a talking picture. Make me famous."

"Me and Angelo and Renzo, too, huh?"

"Oh, sure. Only nobody'll know it but us. We'll all have a big laugh over that, right?"

He was primed now. He kept flapping his gums while Angelo swung us away from the Bay and up into the Brisbane hills. About how swell *Hooch* was, and did Angelo and me want to borrow some copies of this *Black Mask* so we could see if he wasn't right about Hammett and Daly and the other hard-boiled writers. I quit listening after a while. He didn't care. He went right on jabbering to Angelo.

We were up into the thickly wooded part of the hills, nobody around, no lights anywhere, when he finally ran down. "Say," he said, "where we going, anyhow? This road's nothing but a fire trail."

I didn't say anything. Neither did Angelo.

"Joey? How much farther we got to go?"

"This'll do right here," I said, and Angelo pulled the flivver over to the side. "Get out, Bennie."

"Here? What for?"

"Get out. Stand in the lights."

He got out, went around to the front. Stood there looking around, then at me with this puzzled look on his face. Punk kid wasn't even half as smart as he thought he was. He didn't have a clue what was happening until I showed him my rod.

His eyes got big then, round and white as eggs in the headlights. "Christ, Joey, why? *Why?*"

"That book of yours," I said. "That's why."

"*Hooch?* No! No, wait, listen to me—"

"Too late for that."

"Please, Joey, please, you got to listen!"

I shot him twice, then went over and put a third round into him to make sure. I'll give him this—he hadn't tried to beg or run. He stood there and took it like a man.

I opened the door to the Fell Street apartment with the key I'd taken off Sago's body. It wasn't much of a place and it didn't take Angelo and me long to search it top to bottom, every corner, every nook and cranny.

There were a bunch of books in a little case, the ones the kid had talked about and a few he hadn't. A stack of *Black Mask* magazines and some other pulps too.

But there wasn't any *Hooch*.

No manuscript pages, no notes, nothing at all written down. The kid hadn't even owned a typewriting machine.

"He never wrote a word about us and the operation," Angelo said. "Damn fool was just trying to make himself sound important. You didn't need to bump him after all."

"Yeah, I did. Can't trust a punk even thinks about doing something like that."

"Well, you and Renzo don't have to worry about me writing a book. I ain't ever even gonna *read* one."

"That's playing it smart," I said. "All them things do is put ideas in your head."

SNAP

Glenda Rennert

One of the four of us in this cabin is going to be murdered soon. Very soon. Maybe tonight.

I hope I'm wrong, I pray I am, but I can't shed the feeling. The violence is like a presence in these five oh-so-rustic rooms, as alive and deadly as the monster Sierras blizzard that has had us trapped here for the past three days. It grows more intense by the hour, fueled by the enforced togetherness and our mutual hatred. There's no escape from the cabin with the snow drifted up high over doors and windows, no escape from one another. I'm not the only one whose nerves are like exposed wires scraped raw, and I'm afraid none of us is willful enough or strong enough to hold up under the pressure indefinitely. It seems inevitable that before the storm ends one of us will snap.

Who? Which of us the murderer, which the victim?

Bryan is a wimp except when he's been drinking heavily, then he's liable to go off into one of his crazy black rages. He's capable of murder, all right. So is Roger, so is that slut Tracy. Yes, and so am I. None of us is exempt from either the urge or the sudden snap that leads to what the head doctors call a psychotic episode. And the cabin is full of lethal weapons. Handguns and rifles in the gun cabinet next to the fireplace—Roger and his passion for blood sports. Hunting knives, kitchen knives, other sharp instruments. Fireplace tools. Axes and hatchets for chopping wood and kindling. I shudder just thinking about all those things so close at hand.

It hardly seems possible that not so long ago we were all friends. Tracy and me first, when Bry's last book didn't sell as well as expected and we needed some extra money and I lucked into the office job at Beguile Cosmetics where she was assistant sales manager. Then the four of us getting together for dinners, and Bry and Roger seeming to hit it off, and for a while we had some good times in twos and fours. Didn't we? I thought so then, but now I'm not so sure.

Anyhow it all went downhill fast. Tracy snuck out to so many clandestine meetings with her lovers that her work suffered, leaving me no choice but to take over some of it myself. When Mr. Mendelbaum fired her, she blamed me for stealing her job. Roger talked Bry into investing in that Texas oil deal, fifty thousand dollars for God's sake, which he ponied up in cash without even consulting me because Roger promised him a high, quick profit. But the oil company went belly up and we lost our money and the other investors lost theirs, and Bry demanded an accounting that didn't satisfy him and he accused Roger of running some kind of Ponzi scheme.

Then Tracy and Bry started sleeping together, her to get back at me, him to get back at Roger. He had cause, she didn't. I never tried to take her effing job away from her. Well, okay, I did put the bug in Mr. Mendelbaum's ear about her being out of the office so much and sloughing off on her work, but I did it for the good of Beguile. And was I supposed to say no when he offered the assistant manager's position to me after he fired her? As for the affair, Tracy's the one who did the seducing, you can bet on that. Bry wouldn't have the guts, drunk or sober, to make a pass at a woman like her.

Why I ever married him I'll never know. Well, that's not quite true. No other prospects, or at least none with much to offer in the way of security, and a certain glamour in the fact that he makes a nice living writing sleazy sex novels. What a nasty surprise it was to find out he's only hot stuff on the printed page. I hope Tracy was as disappointed in his inept bedroom fumblings as I've been the past five years. Not even someone as practiced as she is, with her string of lovers and her X-rated bragging, could coax even one good lay out of him, I'll bet.

Roger's no prize in that department either, evidently. The rugged outdoors type when he's not brokering phony deals and stealing his clients' money, but his machismo doesn't extend to the bedroom. Another sexual washout. Not quite impotent, to hear Tracy tell it, but he might as well be. Killing animals is how he gets off. All kinds of animals, large and small. Just look in his eyes when he talks about hunting and you know he'd get off on killing a human being, too, if he thought he could away with it.

It's Bry's fault we're in this awful mess. He just had to accept Roger's invitation to spend the weekend up here so the four of us could "work out our differences." Stupid! I told him so, but then I made the mistake of letting him talk me into coming with him, why I don't know. Yes I do. I was afraid he'd lose his temper with Roger over the $50,000 and I wanted to be there to act as peacemaker if that happened. But Roger and the money isn't the only reason he went or I went, or so I thought at the time. I had the idea he'd look for a chance to sneak off with Tracy for an outdoor quickie and I wasn't about to let that happen either.

The snow started coming down hard right after we got here and it hasn't stopped since. One of those freak mountain blizzards, according to Roger, that nobody can predict ahead of time, that just start blowing and go on and on for days. The power went out the first night. If it wasn't for the auxiliary generator in the shed attached to the kitchen we wouldn't have any light other than lanterns and candles, any heat except for the big stone fireplace. Even with electric heaters and a fire going most of the time, it's cold in the living room and even colder in the bedrooms. And the wind makes so much noise even sleep aids don't help—I haven't slept more than a couple of hours the past two nights.

We've been on each other's nerves and at each other's throats ever since it became obvious nothing was going to get worked out and we were snowbound besides. Roger refuses to give us our money back. Last night Bry threatened him with a lawsuit and Roger just laughed, but you could see the hate in his eyes and the twist of his mouth.

Bry keeps giving Tracy bitter looks, not the secretly lustful kind I expected, and she keeps avoiding him. Something must have happened between them to end the affair, not that I care what it was. I wish she'd avoid me, too, but no, she throws snide remarks at me every chance she gets. I got so fed up this afternoon I let her know I knew she was screwing Bry and that I might just tell her husband about it. About all her other affairs, too. She said if I did, she'd fix me good and proper. She practically spit in my face and I came close to spitting in hers.

And then Bry and I had the argument in our bedroom over how much he's been drinking. Yelling and cursing each other, both of us so angry I almost told *him* I knew about the affair. If I had, the fight could have had a lot worse consequences. As it was I said something scathing, I don't remember what, that made him mad enough to slap me and me mad enough to slap him back. He knows I can't stand to be hit.

Bad all around, and getting worse. I just don't see how we can all live together through another night without somebody losing it, really *losing* it.

Bryan Rennert

I poured myself another glass of scotch. Single malt, eighteen years old. I'd helped myself to a lot of it the past three days, and why not? I was entitled to anything of Farrell's I could get after what he did to me. Besides, it's the only way I can stand to be cooped up in this frozen hellhole with him and Tracy and Glenda. I must have been crazy to buy into his "let's get together for the weekend and settle our differences" crap. He didn't mean it. It was just the opening gambit in a sick game, like putting different bugs in a jar and shaking them up and watching to see what happens. Why didn't I realize that before we drove up here? I should have, I've known for some time what a control freak he is.

"Might want to take it a little easy there, Bry." Farrell, sitting over there in his big leather chair cleaning and polishing another of his rifles, half smiling like he didn't have a care in the world. The two of us were alone in the living room with all the dead animal heads on the knotty pine walls. Glenda was sulking in our bedroom because of what happened earlier, and Tracy was doing something in the kitchen. Just as well. When she's close by, I can't help looking at her and remembering the way things ended between us—and perversely, the way it had been with her in bed, a whole kaleidoscope of pornographic images. A hyperactive imagination isn't always a writer's best friend.

I said, "If you don't want me drinking your lousy scotch, just say so."

"Lousy? It costs a hundred bucks a liter, my friend."

"I'm not your friend. Sworn enemy is more like it."

Farrell shrugged and went on polishing.

"Okay," I said, "so you can afford the best. But on whose money, yours or mine and those other poor bastards'?"

"Are you going to start harping on that again?"

"From now until the day you write me a check for fifty thousand dollars."

"That day will never come. Great Lone Star Oil's collapse is responsible for the investors' losses, not me. You'll never prove different."

"We'll just see about that." I tossed off my drink, poured another, and banged the nearly empty bottle down on the wet bar.

"Maybe you didn't notice," Farrell said, "but there's only one more liter of single malt left."

"So what? There're still a couple of fingers left in this one and nobody else is drinking scotch."

"Well, you can always drink yourself sodden on something different if necessary. There's still plenty of bourbon, gin, and vodka. We won't run out before the storm ends."

"Oh, hell, no. Assuming it ever does."

"It should blow itself out sometime tonight."

"You said that last night."

"Can't always predict what a freak blizzard like this will do, I told you that before too, but my guess is it won't last much longer. It'll take us a while to dig our way out of here once it's over, and the road will be impassable when we do. It's five miles cross-country on snowshoes to Compton Village."

"I've never been on snowshoes in my life."

"No, of course you haven't. You don't live life, Rennert, you just make up bullshit stories about it. Don't worry, you won't have to walk the five miles. Neither will the women. The three of you can wait here in comfort while I go for help."

Big man. Mr. Macho. So smug, so arrogant. How I despise the conniving son of a bitch!

I took another slug of single malt. I'd been hitting it pretty hard, yes, but not hard enough to get so drunk I didn't know what I was doing or saying. I had to be careful. If I did get blind drunk, I might just let it slip to Farrell about Tracy and me. He wouldn't like it, that's for sure. I'm not afraid of him, but he's six inches taller and fifty pounds heavier. He'd be mean as hell in a fight, and I have a pretty low pain threshold.

"What's Glenda doing, Rennert? Taking a nap?"

"Who can sleep with that banshee howling outside?"

"I can. You would too if you didn't drink so much."

"Still getting your full eight hours, right? Sleeping like a baby."

"That's right."

"Too bad it's not the sleep of the dead."

Farrell thought that was funny, or pretended to. He said with a wry little chuckle, "Why don't you go wake Glenda and I'll call Tracy. We'll have dinner and then finish what we started to do the other night—play bridge to pass the time."

"You've got to be kidding."

"I don't kid, you know that. We're not going to get out of here any faster by avoiding one another's company."

"It's a hell of a lot better than sitting together at the table playing cards. We couldn't keep it up for more than half an hour the last time. You're crazy if you think it'd be any better tonight."

"It will if we all make an effort to be civilized."

Civilized. Christ. "I hate bridge."

"Anything I like, you hate. That about it?"

Tracy included. She's as conniving and mean-spirited as he

is—a ballbusting, manipulative maneater with the morals of an alley cat and the empathy of a terrorist. The offhand way she ended the affair proved just how uncaring she is, as if I was some stray dog she'd fed a few times and kicked out when she got tired of it. She came on to me that day in the city because she wanted revenge on Glenda, not because she wanted me. I know that now. I may be slow on the uptake sometimes, but I'm not stupid.

"That's it, all right," I said. "Anything you like, I hate."

Tracy Farrell

When I came out of the kitchen with the tray of sandwiches, Bryan was glaring daggers at Roger and Roger was sneering back at him. They make me sick, both of them. Silly, mean little boys pretending to be men, one with rifles and pistols, the other with words. The phony stud hunter and the creepy writer.

I set the tray down on the coffee table. Roger said in his snotty way, "Sandwiches again?"

"What did you expect, a gourmet meal?"

"Something hot. Soup, canned stew."

"There isn't any more of either." There was, but I was sick of standing at the stove. Making sandwiches was enough of a pain in the ass. Let him do the cooking himself if he wanted something hot. Or make that bitch Glenda do it.

The lights flickered again. Every time they did that, I held my breath. If the damn generator went out—

"Don't worry," Roger said, in that way he has of almost reading my mind. "Our auxiliary is the best on the market. It won't quit on us."

"Famous last words."

"You wouldn't freeze even if it did, pet. Too much body heat."

Bryan chuckled at that. I glared a warning at him, then turned away so I wouldn't have to look at his ugly face. I almost wish I hadn't started the affair with him. I never found him attractive and going to bed with him was no fun. I hated the way he kissed and the feel of his hands on my body . . . ugh. I've almost always had to do some acting in bed with a man, but with him I had to give Oscar-caliber performances every time. You read one of his books and you think here's a guy who understands women and a woman's needs, and then you sleep with him and you realize he doesn't know a damn thing. How Glenda could stand to be married to him for five years is beyond me. Maybe she's a masochist in addition to being a miserable back-stabber.

I don't care what she says, she took my job at Beguile away from me on purpose. Went to old Mendelbaum and lied about how l was out of the office more than I was in it and way behind in my work. Of course I was out of the office a lot, an assistant sales manager for a cosmetics company has to do plenty of schmoozing with the customers. So what if sometimes it went farther than that with a good-looking out of town buyer? Maybe I was a little behind in my work, but it was nothing I couldn't make up. Glenda made it sound like I wasn't earning my salary, and at the same time giving Beguile a bad reputation by using sex to sell our products. Oh, she did a terrific job of tearing me down and toadying up to Mendelbaum. Every time I think about it, I see red and I want to scratch her eyes out.

Damn Roger for inviting her and Bryan up here. I know now why he did it and it had nothing to do with patching things up. He's a sadist, he gets a kick out of sticking needles in people and watching them squirm. Does he suspect I slept with Bryan? God, I hope not. He expects me to stay faithful to him even though he hardly ever touches me except when he's been out hunting and killed something. He'd make my life miserable if he found out, maybe divorce me. I won't get a cent if that happens. That lousy pre-nup he made me sign—

"Go make some coffee, pet."

Pet again. I loathe that silly name, and he knows it. "I don't want any more coffee."

"I do. Go make some. And see if you can find some soup."

Sometimes, like right now, I wish he was dead. Dead, dead, dead!

Roger Farrell

Rennert watched Tracy hip-sway out of the room. If I hadn't known before he got here that it was over between them, I would have guessed it from the way he looked at her and she at him. All their briefly shared lust burned out, nothing but ashes left. Neither of them thinks I know about the affair and they're both afraid I'll find out and do something drastic. Perhaps I will. But for now it amuses me to play the cat to their pair of mice.

Listen to that wind! The whole place shook with the last gust and the lights flickered again. Rennert stared up at the ceiling as if he thought the roof was going to cave in. Coward along with all his other faults. Scared, sniveling, booze-swilling candy-ass.

I like storms, even monsters like this one. Nature at its rawest always stirs my blood. Life isn't half as sweet without some excitement, some danger to spice it up. Other kinds of fun and games, too—my special kind. It hadn't been easy, convincing Rennert to come up here with Glenda, but managing it had paid dividends and then some. From my perspective, the sudden blizzard and the snowbound isolation made this a perfect weekend.

I finished pretending to clean the already clean Weatherby Vanguard and carried it over to the cabinet. Sweet rifle. I remember the time I nailed an elk with it at better than three hundred yards, a helluva fine shot. Rennert watched me, licking his lips, while I unlocked the cabinet door and put the Weatherby away. He'd have liked nothing better than to rush over and grab one of the handguns racked inside and shoot me with it. None of the guns are loaded, of course, but he doesn't know that. I felt like laughing. What a joke if he did somehow manage to grab a loaded weapon—he'd never be able to pull the trigger. No guts. He doesn't have enough to wrap around a spool of thread.

I never liked him. Weakling. Loser. Never liked Glenda, either—she's the same kind of scheming leech as my wife. I have to admit it gave me a certain amount of pleasure to screw them out of their investment. Not that I kept all of their $50,000, or all of the other investors' capital—just enough to feather my nest before Great Lone Star Oil went belly up, just enough to make sure I'd have no trouble covering my tracks and getting away with it. Let Rennert file a lawsuit, it won't buy him anything except more financial loss. No proof, no case. Any judge would rule in my favor and he'd be stuck with the legal fees.

I relocked the cabinet door, put the key back in my pocket. The only key, so no worries on that score—not that I ever had any. Rennert was still watching me while he broke the seal on the last liter of single malt. Eventually he would drink that one dry, too, and finally pass out. Until then he was my game, my meat, like any other dumb animal.

The fire in the fireplace had begun to bank. I laid in another log. The supply of cordwood in the shed had dwindled, but there was enough to last another couple of days. I dusted my hands and said to Rennert, "Go wake up Glenda."

"Why the hell should I?"

"It's time to eat, time for her to join the party."

"Party. Jesus."

"We'll have our sandwiches and coffee and then we'll play a rubber or two of bridge until bedtime."

"Dammit, I'm not going to play cards with you!"

"Yes you are. This is my cabin and we're going to do what I say from now until the storm abates and we can start digging out. Don't give me any more argument, just go fetch your wife."

Rennert cut my throat with his eyes, but he didn't argue. He got up and slouched out, just as I'd known he would.

Puppet on a short string, full of sawdust and scotch.

Glenda Rennert

It was cold in the bedroom and I was lying on the bed with the covers pulled up when Bryan staggered in. Staggered is the right word. Still swilling scotch, as if deliberately defying me after our fight—enough already to make him unsteady on his feet, his face red and his eyes shiny. At this rate he'd be falling down drunk by nine or ten. I had to bite my tongue to keep from saying something cutting to him. I didn't want another slap like the one this morning.

"Get up," he said. "The lord and master wants you."

"Roger? Why?"

"Dinner."

"I'm not hungry."

"And then the bastard wants to play bridge."

"What? No! I'm not going through that farce again."

"If I have to, so do you. It's his cabin and he's twice my size, so we're going to do what he says." Bry laughed one of his nasty laughs. "He holds all the cards. For now."

"I won't spend any more time with him or that bitch he's married to. Her especially."

"Why her especially? Just because she blames you for taking her job away from her—"

"That's not the reason I hate her and you know it."

"What are you talking about?"

I tried to stop myself from saying it, but I couldn't. It had built up inside me until I felt as though I'd strangle on it if I didn't spit it out. "Did you think I wouldn't find out you've been sleeping with her? Well, I did. I've known it for weeks now, so don't try to deny it."

". . . All right. It was a mistake and it's over and done with. Does she know you know?"

"Yes."

"You told her?" His mouth had pinched in so tightly I could see little white ridges of muscle along his jawline. "Does Farrell know?"

"I didn't tell him and she wouldn't dare. But maybe I will. I'd love to see what he'd do to her."

"You keep your damn mouth shut."

"Why should I? You—"

He hit me. Not an open-handed slap like last night—with his fist for the first time ever, hard enough to knock me sprawling across the bed. The blow made me cry out, sent sharp pain swirling through my head. I struggled into a sitting position, wincing when I reached up to touch my mouth. My fingers came away bloody.

"Damn you, Bryan. Damn you! You split my lip."

"It's just a little cut. You'll live."

"You shouldn't have hit me like that."

"You asked for it, making stupid threats." He took a step toward me. "Here, give me your hand—"

"Stay away from me! Don't touch me!"

I struggled off the bed, went shakily into the bathroom and slammed the door behind me. Then I looked in the mirror. No, it wasn't a bad cut, but dabbing at it with a wet washcloth didn't stop the bleeding and it wasn't in a place where you could bandage it. And my lip would probably swell until it pulled my whole mouth out of shape.

"Come on out of there, Glenda."

I didn't hurry, but I didn't dawdle either. When I came out I said, "See what you did? It's still bleeding." Already it hurt a little to talk.

"Maybe you'd better stay in here—"

"Oh, no. I want them to see I'm married to a wife-beater."

"Wife-beater, hell. Don't be melodramatic."

"You want me to tell them I ran into a door?"

"I don't care what you tell them about the cut, just keep your mouth shut about Tracy and me. You hear me?"

"I hear you."

"All right. Go ahead, I'll be along in a minute."

I went, holding the washcloth pressed tight against my stinging lip. Saying over and over to myself what I'd said to him: You shouldn't have hit me like that, you shouldn't have hit me like that, you shouldn't have hit me like that . . .

Bryan Rennert

As soon as Glenda was out of the bedroom, I dragged my suitcase out of the closet and slung it open on the bed. The old .32 caliber revolver I'd inherited from my father was tucked inside the spare pair of shoes I'd packed, where not even Glenda would have thought to look for it. I'm nowhere near as partial to firearms as Farrell, don't much like them at all in fact, but the old man taught me how to shoot when I was a kid. It's been years since I did any target practicing, but shooting a pistol is like riding a bicycle, once you've learned you never forget how.

I almost didn't bring the gun. An inadequate weapon compared to the firepower Farrell keeps in the cabin. But the way things were between him and me, I was leery of coming up here without protection if not a method of persuasion. I've been tempted to take it out before this, but I was afraid of what might happen. I'm not a violent man, it takes a lot to provoke me. Well, now I'm provoked. I've had all I'm going to take from Farrell. Enough! No more being pushed around!

The .32 was a five-shot model and I'd loaded in four cartridges before leaving home. I rotated the cylinder to put a round in firing position, then slipped the gun into my coat pocket and went out into the living room.

Farrell and Tracy were sitting at the dining room table, Glenda standing at the wet bar holding a shot of vodka in one hand, the washcloth to her lip with the other. She's never been much of a drinker, her lip must really be hurting. I shouldn't have punched her, but then she shouldn't have provoked me. I'd had enough of her, too. The marriage is over as far as I'm concerned. I just don't give a damn anymore.

I needed a drink myself and went to the wet bar to pour one. Glenda moved aside, not looking at me.

"Sit down, both of you," Farrell said. "I'm hungry even if you're not."

Neither Glenda nor I said anything, just went separately to the table. Farrell told us where to sit, me across from him, Glenda across from Tracy.

"Isn't this nice and cozy," Tracy said. "How's your lip, Glenda?"

No answer, just an up-from-under glare.

"Pretty job you did on her, Bryan. I wish I'd been there to see it."

"It was an accident."

"Sure it was. Wham, bam, just a little accident, ma'am."

Farrell told her to shut up and pour the coffee. He was the only one with any appetite. Tracy ate half a sandwich, I washed down a few bites of mine with scotch, Glenda didn't touch hers. You could have sliced the tension into wedges for dessert.

There was no more conversation until Farrell ordered Tracy to clear the table and bring the cards. "Do we have to play bridge, Roger?" she said. "None of us wants to."

"I do. What the rest of you want doesn't matter." He looked at me. "You and I will partner, Rennert. How does that sound?"

"Torturous."

He chuckled. "The cards, Tracy. I'll deal."

Throughout all of this the wind kept beating at the house, shaking walls and rattling windows, howling and screeching and sandpapering my nerves until I felt like screaming right along with it.

Tracy Farrell

Torture was what it was, all right. Roger was the only one who concentrated on the cards, none of the rest of us even tried. I thought that if he made us sit here like this until midnight, like he'd said he would, I'd get a skillet from the kitchen and belt him with it. But the game didn't last anywhere near that long. It didn't even last fifteen minutes. He bid something in no trumps, and then it was the bitch's turn, but she just sat there like a zombie. Her lip had stopped bleeding and was starting to puff, and I couldn't resist saying, "Go ahead and play, Glenda. Or can't you talk with your mouth all swollen up like a fat-lipped fish?"

She held the zombie pose for three or four seconds and then all of a sudden she threw down her cards and stood up so fast she practically knocked over her chair. "I can't take any more of this, I can't and I won't!"

Roger told her to sit down. She told him what he could do to himself, spun on her fat ankles, and ran out of the room. A few seconds later I heard the spare bedroom door slam.

"Rennert," Roger said, "go get her and bring her back."

"Like hell I will."

"Don't argue, just do what you're told."

"I'm all done following orders from you." Bryan was on his feet now, too. He looked different all of a sudden, in a way that put a chill on the back of my neck. His face was bright red, the look in his eyes scary wild. I'd never seen him like that before, not even when I told him I was through sleeping with him. "I'm fed up with being cheated and lied to and treated like dirt. No more, Farrell—no more."

"You sound like a kid throwing a tantrum—"

"Shut up!"

"What did you say to me?"

"Shut up, shut up!"

"And if I don't?"

"Then I'll shut you up."

"And how do you propose to do that?"

Bryan reached into his pocket, and when his hand came out . . . oh, my God! There was a gun in it, he had a gun!

Roger Farrell

Tracy gasped when she saw the pistol. I admit I was momentarily taken aback myself, but only momentarily. I know guns too well to be frightened by one in the hand of a sorry excuse for a man like Rennert.

"Bryan!" Tracy cried. "Where'd you get that?"

"He brought it with him, obviously," I said, "hidden in his luggage. It's not one of mine, I wouldn't own a puny thirty-two. It's probably not even loaded."

"It's loaded, all right," Rennert said. "It's loaded."

"Even if it is, you won't use it. You're not capable of looking a man in the eye and shooting him. It took you three days just to get up enough nerve to bring your little toy out and show it to me."

"You don't know me, Farrell, you don't know what I'm capable of."

"Don't I?"

"No. But you'll find out if you don't do what *I* say from now on."

"What is it you expect me to do?"

"Write out a confession that you stole my money, sign it, and have Tracy witness it. I'll keep it until we get back to the city. Then you'll write me a check for the fifty thousand and I'll destroy the confession. Otherwise I'll turn it over to the authorities."

I laughed at him, I couldn't help it. "That's as pathetic a scheme as I've ever heard. Typical of a hack writer like you. Either that, or all the scotch has addled your mind."

"I'm not drunk. Not now. Are you going to write a confession?"

"Of course not."

"You'd better. Or else."

"Such trite dialogue. No wonder the critics pan your books."

Rennert's grip on the revolver was steady enough, but he showed his unfamiliarity with handguns by waggling it at me like a character in a cartoon. "Write that confession. I mean it, Farrell."

"No," I said. I got leisurely to my feet. "What I am going to do is take that peashooter away from you."

"Don't try it."

I took a slow, deliberately casual step toward him, then another when he backed up.

Tracy said, "Roger, no!"

I ignored her, watching Rennert. Fear sweat glistened on his face now. His eyes bulged like an amphibian's. Bryan Rennert, the cowardly toad.

"You won't shoot me, we both know that. Give me the gun."

"Don't come any closer, I'm warning you—"

"Give it to me."

I took another slow step, my hand extended. He backed away again, and as soon as he did I moved in to disarm him, my trained reflexes cat-quick as always.

Glenda Rennert

What was that? It sounded like a gunshot—
Oh my God, that was a scream, that's Tracy screaming—
Another explosive noise.
Silence.

I scrambled off the bed and ran to the door, but I didn't touch the knob or the bolt lock. My hands were shaking so badly I couldn't have opened it if I tried. And where would I go if I did leave the bedroom? There's nowhere to go, nowhere to hide—

Hard, fast footsteps. The knob rattled, rattled again. A sudden pounding on the door drove me back away from it, my hand fisting at my sore mouth.

"Unlock the door, Glenda." Bryan's voice, but it didn't sound normal. Thick-tongued, frightening. His black rage voice.

"No! Those shots, the way Tracy screamed... what happened? What did you do?"

"Gave Farrell what he deserved."

"Oh, God, you killed him!"

"That's right. You didn't know I brought a gun with me, did you? He didn't think I'd use it, he tried to take it away from me.

You should have seen the expression on his face when the bullet hit him."

"Tracy . . . ?"

"She got what she deserved too. Boom, boom. Now it's your turn. Wipe the slate clean."

"Oh no, Bryan, please—"

"Begging won't do you any good. Neither will the locked door. I'll break it down if I have to."

"You'll never get away with killing me too!"

"Yes I will. Hyperactive imagination, remember? I'll have plenty of time to think of a way to explain it all to the authorities."

No he won't! *Oh, no, he won't!* I know him, I know exactly what he'll do after he's finished with me. He'll sit down and drink what's left of the scotch, every last drop. And then he'll go to sleep and then *he'll* die because when I was out there by the wet bar I emptied the rest of my sleeping pills, more than twenty of them, into the bottle.

Not just one of us murdered tonight but all four.

Not just one who snapped but two.

GOODBYE, MS. DAMICO

He couldn't believe she was dead.

He didn't believe she'd taken her own life.

The police said that was what it was, a suicide. They said it couldn't be anything else. Ms. Damico had taken a lethal overdose of sleeping pills mixed with alcohol, left a note on her iPad saying she was depressed and tired of living, and been alone in her apartment with the door locked and the safety chain on. Suicide, plain and simple.

He'd been there when she was found, been the one to open up the apartment, and he still didn't believe it.

A woman friend of hers, Ms. Chen, had been trying to reach her because she'd missed a modeling appointment, something she'd never done before, and was not answering her phone. Ms. Chen had come to the building, and when she got no response from ringing Ms. Damico's bell, she'd rung his—Leo Wychek, Bldg. Mgr.—and expressed her concern to him. He'd gone upstairs with her and opened Ms. Damico's door with his passkey. When he saw the safety chain on and received no answer to his hail, he knew for sure something was wrong and hurried down to get his bolt cutters. He went inside after cutting the chain but not into the bedroom where Ms. Chen found Ms. Damico. He was glad he hadn't. It was hard enough imagining her dead without having to see her that way.

Ms. Chen, the other tenants in the building, the people she worked with, the married sister who came to collect her belongings, were as shocked and disbelieving as he was. Why would Ms. Damico do herself in? She had a well-paying job modeling clothes for mail-order catalogues, her health was good, she was always cheerful and seemed happy. He hadn't seen the suicide note, but according to the police there'd been nothing in it to explain the cause of her depression. The precinct officer in charge, a detective named Curtiz, said that some people had a dark side they kept hidden from even those closest to them, and when pressures built up to a breaking point they took the quick way out. Sad, tragic, but it happened more often than you'd think.

Maybe so, but it just didn't feel right to him. She wasn't the type to have a self-destructive dark side. Or to take sleeping pills. Last summer, after he'd chased off an addict who was pestering her in front of the building, she'd said it must be awful to be dependent on drugs and that she would never use any kind of controlled substance. No, not Ms. Damico. Not the nicest, kindest person he'd ever known.

The other tenants treated him as if he weren't a man, a human being, but some sort of unpleasant robotic machine that was best stored away out of sight when not in use. Leo Wychek, building manager—glorified name for rent collector, janitor, handyman. Leo Wychek—fat, middle-aged, with blotchy skin and a liver-spotted bald head that he kept covered with a knitted cap. Leo Wychek—the loneliest man in his little corner of the world. They never considered his feelings, or even if he had feelings. They never asked for his help, they demanded it. They didn't look at him, they looked through him or hid their distaste behind brief, cold glances.

Ms. Damico accepted him as he was, without judgment, as he had learned to accept himself without bitterness or self-pity. Always had a smile for him. A friendly greeting, a caring word. Never resented his reminders when the rent was late, as the others often did. And her expressions of gratitude when he'd done some small chore for her were always sincere. The few times she'd called on him to fix a plumbing or heating problem were the highlight of his days and evenings.

He'd thought of her as a friend, his only sympathetic friend. Once, poor fool that he was, he'd considered asking her to share his company for dinner or a movie. But of course he didn't. He knew she would have turned him down—gently, politely—and he wouldn't have blamed her. No woman as young and attractive as Ms. Damico would want to be seen in public with a hulk like Leo Wychek. He'd had enough rejection in his life, far too much. And he hadn't wanted to spoil the . . . what was the word? . . . the empathy he shared with her.

Now she was dead, dead and gone. If not by her own hand, then she had to have been murdered—a likelihood that filled him with outrage. Who could have done such a thing? She had a lot of friends, men and women both; he knew only a fraction of them and those only by sight. A spiteful woman? A lover, the handsome blond man who'd visited her during the holidays? One of the other tenants? Two of the unmarried men in the building had had dates with her, neither of whom he liked any more than they liked him. Mr. Borden was too aggressive, too full of himself, Mr. Kendall so smooth and slick with women he might have left an oil trail when he crossed the lobby.

Who? And why? And how?

He couldn't get the questions out of his mind. Even when he was tending to his managerial and janitorial duties they plagued him. Usually when he had time to himself, he eased his loneliness by listening to music, reading, watching old movies on TV. When he'd first taken the job here, he'd played Scrabble with old Mr. Sykes—the only social visitor he'd ever had—but Mr. Sykes had died the following year; now, if he felt like playing Scrabble, he played alone. But he couldn't concentrate on any of these activities. Mostly he sat at the kitchen table and drank cup after cup of coffee and thought about Ms. Damico.

The hardest thing to understand, even harder than who had wanted her dead, was the motive. Not money; she hadn't any other than what she earned from her job. A love affair gone sour? A disputed pregnancy? Jealousy? Revenge for some sort of slight? None of those seemed likely to him.

The easiest to understand, after a while, was how her death had been made to look like suicide. She might have given a key to the murderer for one reason or another, or her spare had been stolen; each tenant received two keys when they rented a unit. That explained the locked door. There was an explanation for the chain lock being fastened too. He figured out the method because of his job, but not everyone would. And not everyone was capable of doing it; it would take knowledge of hardware, some practice, a certain amount of dexterity. That narrowed the list of possible suspects down considerably. So did one other thing, one that made him smack the table hard enough to spill coffee when he realized it.

Small hands.

The murderer had to have small hands.

Women had small hands, but his gut feeling was that a man was responsible. He knew one man who fit the bill, and not just in hand size—in the other ways necessary to pull off the trick as well. The man she'd been keeping company with most recently.

Smooth, oily Mr. Kendall in 4B.

There was no real evidence against him, just circumstantial facts. But suppose some proof could be found . . .

Leo Wychek had little to be proud of in his life except for the fact that he was an honest man who respected the privacy of others. He had never used his passkey to enter a tenant's apartment unless he was instructed to do so, or if there was an emergency as in Ms. Damico's case. Never once snooped among a tenant's personal belongings.

Now, for the first time, he felt there was a just reason to compromise his principles.

It was early afternoon when he made up his mind. Mr.

Kendall wouldn't return from his office in a downtown hardware supply firm until after five; there was plenty of time. So he went first to Ms. Damico's apartment and let himself in with his passkey.

It felt strange to be in there alone after what had happened to her. The empty rooms seemed charged with a kind of lingering menace. The faint scent of the perfume she'd worn sharpened the sense of loss he couldn't help feeling. He wouldn't stay long.

The two halves of the severed chain lock still hung from the door and wall brackets. He hadn't replaced them yet because he hadn't wanted to come here for the task, and a good thing he hadn't. He lifted the half out of the slot in the wall bracket, examined the links. The marks he'd anticipated finding were there.

That cemented his resolve. He slid the fastener back into the bracket, letting the chain half dangle as before, then quickly stepped out and relocked the door.

Mr. Kendall's apartment was two floors up, 4B. The hallway there was empty. Leo rang the bell three times to make sure the apartment was likewise empty before letting himself inside.

The living room was expensively furnished, clean and tidy to a fault. Most of the tenants employed a weekly cleaning service, but as far as he knew, Mr. Kendall did all his own cleaning. Fussy. And guarded, too, as if he were afraid something of value might be stolen. The one time Leo had been here before, to unclog a drain, Mr. Kendall had followed him into the bathroom, stood over him while he worked, and followed him out again.

There was nothing in the living room to hold his attention. He opened a few drawers in the immaculate kitchen, careful not to disarrange the contents. Nothing incriminating. But in the medicine cabinet in the bathroom, he found a mostly empty vial of a prescription sleep aid called Temazepam. Could that be the drug that had killed Ms. Damico?

The apartment had two bedrooms. Mr. Kendall had turned the second one into a study—large desk with a computer on a stand beside it, two leather chairs, a small leather couch, a wet bar. None of the desk drawers was locked. One held credit card receipts and paid bills, another a folder of computer printouts; nothing among them connected Mr. Kendall with Ms. Damico. He didn't touch the computer; it was certain to be password-protected.

He hunted through the rest of the room. To one side of the

wet bar was a large closet, its door locked. Was the key he'd noticed in a tray in the middle desk drawer for this door? He tried it and it was.

The closet contained a vacuum cleaner, mop, broom, bucket, several bottled and canned cleaning supplies on a row of shelves. One shelf also held a large plastic case of the type that contained assorted hand tools. Leo's lips pulled in tight against his teeth when he opened the case and saw the one tool he'd hoped to find. But why was the door kept locked? By itself, the tool wasn't incriminating.

There was a light switch by the door but no light had come on when he flipped it. Funny that a burned out bulb wouldn't have been changed. He took a step inside. The closet was not deep but wide, and when he bent to peer past the vacuum cleaner he spotted two small cardboard boxes tucked into a dark corner. He reached for the top box, drew it out.

Photograph albums, half a dozen or more. He opened one—and the color photos mounted inside seared his eyes, set up a sick churning in his stomach. Disgusting, obscene. He couldn't look at more than a couple before slamming the album shut. He raised the cover on the one beneath it just long enough to see that its contents were more of the same. Then he put the lid back on the box, shoved it into the corner where he'd found it.

Damn you, Kendall. God damn you!

He couldn't stand to be in there any longer. He relocked the closet, returned the key to the desk, made sure everything appeared as he'd found it, and hurried out through the living room. The hallway was still empty when he slipped out and used his passkey again. Downstairs in his unit, he put on a coat, exchanged his cap for a rain hat, and then went back through the lobby and outside into a blustery April wind and drizzle.

It was seldom, and only when necessary, that he left the building. He didn't like crowds, the way people looked at him when they bothered to look at him at all. Maybe it was his imagination, maybe it wasn't. But the older he got, the less comfortable he was away from what had become his sanctuary.

It was a six-block walk to the precinct station. The sidewalks were mostly empty, not that it would have mattered today if they'd been teeming. He hurried in his rolling gait, his head down and his shoulders hunched into the collar of his coat.

Detective Curtiz was at his desk in the squad room, and remembered him at a glance. "Wychek, isn't it? What can I do for you?"

Leo sat down and leaned forward with his big hands folded together on his knees. "I'm here about Ms. Damico," he said. "She didn't commit suicide, she was murdered."

"Look, we went through that before—"

"I didn't know for sure then. I do now."

"What do you know?"

"Who killed her. The motive too, I think."

Curtiz gave him a long look. "You're serious, aren't you."

"Dead serious."

"All right, who is it you suspect?"

"One of the other tenants, Robert Kendall, apartment 4B. He had dates with Ms. Damico—I saw them together recently. He must have stolen her spare key—she wouldn't have given it to him. And he has a prescription for sleeping pills."

"So do a lot of people."

"But not Ms. Damico."

"No, but they're easy enough to get. That's not the only reason you think Kendall's guilty?"

"No. He's an executive with a hardware supply company. And he has small hands."

". . . Come on, Wychek. How does that make him a killer?"

"The chain lock. Ms. Damico didn't fasten it inside her apartment, he did from outside in the hallway after he killed her. To do that you need to know hardware and have small hands."

"Wait a minute," Curtiz said. "From *outside* the apartment? How could that be done?"

"With a pair of needle nose pliers. What Kendall did was grip the chain with the pliers just above the end bar, then step out into the hallway, pull the door almost shut, and hold it with his other hand while he maneuvered the bar into the slot in the wall bracket. The opening wasn't wide because of the short length of the chain; that's why a small hand is necessary. I haven't replaced the lock yet—the cut halves of the chain are still there. You can see the marks on the links where he gripped them."

He had the detective's full attention now. "Well, I'll be damned," Curtiz said.

"The pliers he used are in a toolbox in the closet in his study. There's a way to match them to the marks on the chain, isn't there?"

"Probably. How do you know about the toolbox? And his prescription sleeping pills?"

"I saw them," Leo said. "Something else too. Something bad

that might be the reason he murdered Ms. Damico."

"What do you mean, something bad?"

"Two boxes of photographs. Ugly photographs. The worst kind of pornography."

Curtiz's swarthy features hardened perceptibly. "Are you talking about kiddie porn?"

"Yes. There's probably more of it stored on his computer."

"Damn! And you think the Damico woman knew about it and threatened to turn him in?"

"Found out about it somehow, yes. She'd have been horrified."

"If there's one kind of criminal I hate as much as a murderer," Curtiz said, "it's one who traffics in that kind of filth. When did you see the photographs and the other things?"

"This afternoon, before I came here."

"Used your passkey to let yourself into his apartment without his knowledge or consent?"

"Yes. I felt I had to and I'm glad I did."

"So am I. But technically you committed an illegal trespass. Invalidates your testimony as far as getting a search warrant goes."

"Kendall can't get away with what he's done," Leo said fervently. "There must be something you can do."

"Oh, there's something we can do, all right. I hate to say this, Wychek, but if we nail this bastard, and we will if he's as guilty as you say he is, we'll have to keep you out of it. The only way we can get a search warrant and a conviction on both crimes is for what you've told me to go into the record as an anonymous tip and smart police work. No public credit to you."

"I don't care about that," Leo said. "I don't want any credit. All I want is to see him punished."

Robert Kendall was arrested two days later on a charge of possession and transmission of child pornography. The day after that, a charge of homicide was filed against him. He'd broken down and confessed to killing Ms. Damico because she inadvertently overheard part of a private cell phone conversation, confronted him about his "hobby", and was not convinced when he insisted that she'd misunderstood. He was sure that sooner or later she would report him to the police or tell somebody who would, and in a panic to protect himself from exposure he'd hatched his murder scheme.

He went to her apartment the next night and talked her into letting him in, bringing with him a small bottle of Temazepamlaced sherry, the only kind of alcohol she drank. One glass made her woozy enough to offer no resistance when he carried her into the bedroom and forced the lethal amount of the drugged sherry down her throat. Then he wrote the suicide note on her iPad and searched for her spare key. He stayed there until long after midnight to make sure he wouldn't be interrupted while he was performing his trick with the chain lock.

Leo read the account of Kendall's confession in the morning newspaper. Not long afterward he put on his one good suit and went to ride a bus, sitting alone in a corner of the rearmost seat, to the small upstate town where Ms. Damico had been born and where her sister had arranged for her burial. The woman in the florist shop he found told him that the cemetery was at the north edge of town, within walking distance. When he got there, a man in the office looked up the location of the Damico family plot and directed him to it.

The marker on her grave was small, plain, and bore only her name, Julie Ann Damico, and the dates of her birth and death. He stood looking down at it for a long time before he bent to lay the bouquet of flowers he'd bought against the marker.

"Goodbye, Ms. Damico," he said. "Now you can rest in peace."

He imagined as he straightened that if she'd known he came to say goodbye, she would have favored him with one last smile.

CARPENTER & QUINCANNON

GUNPOWDER ALLEY

From where he sat propped behind a copy of the *San Francisco Argonaut*, Quincannon had an unobstructed view of both the entrance to the Hotel Grant's bar parlor and the booth in which his client, Titus Willard, waited nervously. The Seth Thomas clock above the back bar gave the time as one minute past nine, which made the man Willard was waiting for late for their appointment. This was no surprise to Quincannon. Blackmailers seldom missed an opportunity to heap additional pressure on their victims.

Willard fidgeted, looked at the clock for perhaps the twentieth time, and once more pooched out his cheeks—a habitual trick that, combined with his puffy muttonchop whiskers, gave him the look of a large rodent. As per arrangement, he managed to ignore the table where Quincannon sat with his newspaper. The satchel containing the $5,000 cash payoff was on the seat next to him, one corner of it just visible to Quincannon's sharp eye.

The *Argonaut*, like all of the city's papers these days, was full of news of the imminent war with Spain. The Atlantic fleet had been dispatched to Cuban waters, Admiral Dewey's Asiatic Squadron was on its way to the Philippines, and President McKinley had issued a call for volunteer soldiers to join Teddy Roosevelt's Rough Riders. Quincannon, who disdained war as much as he disdained felons of every stripe, paid the inflammatory yellow journalism no mind while pretending to be engrossed in it, and wondered again what his client had done to warrant blackmail demands that now amounted to $10,000.

He had asked Willard, of course, but the banker had refused to divulge the information. Given the fact that the man was in his midfifties, with a prim socialite wife and a grown daughter, and the guilty flush that had stained his features when the question was put to him, his transgressions likely involved one or more young and none-too-respectable members of the opposite sex. In any case, Willard had shown poor judgment in paying the first $5,000 demand, and good judgment in hiring Carpenter and Quincannon, Professional Detective Services, to put an end to the bloodletting after the second demand was made. The man may have been worried, frightened, and guilt-ridden, but he was only half a fool. Pay twice, and he knew he'd be paying for the rest of his life.

Quincannon took a sip of clam juice, his favorite tipple now that he was a confirmed teetotaler, and turned a page of the *Argonaut*. Willard glanced again at the clock, which now read ten past nine, then drained what was left of a double whiskey. And that was when the blackmailer—if it was the blackmailer and not a hireling—finally appeared.

The fellow's entrance into the bar parlor was slow and cautious. This was one thing that alerted Quincannon. The other was the way he was dressed. Threadbare overcoat, slouch hat drawn low on his forehead, wool muffler wound up high inside the coat collar so that it concealed the lower part of his face. This attire might have been somewhat conspicuous at another time of year, but on this damp, chilly November night, he drew only a few casual glances from the patrons, none of which lingered.

He paused just inside the doorway to peer around before his gaze locked in on his prey. Out of the corner of one eye Quincannon watched him approach the booth. What little of the man's face was visible corroborated Willard's description of him from their first meeting: middle-aged, with a hooked nose and sallow complexion, and average to small in size, though it was difficult to tell for certain because of the coat's bulk. Not such-a-much at all.

Titus Willard stiffened when the fellow slipped into the booth opposite. There was a low-voiced exchange of words, after which the banker passed the satchel under the table. The hook-nosed gent opened it just long enough to see that it contained stacks of greenbacks, closed it again, then produced a manila envelope from inside his coat and slid it across the table. Willard opened the envelope and furtively examined the papers it contained—letters of a highly personal nature, judging from the banker's expression.

They would not be the sum total of the blackmail evidence, however. Finding the rest was one part of Quincannon's job, the others being to identify and then yaffle the responsible party or parties.

While the two men were making their exchange, Quincannon casually folded the newspaper and laid it on the table, gathered up his umbrella and derby hat, and strolled out into the hotel lobby. He took a position just inside the corridor that led to the elevators, where he had an oblique view of the bar entrance. His quarry would have to come out that way because there was no other exit from the bar parlor.

The wait this time was less than two minutes. When Hook-nose appeared, he went straight to the swing door that led out to New Montgomery Street. Quincannon followed twenty paces behind. A drizzle of rain had begun and the salt-tinged bay wind had the sting of a whip. It being a poor night for travel by shanks' mare, Quincannon expected his man to take one of the hansom cabs at the stand in front of the Palace Hotel opposite. But this didn't happen. With the satchel clutched inside his overcoat, the fellow angled across Montgomery and turned the far corner into Jessie Street.

Quincannon reached the corner a few seconds later. He paused to peer around it before unfurling his umbrella and turning into Jessie himself, to make sure he wasn't observed. Hook-nose apparently had no fear of pursuit; he was hurrying ahead through the misty rain without a backward glance.

Jessie was a dark, narrow thoroughfare, and something of an anomaly as the new century approached—a mostly residential street that ran for several blocks through the heart of the business district, midway between Market and Mission. Small, old houses and an occasional small business establishment flanked it, fronted by tiny yards and backed by barns and sheds. The electric light glow from Third Street and the now steady drizzle made it a chasm of shadows. The darkness and the thrumming wind allowed Quincannon to quicken his pace without fear of being seen or heard.

After two blocks, his quarry made another turning, this time into a cobblestone cul-de-sac called Gunpowder Alley. The name, or so Quincannon had once been told, derived from the fact that Copperhead sympathizers had stored a large quantity of explosives in one of the houses there during the War Between the States. Gunpowder Alley was even darker than Jessie Street, the frame buildings strung along its short length shabby presences in the wet gloom. The only illumination was strips and daubs of light that leaked palely around a few drawn window curtains.

Not far from the corner, Hook-nose crossed the alley to a squat, dark structure that huddled between the back end of a saloon fronting on Jessie Street and a private residence. The squat building appeared to be a store of some sort, its plate-glass window marked with lettering that couldn't be read at a distance. The man used a key to unlock a door next to the window and disappeared inside.

As Quincannon cut across the alley, lamplight bloomed in pale fragments around the edges of a curtain that covered the store window. He ambled past, pausing in front of the glass to read the lettering: CIGARS, PIPE TOBACCO, SUNDRIES. R.

SONDERBERG, PROP. The curtain was made of heavy muslin; all he could see through the center folds was a slice of narrow counter. He put his ear to the cold glass. The faint whistling voice of the wind was the only sound to be heard.

He moved on. A narrow, ink-black passage separated R. Sonderberg's cigar store from the house on the far side—a low, two-storied structure with a gabled roof and ancient shingles curled by the weather. The parlor window on the lower floor was an uncurtained and palely lamplit rectangle; he could just make out the shape of a white-haired, shawl-draped woman in a high-backed rocking chair, either asleep or keeping a lonely watch on the street. Crowding close along the rear of store and house, paralleling Gunpowder Alley from the Jessie Street corner to its end, was the long back wall of a warehouse, its dark windows steel-shuttered. There was nothing else to see. And nothing to hear except the wind, muted here in the narrow lane.

A short distance beyond the house Quincannon paused to close his umbrella, the drizzle having temporarily ceased. He shook water from the fabric, then turned back the way he'd come. The woman in the rocking chair hadn't moved—asleep, he decided. Lamp glow now outlined a window in the squat building that faced into the side passage; the front part of the shop was once again dark. R. Sonderberg, if that was who the hook-nosed gent was, had evidently entered a room or rooms at the rear—living quarters, like as not.

Quincannon stopped again to listen, and again heard only silence from within. He sidestepped to the door and tried the latch. Bolted. His intention then was to enter the side passage, to determine if access could be gained at the rear. What stopped him was the fact that he was no longer the only pedestrian abroad in Gunpowder Alley.

Heavy footsteps echoed hollowly from the direction of Jessie Street. Even as dark and wet as it was, he recognized almost immediately the brass-buttoned coat, helmet, and handheld dark lantern of a police patrolman. Hell and damn! Of all times for a blasted bluecoat to happen along on his rounds.

Little annoyed Quincannon more than having to abort an investigation in midskulk, but he had no other choice. He turned from the door and moved at an even pace toward the approaching policeman. They met just beyond the joining of the saloon's back wall and the cigar store's far side wall.

Unlike many of his brethren, the bluecoat, an Irishman in his middle years, was a gregarious sort. He stopped, forcing

Quincannon to do likewise, and briefly opened the lantern's shutter so that the beam flicked over his face before saying in a conversational tone, "Evening, sir. Nasty weather, eh?"

"Worse coming, I expect."

"Aye. Heavy rain before morning. Like as not I'll be getting a thorough soaking before my patrol ends."

Quincannon itched to touch his hat and move on. But the bluecoat wasn't done with him yet. "Don't believe I've seen you before, sir. Live in Gunpowder Alley, do you?"

"No. Visiting."

"Which resident, if you don't mind my asking?"

"R. Sonderberg, at the cigar store."

"Ah. I've seen the lad a time or two, but we've yet to meet. I've only been on this beat two weeks now, y'see. Maguire's my name, at your service."

Before Quincannon could frame a lie that would extricate him from Officer Maguire's company, there came in rapid succession a brace of muffled reports. As quiet as the night was, there was no mistaking the fact that they were pistol shots and that the weapon had been fired inside the squat building.

Quincannon's reflexes were superior to the patrolman's; he was already on the run by the time the bluecoat reacted. Behind him Maguire shouted something, but he paid no heed. Another sound, a loudish thump, reached his ears as he charged past the shop's entrance, dropping his umbrella so he could grasp the Navy Colt in its holster. Seconds later he veered into the side passage. The narrow confines appeared deserted, and there were no sounds of movement at its far end. He skidded to a halt in front of the lighted window.

Vertical bars set close together prevented both access and egress. The glass inside was dirty and rain-spotted, but he could make out the figure of a man sprawled supine on the floor of a cluttered room. There was no sign of anyone else.

The spaces between the bars were just wide enough to reach a hand through; he did that, pushing fingers against the pane. It didn't yield to the pressure.

Officer Maguire pounded up beside him, the beam from his lantern cutting jigsaw pieces out of the darkness. The bobbing light illuminated enough of the passage ahead so that Quincannon could see to where it ended at the warehouse wall. He hurried back there while Maguire had his look through the window.

Another short walkway, shrouded in gloom, stretched at right angles to the side passage like the crossbar of the letter *T*.

Quincannon thumbed a lucifer alight as he stepped around behind the cigar store, shielding it with his hand. That section was likewise empty, except for a pair of refuse bins. There was no exit in that direction; the walkway ended in a board fence that joined shop and warehouse walls, built so high that only a monkey could have climbed it. The match's flicker showed him the outlines of a rear door to R. Sonderberg's quarters. He tried the latch, but the heavy door was secure in its frame.

Maguire appeared, his lantern creating more dancing patterns of light and shadow. "See anyone back here?" he demanded.

"No one."

"Would that rear door be open?"

"No. Bolted on the inside."

The bluecoat grunted and pushed past him to try the latch himself. While he was doing that, Quincannon struck another match in order to examine the other half of the walkway. It served the adjacent house, ending in a similarly high and unscalable board fence. The house's rear door, he soon determined, was also bolted within.

The lantern beam again picked him out. "Come away from there, laddie. Out front with me, step lively now."

Quincannon complied. As they hurried along the passage, Maguire said, "Is it your friend Sonderberg lying shot in there?"

No friend of mine or society's, Quincannon thought. But he said only, "I couldn't be sure."

"Didn't seem to be anybody else in the room."

"No."

"Well, we'll soon find out."

When they emerged from the passage, Quincannon saw that the elderly woman had left her rocking chair and was now standing stooped at the edge of her front window, peering out. One other individual had so far been alerted; a man wearing a light overcoat and high hat and carrying a walking stick had appeared from somewhere and stood staring nearby. Quincannon knew from rueful experience that a full gaggle of onlookers would soon follow.

No one had exited the cigar store through the Gunpowder Alley entrance; the door was still locked from within. Maguire grunted again. "We'll be having to break it down," he said. "Sonderberg, or whoever 'tis, may still be alive."

It took the combined weight of both of them to force the door, the bolt finally splintering free with an echoing crack. Once they were inside, Maguire flashed his lantern's beam over displays of cigars and pipe tobacco, partly filled shelves of cheap sundries, then aimed it down behind the low service counter. The shop was cramped and free of hiding places—and completely empty.

The closed door to the rear quarters stood behind a pair of dusty drapes. "By the saints!" Maguire exclaimed when he caught hold of the latch. "This one's bolted, too."

It proved no more difficult to break open than the outer door had. The furnished room beyond covered the entire rear two thirds of the building. The man sprawled on the floor was middle-aged, medium-sized, and hook-nosed—Quincannon's quarry, right enough, though he no longer wore the overcoat, muffler, and slouch hat that had partially disguised him in the Hotel Grant. Blood from a pair of wounds spotted the front of his linsey-woolsey shirt; his open eyes glistened in the light from a table lamp. Maguire went to one knee beside him, felt for a pulse. "Dead," he said unnecessarily.

Quincannon's attention was now on the otherwise empty room. It contained a handful of secondhand furniture, a blanket-covered cot, a potbellied stove that radiated heat, and a table topped with a bottle of whiskey and two empty glasses. The whole was none too tidy and none too clean.

Another pair of curtains partially covered an alcove in the wall opposite the window. Quincannon satisfied himself that the alcove contained nothing more than an icebox and larder cabinet. The only item of furniture large enough to conceal a person was a rickety wardrobe, but all he found when he opened it was a few articles of inexpensive clothing.

Maguire was on his feet again. He said, "I wonder what made him do it."

"Do what?"

"Shoot himself, of course. Suicide's a cardinal sin."

"Is that what you think happened, Officer?"

"Aye, and what else could it be, with all the doors and windows locked and no one else on the premises?"

Suicide? Faugh! Murder was what else it could be, and murder was what it was, despite the circumstances. Three things told Quincannon this beyond any doubt. Sonderberg had been shot twice in the chest, a location handgun suicides seldom chose because it necessitated holding the weapon at an awkward angle, and one of the wounds was high on the left side in a nonlethal spot. The pistol that had fired the two rounds lay some distance away from the dead man, too far for it to have been dropped if he had fired the fatal shot. And the most damning evidence: the satchel containing the $5,000 blackmail payoff was nowhere to be seen here or in the front part of the shop.

But Quincannon shrugged and said nothing. Let the bluecoat believe what he liked. The dispatching of R. Sonderberg was part and parcel to the blackmail game, and that made it John Quincannon's meat.

"I'll be needing to report in to headquarters," Maguire said. "The nearest callbox is on Jessie, two blocks distant. You'll stay here, will you, and keep out any curious citizens until I return, Mr. —?"

"Quinn. That I will, Officer."

"Quinn, is it? You'll be Irish yourself, then?"

"Scotch-Irish," Quincannon said.

Maguire hurried out. As soon as he was alone, Quincannon commenced a search of the premises. The dead man's coat and trouser pockets yielded nothing of value or interest other than an expired insurance card that confirmed his identity as Raymond Sonderberg. The pistol that had done for him was a small-caliber Colt, its chambers fully loaded except for the two fired rounds; it bore no identifying marks of any kind. The $5,000 was not in the room, nor was whatever blackmail evidence had been withheld from Titus Willard tonight.

The bolt on the rear door was tightly drawn, the door itself sturdy in its frame; and for good measure a wooden bar set into brackets spanned its width. Sonderberg had been nothing if not security-conscious, for all the good it had done him. The single window was hinged upward, the swivel latch at the bottom of the sash loosely in place around its stud fastener. Quincannon flipped the hook aside and raised the glass to peer again at the vertical bars. They were set tightly top and bottom; he couldn't budge any of them. And as close together as they were, there was no way in which anything as bulky as the satchel could have passed between them.

Sonderberg had brought the satchel inside with him, there could be no mistaking that. Whoever had shot him had made off with it; that, too, was plain enough. But how the devil could the assassin have committed his crime and then escaped from not one but two sealed rooms in the clutch of seconds that had passed between the firing of the fatal shots and Quincannon's entry into the side passage?

The night's stillness was broken now by the sound of voices out front, but as yet none of the bystanders had attempted to come inside. Muttering to himself, Quincannon lowered the window and made his way out through the cigar store to stand in the broken doorway.

The parlor of the house next door, he noted, was now dark and the white-haired occupant had come out to stand, shawl-draped and leaning on a cane, on the small front porch. The others gathered in Gunpowder Alley numbered less than a dozen, drawn from nearby houses and the Jessie Street watering hole, among them the man in the cape and high hat, who now assailed him with questions. Quincannon provided only enough information, repeating Maguire's false theory of suicide, to dampen the bystanders' enthusiasm; shootings were common in the city, and there was not enough spice in a self-dispatching to hold the jaded citizens' interest. He then sought information of his own, but none of the crowd owned up to seeing Sonderberg or anyone else enter the cigar store after its six o'clock closing.

Some of the men were already moving away to homes and saloon when Maguire returned. The bluecoat dispersed the rest. The elderly woman still stood on the porch; it was not until the alley was mostly deserted again that she doddered back inside the darkened house.

Quincannon asked Maguire if he knew the woman's name and whether or not she lived alone. "I couldn't tell you, lad," the patrolman said. "I've not seen her before—the house has always been dark when I've come by."

The morgue wagon and a trio of other bluecoats arrived shortly. None of them was interested in Quincannon. Neither was Maguire any longer. San Francisco's finest, a misnomer if ever there was one, found suicides and those peripherally involved to be worthy of little time or attention. While the minions of the law were inside with the remains of Raymond Sonderberg, he remembered his dropped umbrella and mounted a brief search, but it was nowhere to be found. One of the onlookers must have made off with it. Faugh! Thieves everywhere in this infernal city!

He crossed to the adjacent house. The parlor window was curtained now, no light showing around its edges. The bell pull beside the door no longer worked; he rapped on the panel instead. There was no immediate response. Mayhap the white-haired woman wanted no truck with visitors after the night's excitement, or had already retired.

Neither. Old boards creaked and a thin, quavery voice asked, "Yes? Who's there?"

"Police officer," Quincannon lied glibly. "A few questions if I may. I won't keep you long."

There was a longish pause, followed by the click of a bolt being thrown; the door squeaked open partway and the old woman appeared. Stooped, still bundled in a shawl over a black dress, she carried her cane in one hand and a lighted candle in the other. A cold draft set the candle flame to flickering in its ceramic holder, so that it cast patterns of light and shadow over her heavily seamed face as she peered out and up at him.

"I know you," she said. "You were here before all the commotion next door."

"You spied me through your parlor window, eh? I thought as much, Mrs. —?"

"Carver. Letitia Carver. Yes, I often sit looking out in the evenings. A person my age has little else to occupy her attention."

"Did you see anyone enter or leave the cigar store at any time tonight?"

"No, no one. What happened to Mr. Sonderberg?"

"Shot dead in his quarters."

"Oh!"

"Possibly by his own hand, more likely by an intruder. You heard the shots, did you?"

"Yes. I thought that's what they were, but I wasn't sure."

"You live here alone, Mrs. Carver?"

"Since my husband passed on, bless his soul."

"And you've had no visitors tonight?"

She sighed wistfully. "Few come to visit me anymore."

"Did you hear anyone moving about in the side or rear passages, before or after the pistol shots?"

"Only you and the other policeman." She sighed again, sadly this time. "Such a tragedy. Poor Mr. Sonderberg."

Poor Mr. Sonderberg, my hat, Quincannon thought. Poor Titus Willard, who was now bereft of $10,000. And poor Carpenter and Quincannon, Professional Detective Services, who were out a substantial fee if the mystery of Sonderberg's death remained unsolved.

The woman said in her quavery voice, "Is there anything more, young man? It's quite chilly standing here."

"Nothing more."

She retreated inside and he returned to the boardwalk. R. Sonderberg's body was in the process of being loaded into the morgue wagon. None of the policemen even glanced in Quincannon's direction as he crossed the alley and made his way to Jessie Street, his thoughts as dark and gloomy as the night around him.

Sabina was already at her desk when he walked into the Market Street offices of Carpenter and Quincannon, Professional Detective Services, the next morning. She was a handsome woman, his partner and unrequited love—the possessor of a fine figure, eyes the color of the sea at dusk, and sleek black hair layered high on her head and fastened with a jeweled comb. Today she wore one of the leg-of-mutton blouses which he usually found enticing, but his mood was such that he took only peripheral notice of her. His night had been a mostly sleepless one in which he'd wrestled unsuccessfully with the problem of how R. Sonderberg had been murdered and by whom. His lack of success was all the more frustrating because he prided himself on having an uncanny knack for unraveling even the knottiest of seemingly impossible problems.

Sabina said, as he shed his umbrella and rain-spotted overcoat, "Titus Willard telephoned a few minutes ago. He was upset that you failed to contact him last night."

"Bah."

"Well, he asked that you get in touch with him as soon as you arrived."

"I'll see him later this morning. He won't be pleased to hear the news I have for him at any time."

"You weren't able to identify the blackmailer, then?"

"On the contrary. The blackmailer's name is, or was, Raymond Sonderberg, the proprietor of a cigar store in Gunpowder Alley. He was murdered in his locked quarters before I could confront him and recover the blackmail evidence and payoff money."

"Murdered? So that's why you're in such a foul humor this morning."

"What makes you think my humor is foul?"

"The scowl you're wearing, for one thing. You look like a pirate on his way to the gibbet."

"Bah," Quincannon said again.

"Exactly what happened last night, John?"

He sat at his desk and provided her with a detailed summary. They often shared information on difficult cases in order to obtain a fresh perspective. Sabina's years as a Pink Rose, one of the select handful of women operatives hired by the Pinkerton Agency, plus the four years of their partnership had honed her skills to a fine edge. He would never have admitted it to her or anyone else, but she was often his equal at the more challenging aspects of the sleuthing game.

"A puzzling series of events, to be sure," Sabina said when he finished his account. "But perhaps not as mysterious as they might seem."

"What do you mean?"

"You know from experience, John, that such mysteries generally have a relatively simple explanation."

He admitted the truth of this. "But I'm hanged if I can see it in this case."

"Well, the first question that occurs to me, was the crime planned or committed on the spur of the moment?"

"If it was planned, it was done in order to silence Sonderberg and make off with the five thousand dollars."

"By an accomplice in the blackmail scheme."

"So it would seem. The accomplice must have been waiting for him in his quarters. The stove there was glowing hot, and there was not enough time for Sonderberg to have stoked the fire to high heat, even if he'd built it up before he left for the Hotel Grant."

"Then why all the mystification?" Sabina asked. "Why not simply shoot Sonderberg and slip away into the night with the loot?"

"To make murder appear to be suicide."

"That could have been accomplished without resorting to such elaborate flummery. Locked rooms and mysterious disappearances smack of deliberate subterfuge."

"Aye, so they do. But to what purpose?"

"The obvious answer is to fool someone in close proximity at the time."

"Who? Not me, surely. No one could have known ahead of time that I would follow Sonderberg from the hotel to Gunpowder Alley."

"The bluecoat, Maguire, then," Sabina said. "From your description of him, he's the sort who makes his rounds on a by-the-clock schedule. Still, it seems rather an intricate game just to confuse a simple patrolman."

"*If* the whole was planned ahead of time, and not a result of circumstance."

"In either case, there has to be a plausible explanation. Are you certain there was no possible means of escape from Sonderberg's building following the shooting?"

"Front and rear entrances bolted from the inside, the door to his living quarters likewise bolted, the only window both barred and locked. Yes, I'm certain of that much."

"Doesn't it follow, then, that if escape was impossible, the murderer was never inside the building?"

"It would," Quincannon said, "except for three facts that indicate otherwise. The missing satchel and greenbacks; the presence of the whiskey bottle and two glasses on the table; the pistol that dispatched Sonderberg lying at a distance from the body. There can be no doubt that both killer and victim were together inside that sealed room."

"The thump you heard just after the shots were fired. Can you find any significance in that?"

"None so far. It might have been a foot striking a wall—that sort of sound."

"But loud enough to carry out to Gunpowder Alley. Did you also hear running steps?"

"No. No other sounds at all." Quincannon stood and began to restlessly pace the office. "The murderer's vanishing act is just as befuddling. Even if he managed to extricate himself from the building, how the devil was he able to disappear so quickly? Not even a cat could have climbed those fences enclosing the rear walkway. Nor the warehouse wall, not that such a scramble would have done him any good with all its windows steel-shuttered."

"Which leaves only one possible escape route."

"The rear door to Letitia Carver's house, yes. But it was bolted when I tried it, and she claims not to have had any visitors."

"She could have been lying."

Quincannon conceded that she could have been.

"I don't suppose there's any chance that she herself could be the culprit?"

"She's eighty if she's a day," he said. "Besides, I saw her sitting in her parlor window not two minutes before the shots were fired."

"Lying to protect the guilty party, possibly. Perhaps a relative. In which case the murderer was hiding in the house while you spoke to her."

"A galling possibility, if true." Quincannon paused, glowering, to run fingers through his thick beard. "The crone seemed innocent enough, yet now that I consider it, there was something . . . odd about her."

"Furtive, you mean?"

"No. Her actions, her words . . . I can't quite put my finger on it."

"Why don't you have another talk with her, John?"

"That," Quincannon said, "is what I intend to do straightaway."

Gunpowder Alley was no more appealing by daylight than it had been under the cloak of darkness. Heavy rain during the early morning hours had slackened into another dreary drizzle, and the buildings encompassing the alley's short length all had a huddled appearance, bleak and sodden under the wet gray sky.

The cul-de-sac was deserted when Quincannon, dry beneath a newly purchased umbrella, turned into it from Jessie Street. Boards had been nailed across the front entrance to the cigar store and a police seal applied to forestall potential looters. At the house next door, tattered curtains still covered the parlor window.

He stood looking at the window for a few seconds, his mind jostled by memory fragments—words spoken to him by Maguire, others by Letitia Carver. Quickly, then, he climbed to the porch and rapped on the front door. Neither that series of knocks nor two more brought a response.

His resolve, sharpened now, prodded him to action. In his pocket he carried a set of lock picks which he'd purchased from an ex-housebreaker living in Warsaw, Illinois, who manufactured burglar tools, advertised them as novelties in the *Police Gazette*, and sold them for ten dollars the set. He set to work with these on the flimsy door lock and within seconds had the bolt snicked free.

In the foyer inside, he paused to listen. No sounds reached his ears save for the random creaks of old, wet timbers. He called loudly, "Hello! Anyone here?" Faint echoes of his voice were all the answer he received.

He moved through an archway into the parlor. The room was cold, decidedly musty; no fire had burned in the grate in a long while, certainly not as recently as last night. The furniture was sparse and had the worn look of discards. One arm of the rocking chair set near the curtained window was broken, bent outward at an angle. The lamp on the rickety table next to it was as cold as the air.

Glowering fiercely now, Quincannon set off on a rapid search of the premises upstairs and down. There were scattered pieces of furniture in two other rooms, including a sagging iron bedstead sans mattress in what might have been the master bedroom; the remaining rooms were empty. A closet in the foyer contained a single item that brought forth a blistering, triple-jointed oath.

He left the house, grumbling and growling, and stepped into the side passage for another examination of the barred window to Sonderberg's quarters. Then he moved on to the cross passage at the rear, where a quick study confirmed his judgments of the night before: there was no possible exit at either end, both fences too tall and slippery to be scaled.

Out front again, he embarked on a rapid canvass of the immediate neighborhood. He spoke to two residents of Gunpowder Alley and the bartender at the saloon on the Jessie Street corner, corroborating one fact he already knew and learning another that surprised him not at all.

The first: The house next to the cigar store had been empty for four months, a possibility he should have suspected much sooner from the pair of conflicting statements he'd finally recalled—Maguire's that in the two weeks he'd patrolled Gunpowder Alley the parlor window had always been dark, the woman calling herself Letitia Carver's that she often sat there at night looking out.

And the second fact: Raymond Sonderberg, a man who kept mostly to himself and eked out a meager living selling cigars and sundries, was known to frequent variety houses and melodeons such as the Bella Union on Portsmouth Square.

The mystery surrounding Sonderberg's death was no longer a mystery. And should not have been one as long as it had; Quincannon felt like a damned rattlepate for allowing himself to be duped and fuddled by what was, as Sabina had suggested, a crime with an essentially simple explanation. For he knew now how and why Sonderberg had been murdered in his locked quarters. And was tolerably sure of who had done the deed—the only person, given the circumstances, it could possibly be.

Titus Willard was alone in his private office at the Montgomery Street branch of Woolworth National Bank when Quincannon arrived there shortly before noon. And none too pleased to have been kept waiting for word as long as he had.

"Why didn't you contact me last night, as we agreed?" he demanded. "Don't tell me you weren't able to follow and identify the blackmailer?"

"One of the blackmailers, yes, the man you paid. Raymond Sonderberg, proprietor of a cigar store in Gunpowder Alley."

"One of the blackmailers? I don't understand."

"His accomplice shot him dead in his quarters and made off with the satchel before I could intervene."

Willard blinked his surprise and consternation. "But who . . . ?"

"I'll have the answer to that question, Mr. Willard, after you've answered a few of mine. Why were you being blackmailed?"

". . . I told you before, I'd rather not say."

"You'll tell me if you want the safe return of your money and the remaining blackmail evidence."

The banker assumed his habitual pooched rodent look.

"A woman, wasn't it?" Quincannon prompted. "An illicit affair?"

"You're, ah, a man of the world, surely you understand that when one reaches my age—"

"I have no interest in reasons or rationalizations, only in the facts of the matter. The woman's name, to begin with."

Willard hemmed and hawed and pooched some more before he finally answered in a scratchy voice, "Pauline Dupree."

"And her profession?"

"Profession? I don't see—oh, very well. She is a stage performer and actress. Yes, and a very good one, I might add."

"I thought as much. Where does she perform?"

"At the Gaiety Theater. But she aspires to be a serious actress one day, perhaps on the New York stage."

"Does she now."

"I, ah, happened to be at the theater one evening two months ago and we chanced to meet—"

Quincannon waved that away. No one "happened to be" at the Gaiety Theater, which was something of a bawdy melodeon on the fringe of the Barbary Coast. The sort of place that catered to middle-aged men with a taste for the exotic, specializing as it did in prurient skits and raucous musical numbers featuring scantily clad young women.

He asked, "You confided in her when you received the first blackmail demand?"

"Of course," Willard said. "She had a right to know . . ."

"Why did she have a right to know?"

"It's . . . letters I wrote to her that are being held against me."

Highly indiscreet letters, no doubt. "And how did the blackmailer get possession of them?"

"They were stolen from her rooms last week, along with a small amount of jewelry. This man Sonderberg . . . a common sneak thief who saw an opportunity for richer gains."

Stolen? Sonderberg a common sneak thief? What a credulous

gent his client was! "Was it Miss Dupree's suggestion that you pay the initial five thousand dollars?"

"Yes, and I agreed. It seemed the most reasonable course of action at the time."

"But when the second demand arrived two days ago, you didn't tell her you'd decided to hire a detective until *after* you came to me."

"That's so, yes. Engaging you was a spur-of-the-moment decision —"

"And when you did tell her, you also explained that I'd be present at the second payoff and that I intended to follow and confront the blackmailer afterward?"

"Why shouldn't I have confided in her? She—" Willard broke off, frowning, then once again performed his rodent imitation. "See here, Quincannon. You're not suggesting that Miss Dupree had anything to do with the extortion scheme?"

It was not yet time to answer that question. "I deal in facts, as I told you, not suggestions," Quincannon hedged. "Where are you keeping her?"

"Her rooms are on Stockton Street," the banker said stiffly.

"Is she likely to be there or at the Gaiety at this hour?"

"I don't know. One or the other, I suppose."

"Come along, then, Mr. Willard," Quincannon said, "and we'll pay a call on the lady. I expect we'll both find it a stimulating rendezvous."

They found Pauline Dupree at the gaudily painted Gaiety Theater, primping in her backstage dressing room. She was more or less what Quincannon had expected—young and rather buxomly attractive, with dark-gold tresses and bold, smoke-hued eyes wise beyond her years. Her high color paled a bit when she saw Quincannon, but she recovered quickly.

"And who is this gentleman, Titus?" she asked Willard.

"John Quincannon, the detective I told you about." The smile the banker bestowed on her was fatuous as well as apologetic. "I'm sorry to trouble you, my dear, but he insisted on seeing you."

"Did he? And for what reason?"

"He wouldn't say, precisely. But he seems to have a notion that you are somehow involved in the blackmail scheme."

There was no need to hold back any longer. Quincannon said, "Not involved in it, the originator of it."

Pauline Dupree's only reaction was a raised eyebrow and a little moue of dismay. A talented actress, to be sure. But then, he'd already had ample evidence of her skills last night.

"I?" she said. "But that's ridiculous."

Quincannon's gaze had roamed the small dressing room. Revealing costumes hung on racks and an array of paints and powders and various theatrical accessories were arranged on tables. He walked over to one, picked up and brandished a long-haired white wig. "Is this the wig you wore last night, Mrs. Carver?" he asked her.

There was no slippage of her composure this time, either. "I have no idea what you're talking about."

"Your portrayal of Letitia Carver was quite good, I admit. The wig, the shawl and black dress and cane, the stooped posture and quavery voice . . . all very accomplished playacting. And of course the darkness and the candlelight concealed the fact that the old-age wrinkles were a product of theatrical makeup."

"And where was I supposed to have given this performance?" Pauline Dupree's eyes were cold and hard now, but her voice remained even.

"The abandoned house next to Raymond Sonderberg's cigar store in Gunpowder Alley. Before and after you murdered Sonderberg in his quarters behind the store."

"Murder?" the banker exclaimed in shocked tones. "See here, Quincannon! An accusation of blackmail is egregious enough, but murder—"

Pauline Dupree said, "It's nonsense, of course. I have no idea where Gunpowder Alley is, nor do I know anyone named Raymond Sonderberg."

"Ah, but you do. Or rather, did. Like Mr. Willard, Sonderberg was drawn to melodeons such as this one. My guess is you made his acquaintance in much the same way as you did my client, and used your no doubt considerable charms to lure him into your blackmail scheme."

"Preposterous!" Willard cried. "Outrageous!"

"But you never intended to share the spoils with him," Quincannon said to the actress. "You wanted the entire ten thousand dollars. To finance your ambition to become a serious actress, may hap? A trip east to New York?"

An eye-flick was his only response. But it was enough to tell him that he'd guessed correctly.

"I give you credit, Miss Dupree," he went on. "You planned it well enough in advance. You had two days to make your arrangements, after learning from Mr. Willard that I would be at the Hotel Grant last night. You found out, likely from

Sonderberg, about the abandoned house next to his building; he may even have helped you gain access. Sometime yesterday evening you went there and made final preparations for your performance—applied makeup, arranged a rocking chair near the window, created the illusion of an old woman seated there."

"Yes? How did I do that?"

"By placing a dressmaker's dummy in the chair, covering the head with the white wig, and draping the rest with a large shawl. This morning I found the dummy where you left it, in the foyer closet."

Willard made disbelieving, spluttering sounds. The actress said, "And why would I have set such an elaborate stage?"

"To flummox me, of course. You knew I would follow Sonderberg from the hotel and that I would be nearby after he arrived home with the satchel. Your plan all along was to eliminate him once he had outlived his usefulness, and to do so by making cold-blooded murder appear to be suicide and staging an apparent vanishing act must have seemed the height of creative challenge."

Willard should have been swayed by this time, but he wasn't. His feelings for Pauline Dupree were stronger than Quincannon had realized. "My dear," he said to his paramour, "you don't have to listen to any more of this slanderous nonsense—"

"Let him finish, Titus. I'd like to know how he thinks I accomplished this creative challenge he speaks of."

"It wasn't difficult," Quincannon said. "So devilishly simple, in fact, it had me buffaloed for a time—something that seldom happens." He paused to fluff his freebooter's beard. "Your actions from the time you set the scene in the house were these: You left the same way you'd entered, by the rear door, crossed along the walkway, and were admitted to Sonderberg's quarters through his rear door. Thus no one could possibly have seen you from the alley. How you explained the old crone's makeup to Sonderberg is of no real import. By then I suspect he would have believed anything you told him.

"You waited there, warm and dry, while he went to the Hotel Grant. When he returned with the satchel, he locked both the entrance to the cigar store and the inside door leading to his quarters. You made haste to convince him by one means or another to let you have the satchel. Then you left him, again through the rear door, no doubt with instructions to lock and bar it behind you."

"Then how am I supposed to have killed him inside his

locked quarters?"

"By slipping around into the side passage and tapping on the window, as if you'd forgotten something. When Sonderberg opened it, raising it high on its hinge, you reached through the bars, shot him twice, then immediately dropped the pistol to the floor. Naturally he released his grip on the window as he staggered backward, and it dropped and clattered shut—the loudish thump I heard before I ran into the passage. The force of impact flipped up the loose swivel catch at the bottom of the sash. Of its own momentum the catch then flipped back down and around the stud fastener, locking the window and adding to the illusion.

"It took you no more than a few seconds, then, to run to the rear walkway and reenter the house, locking that door behind you. While the patrolman and I were responding to the gunshots, you drew the parlor drapes, removed the dressmaker's dummy from the rocking chair, donned the wig, and assumed the role of Letitia Carver. When I came knocking at the door a while later, you could have simply ignored the summons; but you were so confident in your acting ability that you decided instead to have sport with me, holding the candle you'd lighted in such a way that your made-up face remained shadowed the entire time."

A few moments of silence ensued. Willard stood glaring at Quincannon, disbelief still plainly written on the lovesick dolt's pooched features. Pauline Dupree's expression was stoic, but in her eyes was a sparkle that might have been secret amusement.

"Utter rot," the banker said with furious indignation. "Miss Dupree is no more capable of such nefarious trickery than I am."

"Even if I were," she said, "Mr. Quincannon has absolutely no proof of his claims."

"When I find the ten thousand dollars, I'll have all the proof necessary. Hidden here, is it, or in your rooms?"

Again her response was not the one he'd anticipated. "You're welcome to search both," she said. Nor did the sparkle in her eyes diminish; if anything, it brightened. Telling him, he realized, as plainly as if she'd spoken the words, that such searches would prove futile, and that he would never discover where the greenbacks were hidden, no matter how long and hard he searched.

Sharp and bitter frustration goaded Quincannon now. There was no question that his deductions were correct, and he had been sure he could wring a confession from Pauline Dupree, or at the very least convince Titus Willard of her duplicity. But he had succeeded in doing neither. They were a united front against him.

So much so that the banker had moved over to stand protectively in front of her, as if to shield her from further accusations. He said angrily, "Whatever your purpose in attempting to persecute this innocent young woman, Quincannon, I won't stand for any more of it. Consider your services terminated. If you ever dare to bother Miss Dupree or me again, you'll answer to the police and my attorneys."

Behind Willard as he spoke, Pauline Dupree smiled and closed one eye in an exaggerated wink.

"Winked at me!" Quincannon ranted. "Stood there bold as brass and winked at me! The gall of the woman! The sheer mendacity! The —"

Always unflappable, Sabina said, "Calm yourself, John. Remember your blood pressure."

"The devil with my blood pressure. She's going to get away with murder!"

"Of a mean no-account as mendacious as she."

"Murder nonetheless. Murder and blackmail, and with her idiot victim's complicity."

"Unfortunately, there's nothing to be done about it. She was right—you have no proof of her guilt."

There was no gainsaying that. He muttered a frustrated oath.

"John, you know as well as I do that justice isn't always served. At least not immediately. Women like Pauline Dupree seldom go unpunished for long. Ruthlessness, greed, amorality, arrogance . . . all traits that sooner or later combine to bring about a harsh reckoning."

"Not always."

"Often enough. Have faith that it will in her case."

Quincannon knew from experience that Sabina was right, but it mollified him not at all. "And what about our fee? We'll never collect it now."

"Well, we do have Willard's retainer."

"It's not enough. I ought to take the balance out of his blasted hide."

"But you won't. You'll consider the case closed, as I do. And take solace in the fact that once again you solved a baffling crime. Your prowess in that regard remains unblemished."

This, too, was true. Yes, quite true. He *had* done his job

admirably, uncovered the truth with his usual brilliant deductions; the lack of the desired resolution was not his fault.

But the satisfaction, like the retainer, was not enough. "I don't understand the likes of Titus Willard," he growled. "What kind of man goes blithely on making a confounded fool of himself over a woman?"

Sabina cast a look at him, the significance of which he failed to notice. "All kinds, John," she said. "Oh, yes, all kinds."

Nameless Detective

THIN AIR

The man I'd been hired to follow was named Lewis Hornback. He was 43, had dark-brown hair and average features, drove a four-door Dodge Monaco, and lived in a fancy apartment building on Russian Hill. He was also cheating on his wife with an unknown woman and had misappropriated a large sum of money from the interior-design firm they co-owned. Or so Mrs. Hornback alleged. My job was to dig up evidence to support those allegations.

Mrs. Hornback had not told me what she intended to do with any such evidence. Have poor Lewis drawn and quartered, maybe—or at least locked away for the rest of his natural life. She was that kind of women—a thin, pinch-faced harridan ten years older than her husband with vindictive eyes and a desiccated look about her, as if all her vital juices had dried up a long time ago. If Hornback really was cheating on her, maybe he had justifiable cause. But that was not for me to say. It wasn't my job to make moral judgments—all I had to do was make an honest living for myself.

So I took Mrs. Hornback's retainer check, promised to make daily reports, and went to work that same afternoon. Hornback, it seemed, was in the habit of leaving their office at five o'clock most weekdays and not showing up at the Russian Hill apartment until well past midnight. At 4:30 I found a parking space near the garage where he kept his car, on Clay near Van Ness. It was a cold and windy November day, but the sky was clear, with no sign of fog above Twin Peaks or out near the Golden Gate. Which was a relief—tail jobs are tricky enough, especially at night, without the added difficulty of bad weather.

Hornback showed up promptly at five. Eight minutes later he drove his Dodge Monaco down the ramp and turned left on Clay. I gave him a block lead before I pulled out behind him.

He went straight to North Beach, to a little Italian restaurant not far from Washington Square. Meeting the girl friend for dinner, I figured, but it turned out I was wrong. After two drinks at the bar, while I nursed a beer, he took a table alone. I sat at an angle across the room from him, treated myself to *pollo al' diavolo*, and watched him pack away a three-course meal and half a liter of the house wine. Nobody came to talk to him except the waiter; he was just a man having a quiet dinner alone.

He polished off a brandy and three cigarettes for dessert,

lingering the way you do after a heavy meal. When he finally left the restaurant it was almost 7:30. From there he walked over to upper Grant, where he gawked at the young counterculture types who frequent the area, did a little window-shopping, and stopped at a newsstand and a drugstore. I stayed on the opposite side of the street, fifty yards or so behind him. That's about as close to a subject as you want to get on foot. But the walking tail got me nothing except exercise. Hornback was still alone when he led me back to where he had his car.

His next stop was a small branch library at the foot of Russian Hill, where he dropped off a couple of books. Then he headed south on Van Ness, north on Market out of the downtown area, and up the winding expanse of upper Market to the top of Twin Peaks. There was a little shopping area up there, a short distance beyond where Market blends into Portola Drive. He pulled into the parking area in front and went into a neighborhood tavern called Dewey's Place.

I parked down near the end of the lot. Maybe he was meeting the girl friend here or maybe he had just gone into the tavern for a drink; he seemed to like his liquor pretty well. I put on the grey cloth cap I keep in the car, shrugged out of my coat and turned it inside out—it's one of those reversible models—and put it on again that way, just in case Hornback had happened to notice me at the restaurant earlier. Then I stepped out into the cold wind blowing up from the ocean and crossed to Dewey's Place.

There were maybe a dozen customers inside, most of them at the bar. Hornback was down at the far end with a drink in one hand and a cigarette in the other, but the stools on both sides of him were empty. None of the three women in the place looked to be unescorted.

So maybe there wasn't a girl friend. Mrs. Hornback could have been wrong about that, even if she was right about the misappropriation of business funds. It was 9:45 now. If the man had a lady on the side, they would have been together by this time of night. And so far, Hornback had done nothing unusual or incriminating. Hell, he hadn't even done anything interesting.

I sat at the near end of the bar and sipped at a draft beer, watching Hornback in the mirror. He finished his drink, lit a fresh cigarette, and gestured to the bartender for a refill. I thought he looked a little tense, but in the dim lighting I couldn't be sure. He wasn't waiting for anybody, though. I could tell that: no glances at his watch or at the door. Just aimlessly killing time? It could be. For all I knew, this was how he spent each of his evenings out—eating alone, driving alone, drinking alone. And his reason might be the simplest and most innocent of all: he left the office at five and stayed out past midnight because he didn't want to go home to Mrs. Hornback.

When he had downed his second drink he stood up and reached for his wallet. I had already laid a dollar bill on the bar, so I slid off my stool and left ahead of him. I was already in my car when he came out.

Now where? I thought as he fired up the Dodge. Another bar somewhere? A late movie? Home early?

None of those. He surprised me by swinging back east on Portola and then getting into the left-turn lane for Twin Peaks Boulevard. The area up there is residential, at least on the lower part of the hillside. The road itself winds upward at steep angles, makes a figure-eight loop through the empty wooded expanse of Twin Peaks, and curls down on the opposite side of the hill.

Hornback stayed on Twin Peaks Boulevard, climbing toward the park. So he was probably not going to visit anybody in the area; he had by-passed the only intersecting streets on this side, and there were easier ways to get to the residential sections below the park to the north. I wondered if he was just marking more time, if it was his habit to take a long solitary drive around the city before he headed home.

There was almost no traffic and I dropped back several hundred feet to keep my headlights out of his rear-vision mirror on the turns. The view from up there was spectacular; on a night like this you could see for miles in all directions—the ocean, the full-sweep of the Bay, both bridges, the intricate pattern of lights that was San Francisco and its surrounding communities. Inside the park we passed a couple of cars pulled off on the lookouts that dotted the area: people, maybe lovers, taking in the view.

Hornback went through half the figure-eight from the east to west, driving without hurry. Once I saw the brief, faint flare of a match as he lit another cigarette. When he came out on the far side of the park he surprised me again. Instead of continuing down the hill he slowed and turned to the right onto a short, hooked spur road leading to another of the lookouts.

I tapped my brakes as I neared the turn, trying to decide what to do. The spur was a dead end. I could follow him around it or pull off the road and wait for him to come out again. The latter seemed to be the best choice and I cut my headlights and started to glide off onto a turnaround. But then, over on the spur, Hornback swung past a row of cypress trees that lined the near edge of the lookout. The Dodge's brake lights flashed through the trees; then his headlights, too, winked out.

I kept on going, made the turn, and drifted onto a second, tree-shadowed turnaround just beyond the intersection. Diagonally in front of me I could see Hornback ease the Dodge across the flat surface of the lookout and bring it to a stop nose-up against a perimeter guard rail. The distance between us was maybe 75 yards.

What's he up to now? I thought. Well, he had probably stopped there to take in the view and maybe do a little brooding. The other possibility was that he was waiting for someone. A late-evening rendezvous with the alleged girl friend? The police patrol Twin Peaks Park at regular intervals because kids have been known to use it as a lover's lane, but it was hardly the kind of place two adults would pick for an assignation. Why meet up here when the city is full of hotels and motels?

The Dodge gleamed a dullish black in the straight. From where I was I could see all of the passenger side and the rear third of the driver's side; the interior was shrouded in darkness. Pretty soon another match flared, smearing the gloom for an instant with dim yellowish light. Hornback was not quite a chain smoker, but he was the next thing to it—at least a two-pack a day man. I felt a little sorry for him, and a little envious at the same time; I had smoked two packs a day myself until a year and a half ago, when a doctor discovered a benign lesion on one of my lungs. I hadn't had a cigarette since, though there were still times I craved one. Like right now, watching that dark car and waiting for something to happen or not happen.

I slouched down behind the wheel and tried to make myself comfortable. Five minutes passed, ten minutes, fifteen. Behind me, half a dozen sets of headlights came up or went down the hill on Twin Peaks Boulevard, but none of them turned in where we were. And nothing moved that I could see in or around the Dodge.

I occupied my mind by speculating again about Hornback. He was a puzzle, all right. Maybe a cheating husband and a thief, or maybe an innocent on both counts—the victim of a loveless marriage and a shrewish wife. He hadn't done anything of a guilty or furtive nature tonight, and yet here he was, parked alone at 10:40 P.M. on a lookout in Twin Peaks Park. It could go either way. So which way was it going to go?

Twenty minutes.

And I began to feel just a little uneasy. You get intimations like that when you've been a cop of one type or another as long as I have—vague flickers of wrongness that seem at first to have no foundation. The feeling made me fidgety. I sat up and rolled down my window and peered across at the Dodge. Darkness. Stillness. Nothing out of the ordinary.

Twenty-five minutes.

The wind was chill against my face and I rolled the window back up, but the coldness had got into the car. I drew my coat tight around my neck and kept staring at the Dodge and the bright mosaic of lights beyond, like luminous spangles on the black-velvet sky.

Thirty minutes.

The uneasiness grew and became acute. Something was wrong over there, damn it. A half hour was a long time for a man to sit alone on a lookout, whether he was brooding or not. It was even a long time to wait for a rendezvous. But that was only part of the sense of wrongness. There was something else.

Hornback had not lit another cigarette since that one nearly half an hour ago.

The realization made me sit up again. He had been smoking steadily all night long, even during his walk along upper Grant after dinner. When I was a heavy smoker I couldn't have gone half an hour without lighting up; it seemed funny that Hornback could or would, considering that there was nothing else for him to do in there. He might have run out, of course, yet I remembered seeing a full pack in front of him on the bar at Dewey's Place.

What could be wrong? He was alone up here in his car except for my watching eyes; nothing could have happened to him. Unless . . .

Suicide?

The word popped into my mind and made me feel even colder. Suppose Hornback was innocent of infidelity, but suppose he was also despondent over the state of his marriage. Suppose all the aimless wandering tonight had been a prelude to an attempt on his own life—a man trying to work up enough courage to kill himself on a lonely road high above the city. It was possible. I didn't know enough about Hornback to judge his mental stability.

I wrapped both my hands around the wheel, debating with myself. If I went over to his car and checked on him and he was all right, I would have blown not only the tail but my client's trust. But if I stayed here and Hornback had taken pills or done God knew what to himself, I might be sitting passively by while a man died.

Headlights appeared on Twin Peaks Boulevard behind me, then swung in a slow arc onto the spur road. I drifted lower in the seat and waited for them to pass.

Only they did not pass. The car drew abreast of mine and came to a halt. Police patrol. I sensed it even before I saw the darkened dome flasher on the roof. The passenger window was down and the cop on that side extended a flashlight through the opening and flicked it on. The light pinned me for three or four seconds, bright enough to make me squint, then shut off. The patrolman motioned for me to roll down my window.

I glanced past the cruiser to Hornback's Dodge. It remained dark and there was still no movement anywhere in the vicinity. Well, the decision whether or not to check on him was out of my hands now; the cops would want to have a look at the Dodge in any case. And in any case, my assignment was blown.

I let out a breath and wound down the glass. The patrolman, a young guy with a moustache, said, "What's going on here, fella?"

So I told him, keeping it brief, and let him have a look at the photostat of my investigator's license. He seemed half skeptical and half uncertain; he had me get out and stand to one side while he talked things over with his partner, a heavy-set older man with a beer belly larger than mine. After which the partner took out a second flashlight and trotted across the lookout to the Dodge.

The younger cop asked me some questions and I answered them, but my attention was on the older guy. I watched him reach the driver's door and shine his light through the window. A moment later he appeared to reach down for the door handle, but it must have been locked because I didn't see the door open or him lean inside. Instead he put his light up to the window again, slid it over to the window on the rear door, and then turned abruptly to make an urgent semaphoring gesture.

"Sam!" he shouted. "Get over here on the double!"

The young patrolman, Sam, had his right hand on the butt of his service revolver as we ran ahead to the Dodge. I was expecting the worst by this time, but I wasn't at all prepared for what I saw inside that car. I just stood there gaping while the cops' lights crawled through the interior.

There were spots of drying blood across the front seat.

But the seat was empty, and so was the back seat, and so

were the floorboards.

Hornback had disappeared.

One of the two inspectors who arrived on the scene a half hour later was Ben Klein, an old-timer and a casual acquaintance from my own years on the San Francisco cops in the '40s and '50s. I had asked the patrolman to call in Lieutenant Eberhardt, probably my closest friend on or off the force, because I wanted an ally in case matters became dicey. Eb, though, was evidently still on the day shift. I hadn't asked for Klein, but I felt a little better when he showed up.

When he finished checking over the Dodge we went off to one side of it, near the guard rail. From there I could look down a steep slope dotted with stunted trees and underbrush. Search teams were moving along it with flashlights, looking for some sign of Hornback, but so far they didn't seem to be having any luck. Up here the area was swarming with men and vehicles, most but not all of them official. The usual rubberneckers and media types were in evidence along the spur and back on Twin Peaks Boulevard.

"Let me get this straight," Klein said when I had finished giving him my story. He had his hands jammed into his coat pockets and his body hunched against the wind, because the night had turned bitter cold now. "You followed Hornback here around ten-fifteen and you were in a position to watch his car from the time he parked it to the time the two patrolmen showed up."

"That's right."

"You were over on that turnaround?"

"Yes. The whole time."

"And you didn't see anything inside or outside the Dodge?"

"Nothing at all. I couldn't see inside it—too many shadows—but I could see most of the area around it."

"Did you take your eyes off it for any length of time?"

"No. A few seconds now and then, sure, but no more than that."

"Could you see all four doors?"

"Three of the four," I said. "Not the driver's door."

"That's how he disappeared, then."

I nodded. "But what about the dome light? Why didn't I see it go on?"

"It's not working. The bulb's defective. That was one of the first things I checked after we wired up the door lock."

"I also didn't see the door open. I might have missed that, I'll admit, but it's the kind of movement that would have attracted my attention." I paused, working my memory. "Hornback couldn't have gone away toward the road or down the embankment to the east or back into those trees over there. I would have seen him for sure if he had. The only other direction is down this slope, right in front of his car; but if that's it, why didn't I notice any movement when he climbed over the guard rail?"

"Maybe he didn't climb over it. Maybe he crawled under it."

"Why would he have done that?"

"I don't know. I'm only making suggestions."

"Well, I can think of one possibility."

"Which is?"

"The suicide angle," I said. "I told you I was worried about that. What if Hornback decided to do the Dutch, and while he was sitting in the car he used a pocketknife or something else sharp to slash his wrists? That would explain the blood on the front seat. Only he lost his nerve at the last second, panicked, opened the door, fell out of the car, and crawled under the guard rail."

I stopped. The idea was no good. I had realized that even as I laid it out.

Klein knew it too. He was shaking his head. "No blood outside the driver's door or along the side of the car or anywhere under the guard rail. A man with slashed wrists bleeds pretty heavily. Besides, if he'd cut his wrists and had second thoughts, why leave the car at all? Why not just start it up and drive to the nearest hospital?"

"Yeah," I said.

"There's another screwy angle—the locked doors. Who locked them? Hornback? His attacker, if there was one? Why lock them at all?"

I had no answer. I stood brooding out at the city lights.

"Assume he was attacked," Klein said. "By a mugger, say, who's decided to work up here because of the isolation. The attacker would have had to get to the car with you watching, which means coming up this slope, along the side of the car, and in through the driver's door—*if* it wasn't locked at that time. But I don't buy it. It's TV-commando stuff, too farfetched."

"There's another explanation," I said musingly.

"What's that?"

"The attacker was in the car all along."

"Not a mugger, you mean?"

"Right. Somebody who had it in for Hornback."

Klein frowned; he had heavy jowls and it made him look like a bulldog. "I thought you said Hornback was alone the whole night. Didn't meet anybody."

"He didn't. But suppose he was in the habit of frequenting Dewey's Place and this somebody knew it. He or she could have been waiting in the parking lot, slipped inside the Dodge while Hornback and I were in the tavern, hidden on the floor in back, and stayed hidden until Hornback came up here and parked. Then maybe stuck a knife in him."

"Sounds a little melodramatic, but I guess it's possible. Still, what kind of motive fits that explanation?"

"One connected with the money his wife claims Hornback stole from their firm."

"You're not thinking the wife could've attacked him?"

"No. If she was going to do him in, it doesn't make sense she'd hire me to tail him around. Hornback might have had some accomplice in the theft. Maybe they had a falling-out and the accomplice wanted to keep all the money for himself."

"Maybe," Klein said, but he sounded dubious. "The main trouble with that theory is, what happened to Hornback's body? The attacker would have had to get both himself and Hornback out of the car, then drag the body down the slope. Now why in hell would somebody kill a man way up here, with nobody around so far as he knew, and take the corpse away with him instead of just leaving it in the car?"

"I don't know. But I can't figure it any other way."

"Neither can I right now. Let's see what the search teams and the forensic boys turn up."

What the searchers and the lab people turned up, however, was nothing—no sign of Hornback dead or alive, no sign of anybody else in the area, no bloodstains except for those inside the car, no other evidence of any kind. Hornback—or his body—and maybe an attacker as well had not only vanished from the Dodge while I was watching it; he had vanished completely and without a trace. As if into thin air.

It was 1:30 A.M. before Klein let me go home. He asked me to stop in later at the Hall of Justice to sign a statement, but aside from that he seemed satisfied that I had given him all the facts as I knew them. But I was not quite off the hook yet, nor would I be until Hornback turned up. *If* he turned up. My word was all the police had for what had happened on the lookout, and I was the first to admit that it was a pretty bizarre story.

When I got to my Pacific Heights flat I thought about calling

Mrs. Hornback. But it was after two o'clock by then and I saw no point or advantage in phoning a report at this time of night; the police would already have told her about her husband's disappearance. So I drank a glass of milk and crawled into bed and tried to sort things into some kind of order.

How had Hornback vanished? Why? Was he dead or alive? An innocent man, or as guilty as his wife claimed? The victim of suicidal depression, the victim of circumstance, or the victim of premeditated murder?

No good. I was too tired to come up with fresh answers to any of those questions.

After a while I slept and dreamed a lot of nonsense about people dematerializing inside locked cars, vanishing in little puffs of smoke. A long time later the telephone woke me up. I keep the damned thing in the bedroom and it went off six inches from my ear and sat me up in bed, disoriented and grumbling. I pawed at my eyes and got them unstuck. There was grey morning light in the room; the nightstand clock said 6:55. Four hours' sleep and welcome to a new day.

The caller, not surprisingly, was Mrs. Hornback. She berated me for not getting in touch with her, then she demanded my version of last night. I gave it to her.

"I don't believe a word of it," she said.

"That's your privilege, ma'am. But it happens to be the truth."

"We'll see about that." Her voice sounded no different from the way it had when she'd hired me: cold, clipped, and coated with vitriol. There was not a whisper of compassion. "How could you let something like that happen? What kind of detective are you?"

A poor tired one, I thought. But I said, "I did what you asked me to, Mrs. Hornback. What happened on the lookout was beyond my control."

"Yes? Well, if my husband isn't found, and if I don't recover the money I *know* he stole, you'll hear from my lawyer. You can count on that." There was a clattering sound and then the line began to buzz.

Nice lady. A real princess.

I lay back down. I was still half asleep and pretty soon I drifted off again. This time I dreamed I was in a room where half a dozen guys were playing poker. They were all private eyes from the pulp magazines I read and collected—Race Williams, Jim Bennett, Max Latin, some of the best of the bunch. Latin wanted to know what kind of detective I was; his voice sounded just like Mrs. Hornback's. I said I was a pulp detective. They kept saying, "No you're not, you can't play with us because you're not one of us," and I kept saying, "But I am, I'm the same kind of private eye you are."

The jangling of the phone ended that nonsense and sat me up the way it had before. I focused on the clock: 8:40. Conspiracy against my sleep, I thought, and fumbled up the handset.

"Wake you up, hotshot?" a familiar voice said. Eberhardt.

"What do you think?"

"Sorry about that. I've got news for you."

"What news?"

"That funny business up on Twin Peaks last night—your boy Hornback's been found."

I stopped feeling sleepy and the fuzziness cleared out of my mind. "Where? Is he all right?"

"In Golden Gate Park," Eberhardt said. "And no, he's not all right. He's dead—been dead since last night. Stabbed in the chest, probably with a butcher knife."

I got down to the Hall of Justice at ten o'clock, showered, shaved, and full of coffee. Eberhardt was in his office in General Works, gnawing on one of his briar pipes and looking as sour as usual. The sourness was just a facade; he wasn't as grim and grouchy as he liked people to think.

"I've been rereading Klein's report," he said as I sat down. "You get mixed up in the damnedest cases these days."

"Don't I know it. What have you got on Hornback?"

"Nothing much. Guy out jogging found the body at seven-fifteen in a clump of bushes along JFK Drive. Stabbed in the chest, like I told you on the phone—a single wound that penetrated the heart, the probable weapon a butcher knife. The medical examiner says death was instantaneous. I guess that takes care of the suicide theory."

"I guess it does."

"No other marks on the body," he said, "except for a few small scratches on the hands and on one cheek."

"What kind of scratches?"

"Just scratches. The kind you get crawling around in woods or underbrush, or the kind a body might get if it was dragged through the same type of terrain. The ME will have more on that when he finishes his post-mortem."

"What was the condition of Hornback's clothes?"

"Dirty, torn in a couple of places. The same thing applies."

"Anything among his effects?"

"No. The usual stuff—wallet, handkerchief, change, a pack of cigarettes, and a box of matches. Eighty-three dollars in the wallet and a bunch of credit cards. That seems to rule out the robbery motive."

"I don't suppose there was any evidence where he was found."

"None. Killed somewhere else, the way it figures. Like up on that Twin Peaks lookout. Hornback's blood type was AO; it matches the type found on the front seat of his car."

We were silent for a time. I watched Eberhardt break his briar in half and run a pipe-cleaner through the stem. Then I said, "Damn it, Eb, it doesn't make sense. What's the motive behind the whole business? Why would the killer take Hornback's body away and then dump it in Golden Gate Park later? How could he have got it and himself out of the car without me noticing that something was going on?"

"You tell me, mastermind. You were there. You ought to know what you saw or didn't see."

I opened my mouth, closed it again, and blinked at him. "What did you say?"

"You heard me. I said you were there and you ought to know what you saw or didn't see."

What I saw. And what I didn't see.

Eberhardt put his pipe back together and tamped tobacco into the bowl. "We'd better come up with some answers pretty soon," he said. "Klein got back a little while ago from breaking the news to the widow. "He says she blames you for letting Hornback get killed."

Two things I didn't see that I *should* have seen.

"She claims he siphoned off as much as a hundred thousand dollars from that interior-design company of theirs. According to her, he overcharged some customers, pocketed cash payments from others, and phonied up some records. She also figures he took kickbacks from suppliers."

Several things I *did* see.

"Evidently she accused him of it earlier this week. He denied everything. She's got an auditor going over the books, but that takes time. That's why she hired you."

Add them all up, put them all together—a pattern.

"The money is all she cares about, Klein says. She thinks Hornback spent part of it on the alleged girl friend, but she means to get back whatever's left. That kind of woman can stir up a lot of trouble. No telling what kind of accusations she's liable to—"

Sure. A pattern.

"Hey!" Eberhardt said. "Are you listening to me?"

"What?"

"What's the matter with you? I'm not just talking to hear the sound of my own voice."

I stood up and took a couple of turns around the office. "I think I've got something, Eb."

"Got something? You mean answers?"

"Maybe." I sat down again. "Did you see Hornback's body yourself this morning?"

"I saw it. Why?"

"Were there any marks on it besides the stab wound and the scratches? Any other sort of wound, no matter how small?"

He thought. "No. Except for a Band-Aid on one of his fingers, if that matters—"

"You bet it does." I said. "Get Klein in here, would you? I want to ask him a couple of questions."

Eberhardt gave me a narrow look, but he buzzed out to the squad room and asked for Klein. Ben came in a few seconds later.

"When you checked over Hornback's car last night," I asked him, "was the emergency brake set?"

"No, I don't think so."

"What about the transmission? Was the lever in Park or Neutral?"

"Neutral."

"I thought so. That's the answer then."

Eberhardt said, "You know how Hornback's body disappeared from his car?"

"Yes. Only it *didn't* disappear from the car."

"Meaning what?"

"Meaning the body was never inside it," I said. "Hornback wasn't murdered on the lookout. He was killed later on, somewhere else."

"What about the blood on the front seat?"

"He put it there himself, deliberately—by cutting his finger with something sharp, like maybe a razor blade. That's the reason for the Band-Aid."

"Why would he do a crazy thing like that?"

"Because he was planning to disappear."

"Come on, you're talking in riddles."

"No, I'm not. If Mrs. Hornback is right about her husband stealing that money—and she has to be—he was wide open to criminal charges. And she's just the type who would press charges. He had no intention of hanging around to face them; his plan from the beginning had to be to stockpile as much money as he could and, when his wife began to tumble to what he was doing, to split with it. And with this girl friend of his, no doubt.

"But he didn't just want to hop a plane for somewhere; that would have made him an obvious fugitive. So he worked out a clever gimmick, or what he thought was clever anyway. He intended to vanish under mysterious circumstances so it would look like he'd met with foul play—abandon his car in an isolated spot with blood all over the front seat. It's been done before and he knew it probably wouldn't fool anybody but he had nothing to lose by trying."

"O.K. This disappearing act of his was in the works for last night—which is why he stopped at the drugstore in North Beach after dinner, to buy razor blades and Band-Aids. But something happened long before he headed up to Twin Peaks that altered the shape of his plan."

Both Eberhardt and Klein were watching me intently. Ed said, "What was that?"

"He spotted me," I said. "I guess I'm getting old and less careful on a tail job than I used to be; either that or he just tumbled to me by accident. I don't suppose it matters. Anyhow, he realized early in the evening that he had a tail—and it wouldn't have taken much effort for him to figure out I was a private detective hired by his wife to get the goods on him. That was when he shifted gears from a half-clever idea to a really clever one. He'd go through with his disappearing act all right, but he'd do it in front of a witness—and under a set of contrived circumstances that were *really* mysterious."

"It's a pretty good scenario so far," Eberhardt said. "But I'm still waiting to find out how he managed to disappear while you were sitting there watching his car."

"He didn't," I said.

"There you go with the riddles again."

"Follow me through. After he left Dewey's Place—while he was stopped at the traffic light on Portola or when he was driving up Twin Peaks Boulevard—he used the razor blade to slice open his finger and drip blood on the seat. Then he bandaged the cut. That took care of part of the trick. The next part came when he reached the lookout."

"There's a screen of cypress trees along the back edge of the lookout where you turn in off the spur road. They create a blind spot for anybody still on Twin Peaks Boulevard, as I was at the time; I couldn't see all of the lookout until after I'd turned onto the spur. As soon as Hornback came into that blind spot he jammed on his brakes and cut his headlights. I told Ben about that—seeing the brake lights flash through the trees and the headlights go dark. It didn't strike me at the time, but when you think about it it's a little odd somebody would switch off his lights on a lookout like that, with a steep slope at the far end, *before* he stops his car."

Eberhardt said, "I think I see the rest of it coming."

"Sure. He hit the brakes hard enough to bring the Dodge almost, but not quite, to a full stop. At the same time he shoved the transmission into Neutral, shut off the engine, and opened the door. The bulb for the dome light was defective so he didn't have to worry about that. Then he slipped out, pushed down the lock button—a little added mystery—closed the door again, and ran a few steps into the trees where there were enough heavy shadows to hide him and conceal his escape from the area.

"Meanwhile, the car drifted forward nice and slow and came to a halt nose-up against the guard rail. I saw that much, but what I didn't see was the brake lights flash again. As they *should* have if Hornback was still inside the car and stopping it in the normal way."

"One thing," Klein said. "What about that match flare you saw after the car was stopped?"

"That was a nice convincing touch." I said. "When the match flamed, I naturally assumed it was Hornback lighting another cigarette. But I realize now I didn't see anything after that—no sign of a glowing cigarette in the darkness. What really happened is this: he fired a cigarette on his way up to the lookout; I noticed a match flare then too. Before he left the car he put the smoldering butt in the ashtray along with an unused match. As soon as the hot ash burned down far enough it touched off the match. Simple as that."

Eberhardt made chewing sounds on his pipe stem. "O.K.," he said, "you've explained the disappearance. Now explain the murder. Who killed Hornback? Not his wife?"

"No. The last place he would have gone was home and the last person he would have contacted was Mrs. Hornback. It has to be the girl friend. She would be the one who picked him up near the lookout. An argument over the money, maybe—something like that. You'll find out eventually why she did it."

"We won't find out anything unless we know who we're looking for. You got any more rabbits in your hat? Like the name of this girl friend?"

"I don't know her name," I said, "but I think I can tell you where to find her."

He stared at me. "Well?"

"I followed Hornback around to a lot of places last night," I said. "Restaurant, drugstore, newsstand for a pack of cigarette, Dewey's Place for a couple of drinks to shore up his courage—all reasonable stops. But why did he go to the branch library? Why would a man plotting his own disappearance bother to return a couple of library books? Unless the books were just a cover, you see? Unless he really went to the library to tell someone who worked there what he was going to do and where to come pick him up."

"A *librarian?*"

"Why not, Eb? Librarians aren't the stereotypes of fiction. This one figures to be young and attractive, whoever she is. You shouldn't have too much trouble picking out the right one."

He kept on staring at me. Then he shook his head and said, "You know something? You're getting to be a regular Sherlock Holmes in your old age."

"If I am," I said as I stood up, "you're getting to be a regular Lestrade."

That made him scowl. "Who the hell is Lestrade?"

The following day, while I was trying to find a better place to hang the blow-up of the 1932 *Black Mask* cover I keep in my office, Eberhardt called to fill in the final piece. Hornback's girl friend worked at the branch library, all right. Her name was Linda Fields, and she had broken down under police interrogation and confessed to the murder.

The motive behind it was stupid and childish, like a lot of motives behind crimes of passion: Hornback wanted to go to South America, and she wanted to stay in the U.S. They had argued about it on the way to her apartment, the argument had turned nasty after they arrived, Hornback had slapped her, she had picked up a butcher knife, and that was it for him. Afterward she had dragged his body back into her car, taken it to Golden Gate Park, and dumped it. What was left of the stolen money—$98,000 in cash—had been hidden in her apartment. That would make Mrs. Hornback happy—sweet lady that she was—and insure my getting paid for my services.

When Eberhardt finished telling me this, there was a long pause. "Listen," he said, "who's this Lestrade you mentioned yesterday?"

"That's still bothering you, is it?"

"Who is he, damn it? Some character in one of your pulps?"

"Nope. He's a cop in the Sherlock Holmes stories—the one Holmes keeps outwitting."

Eberhardt made a snorting noise, called me something uncomplimentary, and banged the phone down in my ear.

Laughing to myself, I went back to the *Black Mask* poster. Eb was no Lestrade, of course—and I was no Sherlock Holmes. I was the next best thing though. At least to my way of thinking, and in spite of my dream.

A good old-fashioned private eye.

CAT'S-PAW

There are two places that are ordinary enough during the daylight hours but that become downright eerie after dark, particularly if you go wandering around in them by yourself. One is a graveyard; the other is a public zoo. And that goes double for San Francisco's Fleishhacker Zoological Gardens on a blustery winter night, when the fog comes swirling in and makes everything look like capering phantoms or two-dimensional cutouts.

Fleishhacker Zoo was where I was on this foggy winter night—alone, for the most part—and I wished I were somewhere else instead. Anywhere else, as long as it had a heater or a log fire and offered something hot to drink.

I was on my third tour of the grounds, headed past the sea lion tank to make another check of the aviary, when I paused to squint at the luminous dial of my watch. Eleven forty-five. Less than three hours down and better than six left to go. I was already half-frozen, even though I was wearing long johns, two sweaters, two pairs of socks, heavy gloves, a woolen cap, and a long fur-lined overcoat. The ocean was only a thousand yards away, and the icy wind that blew in off it sliced through you to the marrow. If I got through this job without contracting pneumonia, I would consider myself lucky.

Somewhere in the fog, one of the animals made a sudden roaring noise; I couldn't tell what kind of animal or where the noise came from. The first time that sort of thing had happened, two nights ago, I'd jumped a little. Now I was used to it, or as used to it as I would ever get. How guys like Dettlinger and Hammond could work here night after night, month after month, was beyond my comprehension.

I went ahead toward the aviary. The big wind-sculpted cypress trees that grew on my left made looming, swaying shadows, like giant black dancers with rustling headdresses wreathed in mist. Back beyond them, fuzzy yellow blobs of light marked the location of the zoo's cafe. More nightlights burned on the aviary, although the massive fenced-in wing on the near side was dark.

Most of the birds were asleep or nesting or whatever the hell it is birds do at night. But you could hear some of them stirring around, making noise. There were a couple of dozen different varieties in there, including such esoteric types as the crested screamer, the purple gallinule, and the black crake. One esoteric type that used to be in there but wasn't any longer was something called a bunting, a brilliantly colored migratory bird. Three of them had been swiped four days ago, the latest in a rash of thefts the zoological gardens had suffered.

The thief, or thieves, had also got two South American Harris hawks, a bird of prey similar to a falcon; three crab-eating macaques, whatever they were; and half a dozen rare Chiricahua rattlesnakes known as *Crotalus pricei*. He, or they, had picked the locks on buildings and cages, and got away clean each time. Sam Dettlinger, one of the two regular watchmen, had spotted somebody running the night the rattlers were stolen, and given chase, but he hadn't got close enough for much of a description, or even to tell for sure if it was a man or a woman.

The police had been notified, of course, but there was not much they could do. There wasn't much the Zoo Commission could do either, beyond beefing up security—and all that had amounted to was adding one extra night watchman, Al Kirby, on a temporary basis; he was all they could afford. The problem was, Fleishhacker Zoo covers some seventy acres. Long sections of its perimeter fencing are secluded; you couldn't stop somebody determined to climb the fence and sneak in at night if you surrounded the place with a hundred men. Nor could you effectively police the grounds with any less than a hundred men; much of those seventy acres is heavily wooded, and there are dozens of grottoes, brushy fields and slopes, rush-rimmed ponds, and other areas simulating natural habitats for some of the zoo's fourteen hundred animals and birds. Kids, and an occasional grown-up, have gotten lost in there in broad daylight. A thief who knew his way around could hide out on the grounds for weeks without being spotted.

I got involved in the case because I was acquainted with one of the commission members, a guy named Lawrence Factor. He was an attorney, and I had done some investigating for him in the past, and he thought I was the cat's nuts when it came to detective work. So he'd come to see me, not as an official emissary of the commission but on his own; the commission had no money left in its small budget for such as the hiring of a private detective. But Factor had made a million bucks or so in the practice of criminal law, and as a passionate animal lover, he was willing to foot the bill himself. What he wanted me to do was sign on as another night watchman, plus nose around among my contacts to find out if there was any word on the street about the thefts.

It seemed like an odd sort of case, and I told him so. "Why would anybody steal hawks and small animals and rattlesnakes?" I asked. "Doesn't make much sense to me."

"It would if you understood how valuable those creatures are to some people."

"What people?"

"Private collectors, for one," he said. "Unscrupulous individuals who run small independent zoos, for another. They've been known to pay exorbitantly high prices for rare specimens they can't obtain through normal channels—usually because of the state or federal laws protecting endangered species."

"You mean there's a thriving black market in animals?"

"You bet there is. Animals, reptiles, birds—you name it. Take the *pricei*, the southwestern rattler, for instance. Several years ago, the Arizona Game and Fish Department placed it on a special permit list; people who want the snake first have to obtain a permit from the Game and Fish authority before they can go out into the Chiricahua Mountains and hunt one. Legitimate researchers have no trouble getting a permit, but hobbyists and private collectors are turned down. Before the permit list, you could get a *pricei* for twenty-five dollars; now, some snake collectors will pay two hundred and fifty dollars and up for one."

"The same high prices apply on the other stolen specimens?"

"Yes," Factor said. "Much higher, in the case of the Harris hawk."

"How much higher?"

"From three to five thousand dollars, after it has been trained for falconry."

I let out a soft whistle. "You have any idea who might be pulling the thefts?"

"Not specifically, no. It could be anybody with a working knowledge of zoology and the right—or wrong—contacts for disposal of the specimens."

"Someone connected with Fleishhacker, maybe?"

"That's possible. But I damned well hope not."

"So your best guess is what?"

"A professional at this sort of thing," Factor said. "They don't usually rob large zoos like ours—there's too much risk and too much publicity; mostly they hit small zoos or private collectors, and do some poaching on the side. But it has been known to happen when they hook up with buyers who are willing to pay premium prices."

"What makes you think it's a pro in this case? Why not an amateur? Or even kids out on some kind of crazy lark?"

"Well, for one thing, the thief seemed to know exactly what he was after each time. Only expensive and endangered specimens were taken. For another thing, the locks on the building and cage doors were picked by an expert—and that's not my theory, it's the police's."

"You figure he'll try it again."

"Well, he's four-for-four so far, with no hassle except for the minor scare Sam Dettlinger gave him; that has to make him feel pretty secure. And there are dozens more valuable, prohibited specimens in the gardens. I like the odds that he'll push his luck and go for five straight."

But so far the thief hadn't pushed his luck. This was the third night I'd been on the job and nothing had happened. Nothing had happened during my daylight investigation either; I had put out feelers all over the city, but nobody admitted to knowing anything about the zoo thefts. Nor had I been able to find out anything from any of the Fleishhacker employees I'd talked to. All the information I had on the case, in fact, had been furnished by Lawrence Factor in my office three days ago.

If the thief was going to make another hit, I wished he would do it pretty soon and get it over with. Prowling around here in the dark and the fog and that damned icy wind, waiting for something to happen, was starting to get on my nerves. Even if I was being well paid, there were better ways to spend long, cold winter nights. Like curled up in bed with a copy of *Black Mask* or *Detective Tales* or one of the other pulps in my collection. Like curled up in bed with Kerry . . .

I moved ahead to the near doors of the aviary and tried them to make sure they were still locked. They were. But I shone my flash on them anyway, just to be certain that they hadn't been tampered with since the last time one of us had been by. No problem there, either.

There were four of us on the grounds—Dettlinger, Hammond, Kirby, and me—and the way we'd been working it was to spread out to four corners and then start moving counterclockwise in a set but irregular pattern; that way, we could cover the grounds thoroughly without all of us congregating in one area, and without more than fifteen minutes going by from one building check to another. We each had a walkie-talkie clipped to our belts, so one could summon the others if anything went down. We also used the things to radio our positions periodically, so we'd be sure to stay spread out from each other.

I went around the other side of the aviary, to the entrance that faced the long, shallow pond where the bigger tropical birds had their sanctuary. The doors there were also secure. The wind gusted over the pond as I was checking the doors, like a williwaw off the frozen Arctic tundra; it made the cypress trees genuflect, shredded the fog for an instant so that I could see all the way across to the construction site of the new Primate Discovery Center, and cracked my teeth together with a sound like rattling bones. I flexed the cramped fingers of my left hand, the one that had suffered some slight nerve damage in a shooting scrape a few months back; extreme cold aggravated the chronic stiffness. I thought longingly of the hot coffee in my thermos. But the thermos was over at the zoo office behind the carousel, along with my brown-bag supper, and I was not due for a break until one o'clock.

The path that led to Monkey Island was on my left; I took it, hunching forward against the wind. Ahead, I could make out the high dark mass of man-made rocks that comprised the island home of sixty or seventy spider monkeys. But the mist was closing in again, like wind-driven skeins of shiny gray cloth being woven together magically; the building that housed the elephants and pachyderms, only a short distance away, was invisible.

One of the male peacocks that roam the grounds let loose with its weird cry somewhere behind me. The damned things were always doing that, showing off even in the middle of the night. I had never cared for peacocks much, and I liked them even less now. I wondered how one of them would taste roasted with garlic and anchovies. The thought warmed me a little as I moved along the path between the hippo pen and the brown bear grottoes, turned onto the wide concourse that led past the front of the Lion House.

In the middle of the concourse was an extended oblong pond, with a little center island overgrown with yucca trees and pampas grass. The vegetation had an eerie look in the fog, like fantastic creatures waving their appendages in a low-budget science fiction film. I veered away from them, over toward the glass-and-wire cages that had been built onto the Lion House's stucco facade. The cages were for show: inside was the Zoological Society's current pride and joy, a year-old white tiger named Prince Charles, one of only fifty known white tigers in the world. Young Charley was the zoo's rarest and most valuable possession, but the thief hadn't attempted to steal him. Nobody in his right mind would try to make off with a frisky, five-hundred-pound tiger in the middle of the night.

Charley was asleep; so was his sister, a normally marked Bengal tiger named Whiskers. I looked at them for a few seconds, decided I wouldn't like to have to pay their food bill, and started to turn away.

Somebody was hurrying toward me, from over where the otter pool was located.

I could barely see him in the mist; he was just a moving black shape. I tensed a little, taking the flashlight out of my pocket, putting my cramped left hand on the walkie-talkie so I could use the thing if it looked like trouble. But it wasn't trouble. The figure called my name in a familiar voice, and when I put my flash on for a couple of seconds I saw that it was Sam Dettlinger.

"What's up?" I said when he got to me. "You're supposed to be over by the gorillas about now."

"Yeah," he said, "but I thought I saw something about fifteen minutes ago, out back by the cat grottoes."

"Saw what?"

"Somebody moving around in the bushes," he said. He tipped back his uniform cap, ran a gloved hand over his face to wipe away the thin film of moisture the fog had put there. He was in his forties, heavyset, owl-eyed, with carrot-colored hair and a mustache that looked like a dead caterpillar draped across his upper lip.

"Why didn't you put out a call?"

"I couldn't be sure I actually saw somebody and I didn't want to sound a false alarm; this damn fog distorts everything, makes you see things that aren't there. Wasn't anybody in the bushes when I went to check. It might have been a squirrel or something. Or just the fog. But I figured I'd better search the area to make sure."

"Anything?"

"No. Zip."

"Well, I'll make another check just in case."

"You want me to come with you?"

"No need. It's about time for your break, isn't it?"

He shot the sleeve of his coat and peered at his watch. "You're right, it's almost midnight—"

Something exploded inside the Lion House—a flat cracking noise that sounded like a gunshot.

Both Dettlinger and I jumped. He said, "What the hell was that?"

"I don't know. Come on!"

We ran the twenty yards or so to the front entrance. The noise had awakened Prince Charles and his sister; they were up and starting to prowl their cage as we rushed past. I caught hold of the door handle and tugged on it, but the lock was secure.

I snapped at Dettlinger, "Have you got a key?"

"Yeah, to all the buildings . . ."

He fumbled his key ring out, and I switched on my flash to help him find the right key. From inside, there was cold dead silence; I couldn't hear anything anywhere else in the vicinity except for faint animal sounds lost in the mist. Dettlinger got the door unlocked, dragged it open. I crowded in ahead of him, across a short foyer and through another door that wasn't locked, into the building's cavernous main room.

A couple of the ceiling lights were on; we hadn't been able to tell from outside because the Lion House had no windows. The interior was a long rectangle with a terra-cotta tile floor, now-empty feeding cages along the entire facing wall and the near side wall, another set of entrance doors in the far side wall, and a kind of indoor garden full of tropical plants flanking the main entrance to the left. You could see all of the enclosure from two steps inside, and there wasn't anybody in it. Except—

"Jesus!" Dettlinger said. "Look!"

I was looking, all right. And having trouble accepting what I saw. A man lay sprawled on his back inside one of the cages diagonally to our right; there was a small glistening stain of blood on the front of his heavy coat and a revolver of some kind in one of his outflung hands. The small access door at the front of the cage was shut, and so was the sliding panel at the rear that let the big cats in and out at feeding time. In the pale light, I could see the man's face clearly: his teeth were bared in the rictus of death.

"It's Kirby," Dettlinger said in a hushed voice. "Sweet Christ, what—?"

I brushed past him and ran over and climbed the brass railing that fronted all the cages. The access door, a four-by-two-foot barred inset, was locked tight. I poked my nose between two of the bars, peering in at the dead man. Kirby, Al Kirby. The temporary night watchman the Zoo Commission had hired a couple of weeks ago. It looked as though he had been shot in the chest at close range; I could see where the upper middle of his coat had been scorched by the powder discharge.

My stomach jumped a little, the way it always does when I

come face-to-face with violent death. The faint, gamy, big-cat smell that hung in the air didn't help it any. I turned toward Dettlinger, who had come up beside me.

"You have a key to this access door?" I asked him.

"No. There's never been a reason to carry one. Only the cat handlers have them." He shook his head in an awed way. "How'd Kirby get in there? What happened?"

"I wish I knew. Stay put for a minute."

I left him and ran down to the doors in the far side wall. They were locked. Could somebody have had time to shoot Kirby, get out through these doors, then relock them before Dettlinger and I busted in? It didn't seem likely. We'd been inside less than thirty seconds after we'd heard the shot.

I hustled back to the cage where Kirby's body lay. Dettlinger had backed away from it, around in front of the side-wall cages; he looked a little queasy now himself, as if the implications of violent death had finally registered on him. He had a pack of cigarettes in one hand, getting ready to soothe his nerves with some nicotine. But this wasn't the time or the place for a smoke; I yelled at him to put the things away, and he quickly complied.

When I reached him I said, "What's behind these cages? Some sort of rooms back there, aren't there?"

"Yeah. Where the handlers store equipment and meat for the cats. Chutes, too, that lead out to the grottoes."

"How do you get to them?"

He pointed over at the rear side wall. "That door next to the last cage."

"Any other way in or out of those rooms?"

"No. Except through the grottoes, but the cats are out there."

I went around to the interior door he'd indicated. Like all the others, it was locked. I said to Dettlinger, "You have a key to this door?"

He nodded, got it out, and unlocked the door. I told him to keep watch out here, switched on my flashlight, and went on through. The flash beam showed me where the light switches were; I flicked them on and began a cautious search. The door to one of the meat lockers was open, but nobody was hiding inside. Or anywhere else back there.

When I came out I shook my head in answer to Dettlinger's silent question. Then I asked him, "Where's the nearest phone?"

"Out past the grottoes, by the popcorn stand."

"Hustle out there and call the police. And while you're at it, radio Hammond to get over here on the double—"

"No need for that," a new voice said from the main entrance.

"I'm already here."

I glanced in that direction and saw Gene Hammond, the other regular night watchman. You couldn't miss him; he was six-five, weighed in at a good two-fifty, and had a face like the back end of a bus. Disbelief was written on it now as he stared across at Kirby's body.

"Go," I told Dettlinger. "I'll watch things here."

"Right."

He hurried out past Hammond, who was on his way toward where I stood in front of the cage. Hammond said as he came up, "God—what happened?"

"We don't know yet."

"How'd Kirby get in there?"

"We don't know that either." I told him what we did know, which was not much. "When did you last see Kirby?"

"Not since the shift started at nine."

"Any idea why he'd have come in here?"

"No. Unless he heard something and came in to investigate. But he shouldn't have been in this area, should he?"

"Not for another half hour, no."

"Christ, you don't think that he—"

"What?"

"Killed himself," Hammond said.

"It's possible. Was he despondent for some reason?"

"Not that I know about. But it sure looks like suicide. I mean, he's got that gun in his hand, he's all alone in the building, all the doors are locked. What else could it be?"

"Murder," I said.

"How? Where's the person who killed him, then?"

"Got out through one of the grottoes, maybe."

"No way," Hammond said. "Those cats would maul anybody who went out among 'em—and I mean anybody; not even any of the handlers would try a stunt like that. Besides, even if somebody made it down into the moat, how would he scale that twenty-foot back wall to get out of it?"

I didn't say anything.

Hammond said, "And another thing: why would Kirby be locked in this cage if it was murder?"

"Why would he lock himself in to commit suicide?"

He made a bewildered gesture with one of his big hands. "Crazy," he said. "The whole thing's crazy."

He was right. None of it seemed to make any sense at all.

I knew one of the homicide inspectors who responded to

Dettlinger's call. His name was Branislaus and he was a pretty decent guy, so the preliminary questions-and-answers went fast and hassle-free. After which he packed Dettlinger and Hammond and me off to the zoo office while he and the lab crew went to work inside the Lion House.

I poured some hot coffee from my thermos, to help me thaw out a little, and then used one of the phones to get Lawrence Factor out of bed. He was paying my fee and I figured he had a right to know what had happened as soon as possible. He made shocked noises when I told him, asked a couple of pertinent questions, said he'd get out to Fleishhacker right away, and rang off.

An hour crept away. Dettlinger sat at one of the desks with a pad of paper and a pencil and challenged himself in a string of tick-tack-toe games. Hammond chain-smoked cigarettes until the air in there was blue with smoke. I paced around for the most part, now and then stepping out into the chill night to get some fresh air: all that cigarette smoke was playing merry hell with my lungs. None of us had much to say. We were all waiting to see what Branislaus and the rest of the cops turned up.

Factor arrived at one-thirty, looking harried and upset. It was the first time I had ever seen him without a tie and with his usually immaculate Robert Redford hairdo in some disarray. A patrolman accompanied him into the office, and judging from the way Factor glared at him, he had had some difficulty getting past the front gate. When the patrolman left, I gave Factor a detailed account of what had taken place as far as I knew it, with embellishments from Dettlinger. I was just finishing when Branislaus came in.

Branny spent a couple of minutes discussing matters with Factor. Then he said he wanted to talk to the rest of us one at a time, picked me to go first, and herded me into another room.

The first thing he said was, "This is the screwiest shooting case I've come up against in twenty years on the force. What in bloody hell is going on here?"

"I was hoping maybe you could tell me."

"Well, I can't—yet. So far it looks like a suicide, but if that's it, it's a candidate for Ripley. Whoever heard of anybody blowing himself away in a lion cage at the zoo?"

"Any indication he locked himself in there?"

"We found a key next to his body that fits the access door in front."

"Just one loose key?"

"That's right."

"So it could have been dropped in there by somebody else after Kirby was dead and after the door was locked. Or thrown in through the bars from outside."

"Granted."

"And suicides don't usually shoot themselves in the chest," I said.

"Also granted, although it's been known to happen."

"What kind of weapon was he shot with? I couldn't see it too well from outside the cage, the way he was lying."

"Thirty-two Iver Johnson."

"Too soon to tell yet if it was his, I guess."

"Uh-huh. Did he come on the job armed?"

"Not that I know about. The rest of us weren't, or weren't supposed to be."

"Well, we'll know more when we finish running a check on the serial number," Branislaus said. "It was intact, so the thirty-two doesn't figure to be a Saturday night special."

"Was there anything in Kirby's pockets?"

"The usual stuff. And no sign of a suicide note. But you don't think it was suicide anyway, right?"

"No, I don't."

"Why not?"

"No specific reason. It's just that a suicide under those circumstances rings false. And so does a suicide on the heels of the thefts the zoo's been having lately."

"So you figure there's a connection between Kirby's death and the thefts?"

"Don't you?"

"The thought crossed my mind," Branislaus said dryly. "Could be the thief slipped back onto the grounds tonight, something happened before he had a chance to steal something, and he did for Kirby—I'll admit the possibility. But what were the two of them doing in the Lion House? Doesn't add up that Kirby caught the guy in there. Why would the thief enter it in the first place? Not because he was trying to steal a lion or a tiger, that's for sure."

"Maybe Kirby stumbled on him somewhere else, somewhere nearby. Maybe there was a struggle; the thief got the drop on Kirby, then forced him to let both of them into the Lion House with his key."

"Why?"

"To get rid of him where it was private."

"I don't buy it," Branny said. "Why wouldn't he just knock

Kirby over the head and run for it?"

"Well, it could be he's somebody Kirby knew."

"Okay. But the Lion House angle is still too much trouble for him to go through. It would've been much easier to shove the gun into Kirby's belly and shoot him on the spot. Kirby's clothing would have muffled the sound of the shot; it wouldn't have been audible more than fifty feet away."

"I guess you're right," I said.

"But even supposing it happened the way you suggest, it still doesn't add up. You and Dettlinger were inside the Lion House thirty seconds after the shot, by your own testimony. You checked the side entrance doors almost immediately and they were locked; you looked around behind the cages and nobody was there. So how did the alleged killer get out of the building?"

"The only way he could have got out was through one of the grottoes in back."

"Only he couldn't have, according to what both Dettlinger and Hammond say."

I paced over to one of the windows—nervous energy—and looked out at the fog-wrapped construction site for the new monkey exhibit. Then I turned and said, "I don't suppose your men found anything in the way of evidence inside the Lion House?"

"Not so you could tell it with the naked eye."

"Or anywhere else in the vicinity."

"No."

"Any sign of tampering on any of the doors?"

"None. Kirby used his key to get in, evidently."

I came back to where Branislaus was leaning hipshot against somebody's desk. "Listen, Branny," I said, "this whole thing is too screwball. Somebody's playing games here, trying to muddle our thinking—and that means murder."

"Maybe," he said. "Hell, probably. But how was it done? I can't come up with an answer, not even one that's believably far-fetched. Can you?"

"Not yet."

"Does that mean you've got an idea?"

"Not an idea; just a bunch of little pieces looking for a pattern."

He sighed. "Well, if they find it, let me know."

When I went back into the other room I told Dettlinger that he was next on the grill. Factor wanted to talk some more, but I put him off. Hammond was still polluting the air with his damned cigarettes, and I needed another shot of fresh air; I also needed to be alone for a while.

I put my overcoat on and went out and wandered past the cages where the smaller cats were kept, past the big open fields that the giraffes and rhinos called home. The wind was stronger and colder than it had been earlier; heavy gusts swept dust and twigs along the ground, broke the fog up into scudding wisps. I pulled my cap down over my ears to keep them from numbing.

The path led along to the concourse at the rear of the Lion House, where the open cat-grottoes were. Big, portable electric lights had been set up there and around the front so the police could search the area. A couple of patrolmen glanced at me as I approached, but they must have recognized me because neither of them came over to ask what I was doing there.

I went to the low, shrubberied wall that edged the middle cat-grotto. Whatever was in there, lions or tigers, had no doubt been aroused by all the activity; but they were hidden inside the dens at the rear. These grottoes had been newly renovated—lawns, jungly vegetation, small trees, everything to give the cats the illusion of their native habitat. The side walls separating this grotto from the other two were man-made rocks, high and unscalable. The moat below was fifty feet wide, too far for either a big cat or a man to jump; and the near moat wall was sheer and also unscalable from below, just as Hammond and Dettlinger had said.

No way anybody could have got out of the Lion House through the grottoes, I thought. Just no way.

No way it could have been murder then. Unless . . .

I stood there for a couple of minutes, with my mind beginning, finally, to open up. Then I hurried around to the front of the Lion House and looked at the main entrance for a time, remembering things.

And then I knew.

Branislaus was in the zoo office, saying something to Factor, when I came back inside. He glanced over at me as I shut the door.

"Branny," I said, "those little pieces I told you about finally found their pattern."

He straightened. "Oh? Some of it or all of it?"

"All of it, I think."

Factor said, "What's this about?"

"I figured out what happened at the Lion House tonight," I said. "Al Kirby didn't commit suicide; he was murdered. And I can name the man who killed him."

I expected a reaction, but I didn't get one beyond some widened eyes and opened mouths. Nobody said anything and nobody moved much. But you could feel the sudden tension in the room, as thick in its own intangible way as the layers of smoke from Hammond's cigarettes.

"Name him," Branislaus said.

But I didn't, not just yet. A good portion of what I was going to say was guesswork—built on deduction and logic, but still guesswork—and I wanted to choose my words carefully. I took off my cap, unbuttoned my coat, and moved away from the door, over near where Branny was standing.

He said, "Well? Who do you say killed Kirby?"

"The same person who stole the birds and other specimens. And I don't mean a professional animal thief, as Mr. Factor suggested when he hired me. He isn't an outsider at all; and he didn't climb the fence to get onto the grounds."

"No?"

"No. He was already in here on those nights and on this one, because he works here as a night watchman. The man I'm talking about is Sam Dettlinger."

That got some reaction. Hammond said, "I don't believe it," and Factor said, "My God!" Branislaus looked at me, looked at Dettlinger, looked at me again—moving his head like a spectator at a tennis match.

The only one who didn't move was Dettlinger. He sat still at one of the desks, his hands resting easily on its blotter; his face betrayed nothing.

He said, "You're a liar," in a thin, hard voice.

"Am I? You've been working here for some time; you know the animals and which ones are endangered and valuable. It was easy for you to get into the buildings during your rounds: just use your key and walk right in. When you had the specimens, you took them to some prearranged spot along the outside fence and passed them over to an accomplice."

"What accomplice?" Branislaus asked.

"I don't know. You'll get it out of him, Branny, or you'll find out some other way. But that's how he had to have worked it."

"What about the scratches on the locks?" Hammond asked. "The police told us the locks were picked—"

"Red herring," I said. "Just like Dettlinger's claim that he chased a stranger on the grounds the night the rattlers were stolen. Designed to cover up the fact that it was an inside job." I looked back at Branislaus. "Five'll get you ten Dettlinger's had some sort of locksmithing experience. It shouldn't take much digging to find out."

Dettlinger started to get out of his chair, thought better of it, and sat down again. We were all staring at him, but it did not seem to bother him much; his owl eyes were on my neck, and if they'd been hands I would have been dead of strangulation.

Without shifting his gaze, he said to Factor, "I'm going to sue this son of a bitch for slander. I can do that, can't I, Mr. Factor?"

"If what he says isn't true, you can," Factor said.

"Well, it isn't true. It's all a bunch of lies. I never stole anything. And I sure never killed Al Kirby. How the hell could I? I was with this guy, outside the Lion House, when Al died inside."

"No, you weren't," I said.

"What kind of crap is that? I was standing right next to you, we both heard the shot."

"That's right, we both heard the shot. And that's the first thing that put me onto you, Sam. Because we damned well shouldn't have heard it."

"No? Why not?"

"Kirby was shot with a thirty-two-caliber revolver. A thirty-two is a small gun; it doesn't make much of a bang. Branny, you remember saying to me a little while ago that if somebody had shoved that thirty-two into Kirby's middle, you wouldn't have been able to hear the pop more than fifty feet away? Well, that's right. But Dettlinger and I were a lot more than fifty feet from the cage where we found Kirby—twenty yards from the front entrance, thick stucco walls, a ten-foot foyer, and another forty feet or so of floor space to the cage. Yet we not only heard a shot, we heard it loud and clear."

Branislaus said, "So how is that possible?"

I didn't answer him. Instead I looked at Dettlinger and I said, "Do you smoke?"

That got a reaction out of him. The one I wanted: confusion. "What?"

"Do you smoke?"

"What kind of question is that?"

"Gene must have smoked half a pack since we've been in here, but I haven't seen you light up once. In fact, I haven't seen you light up the whole time I've been working here. So answer me, Sam—do you smoke or not?"

"No, I don't smoke. You satisfied?"

"I'm satisfied," I said. "Now suppose you tell me what it was you had in your hand in the Lion House, when I came back from checking the side doors?"

He got it, then—the way I'd trapped him. But he clamped his lips together and sat still.

"What are you getting at?" Branislaus asked me. "What did he have in his hand?"

"At the time I thought it was a pack of cigarettes; that's what it looked like from a distance. I took him to be a little queasy, a delayed reaction to finding the body, and I figured he wanted some nicotine to calm his nerves. But that wasn't it at all; he wasn't queasy, he was scared—because I'd seen what he had in his hand before he could hide it in his pocket."

"So what was it?"

"A tape recorder," I said. "One of those small battery-operated jobs they make nowadays, a white one that fits in the palm of the hand. He'd just picked it up from wherever he'd stashed it earlier, maybe behind one of the bars in the cage. I didn't notice it because it was so small and because my attention was on Kirby's body."

"You're saying the shot you heard was on tape?"

"Yes. My guess is, he recorded it right after he shot Kirby. Fifteen minutes or so earlier."

"Why did he shoot Kirby? And why in the Lion House?"

"Well, he and Kirby could have been in on the thefts together; they could have had some kind of falling-out, and Dettlinger decided to get rid of him. But I don't like that much. As a premeditated murder, it's too elaborate. No, I think the recorder was a spur-of-the-moment idea. I doubt if it belonged to Dettlinger, in fact. Ditto the thirty-two. He's clever, but he's not a planner, he's an improviser."

"If the recorder and the gun weren't his, whose were they? Kirby's?"

I nodded. "The way I see it, Kirby found out about Dettlinger pulling the thefts; saw him do the last one, maybe. Instead of reporting it, he did some brooding and then decided tonight to try a little shakedown. But Dettlinger's bigger and tougher than he was, so he brought the thirty-two along for protection. He also brought the recorder, the idea probably being to tape his conversation with Dettlinger, without Dettlinger's knowledge, for further blackmail leverage.

"He buttonholed Dettlinger in the vicinity of the Lion House and the two of them went inside to talk it over in private. Then something happened. Dettlinger tumbled to the recorder, got rough, Kirby pulled the gun, they struggled for it, Kirby got shot dead—that sort of scenario.

"So then Dettlinger had a corpse on his hands. What was he going to do? He could drag it outside, leave it somewhere, make it look like the mythical fence-climbing thief killed him; but if he did that he'd be running the risk of me or Hammond appearing suddenly and spotting him. Instead he got what he thought was a bright idea: he'd create a big mystery and confuse hell out of everybody, plus give himself a dandy alibi for the apparent time of Kirby's death.

"He took the gun and the recorder to the storage area behind the cages. Erased what was on the tape, used the fast-forward and the timer to run off fifteen minutes of tape, then switched to record and fired a second shot to get the sound of it on tape. I don't know for sure what he fired the bullet into; but I found one of the meat locker doors open when I searched back there, so maybe he used a slab of meat for a target. And then piled a bunch of other slabs on top to hide it until he could get rid of it later on. The police wouldn't be looking for a second bullet, he thought, so there wasn't any reason for them to rummage around in the meat.

"His next moves were to rewind the tape, go back out front, and stash the recorder—turned on, with the volume all the way up. That gave him fifteen minutes. He picked up Kirby's body . . . most of the blood from the wound had been absorbed by the heavy coat Kirby was wearing, which was why there wasn't any blood on the floor and why Dettlinger didn't get any on him. And why I didn't notice, fifteen minutes later, that it was starting to coagulate. He carried the body to the cage, put it inside with the thirty-two in Kirby's hand, relocked the access door—he told me he didn't have a key, but that was a lie—and then threw the key in with the body. But putting Kirby in the cage was his big mistake. By doing that he made the whole thing too bizarre. If he'd left the body where it was, he'd have had a better chance of getting away with it.

"Anyhow, he slipped out of the building without being seen and hid over by the otter pool. He knew I was due there at midnight, because of the schedule we'd set up; and he wanted to be with me when that recorded gunshot went off. Make me the cat's-paw, if you don't mind a little grim humor, for what he figured would be his perfect alibi.

"Later on, when I sent him to report Kirby's death, he disposed of the recorder. He couldn't have gone far from the Lion House to get rid of it; he made the call, and he was back within fifteen minutes. With any luck, his fingerprints will be on the recorder when your men turn it up.

"And if you want any more proof I'll swear in court I didn't smell cordite when we entered the Lion House; all I smelled was the gamy odor of jungle cats. I should have smelled cordite if that thirty-two had just been discharged. But it hadn't, and the cordite smell from the earlier discharges had already faded."

That was a pretty long speech and it left me dry-mouthed. But it had made its impression on the others in the room, Branislaus in particular.

He asked Dettlinger, "Well? You have anything to say for yourself?"

"I never did any of those things he said—none of 'em, you hear?"

"I hear."

"And that's all I'm saying until I see a lawyer."

"You've got one of the best sitting next to you. How about it, Mr. Factor? You want to represent Dettlinger?"

"Pass," Factor said thinly. "This is one case where I'll be glad to plead bias."

Dettlinger was still strangling me with his eyes. I wondered if he would keep on proclaiming his innocence even in the face of stronger evidence than what I'd just presented. Or if he'd crack under pressure, as most amateurs do.

I decided he was the kind who'd crack eventually, and I quit looking at him and at the death in his eyes.

"Well, I was wrong about that much," I said to Kerry the following night. We were sitting in front of a log fire in her Diamond Heights apartment, me with a beer and her with a glass of wine, and I had just finished telling her all about it. "Dettlinger hasn't cracked and it doesn't look as if he's going to. The DA'll have to work for his conviction."

"But you were right about most of it?"

"Pretty much. I probably missed a few details; with Kirby dead, and unless Dettlinger talks, we may never know some of them for sure. But for the most part I think I got it straight."

"My hero," she said, and gave me an adoring look.

She does that sometimes—puts me on like that. I don't understand women, so I don't know why. But it doesn't matter. She has auburn hair and green eyes and a fine body; she's also smarter than I am—she works as an advertising copywriter— and she is stimulating to be around. I love her to pieces, as the boys in the back room used to say.

"The police found the tape recorder," I said. "Took them until late this morning, because Dettlinger was clever about hiding it. He'd buried it in some rushes inside the hippo pen, probably with the idea of digging it up again later on and getting rid of it permanently. There was one clear print on the fast-forward button—Dettlinger's."

"Did they also find the second bullet he fired?"

"Yep. Where I guessed it was: in one of the slabs of fresh meat in the open storage locker."

"And did Dettlinger have locksmithing experience?"

"Uh-huh. He worked for a locksmith for a year in his mid-twenties. The case against him, even without a confession, is pretty solid."

"What about his accomplice?"

"Branislaus thinks he's got a line on the guy," I said. "From some things he found in Dettlinger's apartment. Man named Gerber—got a record of animal poaching and theft. I talked to Larry Factor this afternoon and he's heard of Gerber. The way he figures it, Dettlinger and Gerber had a deal for the specimens they stole with some collectors in Florida. That seems to be Gerber's usual pattern of operation anyway."

"I hope they get him too," Kerry said. "I don't like the idea of stealing birds and animals out of the zoo. It's ... obscene, somehow."

"So is murder."

We didn't say anything for a time, looking into the fire, working on our drinks.

"You know," I said finally, "I have a lot of empathy for animals myself. Take gorillas, for instance."

"Why gorillas?"

"Because of their mating habits."

"What are their mating habits?"

I had no idea, but I made up something interesting. Then I gave her a practical demonstration.

No gorilla ever had it so good.

SKELETON RATTLE YOUR MOULDY LEG

He was one of the oddest people I had ever met. Sixty years old, under five and a half feet tall, slight, with great bony knobs for elbows and knees, with bat-winged ears and a bent nose and eyes that danced left and right, left and right, and had sparkly little lights in them. He wore baggy clothes—sweaters and jeans, mostly, crusted with patches—and a baseball cap turned around so that the bill poked out from the back of his head. In his back pocket he carried a whisk broom, and if he knew you, or wanted to, he would come up and say, "I know you—you've got a speck on your coat," and he would brush it off with the broom. Then he would talk, or maybe recite or even sing a little: a gnarled old harlequin cast up from another age.

These things were odd enough, but the oddest of all was his obsession with skeletons.

His name was Nick Damiano and he lived in the building adjacent to the one where Eberhardt and I had our new office—lived in a little room in the basement. Worked there, too, as a janitor and general handyman; the place was a small residence hotel for senior citizens, mostly male, called the Medford. So it didn't take long for our paths to cross. A week or so after Eb and I moved in, I was coming up the street one morning and Nick popped out of the alley that separated our two buildings.

He said, "I know you—you've got a speck on your coat," and out came the whisk broom. Industriously he brushed away the imaginary speck. Then he grinned and said, "Skeleton rattle your mouldy leg."

"Huh?"

"That's poetry," he said. "From archy and mehitabel. You know archy and mehitabel?"

"No," I said, "I don't."

"They're lower case; they don't have capitals like we do. Archy's a cockroach and mehitabel's a cat and they were both poets in another life. A fellow named don marquis created them a long time ago. He's lower case too."

"Uh . . . I see."

"One time mehitabel went to Paris," he said, "and took up with a tom cat named francy, who was once the poet Francois Villon, and they used to go to the catacombs late at night. They'd dance and sing among those old bones."

And he began to recite:

"prince if you pipe and plead and beg
you may yet be crowned with a grisly kiss
skeleton rattle your mouldy leg
all men's lovers come to this"

That was my first meeting with Nick Damiano; there were others over the next four months, none of which lasted more than five minutes. Skeletons came into all of them, in one way or another. Once he sang half a dozen verses of the old spiritual, "Dry Bones," in a pretty good baritone. Another time he quoted, "'The Knight's bones are dust/And his good sword rust—/His Soul is with the saints, I trust.'" Later I looked it up and it was a rhyme from an obscure work by Coleridge. On the other days he made sly little comments: "Why, hello there, I knew it was you coming—I heard your bones chattering and clacking all the way down the street." And, "Cleaned out your closet lately? Might be skeletons hiding in there." And, "Sure is hot today. Sure would be fine to take off our skins and just sit around in our bones."

I asked one of the Medford's other residents, a guy named Irv Feinberg, why Nick seemed to have such a passion for skeletons. Feinberg didn't know; nobody knew, he said, because Nick wouldn't discuss it. He told me that Nick even owned a genuine skeleton, liberated from some medical facility, and that he kept it wired to the wall of his room and burned candles in its skull.

A screwball, this Nick Damiano—sure. But he did his work and did it well, and he was always cheerful and friendly, and he never gave anybody any trouble. Harmless old Nick. A happy whack, marching to the rhythm of dry old bones chattering and clacking together inside his head. Everybody in the neighborhood found him amusing, including me: San Francisco has always been proud of its characters, its kooks. Yeah, everyone liked old Nick.

Except that somebody didn't like him, after all.

Somebody took hold of a blunt instrument one raw November night, in that little basement room with the skeleton leering on from the wall, and beat Nick Damiano to death.

It was four days after the murder that Irv Feinberg came to see me. He was a rotund little guy in his sixties, very energetic, a retired plumber who wore loud sports coats and spent most of his time doping out the races at Golden Gate Fields and a variety of other tracks. He had known Nick as well as anyone could, had called him his friend.

I was alone in the office when Feinberg walked in; Eberhardt was down at the Hall of Justice, trying to coerce some of his former cop pals into giving him background information on a missing-person case he was working. Feinberg said by way of greeting, "Nice office you got here," which was a lie, and came over and plopped himself into one of the clients' chairs. "You busy? Or you got a few minutes we can talk?"

"What can I do for you, Mr. Feinberg?"

"The cops have quit on Nick's murder," he said. "They don't come around anymore, they don't talk to anybody in the hotel. I called down to the Hall of Justice, I wanted to know what's happening; I got the big runaround."

"The police don't quit a homicide investigation—"

"The hell they don't. A guy like Nick Damiano? It's no big deal to them. They figure it was somebody looking for easy money, a drug addict from over in the Tenderloin. On account of Dan Cady, he's the night clerk, found the door to the alley unlocked just after he found Nick's body."

"That sounds like a reasonable theory," I said.

"Reasonable, hell. The door wasn't tampered with or anything; it was just unlocked. So how'd the drug addict get in? Nick wouldn't have left that door unlocked; he was real careful about things like that. And he wouldn't have let a stranger in, not at that time of night."

"Well, maybe the assailant came in through the front entrance and went out through the alley door..."

"No way," Feinberg said. "Front door's on a night security lock from eight o'clock on; you got to buzz the desk from outside and Dan Cady'll come see who you are. If he don't know you, you don't get in."

"All right, maybe the assailant wasn't a stranger. Maybe he's somebody Nick knew."

"Sure, that's what I think. But not somebody outside the hotel. Nick never let people in at night, not anybody, not even somebody lives there; you had to go around to the front door and buzz the desk. Besides, he didn't have any outside friends that came to see him. He didn't go out himself either. He had to tend to the heat, for one thing, do other chores, so he stayed put. I know all that because I spent plenty of evenings with him, shooting craps for pennies... Nick liked to shoot craps, he called it 'rolling dem bones.'"

Skeletons, I thought. I said, "What do you think then, Mr. Feinberg? That somebody from the hotel killed Nick?"

"That's what I think," he said. "I don't like it, most of those people are my friends, but that's how it looks to me."

"You have anybody specific in mind?"

"No. Whoever it was, he was in there arguing with Nick before he killed him."

"Oh? How do you know that?"

"George Weaver heard them. He's our newest tenant, George is, moved in three weeks ago. Used to be a bricklayer in Chicago, came out here to be with his daughter when he retired, only she had a heart attack and died last month. His other daughter died young and his wife died of cancer; now he's all alone." Feinberg shook his head. "It's a hell of a thing to be old and alone."

I agreed that it must be.

"Anyhow, George was in the basement getting something out of his storage bin and he heard the argument. Told Charley Slattery a while later that it didn't sound violent or he'd have gone over and banged on Nick's door. As it was, he just went back upstairs."

"Who's Charley Slattery?"

"Charley lives at the Medford and works over at Monahan's Gym on Turk Street. Used to be a small-time fighter; now he just hangs around doing odd jobs. Not too bright, but he's okay."

"Weaver didn't recognize the other voice in the argument?"

"No. Couldn't make out what it was all about either."

"What time was that?"

"Few minutes before eleven, George says."

"Did anyone else overhear the argument?"

"Nobody else around at the time."

"When was the last anybody saw Nick alive?"

"Eight o'clock. Nick came up to the lobby to fix one of the lamps wasn't working. Dan Cady talked to him a while when he was done."

"Cady found Nick's body around two a.m., wasn't it?"

"Two-fifteen."

"How did he happen to find it? That wasn't in the papers."

"Well, the furnace was still on. Nick always shuts it off by midnight or it gets to be too hot upstairs. So Dan went down to find out why, and there was Nick lying on the floor of his room with his head all beat in."

"What kind of guy is Cady?"

"Quiet, keeps to himself, spends most of his free time reading library books. He was a college history teacher once, up in Oregon. But he got in some kind of trouble with a woman—

this was back in the forties, teachers had to watch their morals—and the college fired him and he couldn't get another teaching job. He fell into the booze for a lot of years afterward. But he's all right now. Belongs to AA."

I was silent for a time. Then I asked, "The police didn't find anything that made them suspect one of the other residents?"

"No, but that don't mean much." Feinberg made a disgusted noise through his nose. "Cops. They don't even know what it was bashed in Nick's skull, what kind of weapon. Couldn't find it anywhere. They figure the killer took it away through that unlocked alley door and got rid of it. I figure the killer unlocked the door to make it look like an outside job, then went upstairs and hid the weapon somewhere till next day."

"Let's suppose you're right. Who might have a motive to've killed Nick?"

"Well . . . nobody, far as I know. But somebody's got one, you can bet on that."

"Did Nick get along with everybody at the Medford?"

"Sure," Feinberg said. Then he frowned a little and said, "Except Wesley Thane, I guess. But I can't see Wes beating anybody's head in. He pretends to be tough but he's a wimp. And a goddamn snob."

"Oh?"

"He's an actor. Little theater stuff these days, but once he was a bit player down in Hollywood, made a lot of crappy B movies where he was one of the minor bad guys. Hear him tell it, he was Clark Gable's best friend back in the forties. A windbag who thinks he's better than the rest of us. He treated Nick like a freak."

"Was there ever any trouble between them?"

"Well, he hit Nick once, just after he moved in five years ago and Nick tried to brush off his coat. I was there and I saw it."

"Hit him with what?"

"His hand. A kind of slap. Nick shied away from him after that."

"How about recent trouble?"

"Not that I know about. I didn't even have to noodge him into kicking in twenty bucks to the fund. But hell, everybody in the building kicked in something except old lady Howsam; she's bedridden and can barely make ends meet on her pension, so I didn't even ask her."

I said, "Fund?"

Feinberg reached inside his gaudy sport jacket and produced a bulky envelope. He put the envelope on my desk and pushed it toward me with the tips of his fingers. "There's two hundred bucks in there," he said. "What'll that hire you for? Three-four days?"

I stared at him. "Wait a minute, Mr. Feinberg. Hire me to do what?"

"Find out who killed Nick. What do you think we been talking about here?"

"I thought it was only talk you came for. A private detective can't investigate a homicide in this city, not without police permission . . ."

"So get permission," Feinberg said. "I told you, the cops have quit on it. Why should they try to keep you from investigating?"

"Even if I did get permission, I doubt if there's much I could do that the police haven't already—"

"Listen, don't go modest on me. You're a good detective, I see your name in the papers all the time. I got confidence in you; we all do. Except maybe the guy who killed Nick."

There was no arguing him out of it; his mind was made up, and he'd convinced the others in the Medford to go along with him. So I quit trying finally and said all right, I would call the Hall of Justice and see if I could get clearance to conduct a private investigation. And if I could, then I'd come over later and see him and take a look around and start talking to people. That satisfied him. But when I pushed the envelope back across the desk, he wouldn't take it.

"No," he said, "that's yours, you just go ahead and earn it." And he was on his feet and gone before I could do anything more than make a verbal protest.

I put the money away in the lock-box in my desk and telephoned the Hall. Eberhardt was still hanging around, talking to one of his old cronies in General Works, and I told him about Feinberg and what he wanted. Eb said he'd talk to the homicide inspector in charge of the Nick Damiano case and see what was what; he didn't seem to think there'd be any problem getting clearance. There were problems, he said, only when private eyes tried to horn in on VIP cases, the kind that got heavy media attention.

He used to be a homicide lieutenant so he knew what he was talking about. When he called back a half hour later he said, "You got your clearance. Feinberg had it pegged: the case is already in the Inactive File for lack of leads and evidence. I'll see if I can finagle a copy of the report for you."

Some case, I thought as I hung up. In a way it was ghoulish, like poking around in a fresh grave. And wasn't that an appropriate image; I could almost hear Nick's sly laughter.

Skeleton rattle your mouldy leg.

The basement of the Medford Hotel was dimly lighted and too warm: a big, old-fashioned oil furnace rattled and roared in one corner, giving off shimmers of heat. Much of the floor space was taken up with fifty-gallon trash receptacles, some full and some empty and one each under a pair of garbage chutes from the upper floors. Over against the far wall, and throughout a small connecting room beyond, were rows of narrow storage cubicles made out of wood and heavy wire, with padlocks on each of the doors.

Nick's room was at the rear, opposite the furnace and alongside the room that housed the hot-water heaters. But Feinberg didn't take me there directly; he said something I didn't catch, mopping his face with a big green handkerchief, and detoured over to the furnace and fiddled with the controls and got it shut down.

"Damn thing," he said. "Owner's too cheap to replace it with a modern unit that runs off a thermostat. Now we got some young snot he hired to take Nick's job, don't live here and don't stick around all day and leaves the furnace turned on too long. It's like a goddamn sauna in here."

There had been a police seal on the door to Nick's room, but it had been officially removed. Feinberg had the key; he was a sort of building mayor, by virtue of seniority—he'd lived at the Medford for more than fifteen years—and he had got custody of the key from the owner. He opened the lock, swung the thick metal door open, and clicked on the lights.

The first thing I saw was the skeleton. It hung from several pieces of shiny wire on the wall opposite the door, and it was a grisly damned thing streaked with blobs of red and green and orange candle wax. The top of the skull had been cut off and a fat red candle jutted up from the hollow inside, like some sort of ugly growth. Melted wax rimmed and dribbled from the grinning mouth, giving it a bloody look.

"Cute, ain't it?" Feinberg said. "Nick and his frigging skeletons."

I moved inside. It was just a single room with a bathroom alcove, not more than fifteen feet square. Cluttered, but in a way that suggested everything had been assigned a place. Army cot against one wall, a small table, two chairs, one of those little waist-high refrigerators with a hot plate on top, a standing cupboard full of pots and dishes; stacks of newspapers and magazines, some well-used books—volumes of poetry, an anatomical text, two popular histories about ghouls and graverobbers, a dozen novels with either "skeleton" or "bones" in the title; a broken wooden wagon, a Victrola without its eartrumpet amplifier, an ancient Olivetti typewriter, a collection of oddball tools, a scabrous iron-bound steamer trunk, an open box full of assorted pairs of dice, and a lot of other stuff, most of which appeared to be junk.

A thick fiber mat covered the floor. On it, next to the table, was the chalked outline of Nick's body and some dark stains. My stomach kicked a little when I looked at the stains; I had seen corpses of bludgeon victims and I knew what those stains looked like when they were fresh. I went around the table on the other side and took a closer look at the wax-caked skeleton. Feinberg tagged along at my heels.

"Nick used to talk to that thing," he said. "Ask it questions, how it was feeling, could he get it anything to eat or drink. Gave me the willies at first. He even put his arm around it once and kissed it, I swear to God. I can still see him do it."

"He get it from a medical facility?"

"One that was part of some small college he worked at before he came to San Francisco. He mentioned that once."

"Did he say where the college was?"

"No."

"Where did Nick come from? Around here?"

Feinberg shook his head. "Midwest somewhere, that's all I could get out of him."

"How long had he been in San Francisco?"

"Ten years. Worked here the last eight; before that, he helped out at a big apartment house over on Geary."

"Why did he come to the city? He have relatives here or what?"

"No, no relatives, he was all alone. Just him and his bones—he said that once."

I poked around among the clutter of things in the room, but if there had been anything here relevant to the murder, the police would have found it and probably removed it and it would be mentioned in their report. So would anything found among Nick's effects that determined his background. Eberhardt would have a copy of the report for me to look at later; when he said he'd try to do something he usually did it.

When I finished with the room, we went out and Feinberg locked the door. We took the elevator up to the lobby. It was dim up there, too, and a little depressing. There was a lot of plaster and wood and imitation marble, and some antique furniture and dusty potted plants, and it smelled of dust and faintly of decay. A sense of age permeated the place: you felt it and you smelled it and you saw it in the surroundings, in the half-dozen men and one woman sitting on the sagging chairs, reading or staring out through the windows at O'Farrell Street, people with nothing to do and nobody to do it with, waiting like doomed prisoners for the sentence of death to be carried out. Dry witherings and an aura of hopelessness—that was the impression I would carry away with me and that would linger in my mind.

I thought: I'm fifty-four, another few years and I could be stuck in here too. But that wouldn't happen. I had work I could do pretty much to the end and I had Kerry and I had some money in the bank and a collection of six thousand pulp magazines that were worth plenty on the collectors' market. No, this kind of place wouldn't happen to me. In a society that ignored and showed little respect for its elderly, I was one of the lucky ones.

Feinberg led me to the desk and introduced me to the day clerk, a sixtyish barrel of a man named Bert Norris. If there was anything he could do to help, Norris said, he'd be glad to oblige; he sounded eager, as if nobody had needed his help in a long time. The fact that Feinberg had primed everyone here about my investigation made things easier in one respect and more difficult in another. If the person who had killed Nick Damiano was a resident of the Medford, I was not likely to catch him off guard.

When Norris moved away to answer a switchboard call, Feinberg asked me, "Who're you planning to talk to now?"

"Whoever's available," I said.

"Dan Cady? He lives here—two-eighteen. Goes to the library every morning after he gets off, but he's always back by noon. You can probably catch him before he turns in."

"All right, good."

"You want me to come along?"

"That's not necessary, Mr. Feinberg."

"Yeah, I get it. I used to hate that kind of thing too when I was out on a plumbing job."

"What kind of thing?"

"Somebody hanging over my shoulder, watching me work. Who needs crap like that? You want me, I'll be in my room with the scratch sheets for today's races."

Dan Cady was a thin, sandy-haired man in his mid-sixties, with cheeks and nose road-mapped by ruptured blood vessels—the badge of the alcoholic, practicing or reformed. He wore thick glasses, and behind them his eyes had a strained, tired look, as if from too much reading.

"Well, I'll be glad to talk to you," he said, "but I'm afraid I'm not very clear-headed right now. I was just getting ready for bed."

"I won't take up much of your time, Mr. Cady."

He let me in. His room was small and strewn with library books, most of which appeared to deal with American history; a couple of big maps, an old one of the United States and an even older parchment map of Asia, adorned the walls, and there were plaster busts of historical figures I didn't recognize, and a huge globe on a wooden stand. There was only one chair; he let me have that and perched himself on the bed.

I asked him about Sunday night, and his account of how he'd come to find Nick Damiano's body coincided with what Feinberg had told me. "It was a frightening experience," he said. "I'd never seen anyone dead by violence before. His head . . . well, it was awful."

"Were there signs of a struggle in the room?"

"Yes, some things were knocked about. But I'd say it was a brief struggle—there wasn't much damage."

"Is there anything unusual you noticed? Something that should have been there but wasn't, for instance?"

"No. I was too shaken to notice anything like that."

"Was Nick's door open when you got there?"

"Wide open."

"How about the door to the alley?"

"No. Closed."

"How did you happen to check it, then?"

"Well, I'm not sure," Cady said. He seemed faintly embarrassed; his eyes didn't quite meet mine. "I was stunned and frightened; it occurred to me that the murderer might still be around somewhere. I took a quick look around the basement and then opened the alley door and looked out there . . . I wasn't thinking very clearly. It was only when I shut the door again that I realized it had been unlocked."

"Did you see or hear anything inside or out?"

"Nothing. I left the door unlocked and went back to the lobby to call the police."

"When you saw Nick earlier that night, Mr. Cady, how did he seem to you?"

"Seem? Well, he was cheerful; he usually was. He said he'd have come up sooner to fix the lamp but his old bones wouldn't allow it. That was the way he talked . . ."

"Yes, I know. Do you have any idea who he might have argued with that night, who might have killed him?"

"None," Cady said. "He was such a gentle soul . . . I still can't believe a thing like that could happen to him."

Down in the lobby again, I asked Bert Norris if Wesley Thane, George Weaver, and Charley Slattery were on the premises. Thane was, he said, Room 315; Slattery was at Monahan's Gym and would be until six o'clock. He started to tell me that Weaver was out, but then his eyes shifted past me and he said, "No, there he is now just coming in."

I turned. A heavyset, stooped man of about seventy had just entered from the street, walking with the aid of a hickory cane; but he seemed to get along pretty good. He was carrying a grocery sack in his free hand and a folded newspaper under his arm.

I intercepted him halfway to the elevator and told him who I was. He looked me over for about ten seconds, out of alert blue eyes that had gone a little rheumy, before he said, "Irv Feinberg said you'd be around." His voice was surprisingly strong and clear for a man his age. "But I can't help you much. Don't know much."

"Should we talk down here or in your room?"

"Down here's all right with me."

We crossed to a deserted corner of the lobby and took chairs in front of a fireplace that had been boarded up and painted over. Weaver got a stubby little pipe out of his coat pocket and began to load up.

I said, "About Sunday night, Mr. Weaver. I understand you went down to the basement to get something out of your storage locker . . ."

"My old radio," he said. "New one I bought a while back quit playing and I like to listen to the eleven o'clock news before I go to sleep. When I got down there I heard Damiano and some fella arguing."

"Just Nick and one other man?"

"Sounded that way."

"Was the voice familiar to you?"

"Didn't sound familiar. But I couldn't hear it too well; I was over by the lockers. Couldn't make out what they were saying either."

"How long were you in the basement?"

"Three or four minutes, is all."

"Did the argument get louder, more violent, while you were there?"

"Didn't seem to. No." He struck a kitchen match and put the flame to the bowl of his pipe. "If it had, I guess I'd've gone over and banged on the door, announced myself. I'm as curious as the next man when it comes to that."

"But as it was you went straight back to your room?"

"That's right. Ran into Charley Slattery when I got out of the elevator; his room's just down from mine on the third floor."

"What was his reaction when you told him what you'd heard?"

"Didn't seem to worry him much," Weaver said. "So I figured it was nothing for me to worry about either."

"Slattery didn't happen to go down to the basement himself, did he?"

"Never said anything about it if he did."

I don't know what I expected Wesley Thane to be like—the Raymond Massey or John Carradine type, maybe, something along those shabbily aristocratic and vaguely sinister lines—but the man who opened the door to Room 315 looked about as much like an actor as I do. He was a smallish guy in his late sixties, he was bald, and he had a nondescript face except for mean little eyes under thick black brows that had no doubt contributed to his career as a B-movie villain. He looked somewhat familiar, but even though I like old movies and watch them whenever I can, I couldn't have named a single film he had appeared in.

He said, "Yes? What is it?" in a gravelly, staccato voice. That was familiar, too, but again I couldn't place it in any particular context.

I identified myself and asked if I could talk to him about Nick Damiano. "That cretin," he said, and for a moment I thought he was going to shut the door in my face. But then he said, "Oh, all right, come in. If I don't talk to you, you'll probably think I had something to do with the poor fool's murder."

He turned and moved off into the room, leaving me to shut the door. The room was larger than Dan Cady's and jammed with stage and screen memorabilia: framed photographs, playbills, film posters, blown-up black-and-white stills; and a variety of salvaged props, among them the plumed helmet off a suit of armor and a Napoleonic uniform displayed on a dressmaker's dummy.

Thane stopped near a lumpy-looking couch and did a theatrical about-face. The scowl he wore had a practiced look, and it occurred to me that under it he might be enjoying himself. "Well?" he said.

I said, "You didn't like Nick Damiano, did you, Mr. Thane," making it a statement instead of a question.

"No, I didn't like him. And no, I didn't kill him, if that's your next question."

"Why didn't you like him?"

"He was a cretin. A gibbering moron. All that nonsense about skeletons—he ought to have been locked up long ago."

"You have any idea who did kill him?"

"No. The police seem to think it was a drug addict."

"That's one theory," I said. "Irv Feinberg has another: he thinks the killer is a resident of this hotel."

"I know what Irv Feinberg thinks. He's a damned meddler who doesn't know when to keep his mouth shut."

"You don't agree with him then?"

"I don't care one way or another."

Thane sat down and crossed his legs and adopted a sufferer's pose; now he was playing the martyr. I grinned at him, because it was something he wasn't expecting, and went to look at some of the stuff on the walls. One of the black-and-white stills depicted Thane in Western garb, with a smoking six-gun in his hand. The largest of the photographs was of Clark Gable, with an ink inscription that read, "For my good friend, Wes."

Behind me he said impatiently, "I'm waiting."

I let him wait a while longer. Then I moved back near the couch and grinned at him again and said, "Did you see Nick Damiano the night he was murdered?"

"I did not."

"Talk to him at all that day?"

"No."

"When was the last you had trouble with him?"

"Trouble? What do you mean, trouble?"

"Irv Feinberg told me you hit Nick once, when he tried to brush off your coat."

"My God," Thane said, "that was years ago. And it was only a slap. I had no problems with him after that. He avoided me and I ignored him; we spoke only when necessary." He paused, and his eyes got bright with something that might have been malice. "If you're looking for someone who had trouble with

Damiano recently, talk to Charley Slattery."

"What kind of trouble did Slattery have with Nick?"

"Ask him. It's none of my business."

"Why did you bring it up then?"

He didn't say anything. His eyes were still bright.

"All right, I'll ask Slattery," I said. "Tell me, what did you think when you heard about Nick? Were you pleased?"

"Of course not. I was shocked. I've played many violent roles in my career, but violence in real life always shocks me."

"The shock must have worn off pretty fast. You told me a couple of minutes ago you don't care who killed him."

"Why should I, as long as no one else is harmed?"

"So why did you kick in the twenty dollars?"

"What?"

"Feinberg's fund to hire me. Why did you contribute?"

"If I hadn't it would have made me look suspicious to the others. I have to live with these people; I don't need that sort of stigma." He gave me a smug look. "And if you repeat that to anyone, I'll deny it."

"Must be tough on you," I said.

"I beg your pardon?"

"Having to live in a place like this, with a bunch of broken-down old nobodies who don't have your intelligence or compassion or great professional skill."

That got to him; he winced, and for a moment the actor's mask slipped and I had a glimpse of the real Wesley Thane—a defeated old man with faded dreams of glory, a never-was with a small and mediocre talent, clinging to the tattered fringes of a business that couldn't care less. Then he got the mask in place again and said with genuine anger, "Get out of here. I don't have to take abuse from a cheap gumshoe."

"You're dating yourself, Mr. Thane; nobody uses the word 'gumshoe' any more. It's forties B-movie dialogue."

He bounced up off the couch, pinch-faced and glaring. "Get out, I said. Get out!"

I got out. And I was on my way to the elevator when I realized why Thane hadn't liked Nick Damiano. It was because Nick had taken attention away from him—upstaged him. Thane was an actor, but there wasn't any act he could put on more compelling than the real-life performance of Nick and his skeletons.

Monahan's Gym was one of those tough, men-only places that catered to ex-pugs and oldtimers in the fight game, the kind of place you used to see a lot of in the forties and fifties but that have become an anachronism in this day of chic health clubs, fancy spas, and dwindling interest in the art of prizefighting. It smelled of sweat and steam and old leather, and it resonated with the grunts of weightlifters, the smack and thud of gloves against leather bags, the profane talk of men at liberty from a more or less polite society.

I found Charley Slattery in the locker room, working there as an attendant. He was a short, beefy guy, probably a light-heavyweight in his boxing days, gone to fat around the middle in his old age; white-haired, with a face as seamed and time-eroded as a chunk of desert sandstone. One of his eyes had a glassy look; his nose and mouth were lumpy with scar tissue. A game fighter in his day, I thought, but not a very good one. A guy who had never quite learned how to cover up against the big punches, the hammerblows that put you down and out.

"Sure, I been expectin' you," he said when I told him who I was. "Irv Feinberg, he said you'd be around. You findin' out anything the cops dint?"

"It's too soon to tell, Mr. Slattery."

"Charley," he said, "I hate that Mr. Slattery crap."

"All right, Charley."

"Well, I wish I could tell you somethin' would help you, but I can't think of nothin'. I dint even see Nick for two-three days before he was murdered."

"Any idea who might have killed him?"

"Well, some punk off the street, I guess. Guy Nick was arguin' with that night—George Weaver, he told you about that, dint he? What he heard?"

"Yes. He also said he met you upstairs just afterward."

Slattery nodded. "I was headin' down the lobby for a Coke, they got a machine down there, and George, he come out of the elevator with his cane and this little radio unner his arm. He looked kind of funny and I ast him what's the matter and that's when he told me about the argument."

"What did you do then?"

"What'd I do? Went down to get my Coke."

"You didn't go to the basement?"

"Nah, damn it. George, he said it was just a argument Nick was havin' with somebody. I never figured it was nothin', you know, violent. If I had—Yeah, Eddie? You need somethin'?"

A muscular black man in his mid-thirties, naked except for a pair of silver-blue boxing trunks, had come up. He said, "Towel and some soap, Charley. No soap in the showers again."

"Goddamn. I catch the guy keeps swipin' it," Slattery said, "I'll kick his ass." He went and got a clean towel and a bar of soap, and the black man moved off with them to a back row of lockers. Slattery watched him go; then he said to me, "That's Eddie Jordan. Pretty fair welterweight once, but he never trained right, never had the right manager. He could of been good, that boy, if—" He broke off, frowning. "I shouldn't ought to call him that, I guess. 'Boy.' Blacks, they don't like to be called that nowadays."

"No," I said, "they don't."

"But I don't mean nothin' by it I mean, we always called 'em 'boy'. It was just somethin' we called 'em. It wasn't nothin' personal, you know?"

I knew, all right, but it was not something I wanted to or ever could explain to Charley Slattery. Race relations, the whole question of race, was too complex an issue. In his simple world, "boy" and all the other pejoratives and epithets were just words, meaningless without a couple of centuries of hatred and malice behind them, and it really wasn't anything personal

"Let's get back to Nick," I said. "You liked him, didn't you, Charley?"

"Sure I did. He was goofy, him and his skeletons, but he worked hard and he never bothered nobody."

"I had a talk with Wesley Thane a while ago. He told me you had some trouble with Nick not long ago."

Slattery's eroded face arranged itself into a scowl. "That damn actor, he don't know what he's talkin' about. Why don't he mind his own damn business? I never had no trouble with Nick."

"Not even a little? A disagreement of some kind, maybe?"

He hesitated. Then he shrugged and said, "Well, yeah, I guess we had that. A kind of disagreement."

"When was this?"

"I dunno. Couple of weeks ago."

"What was it about?"

"Garbage," Slattery said.

"Garbage?"

"Nick, he dint like nobody touchin' the cans in the basement. But hell, I was in there one night and the cans unner the chutes was full, so I switched 'em for empties. Well, Nick come around and yelled at me, and I wasn't feelin' too good so I yelled back at him. Next thing, I got sore and kicked over one of the cans and spilled out some garbage. Dan Cady, he heard the noise clear up in the lobby and come down and that son of a bitch Wes

Thane was with him. Dan, he got Nick and me calmed down. That's all there was to it."

"How were things between you and Nick after that?"

"Okay. He forgot it and so did I. It dint mean nothin'. Just one of them things."

"Did Nick have problems with any other people in the hotel?" I asked.

"Nah. I don't think so."

"What about Wes Thane? He admitted he and Nick didn't get along very well."

"I never heard about them havin' no fight or anythin' like that."

"How about trouble Nick might have had with somebody outside the Medford?"

"Nah," Slattery said. "Nick, he got along with everybody, you know? Everybody liked Nick, even if he was goofy."

Yeah, I thought, everybody liked Nick, even if he was goofy. Then why is he dead?

I went back to the Medford and talked with three more residents, none of whom could offer any new information or any possible answers to that question of motive. It was almost five when I gave it up for the day and went next door to the office.

Eberhardt was there, but I didn't see him at first because he was on his hands and knees behind his desk. He poked his head up as I came inside and shut the door.

"Fine thing," I said, "you down on your knees like that. What if I'd been a prospective client?"

"So? I wouldn't let somebody like you hire me."

"What're you doing down there anyway?"

"I was cleaning my pipe and I dropped the damn bit." He disappeared again for a few seconds, muttered, "Here it is," reappeared, and hoisted himself to his feet.

There were pipe ashes all over the front of his tie and his white shirt; he'd even managed to get a smear of ash across his jowly chin. He was something of a slob, Eberhardt was, which gave us one of several common bonds: I was something of a slob myself. We had been friends for more than thirty years, and we'd been through some hard times together—some very hard times in the recent past. I hadn't been sure at first that taking him in as a partner after his retirement was a good idea, for a variety of reasons; but it had worked out so far.

He sat down and began brushing pipe dottle off his desk—he must have dropped a bowlful on it as well as on himself. He said as I hung up my coat, "How goes the Nick Damiano investigation?"

"Not too good. Did you manage to get a copy of the police report?"

"On your desk. But I don't think it'll tell you much."

The report was in an unmarked manila envelope; I read it standing up. Eberhardt was right that it didn't enlighten me much. Nick Damiano had been struck on the head at least three times by a heavy blunt instrument and had died of a brain hemorrhage, probably within seconds of the first blow. The wounds were "consistent with" a length of three-quarter-inch steel pipe, but the weapon hadn't been positively identified because no trace of it had been found. As for Nick's background, nothing had been found there either. No items of personal history among his effects, no hint of relatives or even of his city of origin. They'd run a check on his fingerprints through the FBI computer, with negative results: he had never been arrested on a felony charge, never been in military service or applied for a civil service job, never been fingerprinted at all.

When I put the report down Eberhardt said, "Anything?"

"Doesn't look like it." I sat in my chair and looked out the window for a time, at heavy rainclouds massing above the Federal Building down the hill. "There's just nothing to go on in this thing, Eb—no real leads or suspects, no apparent motive."

"So maybe it's random. A street-killing, drug-related, like the report says."

"Maybe."

"You don't think so?"

"Our client doesn't think so."

"You want to talk over the details?"

"Sure. But let's do it over a couple of beers and some food."

"I thought you were on a diet."

"I am. Whenever Kerry's around. But she's working late tonight—new ad campaign she's writing. A couple of beers won't hurt me. And we'll have something non-fattening to eat."

"Sure we will," Eberhardt said.

We went to an Italian place out on Clement and had four beers apiece and plates of fettucine alfredo and half a loaf of garlic bread. But the talking we did got us nowhere. If one of the residents of the Medford had killed Nick Damiano, what was the damn motive? A broken-down old actor's petulant jealousy? A mindless dispute over garbage cans? Just what was the argument all about that George Weaver had overheard?

Eberhardt and I split up early and I drove home to my flat in

Pacific Heights. The place had a lonely feel; after spending most of the day in and around the Medford, I needed something to cheer me up—I needed Kerry. I thought about calling her at Bates and Carpenter, her ad agency, but she didn't like to be disturbed while she was working. And she'd said she expected to be there most of the evening.

I settled instead for cuddling up to my collection of pulp magazines—browsing here and there, finding something to read. On nights like this the pulps weren't much of a substitute for human companionship in general and Kerry in particular, but at least they kept my mind occupied. I found a 1943 issue of *Dime Detective* that looked interesting, took it into the bathtub, and lingered there reading until I got drowsy. Then I went to bed, went right to sleep for a change—

—and woke up at three a.m. by the luminous dial of the nightstand clock, because the clouds had finally opened up and unleashed a wailing torrent of wind-blown rain; the sound of it on the roof and on the rainspouts outside the window was loud enough to wake up a deaf man. I lay there half groggy, listening to the storm and thinking about how the weather had gone all screwy lately.

And then all of a sudden I was thinking about something else, and I wasn't groggy anymore. I sat up in bed, wide awake. And inside of five minutes, without much effort now that I had been primed, I knew what it was the police had overlooked and I was reasonably sure I knew who had murdered Nick Damiano.

But I still didn't know why. I didn't have an inkling of *why*.

The Medford's front door was still on its night security lock when I got there at a quarter to eight. Dan Cady let me in. I asked him a couple of questions about Nick's janitorial habits, and the answers he gave me pretty much confirmed my suspicions. To make absolutely sure, I went down to the basement and spent ten minutes poking around in its hot and noisy gloom.

Now the hard part, the part I never liked. I took the elevator to the third floor and knocked on the door to Room 304. He was there; not more than five seconds passed before he called out, "Door's not locked." I opened it and stepped inside.

He was sitting in a faded armchair near the window, staring out at the rain and the wet streets below. He turned his head briefly to look at me, then turned it back again to the window. The stubby little pipe was between his teeth and the overheated air smelled of his tobacco, a kind of dry, sweet scent, like withered roses.

"More questions?" he said.

"Not exactly, Mr. Weaver. You mind if I sit down?"

"Bed's all there is."

I sat on the bottom edge of the bed, a few feet away from him. The room was small, neat—not much furniture, not much of anything; old patterned wallpaper and a threadbare carpet, both of which had a patina of gray. Maybe it was my mood and the rain-dull day outside, but the entire room seemed gray, full of that aura of age and hopelessness.

"Hot in here," I said. "Furnace is going full blast down in the basement."

"I don't mind it hot."

"Nick Damiano did a better job of regulating the heat, I understand. He'd turn it on for a few hours in the morning, leave it off most of the day, turn it back on in the evenings, and then shut it down again by midnight. The night he died, though, he didn't have time to shut it down."

Weaver didn't say anything.

"It's pretty noisy in the basement when that furnace is on," I said. "You can hardly hold a normal conversation with somebody standing right next to you. It'd be almost impossible to hear anything, even raised voices, from a distance. So you couldn't have heard an argument inside Nick's room, not from back by the storage lockers. And probably not even if you stood right next to the door, because the door's thick and made of metal."

He still didn't stir, didn't speak.

"You made up the argument because you ran into Charley Slattery. He might have told the police he saw you come out of the elevator around the time Nick was killed, and that you seemed upset; so you had to protect yourself. Just like you protected yourself by unlocking the alley door after the murder."

More silence.

"You murdered Nick, all right. Beat him to death with your cane—hickory like that is as thick and hard as three-quarter-inch steel pipe. Charley told me you had it under your arm when you got off the elevator. Why under your arm? Why weren't you walking with it like you usually do? Has to be that you didn't want your fingers around the handle, the part you clubbed Nick with, even if you did wipe off most of the blood and gore."

He was looking at me now, without expression—just a dull, steady, waiting look.

"How'd you clean the cane once you were here in your room? Soap and water? Cleaning fluid of some kind? It doesn't matter, you know. There'll still be minute traces of blood on it that the forensics lab can match up to Nick's."

He put an end to his silence then; by saying in a clear, toneless voice, "All right. I done it," and that made it a little easier on both of us. The truth is always easier, no matter how painful it might be.

I said, "Do you want to tell me about it, Mr. Weaver?"

"Not much to tell," he said. "I went to the basement to get my other radio, like I told you before. He was fixing the door to one of the storage bins near mine. I looked at him up close, and I knew he was the one. I'd had a feeling he was ever since I moved in, but that night, up close like that, I knew it for sure."

He paused to take the pipe out of his mouth and lay it carefully on the table next to his chair. Then he said, "I accused him point blank. He put his hands over his ears like a woman, like he couldn't stand to hear it, and ran to his room. I went after him. Got inside before he could shut the door. He started babbling, crazy things about skeletons, and I saw that skeleton of his grinning across the room, and I . . . I don't know, I don't remember that part too good. He pushed me, I think, and I hit him with my cane, I kept hitting him . . ."

His voice trailed off and he sat there stiffly, with his big gnarled hands clenched in his lap.

"Why, Mr. Weaver? You said he was the one, that you accused him. Accused him of what?"

He didn't seem to hear me. He said, "After I come to my senses, I couldn't breathe. Thought I was having a heart attack. God, it was hot in there . . . hot as hell. I opened the alley door to get some air and I guess I must have left it unlocked. I never did that on purpose. Only the story about the argument."

"Why did you kill Nick Damiano?"

No answer for a few seconds; I thought he still wasn't listening and I was about to ask the question again. But then he said, "My Bible's over on the desk. Look inside the front cover."

The Bible was a well-used Gideon and inside the front cover was a yellowed newspaper clipping. I opened the clipping. It was from the *Chicago Sun-Times*, dated June 23, 1957—a news story, with an accompanying photograph, that bore the headline: FLOWER SHOP BOMBER IDENTIFIED.

I took it back to the bed and sat again to read it. It said that the person responsible for a homemade bomb that had exploded in a crowded florist shop the day before, killing seven people, was a handyman named Nicholas Donato. One of the dead was Marjorie Donato, the bomber's estranged wife and an employee of the shop; another victim was the shop's owner, Arthur Cullen, with whom Mrs. Donato had apparently been having an affair. According to friends, Nicholas Donato had been despondent over the estrangement and the affair, had taken to drinking heavily, and had threatened "to do something drastic" if his wife didn't move back in with him. He had disappeared the morning of the explosion and had not been apprehended at the time the news story was printed. His evident intention had been to blow up only his wife and her lover; but Mrs. Donato had opened the package containing the bomb immediately after it was brought by messenger, in the presence of several customers, and the result had been mass slaughter.

I studied the photograph of Nicholas Donato. It was a head-and-shoulders shot, of not very good quality, and I had to look at it closely for a time to see the likeness. But it was there: Nicholas Donato and Nick Damiano had been the same man.

Weaver had been watching me read. When I looked up from the clipping he said, "They never caught him. Traced him to Indianapolis, but then he disappeared for good. All these years, twenty-seven years, and I come across him here in San Francisco. Coincidence. Or maybe it was supposed to happen that way. The hand of the Lord guides us all, and we don't always understand the whys and wherefores."

"Mr. Weaver, what did that bombing have to do with you?"

"One of the people he blew up was my youngest daughter. Twenty-two that year. Went to that flower shop to pick out an arrangement for her wedding. I saw her after it happened, I saw what his bomb did to her . . ."

He broke off again; his strong voice trembled a little now. But his eyes were dry. He'd cried once, he'd cried many times, but that had been long ago. There were no tears left any more.

I got slowly to my feet. The heat and the sweetish tobacco scent were making me feel sick to my stomach. And the grayness, the aura of age and hopelessness and tragedy, were like an oppressive weight.

I said, "I'll be going now."

"Going?" he said. "Telephone's right over there."

"I won't be calling the police, Mr. Weaver. From here or from anywhere else."

"What's that? But . . . you know I killed him . . ."

"I don't know anything," I said. "I don't even remember coming here today."

I left him quickly, before he could say anything else, and went downstairs and out to O'Farrell Street. Wind-hurled rain buffeted me, icy and stinging, but the feel and smell of it was a relief. I pulled up the collar on my overcoat and hurried next door.

Upstairs in the office I took Irv Feinberg's two hundred dollars out of the lock-box in the desk and slipped the envelope into my coat pocket. He wouldn't like getting it back; he wouldn't like my calling it quits on the investigation, just as the police had done. But that didn't matter. Let the dead lie still, and the dying find what little peace they had left. The judgment was out of human hands anyway.

I tried not to think about Nick Damiano any more, but it was too soon and I couldn't blot him out yet. Harmless old Nick, the happy whack. Jesus Christ. Seven people—he had slaughtered seven people that day in 1957. And for what? For a lost woman; for a lost love. No wonder he'd gone batty and developed an obsession for skeletons. He had lived with them, seven of them, all those years, heard them clattering and clacking all those thousands of nights. And now, pretty soon, he would be one himself.

Skeleton rattle your mouldy leg.

All men's lovers come to this.

INCIDENT IN A NEIGHBORHOOD TAVERN

When the holdup went down I was sitting at the near end of the Foghorn Tavern's scarred mahogany bar talking to the owner, Matt Candiotti.

It was a little before seven of a midweek evening, lull-time in working-class neighborhood saloons like this one. Blue-collar locals would jam the place from four until about six-thirty, when the last of them headed home for dinner; the hard-core drinkers wouldn't begin filtering back in until about seven-thirty or eight. Right now there were only two customers, and the jukebox and computer hockey games were quiet. The TV over the back bar was on, but with the sound turned down to a tolerable level. One of the customers, a porky guy in his fifties, drinking Anchor Steam out of the bottle, was watching the last of the NBC national news. The other customer, an equally porky and middle-aged female barfly, half in the bag on red wine, was trying to convince him to pay attention to her instead of Tom Brokaw.

I had a draft beer in front of me, but that wasn't the reason I was there. I'd come to ask Candiotti, as I had asked two dozen other merchants here in the Outer Mission, if he could offer any leads on the rash of burglaries that were plaguing small businesses in the neighborhood. The police hadn't come up with anything positive after six weeks, so a couple of the victims had gotten up a fund and hired me to see what I could find out. They'd picked me because I had been born and raised in the Outer Mission, I still had friends and shirttail relatives living here, and I understood the neighborhood a good deal better than any other private detective in San Francisco.

But so far I wasn't having any more luck than the SFPD. None of the merchants I'd spoken with today had given me any new ideas. And Candiotti was proving to be no exception. He stood slicing limes into wedges as we talked. They might have been onions the way his long, mournful face was screwed up, like a man trying to hold back tears. His gray-stubbled jowls wobbled every time he shook his head. He reminded me of a tired old hound, friendly and sad, as if life had dealt him a few kicks but not quite enough to rob him of his good nature.

"Wish I could help," he said. "But hell, I don't hear nothing. Must be pros from Hunters Point or the Fillmore, hah?"

Hunters Point and the Fillmore were black sections of the city, which was a pretty good indicator of where his head was at. I said, "Some of the others figure it for local talent."

"Out of this neighborhood, you mean?"

I nodded, drank some of my draft.

"Nah, I doubt it," he said. "Guys that organized, they don't shit where they eat. Too smart, you know?"

"Maybe. Any break-ins or attempted break-ins here?"

"Not so far. I got bars on all the windows, double dead-bolt locks on the storeroom door off the alley. Besides, what's for them to steal besides a few cases of whiskey?"

"You don't keep cash on the premises overnight?"

"Fifty bucks in the till," Candiotti said, "that's all; that's my limit. Everything else goes out of here when I close up, down to the night deposit at the B of A on Mission. My mama didn't raise no airheads." He scraped the lime wedges off his board into a plastic container, and racked the serrated knife he'd been using. "One thing I did hear," he said. "I heard some of the loot turned up down in San Jose. You know about that?"

"Not much of a lead there. Secondhand dealer named Pitman had a few pieces of stereo equipment stolen from the factory outlet store on Geneva. Said he bought it from a guy at the San Jose flea market, somebody he didn't know, never saw before."

"Yeah, sure," Candiotti said wryly. "What do the cops think?"

"That Pitman bought it off a fence."

"Makes sense. So maybe the boosters are from San Jose, hah?"

"Could be," I said, and that was when the kid walked in.

He brought bad air in with him; I sensed it right away and so did Candiotti. We both glanced at the door when it opened, the way you do, but we didn't look away again once we saw him. He was in his early twenties, dark-skinned, dressed in chinos, a cotton windbreaker, sharp-toed shoes polished to a high gloss. But it was his eyes that put the chill on my neck, the sudden clutch of tension down low in my belly. They were bright, jumpy, on the wild side, and in the dim light of the Foghorn's interior, the pupils were so small they seemed nonexistent. He had one hand in his jacket pocket and I knew it was clamped around a gun even before he took it out and showed it to us.

He came up to the bar a few feet on my left, the gun jabbing the air in front of him. He couldn't hold it steady; it kept jerking up and down, from side to side, as if it had a kind of spasmodic life of its own. Behind me, at the other end of the bar, I heard Anchor Steam suck in his breath, the barfly make a sound like a stifled moan. I eased back a little on the stool, watching the gun and the kid's eyes flick from Candiotti to me to the two customers and back around again. Candiotti didn't move at all, just stood there staring with his hound's face screwed up in that holding-back-tears way.

"All right all right," the kid said. His voice was high pitched, excited, and there was drool at one corner of his mouth. You couldn't get much more stoned than he was and still function. Coke, crack, speed—maybe a combination. The gun that kept flicking this way and that had to be a goddamn Saturday night special. "Listen good, man, everybody listen good. I don't want to kill none of you, man, but I will if I got to, you better believe it."

None of us said anything. None of us moved.

The kid had a folded-up paper sack in one pocket; he dragged it out with his free hand, dropped it, broke quickly at the middle to pick it up without lowering his gaze. When he straightened again there was sweat on his forehead, more drool coming out of his mouth. He threw the sack on the bar.

"Put the money in there Mr. Cyclone Man," he said to Candiotti. "All the money in the register but not the coins, I don't want the fuckin' coins, you hear me?"

Candiotti nodded; reached out slowly, caught up the sack, turned toward the back bar with his shoulders hunched up against his neck. When he punched No Sale on the register, the ringing thump of the cash drawer sliding open seemed overloud in the electric hush. For a few seconds the kid watched him scoop bills into the paper sack; then his eyes and the gun skittered my way again. I had looked into the muzzle of a handgun before and it was the same feeling each time: dull fear, helplessness, a kind of naked vulnerability.

"Your wallet on the bar, man, all your cash." The gun barrel and the wild eyes flicked away again, down the length of the plank, before I could move to comply. "You down there, dude, you and fat mama put your money on the bar. All of it, hurry up."

Each of us did as we were told. While I was getting my wallet out I managed to slide my right foot off the stool, onto the brass rail, and to get my right hand pressed tight against the beveled edge of the bar. If I had to make any sudden moves, I would need the leverage.

Candiotti finished loading the sack, turned from the register. There was a grayish cast to his face now—the wet gray color of fear. The kid said to him, "Pick up their money, put it in the sack with the rest. Come on come on come on!"

Candiotti went to the far end of the plank, scooped up the wallets belonging to Anchor Steam and the woman; then he came back my way, added my wallet to the contents of the paper sack, put the sack down carefully in front of the kid.

"Okay," the kid said, "okay all right." He glanced over his shoulder at the street door, as if he'd heard something there; but it stayed closed. He jerked his head around again. In his sweaty agitation the Saturday night special almost slipped free of his fingers; he fumbled a tighter grip on it, and when it didn't go off I let the breath I had been holding come out thin and slow between my teeth. The muscles in my shoulders and back were drawn so tight I was afraid they might cramp.

The kid reached out for the sack, dragged it in against his body. But he made no move to leave with it. Instead he said, "Now we go get the big pile, man."

Candiotti opened his mouth, closed it again. His eyes were almost as big and starey as the kid's.

"Come on Mr. Cyclone Man, the safe, the safe in your office. We goin' back there now."

"No money in that safe," Candiotti said in a thin, scratchy voice. "Nothing valuable."

"Oh man I'll kill you man I'll blow your fuckin' head off! I ain't playin' no games I want that money!"

He took two steps forward, jabbing with the gun up close to Candiotti's gray face. Candiotti backed off a step, brought his hands up, took a tremulous breath.

"All right," he said, "but I got to get the key to the office. It's in the register."

"Hurry up hurry up!"

Candiotti turned back to the register, rang it open, rummaged inside with his left hand. But with his right hand, shielded from the kid by his body, he eased up the top on a large wooden cigar box adjacent. The hand disappeared inside; came out again with metal in it, glinting in the back bar lights. I saw it and I wanted to yell at him, but it wouldn't have done any good, would only have warned the kid . . . and he was already turning with it, bringing it up with both hands now—the damn gun of his own he'd had hidden inside the cigar box. There was no time for me to do anything but shove away from the bar and sideways off the stool just as Candiotti opened fire.

The state he was in, the kid didn't realize what was happening until it was too late for him to react; he never even got a shot off. Candiotti's first slug knocked him halfway around, and one of the three others that followed it opened up his face like a piece of ripe fruit smacked by a hammer. He was dead before his body, driven backward, slammed into the cigarette machine near the door, slid down it to the floor.

The half-drunk woman was yelling in broken shrieks, as if she couldn't get enough air for a sustained scream. When I came up out of my crouch I saw that Anchor Steam had hold of her, clinging to her as much for support as in an effort to calm her down. Candiotti stood flat-footed, his arms down at his sides, the gun out of sight below the bar, staring at the bloody remains of the kid as if he couldn't believe what he was seeing, couldn't believe what he'd done.

Some of the tension in me eased as I went to the door, found the lock on its security gate, fastened it before anybody could come in off the street. The Saturday night special was still clutched in the kid's hand; I bent, pulled it free with my thumb and forefinger, and broke the cylinder. It was loaded, all right—five cartridges. I dropped it into my jacket pocket, thought about checking the kid's clothing for identification, didn't do it. It wasn't any of my business, now, who he'd been. And I did not want to touch him or any part of him. There was a queasiness in my stomach, a fluttery weakness behind my knees—the same delayed reaction I always had to violence and death—and touching him would only make it worse.

To keep from looking at the red ruin of the kid's face, I pivoted back to the bar. Candiotti hadn't moved. Anchor Steam had gotten the woman to stop screeching and had coaxed her over to one of the handful of tables near the jukebox; now she was sobbing, "I've got to go home, I'm gonna be sick if I don't go home." But she didn't make any move to get up and neither did Anchor Steam.

I walked over near Candiotti and pushed hard words at him in an undertone. "That was a damn fool thing to do. You could have got us all killed."

"I know," he said. "I know."

"Why'd you do it?"

"I thought . . . hell, you saw the way he was waving that piece of his . . ."

"Yeah," I said. "Call the police. Nine-eleven."

"Nine-eleven. Okay."

"Put that gun of yours down first. On the bar."

He did that. There was a phone on the back bar; he went away to it in shaky strides. While he was talking to the Emergency operator I picked up his weapon, saw that it was a

.32 Charter Arms revolver. I held it in my hand until Candiotti finished with the call, then set it down again as he came back to where I stood.

"They'll have somebody here in five minutes," he said.

I said, "You know that kid?"

"Christ, no."

"Ever see him before? Here or anywhere else?"

"No."

"So how did he know about your safe?"

Candiotti blinked at me. "What?"

"The safe in your office. Street kid like that... how'd he know about it?"

"How should I know? What difference does it make?"

"He seemed to think you keep big money in that safe."

"Well, I don't. There's nothing in it."

"That's right, you told me you don't keep more than fifty bucks on the premises overnight. In the till."

"Yeah."

"Then why have you got a safe, if it's empty?"

Candiotti's eyes narrowed. "I used to keep my receipts in it, all right? Before all these burglaries started. Then I figured I'd be smarter to take the money to the bank every night."

"Sure, that explains it," I said. "Still, a kid like that, looking for a big score to feed his habit, he wasn't just after what was in the till and our wallets. No, it was as if he'd gotten wind of a heavy stash—a few grand or more."

Nothing from Candiotti.

I watched him for a time. Then I said, "Big risk you took, using that thirty-two of yours. How come you didn't make your play the first time you went to the register? How come you waited until the kid mentioned your office safe?"

"I didn't like the way he was acting, like he might start shooting any second. I figured it was our only chance. Listen, what're you getting at, hah?"

"Another funny thing," I said, "is the way he called you 'Mr. Cyclone Man.' Now why would a hopped-up kid use a term like that to a bar owner he didn't know?"

"How the hell should I know?"

"Cyclone," I said. "What's a cyclone but a big destructive wind? Only one other thing I can think of."

"Yeah? What's that?"

"A fence. A cyclone fence."

Candiotti made a fidgety movement. Some of the wet gray pallor was beginning to spread across his cheeks again, like a fungus.

I said, "And a fence is somebody who receives and distributes stolen goods. A Mr. Fence Man. But then you know that, don't you, Candiotti? We were talking about that kind of fence before the kid came in . . . how Pitman, down in San Jose, bought some hot stereo equipment off of one. That fence could just as easily be operating here in San Francisco, though. Right here in this neighborhood, in fact. Hell, suppose the stuff taken in all those burglaries never left the neighborhood. Suppose it was brought to a place nearby and stored until it could be trucked out to other cities—a tavern storeroom, for instance. Might even be some of it is still in that storeroom. And the money he got for the rest he'd keep locked up in his safe, right? Who'd figure it? Except maybe a poor junkie who picked up a whisper on the street somewhere—"

Candiotti made a sudden grab for the .32, caught it and backed up a step with it leveled at my chest. "You smart son of a bitch," he said. "I ought to kill you too."

"In front of witnesses? With the police due any minute?"

He glanced over at the two customers. The woman was still sobbing, lost in a bleak outpouring of self-pity; but Anchor Steam was staring our way, and from the expression on his face he'd heard every word of my exchange with Candiotti.

"There's still enough time for me to get clear," Candiotti said grimly. He was talking to himself, not to me. Sweat had plastered his lank hair to his forehead; the revolver was not quite steady in his hand. "Lock you up in my office, you and those two back there . . ."

"I don't think so," I said.

"Goddamn you, you think I won't use this gun again?"

"I know you won't use it. I emptied out the last two cartridges while you were on the phone."

I took the two shells from my left-hand jacket pocket and held them up where he could see them. At the same time I got the kid's Saturday night special out of the other pocket, held it loosely pointed in his direction. "You want to put your piece down now, Candiotti? You're not going anywhere, not for a long time."

He put it down—dropped it clattering onto the bartop. And as he did, his sad hound's face screwed up again, only this time he didn't even try to keep the wetness from leaking out of his eyes. He was leaning against the bar, crying like the woman, submerged in his own outpouring of self-pity, when the cops showed up a few minutes later.

STAKEOUT

Four o'clock in the morning. And I was sitting huddled and ass-numb in my car in a freezing rainstorm, waiting for a guy I had never seen in person to get out of a nice warm bed and drive off in his Mercedes, thus enabling me to follow him so I could find out where he lived.

Thrilling work if you can get it. The kind that makes any self-respecting detective wonder why he didn't become a plumber instead.

Rain hammered against the car's metal surfaces, sluiced so thickly down the windshield that it transformed the glass into an opaque screen; all I could see were smeary blobs of light that marked the street lamps along this block of Forty-Seventh Avenue. Wind buffeted the car in forty-mile-an-hour gusts off the ocean nearby. Condensation had formed again on the driver's door window, even though I had rolled it down half an inch; I rubbed some of the mist away and took another bleary-eyed look across the street.

This was one of San Francisco's older middle-class residential neighborhoods, desirable as long as you didn't mind fog-belt living because Sutro Heights Park was just a block away and you were also within walking distance of Ocean Beach, the Cliff House, and Land's End. Most of the houses had been built in the thirties and stood shoulder-to-shoulder with their neighbors, but they seemed to have more individuality than the bland row houses dominating the avenues farther inland; out here, California Spanish was the dominant style. Asians had bought up much of the city's west side housing in recent years, but fewer of those close to the ocean than anywhere else. A lot of homes in pockets such as this were still owned by older-generation, blue-collar San Franciscans.

The house I had under surveillance, number 9279, was one of the Spanish stucco jobs, painted white with a red tile roof. Yucca palms, one large and three small, dominated its tiny front yard. The three-year-old Mercedes with the Washington state license plates was still parked, illegally, across the driveway. Above it, the house's front windows remained dark. If anybody was up yet I couldn't tell it from where I was sitting.

I shifted position for the hundredth time, wincing as my stiffened joints protested with creaks and twinges. I had been here four and a half hours now, with nothing to do except to sit and wait and try not to fall asleep; to listen to the rain and the rattle and stutter of my thoughts. I was weary and irritable and I wanted some hot coffee and my own warm bed. It would be well past dawn, I thought bleakly, before I got either one.

Stakeouts. God, how I hated them. The passive waiting, the boredom, the slow, slow passage of dead time. How many did this make over the past thirty-odd years? How many empty, wasted, lost hours? Too damn many, whatever the actual figure. The physical discomfort was also becoming less tolerable, especially on nights like this, when not even a heavy overcoat and gloves kept the chill from penetrating bone deep. I had lived fifty-eight years; fifty-eight is too old to sit all-night stakeouts on the best of cases, much less on a lousy split-fee skip-trace.

I was starting to hate Randolph Hixley, too, sight unseen. He was the owner of the Mercedes across the street and my reason for being here. To his various and sundry employers, past and no doubt present, he was a highly paid freelance computer consultant. To his ex-wife and two kids, he was a probable deadbeat who currently owed some twenty-four thousand in back alimony and child support. To me and Puget Sound Investigations of Seattle, he was what should have been a small but adequate fee for routine work. Instead, he had developed into a minor pain in the ass. Mine.

Hixley had quit Seattle for parts unknown some four months ago, shortly after his wife divorced him for what she referred to as "sexual misconduct," and had yet to make a single alimony or child support payment. For reasons of her own, the wife had let the first two barren months go by without doing anything about it. On the occasion of the third due date, she had received a brief letter from Hixley informing her in tear-jerk language that he was so despondent over the breakup of their marriage he hadn't worked since leaving Seattle and was on the verge of becoming one of the homeless. He had every intention of fulfilling his obligations, though, the letter said; he would send money as soon as he got back on his feet. So would she bear with him for a while and please not sic the law on him? The letter was postmarked San Francisco, but with no return address.

The ex-wife, who was no dummy, smelled a rat. But because she still harbored some feelings for him, she had gone to Puget Sound Investigations rather than to the authorities, the object being to locate Hixley and determine if he really was broke and despondent. If so, then she would show the poor dear compassion and understanding. If not, then she would obtain a judgment against the son of a bitch and force him to pay up or get thrown in the slammer.

Puget Sound had taken the job, done some preliminary work, and then called a San Francisco detective—me—and farmed out the tough part for half the fee. That kind of cooperative thing is done all the time when the client isn't wealthy enough and the fee isn't large enough for the primary agency to send one of its own operatives to another state. No private detective likes to split fees, particularly when he's the one doing most of the work, but ours is sometimes a back-scratching business. Puget Sound had done a favor for me once; now it was my turn.

Skip-tracing can be easy or it can be difficult, depending on the individual you're trying to find. At first I figured Randolph Hixley, broke or not, might be one of the difficult ones. He had no known relatives or friends in the Bay Area. He had stopped using his credit cards after the divorce, and had not applied for new ones, which meant that if he was working and had money, he was paying his bills in cash. In Seattle, he'd provided consultancy services to a variety of different companies, large and small, doing most of the work at home by computer link. If he'd hired out to one or more outfits in the Bay Area, Puget Sound had not been able to turn up a lead as to which they might be, so I probably wouldn't be able to either. There is no easy way to track down that information, not without some kind of insider pull with the IRS.

And yet despite all of that, I got lucky right away—so lucky I revised my thinking and decided, prematurely and falsely, that Hixley was going to be one of the easy traces after all. The third call I made was to a contact in the San Francisco City Clerk's office, and it netted me the information that the 1987 Mercedes 560 SL registered in Hixley's name had received two parking tickets on successive Thursday mornings, the most recent of which was the previous week. The tickets were for identical violations: illegal parking across a private driveway and illegal parking during posted street-cleaning hours. Both citations had been issued between seven and seven-thirty a.m. And in both instances, the address was the same: 9279 Forty-Seventh Avenue.

I looked up the address in my copy of the reverse city directory; 9279 Forty-Seventh Avenue was a private house occupied by one Anne Carswell, a commercial artist, and two other Carswells, Bonnie and Margo, whose ages were given as eighteen and nineteen, respectively, and who I presumed were her daughters. The Carswells didn't own the house; they had been renting it for a little over two years.

Since there had been no change of registration on the Mercedes—I checked on that with the DMV—I assumed that the car still belonged to Randolph Hixley. And I figured things this way: Hixley, who was no more broke and despondent than I was, had met and established a relationship with Anne Carswell, and taken to spending Wednesday nights at her house. Why only Wednesdays? For all I knew, once a week was as much passion as Randy and Anne could muster up. Or it could be the two daughters slept elsewhere that night. In any case, Wednesday was Hixley's night to howl.

So the next Wednesday evening I drove out there, looking for his Mercedes. No Mercedes. I made my last check at midnight, went home to bed, got up at six a.m., and drove back to Forty-Seventh Avenue for another look. Still no Mercedes.

Well, I thought, they skipped a week. Or for some reason they'd altered their routine. I went back on Thursday night. And Friday night and Saturday night. I made spot checks during the day. On one occasion I saw a tall, willowy redhead in her late thirties—Anne Carswell, no doubt—driving out of the garage. On another occasion I saw the two daughters, one blond, one brunette, both attractive, having a conversation with a couple of sly college types. But that was all I saw. Still no Mercedes, still no Randolph Hixley.

I considered bracing one of the Carswell women on a ruse, trying to find out that way where Hixley was living. But I didn't do it. He might have put them wise to his background and the money he owed, and asked them to keep mum if anyone ever approached them. Or I might slip somehow in my questioning and make her suspicious enough to call Hixley. I did not want to take the chance of warning him off.

Last Wednesday had been another bust. So had early Thursday—I drove out there at five a.m. that time. And so had the rest of the week. I was wasting time and gas and sleep, but it was the only lead I had. All the other skip-trace avenues I'd explored had led me nowhere near my elusive quarry.

Patience and perseverance are a detective's best assets; hang in there long enough and as often as not you find what you're looking for.

Tonight I'd finally found Hixley and his Mercedes, back at the Carswell house after a two-week absence.

The car hadn't been there the first two times I drove by, but when I made what would have been my last pass, at twenty of twelve, there it was, once again illegally parked across the driveway. Maybe he didn't give a damn about parking tickets because he had no intention of paying them. Or maybe he disliked walking fifty feet or so, which was how far away the nearest legal curb space was. Or, hell, maybe he was just an arrogant bastard who thumbed his nose at the law any time it inconvenienced him. Whatever his reason for blocking Anne Carswell's driveway, it was his big mistake.

The only choice I had, spotting his car so late, was to stake it out and wait for him to show. I would have liked to go home and catch a couple of hours' sleep, but for all I knew he wouldn't spend the entire night this time. If I left and came back and he was gone, I'd have to go through this whole rigmarole yet again.

So I parked and settled in. The lights in the Carswell house had gone off at twelve-fifteen and hadn't come back on since. It had rained off and on all evening, but the first hard rain started a little past one. The storm had steadily worsened until, now, it was a full-fledged howling, ripping blow. And still I sat and still I waited . . .

A blurred set of headlights came boring up Forty-Seventh toward Geary, the first car to pass in close to an hour. When it went swishing by I held my watch up close to my eyes: 4:07. Suppose he stays in there until eight or nine? I thought. Four or five more hours of this and I'd be too stiff to move. It was meatlocker cold in the car. I couldn't start the engine and put the heater on because the exhaust, if not the idle, would call attention to my presence. I'd wrapped my legs and feet in the car blanket, which provided some relief; even so, I could no longer feel my toes when I tried to wiggle them.

The hard drumming beat of the rain seemed to be easing a little. Not the wind, though; a pair of back-to-back gusts shook the car, as if it were a toy in the hands of a destructive child. I shifted position again, pulled the blanket more tightly around my ankles.

A light went on in the Carswell house.

I scrubbed mist off the driver's door window, peered through the wet glass. The big front window was alight over there, behind drawn curtains. That was a good sign: People don't usually put their living room lights on at four a.m. unless somebody plans to be leaving soon.

Five minutes passed while I sat chafing my gloved hands together and moving my feet up and down to improve circulation. Then another light went on—the front porch light this time. And a few seconds after that, the door opened and somebody came out onto the stoop.

It wasn't Randolph Hixley; it was a young blond woman wearing a trenchcoat over what looked to be a lacy nightgown. One of the Carswell daughters. She stood still for a moment, looking out over the empty street. Then she drew the trenchcoat collar up around her throat and ran down the stairs and over to Hixley's Mercedes.

For a few seconds she stood hunched on the sidewalk on the passenger side, apparently unlocking the front door with a set of keys. She pulled the door open, as if making sure it was unlocked, then slammed it shut again. She turned and ran back up the stairs and vanished into the house.

I thought: Now what was that all about?

The porch light stayed on. So did the light in the front room. Another three minutes dribbled away. The rain slackened a little more, so that it was no longer sheeting; the wind continued to wail and moan. And then things got even stranger over there.

First the porch light went off. Then the door opened and somebody exited onto the stoop, followed a few seconds later by a cluster of shadow-shapes moving in an awkward, confused fashion. I couldn't identify them or tell what they were doing while they were all grouped on the porch; the tallest yucca palm cast too much shadow and I was too far away. But when they started down the stairs, there was just enough extension of light from the front window to individuate the shapes for me.

There were four of them, by God—three in an uneven line on the same step, the fourth backing down in front of them as though guiding the way. Three women, one man. The man—several inches taller, wearing an overcoat and hat, head lolling forward as if he were drunk or unconscious—was being supported by two of the women.

They all managed to make it down the slippery stairs without any of them suffering a misstep. When they reached the sidewalk, the one who had been guiding ran ahead to the Mercedes and dragged the front passenger door open. In the faint outspill from the dome light, I watched the other two women, with the third one's help, push and prod the man inside. Once they had the door shut again, they didn't waste any time catching their breaths. Two of them went running back to the house; the third hurried around to the driver's door, bent to unlock it. She was the only one of the three, I realized then, who was fully dressed: raincoat, rainhat, slacks, boots. When she slid in under the wheel I had a dome-lit glimpse of reddish hair and a white, late-thirties face under the rainhat. Anne Carswell.

She fired up the Mercedes, let the engine warm for all of five seconds, switched on the headlights, and eased away from the curb at a crawl, the way you'd drive over a surface of broken glass. The two daughters were already back inside the house, with the door shut behind them.

I had long since unwrapped the blanket from around my legs; I didn't hesitate in starting my car. Or in trying to start it: The engine was cold and it took three whiffing tries before it caught and held. If Anne Carswell had been driving fast, I might have lost her. As it was, with her creeping along, she was only halfway along the next block behind me when I swung out into a tight U-turn.

I ran dark through the rain until she completed a slow turn west on Point Lobos and passed out of sight. Then I put on my lights and accelerated across Geary to the Point Lobos intersection. I got there in time to pick up the Mercedes' taillights as it went through the flashing yellow traffic signal at Forty-Eighth Avenue. I let it travel another fifty yards downhill before I turned onto Point Lobos in pursuit.

Five seconds later, Anne Carswell had another surprise for me.

I expected her to continue down past the Cliff House and around onto the Great Highway; there is no other through direction once you pass Forty-Eighth. But she seemed not to be leaving the general area after all. The Mercedes' brake lights came on and she slow-turned into the Merrie Way parking area above the ruins of the old Sutro Baths. The combination lot and overlook had only the one entrance/exit; it was surrounded on its other three sides by cliffs and clusters of wind-shaped cypress trees and a rocky nature trail that led out beyond the ruins to Land's End.

Without slowing, I drove on past. She was crawling straight down the center of the unpaved, potholed lot, toward the trees at the far end. Except for the Mercedes, the rain-drenched expanse appeared deserted.

Below Merrie Way, on the other side of Point Lobos, there is a newer, paved parking area carved out of Sutro Heights Park for sightseers and patrons of Louis' Restaurant opposite and the Cliff House bars and eateries farther down. It, too, was deserted at this hour. From the overlook above, you can't see this curving downhill section of Point Lobos; I swung across into the paved lot, cut my lights, looped around to where I had a clear view of the Merrie Way entrance. Then I parked, shut off the engine, and waited.

For a few seconds I could see a haze of slowly moving light up there, but not the Mercedes itself. Then the light winked out and there was nothing to see except wind-whipped rain and dark. Five minutes went by. Still nothing to see. She must have parked, I thought, but to do what?

Six minutes, seven. At seven and a half, a shape materialized out of the gloom above the entrance—somebody on foot, walking fast, bent against the lashing wind. Anne Carswell. She was moving at an uphill angle out of the overlook, climbing to Forty-Eighth Avenue.

When she reached the sidewalk, a car came through the flashing yellow at the intersection and its headlight beams swept over her; she turned away from them, as if to make sure her face wasn't seen. The car swished down past where I was, disappeared beyond the Cliff House. I watched Anne Carswell cross Point Lobos and hurry into Forty-Eighth at the upper edge of the park.

Going home, I thought. Abandoned Hixley and his Mercedes on the overlook and now she's hoofing it back to her daughters.

What the hell?

I started the car and drove up to Forty-Eighth and turned there. Anne Carswell was now on the opposite side of the street, near where Geary dead-ends at the park; when my lights caught her she turned her head away as she had a couple of minutes ago. I drove two blocks, circled around onto Forty-Seventh, came back a block, and then parked and shut down again within fifty yards of the Carswell house. Its porch light was back on, which indicated that the daughters were anticipating her imminent return. Two minutes later she came fast-walking out of Geary onto Forty-Seventh. One minute after that, she climbed the stairs to her house and let herself in. The porch light went out immediately, followed fifteen seconds later by the light in the front room.

I got the car moving again and made my way back down to the Merrie Way overlook.

The Mercedes was still the only vehicle on the lot, parked at an angle just beyond the long terraced staircase that leads down the cliffside to the pitlike bottom of the ruins. I pulled in alongside, snuffed my lights. Before I got out, I armed myself with the flashlight I keep clipped under the dash.

Icy wind and rain slashed at me as I crossed to the Mercedes. Even above the racket made by the storm, I could hear the barking of sea lions on the offshore rocks beyond the Cliff House. Surf boiled frothing over those rocks, up along the cliffs and among the concrete foundations that are all that's left of the old bathhouse. Nasty night, and a nasty business here to go with it. I was sure of that now.

I put the flashlight up against the Mercedes' passenger window, flicked it on briefly. He was in there, all right; she'd shoved him over so that he lay half sprawled under the wheel, his head tipped back against the driver's door. The passenger door was unlocked. I opened it and got in and shut the door again to extinguish the dome light. I put the flash beam on his face, shielding it with my hand.

Randolph Hixley, no doubt of that; the photograph Puget Sound Investigations had sent me was a good one. No doubt, either, that he was dead. I checked for a pulse, just to make sure. Then I moved the light over him, slowly, to see if I could find out what had killed him.

There weren't any discernible wounds or bruises or other marks on his body; no holes or tears or bloodstains on his damp clothing. Poison? Not that, either. Most any deadly poison produces convulsions, vomiting, rictus; his facial muscles were smooth and when I sniffed at his mouth I smelled nothing except Listerine.

Natural causes, then? Heart attack, stroke, aneurysm? Sure, maybe. But if he'd died of natural causes, why would Anne Carswell and her daughters have gone to all the trouble of moving his body and car down here? Why not just call Emergency Services?

On impulse I probed Hixley's clothing and found his wallet. It was empty—no cash, no credit cards, nothing except some old photos. Odd. He'd quit using credit cards after his divorce; he should have been carrying at least a few dollars. I took a close look at his hands and wrists. He was wearing a watch, a fairly new and fairly expensive one. No rings or other jewelry but there was a white mark on his otherwise tanned left pinkie, as if a ring had been recently removed.

They rolled him, I thought. All the cash in his wallet and a ring off his finger. Not the watch because it isn't made of gold or platinum and you can't get much for a watch, anyway, these days.

But why? Why would they kill a man for a few hundred bucks? Or rob a dead man and then try to dump the body? In either case, the actions of those three women made no damn sense . . .

Or did they?

I was beginning to get a notion.

I backed out of the Mercedes and went to sit and think in my own car. I remembered some things, and added them together with some other things, and did a little speculating, and the notion wasn't a notion anymore—it was the answer.

Hell, I thought then, I'm getting old. Old and slow on the uptake. I should have seen this part of it as soon as they brought the body out. And I should have tumbled to the other part a week ago, if not sooner.

I sat there for another minute, feeling my age and a little sorry for myself because it was going to be quite a while yet before I got any sleep. Then, dutifully, I hauled up my mobile phone and called in the law.

They arrested the three women a few minutes past seven a.m. at the house on Forty-Seventh Avenue. I was present for identification purposes. Anne Carswell put up a blustery protest of innocence until the inspector in charge, a veteran named Ginzberg, tossed the words "foul play" into the conversation; then the two girls broke down simultaneously and soon there were loud squawks of denial from all three: "We didn't hurt him! He had a heart attack, he died of a heart attack!" The girls, it turned out, were not named Carswell and were not Anne Carswell's daughters. The blonde was Bonnie Harper; the brunette was Margo LaFond. They were both former runaways from southern California.

The charges against the trio included failure to report a death, unlawful removal of a corpse, and felony theft. But the main charge was something else entirely.

The main charge was operating a house of prostitution.

Later that day, after I had gone home for a few hours' sleep, I laid the whole thing out for my partner, Eberhardt.

"I should have known they were hookers and Hixley was a customer," I said. "There were enough signs. His wife divorced him for 'sexual misconduct'; that was one. Another was how unalike those three women were—different hair colors, which isn't typical in a mother and her daughters. Then there were those sly young guys I saw with the two girls. They weren't boyfriends, they were customers too."

"Hixley really did die of a heart attack?" Eberhardt asked.

"Yeah. Carswell couldn't risk notifying Emergency Services; she didn't know much about Hixley and she was afraid somebody would come around asking questions. She had a nice discreet operation going there, with a small but high-paying clientele, and she didn't want a dead man to rock the boat. So she and the girls dressed the corpse and hustled it out of there. First, though, they emptied Hixley's wallet and she stripped a valuable garnet ring off his pinkie. She figured it was safe to do that; if anybody questioned the empty wallet and missing ring, it would look like the body had been rolled on the Merrie Way overlook, after he'd driven in there himself and had his fatal heart attack. As far as she knew, there was nothing to tie Hixley to her and her girls—no direct link, anyhow. He hadn't told her about the two parking tickets."

"Uh-huh. And he was in bed with all three of them when he croaked?"

"So they said. Right in the middle of a round of fun and games. That was what he paid them for each of the times he went there—seven hundred and fifty bucks for all three, all night."

"Jeez, three women at one time." Eberhardt paused, thinking about it. Then he shook his head. "How?" he said.

I shrugged. "Where there's a will, there's a way."

"Kinky sex—I never did understand it. I guess I'm old fashioned."

"Me too. But Hixley's brand is pretty tame, really, compared to some of the things that go on nowadays."

"Seems like the whole damn world gets a little kinkier every day," Eberhardt said. "A little crazier every day, too. You know what I mean?"

"Yeah," I said, "I know what you mean."

SOULS BURNING

Hotel Majestic, Sixth Street, downtown San Francisco. A hell of an address—a hell of a place for an ex-con not long out of Folsom to set up housekeeping. Sixth Street, south of Market—South of the Slot, it used to be called—is the heart of the city's Skid Road and has been for more than half a century.

Eddie Quinlan. A name and a voice out of the past, neither of which I'd recognized when he called that morning. Close to seven years since I had seen or spoken to him, six years since I'd even thought of him. Eddie Quinlan. Edgewalker, shadowman with no real substance or purpose, drifting along the narrow catwalk that separates conventional society from the underworld. Information seller, gofer, small-time bagman, doer of any insignificant job, legitimate or otherwise, that would help keep him in food and shelter, liquor and cigarettes. The kind of man you looked at but never really saw: a modern-day Yehudi, the little man who wasn't there. Eddie Quinlan. Nobody, loser—fall guy. Drug bust in the Tenderloin one night six and a half years ago; one dealer setting up another, and Eddie Quinlan, small-time bagman, caught in the middle; hard-assed judge, five years in Folsom, goodbye Eddie Quinlan. And the drug dealers? They walked, of course. Both of them.

And now Eddie was out, had been out for six months. And after six months of freedom, he'd called me. Would I come to his room at the Hotel Majestic tonight around eight? He'd tell me why when he saw me. It was real important—would I come? All right, Eddie. But I couldn't figure it. I had bought information from him in the old days, bits and pieces for five or ten dollars; maybe he had something to sell now. Only I wasn't looking for anything and I hadn't put the word out, so why pick me to call?

If you're smart you don't park your car on the street at night South of the Slot. I put mine in the Fifth and Mission Garage at seven forty-five and walked over to Sixth. It had rained most of the day and the streets were still wet, but now the sky was cold and clear. The kind of night that is as hard as black glass, so that light seems to bounce off the dark instead of shining through it; lights and their colors so bright and sharp reflecting off the night and the wet surfaces that the glare is like splinters against your eyes.

Friday night, and Sixth Street was teeming. Sidewalks jammed—old men, young men, bag ladies, painted ladies, blacks, whites, Asians, addicts, pushers, muttering mental cases, drunks leaning against walls in tight little clusters while they shared paper-bagged bottles of sweet wine and cans of malt liquor; men and women in filthy rags, in smart new outfits topped off with sunglasses, carrying ghetto blasters and red-and-white canes, some of the canes in the hands of individuals who could see as well as I could, carrying a hidden array of guns and knives and other lethal instruments. Cheap hotels, greasy spoons, seedy taverns, and liquor stores complete with barred windows and cynical proprietors that stayed open well past midnight. Laughter, shouts, curses, threats; bickering and dickering. The stenches of urine and vomit and unwashed bodies and rotgut liquor, and over those like an umbrella, the subtle effluvium of despair. Predators and prey, half hidden in shadow, half revealed in the bright, sharp dazzle of fluorescent lights and bloody neon.

It was a mean street, Sixth, one of the meanest, and I walked it warily. I may be fifty-eight but I'm a big man and I walk hard too; and I look like what I am. Two winos tried to panhandle me and a fat hooker in an orange wig tried to sell me a piece of her tired body, but no one gave me any trouble.

The Majestic was five stories of old wood and plaster and dirty brick, just off Howard Street. In front of its narrow entrance, a crack dealer and one of his customers were haggling over the price of a baggie of rock cocaine; neither of them paid any attention to me as I moved past them. Drug deals go down in the open here, day and night. It's not that the cops don't care, or that they don't patrol Sixth regularly; it's just that the dealers outnumber them ten to one. On Skid Road any crime less severe than aggravated assault is strictly low priority.

Small, barren lobby: no furniture of any kind. The smell of ammonia hung in the air like swamp gas. Behind the cubbyhole desk was an old man with dead eyes that would never see anything they didn't want to see. I said, "Eddie Quinlan," and he said, "Two-oh-two" without moving his lips. There was an elevator but it had an Out of Order sign on it; dust speckled the sign. I went up the adjacent stairs.

The disinfectant smell permeated the second floor hallway as well. Room 202 was just off the stairs, fronting on Sixth; one of the metal 2s on the door had lost a screw and was hanging upside down. I used my knuckles just below it. Scraping noise inside, and a voice said, "Yeah?"

I identified myself. A lock clicked, a chain rattled, the door wobbled and for the first time in nearly seven years I was looking at Eddie Quinlan.

He hadn't changed much. Little guy, about five-eight, and past forty now. Thin, nondescript features, pale eyes, hair the color of sand. The hair was thinner and the lines in his face were longer and deeper, almost like incisions where they bracketed his nose. Otherwise he was the same Eddie Quinlan.

"Hey," he said, "thanks for coming. I mean it, thanks."

"Sure, Eddie."

"Come on in."

The room made me think of a box—the inside of a huge rotting packing crate. Four bare walls with the scaly remnants of paper on them like psoriatic skin, bare uncarpeted floor, unshaded bulb hanging from the center of a bare ceiling. The bulb was dark; what light there was came from a low-wattage reading lamp and a wash of red-and-green neon from the hotel's sign that spilled in through a single window. Old iron-framed bed, unpainted nightstand, scarred dresser, straight-backed chair next to the bed and in front of the window, alcove with a sink and toilet and no door, closet that wouldn't be much larger than a coffin.

"Not much, is it," Eddie said.

I didn't say anything.

He shut the hall door, locked it. "Only place to sit is that chair there. Unless you want to sit on the bed? Sheets are clean. I try to keep things clean as I can."

"Chair's fine."

I went across to it; Eddie put himself on the bed. A room with a view, he'd said on the phone. Some view. Sitting here you could look down past Howard and up across Mission—almost two full blocks of the worst street in the city. It was so close you could hear the beat of its pulse, the ugly sounds of its living and its dying.

"So why did you ask me here, Eddie? If it's information for sale, I'm not buying right now."

"No, no, nothing like that, I ain't in the business anymore."

"Is that right?"

"Prison taught me a lesson. I got rehabilitated." There was no sarcasm or irony in the words; he said them matter-of-factly.

"I'm glad to hear it."

"I been a good citizen ever since I got out. No lie. I haven't had a drink, ain't even been in a bar."

"What are you doing for money?"

"I got a job," he said. "Shipping department at a wholesale sporting goods outfit on Brannan. It don't pay much but it's honest work."

I nodded. "What is it you want, Eddie?"

"Somebody I can talk to, somebody who'll understand— that's all I want. You always treated me decent. Most of 'em, no matter who they were, they treated me like I wasn't even human. Like I was a turd or something."

"Understand what?"

"About what's happening down there."

"Where? Sixth Street?"

"Look at it," he said. He reached over and tapped the window; stared through it. "Look at the people . . . there, you see that guy in the wheelchair and the one pushing him? Across the street there?"

I leaned closer to the glass. The man in the wheelchair wore a military camouflage jacket, had a heavy wool blanket across his lap; the black man manipulating him along the crowded sidewalk was thick-bodied, with a shiny bald head. "I see them."

"White guy's name is Baxter," Eddie said. "Grenade blew up under him in 'Nam and now he's a paraplegic. Lives right here in the Majestic, on this floor down at the end. Deals crack and smack out of his room. Elroy, the black dude, is his bodyguard and roommate. Mean, both of 'em. Couple of months ago, Elroy killed a guy over on Minna that tried to stiff them. Busted his head with a brick. You believe it?"

"I believe it."

"And they ain't the worst on the street. Not the worst."

"I believe that too."

"Before I went to prison I lived and worked with people like that and I never saw what they were. I mean I just never saw it. Now I do, I see it clear—every day walking back and forth to work, every night from up here. It makes you sick after a while, the things you see when you see 'em clear."

"Why don't you move?"

"Where to? I can't afford no place better than this."

"No better room, maybe, but why not another neighborhood? You don't have to live on Sixth Street."

"Wouldn't be much better, any other neighborhood I could buy into. They're all over the city now, the ones like Baxter and Elroy. Used to be it was just Skid Road and the Tenderloin and the ghettos. Now they're everywhere, more and more every day. You know?"

"I know."

"Why? It don't have to be this way, does it?"

Hard times, bad times: alienation, poverty, corruption, too

much government, not enough government, lack of social services, lack of caring, drugs like a cancer destroying society. Simplistic explanations that were no explanations at all and as dehumanizing as the ills they described. I was tired of hearing them and I didn't want to repeat them, to Eddie Quinlan or anybody else. So I said nothing.

He shook his head. "Souls burning everywhere you go," he said, and it was as if the words hurt his mouth coming out.

Souls burning. "You find religion at Folsom, Eddie?"

"Religion? I don't know, maybe a little. Chaplain we had there, I talked to him sometimes. He used to say that about the hardtimers, that their souls were burning and there wasn't nothing he could do to put out the fire. They were doomed, he said, and they'd doom others to burn with 'em."

I had nothing to say to that either. In the small silence a voice from outside said distinctly, "Dirty bastard, what you doin' with my pipe?" It was cold in there, with the hard bright night pressing against the window. Next to the door was a rusty steam radiator but it was cold too; the heat would not be on more than a few hours a day, even in the dead of winter, in the Hotel Majestic.

"That's the way it is in the city," Eddie said. "Souls burning. All day long, all night long, souls on fire."

"Don't let it get to you."

"Don't it get to you?"

"... Yes, Sometimes."

He bobbed his head up and down. "You want to do something, you know? You want to try to fix it somehow, put out the fires, There has to be a way."

"I can't tell you what it is," I said.

He said, "If we all just did something. It ain't too late. You don't think it's too late?"

"No."

"Me neither. There's still hope."

"Hope, faith, blind optimism—sure."

"You got to believe," he said, nodding. "That's all, you just got to believe."

Angry voices rose suddenly from outside; a woman screamed, thin and brittle. Eddie came off the bed, hauled up the window sash. Chill, damp air and street noises came pouring in: shouts, cries, horns honking, cars whispering on the wet pavement, a Muni bus clattering along Mission; more shrieks. He leaned out, peering downward.

"Look," he said, "look."

I stretched forward and looked. On the sidewalk below, a hooker in a leopard-skin coat was running wildly toward Howard; she was the one doing the yelling. Chasing behind her, tight black skirt hiked up over the tops of net stockings and hairy thighs, was a hideously rouged transvestite waving a pocket knife. A group of winos began laughing and chanting, "Rape! Rape!" as the hooker and the transvestite ran zigzagging out of sight on Howard.

Eddie pulled his head back in. The flickery neon wash made his face seem surreal, like a hallucinogenic vision. "That's the way it is," he said sadly. "Night after night, day after day."

With the window open, the cold was intense; it penetrated my clothing and crawled on my skin. I'd had enough of it, and of this room and Eddie Quinlan and Sixth Street.

"Eddie, just what is it you want from me?"

"I already told you. Talk to somebody who understands how it is down there."

"Is that the only reason you asked me here?"

"Ain't it enough?"

"For you, maybe." I got to my feet. "I'll be going now."

He didn't argue. "Sure, you go ahead."

"Nothing else you want to say?"

"Nothing else." He walked to the door with me, unlocked it, and then put out his hand. "Thanks for coming. I appreciate it, I really do."

"Yeah. Good luck, Eddie."

"You too," he said. "Keep the faith."

I went out into the hall, and the door shut gently and the lock clicked behind me.

Downstairs, out of the Majestic, along the mean street and back to the garage where I'd left my car. And all the way I kept thinking: There's something else, something more he wanted from me . . . and I gave it to him by going there and listening to him. But what? What did he really want?

I found out later that night. It was all over the TV—special bulletins and then the eleven o'clock news.

Twenty minutes after I left him, Eddie Quinlan stood at the window of his room-with-a-view, and in less than a minute, using a high-powered semiautomatic rifle he'd taken from the sporting goods outfit where he worked, he shot down fourteen people on the street below. Nine dead, five wounded, one of the wounded in critical condition and not expected to live. Six of the victims were known drug dealers; all of the others also had arrest records, for crimes ranging from prostitution to burglary. Two of the dead were Baxter, the paraplegic ex-Vietnam vet, and his bodyguard, Elroy.

By the time the cops showed up, Sixth Street was empty except for the dead and the dying. No more targets, and up in his room, Eddie Quinlan had sat on the bed and put the rifle's muzzle in his mouth and used his big toe to pull the trigger.

My first reaction was to blame myself. But how could I have known or even guessed? Eddie Quinlan. Nobody, loser, shadowman without substance or purpose. How could anyone have figured him for a thing like that?

Somebody I can talk to, somebody who'll understand—that's all I want.

No. What he'd wanted was somebody to help him justify to himself what he was about to do. Somebody to record his verbal suicide note. Somebody he could trust to pass it on afterward, tell it right and true to the world.

You want to do something, you know? You want to try to fix it somehow, put out the fires. There has to be a way.

Nine dead, five wounded, one of the wounded in critical condition and not expected to live. Not that way.

Souls burning. All day long, all night long, souls on fire.

The soul that had burned tonight was Eddie Quinlan's.

LA BELLEZZA DELLE BELLEZZE

1

That Sunday, the day before she died, I went down to Aquatic Park to watch the old men play bocce. I do that sometimes on weekends when I'm not working, when Kerry and I have nothing planned. More often than I used to, out of nostalgia and compassion and maybe just a touch of guilt, because in San Francisco bocce is a dying sport.

Only one of the courts was in use. Time was, all six were packed throughout the day and there were spectators and waiting players lined two and three deep at courtside and up along the fence on Van Ness. No more. Most of the city's older Italians, to whom bocce was more a religion than a sport, have died off. The once large and closeknit North Beach Italian community has been steadily losing its identity since the fifties—families moving to the suburbs, the expansion of Chinatown, and the gobbling up of North Beach real estate by wealthy Chinese—and even though there has been a small new wave of immigrants from Italy in recent years, they're mostly young and upscale. Young, upscale Italians don't play bocce much, if at all; their interests lie in soccer, in the American sports where money and fame and power have replaced a love of the game itself. The Di Massimo bocce courts at the North Beach Playground are mostly closed now; the only place you can find a game every Saturday and Sunday is on the one Aquatic Park court. And the players get older, and sadder, and fewer each year.

There were maybe fifteen players and watchers on this Sunday, almost all of them older than my fifty-eight. The two courts nearest the street are covered by a high, pillar-supported roof, so that contests can be held even in wet weather; and there are wooden benches set between the pillars. I parked myself on one of the benches midway along. The only other seated spectator was Pietro Lombardi, in a patch of warm May sunlight at the far end, and this surprised me. Even though Pietro was in his seventies, he was one of the best and spryest of the regulars, and also one of the most social. To see him sitting alone, shoulders slumped and head bowed, was puzzling.

Pining away for the old days, maybe, I thought—as I had just been doing. And a phrase popped into my head, a line from Dante that one of my uncles was fond of quoting when I was growing up in the Outer Mission: *Nessun maggior dolore che ricordarsi del tempo felice nella miseria.* The bitterest of woes is to remember old happy days.

Pietro and his woes didn't occupy my attention for long. The game in progress was spirited and voluble, as only a game of bocce played by elderly *paesanos* can be, and I was soon caught up in it.

Bocce is simple—deceptively simple. You play it on a long narrow packed-earth pit with low wooden sides. A wooden marker ball the size of a walnut is rolled to one end; the players stand at the opposite end and in turn roll eight larger, heavier balls, grapefruit-sized, in the direction of the marker, the object being to see who can put his bocce ball closest to it. One of the required skills is slow-rolling the ball, usually in a curving trajectory, so that it kisses the marker and then lies up against it—the perfect shot—or else stops an inch or two away. The other required skill is knocking an opponent's ball away from any such close lie without disturbing the marker. The best players, like Pietro Lombardi, can do this two out of three times on the fly—no mean feat from a distance of fifty feet. They can also do it by caroming the ball off the pit walls, with topspin or reverse spin after the fashion of pool-shooters.

Nobody paid much attention to me until after the game in progress had been decided. Then I was acknowledged with hand gestures and a few words—the tolerant acceptance accorded to known spectators and occasional players. Unknowns got no greeting at all; these men still clung to the old ways, and one of the old ways was clannishness.

Only one of the group, Dominick Marra, came over to where I was sitting. And that was because he had something on his mind. He was in his mid-seventies, white-haired, white-mustached; a bantamweight in baggy trousers held up by galluses. He and Pietro Lombardi had been close friends for most of their lives. Born in the same town—Agropoli, a village on the Gulf of Salerno not far from Naples; moved to San Francisco with their families a year apart, in the late twenties; married cousins, raised large families, were widowered at almost the same time a few years ago. The kind of friendship that is almost a blood tie. Dominick had been a baker; Pietro had owned a North Beach trattoria that now belonged to one of his daughters.

What Dominick had on his mind was Pietro. "You see how he sits over there, hah? He's got trouble—*la miseria.*"

"What kind of trouble?"

"His granddaughter. Gianna Fornessi."

"Something happen to her?"

"She's maybe go to jail," Dominick said.

"What for?"

"Stealing money."

"I'm sorry to hear it. How much money?"

"Two thousand dollars."

"Who did she steal it from?"

"*Che?*"

"Who did she steal the money from?"

Dominick gave me a disgusted look. "She don't steal it. Why you think Pietro he's got *la miseria*, hah?"

I knew what was coming now; I should have known it the instant Dominick started confiding to me about Pietro's problem. I said, "You want me to help him and his granddaughter."

"Sure. You a detective."

"A busy detective."

"You got no time for old man and young girl? *Compaesani?*"

I sighed, but not so he could hear me do it. "All right, I'll talk to Pietro. See if he wants my help, if there's anything I can do."

"Sure he wants your help. He just don't know it yet."

We went to where Pietro was sitting alone in the sun. He was taller than Dominick, heavier, balder. And he had a fondness for Toscanas, those little twisted black Italian cigars; one protruded now from a corner of his mouth. He didn't want to talk at first, but Dominick launched into a monologue in Italian that changed his mind and put a glimmer of hope in his sad eyes. Even though I've lost a lot of the language over the years, I can understand enough to follow most conversations. The gist of Dominick's monologue was that I was not just a detective but a miracle worker, a cross between Sherlock Holmes and the Messiah. Italians are given to hyperbole in times of excitement or stress, and there isn't much you can do to counteract it—especially when you're one of the *compaesani* yourself.

"My Gianna, she's good girl," Pietro said. "Never give trouble, even when she's little one. *La bellezza delle bellezze*, you understand?"

The beauty of beauties. His favorite grandchild, probably.

I said, "I understand. Tell me about the money, Pietro."

"She don't steal it," he said. "*Una ladra*, my Gianna? No, no, it's all big lie."

"Did the police arrest her?"

"They got no evidence to arrest her."

"But somebody filed charges, is that it?"

"Charges," Pietro said. "Bah," he said and spat.

"Who made the complaint?"

Dominick said, "Ferry," as if the name were an obscenity.

"Who's Ferry?"

He tapped his skull. "*Caga di testa*, this man."

"That doesn't answer my question."

"He live where she live. Same apartment building."

"And he says Gianna stole two thousand dollars from him."

"Liar," Pietro said. "He lies."

"Stole it how? Broke in or what?"

"She don't break in nowhere, not my Gianna. This Ferry, this *bastardo*, he says she take the money when she's come to pay rent and he's talk on telephone. But how she knows where he keep his money? Hah? How she knows he have two thousand dollars in his desk?"

"Maybe he told her."

"Sure, that's what he says to police," Dominick said. "Maybe he told her, he says. He don't tell her nothing."

"Is that what Gianna claims?"

Pietro nodded. Threw down what was left of his Toscana and ground in into the dirt with his shoe—a gesture of anger and frustration. "She don't steal that money," he said. "What she need to steal money for? She got good job, she live good, she don't have to steal."

"What kind of job does she have?"

"She sell drapes, curtains. In . . . what you call that business, Dominick?"

"Interior decorating business," Dominick said.

"*Si*. In interior decorating business."

"Where does she live?" I asked.

"Chestnut Street."

"Where on Chestnut Street? What number?"

"Seventy-two fifty."

"You make that Ferry tell the truth, hah?" Dominick said to me. "You fix it up for Gianna and her goombah?"

"I'll do what I can."

"*Va bene*. Then you come tell Pietro right away."

"If Pietro will tell me where he lives—"

There was a sharp whacking sound as one of the bocce balls caromed off the side wall near us, then a softer clicking of ball meeting ball, and a shout went up from the players at the far end: another game won and lost. When I looked back at

Dominick and Pietro they were both on their feet. Dominick said, "You find Pietro okay, good detective like you," and Pietro said, "*Grazie, mi amico,*" and before I could say anything else the two of them were off arm in arm to join the others.

Now I was the one sitting alone in the sun, holding up a burden. Primed and ready to do a job I didn't want to do, probably couldn't do, and would not be paid well for if at all. Maybe this man Ferry wasn't the only one involved who had *caga di testa*—shit for brains. Maybe I did too.

2

The building at 7250 Chestnut Street was an old three-story, brown-shingled job, set high in the shadow of Coit Tower and across from the retaining wall where Telegraph Hill falls off steeply toward the Embarcadero. From each of the apartments, especially the ones on the third floor, you'd have quite a view of the bay, the East Bay, and both bridges. Prime North Beach address, this. The rent would be well in excess of two thousand a month.

A man in a tan trenchcoat was coming out of the building as I started up the steps to the vestibule. I called out to him to hold the door for me—it's easier to get apartment dwellers to talk to you once you're inside the building—but either he didn't hear me or he chose to ignore me. He came hurrying down without a glance my way as he passed. City-bred paranoia, I thought. It was everywhere these days, rich and poor neighborhoods both, like a nasty strain of social disease. Bumpersticker for the nineties: Fear Lives.

There were six mailboxes in the foyer, each with Dymo-Label stickers identifying the tenants. Gianna Fornessi's name was under box #4, along with a second name: Ashley Hansen. It figured that she'd have a roommate; salespersons working in the interior design trade are well but not extravagantly paid. Box #1 bore the name George Ferry and that was the bell I pushed. He was the one I wanted to talk to first.

A minute died away, while I listened to the wind that was savaging the trees on the hillside below. Out on the bay hundreds of sailboats formed a mosaic of white on blue. Somewhere among them a ship's horn sounded—to me, a sad false note. Shipping was all but dead on this side of the bay, thanks to wholesale mismanagement of the port over the past few decades.

The intercom crackled finally and a male voice said, "Who is it?" in wary tones.

I asked if he was George Ferry, and he admitted it, even more guardedly. I gave him my name, said that I was there to ask him a few questions about his complaint against Gianna Fornessi. He said, "Oh Christ." There was a pause, and then, "I called you people yesterday, I told Inspector Cullen I was dropping the charges. Isn't that enough?"

He thought I was a cop. I could have told him I wasn't; I could have let the whole thing drop right there, since what he'd just said was a perfect escape clause from my commitment to Pietro Lombardi. But I have too much curiosity to let go of something, once I've got a piece of it, without knowing the particulars. So I said, "I won't keep you long, Mr. Ferry. Just a few questions."

Another pause. "Is it really necessary?"

"I think it is, yes."

An even longer pause. But then he didn't argue, didn't say anything else—just buzzed me in.

His apartment was on the left, beyond a carpeted, dark-wood staircase. He opened the door as I approached it. Mid-forties, short, rotund, with a nose like a blob of putty and a Friar Tuck fringe of reddish hair. And a bruise on his left cheekbone, a cut along the right corner of his mouth. The marks weren't fresh, but then they weren't very old either. Twenty-four hours, maybe less.

He didn't ask to see a police ID; if he had, I would have told him immediately that I was a private detective, because nothing can lose you a California investigator's license faster than impersonating a police officer. On the other hand, you can't be held accountable for somebody's false assumption. Ferry gave me a nervous once-over, holding his head tilted downward as if that would keep me from seeing his bruise and cut, then stood aside to let me come in.

The front room was neat, furnished in a self-consciously masculine fashion: dark woods, leather, expensive sporting prints. It reeked of leather, dust, and his lime-scented cologne.

As soon as he shut the door, Ferry went straight to a liquor cabinet and poured himself three fingers of Jack Daniels, no water or mix, no ice. Just holding the drink seemed to give him courage. He said, "So. What is it you want to know?"

"Why you dropped your complaint against Gianna Fornessi."

"I explained to Inspector Cullen."

"Explain to me, if you don't mind."

He had some of the sour mash. "Well, it was all a

mistake . . . just a silly mistake. She didn't take the money after all."

"You know who did take it, then?"

"Nobody took it. I . . . misplaced it."

"Misplaced it. Uh-huh."

"I thought it was in my desk," Ferry said. "That's where I usually keep the cash I bring home. But I'd put it in my safe deposit box along with some other papers, without realizing it. It was in an envelope, you see, and the envelope got mixed up with the other papers."

"Two thousand dollars is a lot of cash to keep at home. You make a habit of that sort of thing?"

"In my business . . ." The rest of the sentence seemed to hang up in his throat; he oiled the route with the rest of his drink. "In my business I need to keep a certain amount of cash on hand, both here and at the office. The amount I keep here isn't usually as large as two thousand dollars, but I—"

"What business are you in, Mr. Ferry?"

"I run a temp employment agency for domestics."

"Temp?"

"Short for temporary," he said. "I supply domestics for part-time work in offices and private homes. A lot of them are poor, don't have checking accounts, so they prefer to be paid in cash. Most come to the office, but a few—"

"Why did you think Gianna Fornessi had stolen the two thousand dollars?"

". . . What?"

"Why Gianna Fornessi? Why not somebody else?"

"She's the only one who was here. Before I thought the money was missing, I mean. I had no other visitors for two days and there wasn't any evidence of a break-in."

"You and she are good friends, then?"

"Well . . . no, not really. She's a lot younger . . ."

"Then why was she here?"

"The rent," Ferry said. "She was paying her rent for the month. I'm the building manager, I collect for the owner. Before I could write out a receipt I had a call, I was on the phone for quite a while and she . . . I didn't pay any attention to her and I thought she must have . . . you see why I thought she'd taken the money?"

I was silent.

He looked at me, looked at his empty glass, licked his lips, and went to commune with Jack Daniels again.

While he was pouring I asked him, "What happened to your

face, Mr. Ferry?"

His hand twitched enough to clink bottle against glass. He had himself another taste before he turned back to me. "Clumsy," he said, "I'm clumsy as hell. I fell down the stairs, the front stairs, yesterday morning." He tried a laugh that didn't come off. "Fog makes the steps slippery. I just wasn't watching where I was going."

"Looks to me like somebody hit you."

"Hit me? No, I told you . . . I fell down the stairs."

"You're sure about that?"

"Of course I'm sure. Why would I lie about it?"

That was a good question. Why would he lie about that, and about all the rest of it too? There was about as much truth in what he'd told me as there is value in a chunk of fool's gold.

3

The young woman who opened the door of apartment #4 was not Gianna Fornessi. She was blonde, with the kind of fresh-faced Nordic features you see on models for Norwegian ski wear. Tall and slender in a pair of green silk lounging pajamas; arms decorated with hammered gold bracelets, ears with dangly gold triangles. Judging from the expression in her pale eyes, there wasn't much going on behind them. But then, with her physical attributes, not many men would care if her entire brain had been surgically removed.

"Well," she said, "hello."

"Ashley Hansen?"

"That's me. Who're you?"

When I told her my name her smile brightened, as if I'd said something amusing or clever. Or maybe she just liked the sound of it.

"I knew right away you were Italian," she said. "Are you a friend of Jack's?"

"Jack?"

"Jack Bisconte." The smile dulled a little. "You are, aren't you?"

"No," I said, "I'm a friend of Pietro Lombardi."

"Who?"

"Your roommate's grandfather. I'd like to talk to Gianna, if she's home."

Ashley Hansen's smile was gone now; her whole demeanor had changed, become less self-assured. She nibbled at a corner of her lower lip, ran a hand through her hair, fiddled with one

of her bracelets. Finally she said, "Gianna isn't here."
"When will she be back?"
"She didn't say."
"You know where I can find her?"
"No. What do you want to talk to her about?"
"The complaint George Ferry filed against her."
"Oh, that," she said. "That's all been taken care of."
"I know. I just talked to Ferry."
"He's a creepy little prick, isn't he?"
"That's one way of putting it."
"Gianna didn't take his money. He was just trying to hassle her, that's all."
"Why would he do that?"
"Well, why do you think?"
I shrugged. "Suppose you tell me."
"He wanted her to do things."
"You mean go to bed with him?"
"Things," she said. "Kinky crap, *real* kinky."
"And she wouldn't have anything to do with him."
"No way, Jose. What a creep."
"So he made up the story about the stolen money to get back at her, is that it?"
"That's it."
"What made him change his mind, drop the charges?"
"He didn't tell you?"
"No."
"Who knows?" She laughed. "Maybe he got religion."
"Or a couple of smacks in the face."
"Huh?"
"Somebody worked him over yesterday," I said. "Bruised his cheek and cut his mouth. You have any idea who?"
"Not me, mister. How come you're so interested, anyway?"
"I told you, I'm a friend of Gianna's grandfather."
"Yeah, well . . ."
"Gianna have a boyfriend, does she?"
". . . Why do you want to know that?"
"Jack Bisconte, maybe? Or is he yours?"
"He's just somebody I know." She nibbled at her lip again, did some more fiddling with her bracelets. "Look, I've got to go. You want me to tell Gianna you were here?"
"Yes." I handed her one of my business cards. "Give her this and ask her to call me."
She looked at the card; blinked at it and then blinked at me. "You . . . you're a detective?"

"That's right."

"My God," she said, and backed off, and shut the door in my face.

I stood there for a few seconds, remembering her eyes—the sudden fear in her eyes when she'd realized she had been talking to a detective.

What the hell?

4

North Beach used to be the place you went when you wanted pasta fino, espresso and biscotti, conversation about *la dolce vita* and *il patria d'Italia*. Not anymore. There are still plenty of Italians in North Beach, and you can still get the good food and some of the good conversation; but their turf continues to shrink a little more each year, and despite the best efforts of the entrepreneurial new immigrants, the vitality and most of the Old World atmosphere are just memories.

The Chinese are partly responsible, not that you can blame them for buying available North Beach real estate when Chinatown, to the west, began to burst its boundaries. Another culprit is the Bohemian element that took over upper Grant Avenue in the fifties, paving the way for the hippies and the introduction of hard drugs in the sixties, which in turn paved the way for the jolly current mix of motorcycle toughs, aging hippies, coke and crack dealers, and the pimps and smalltime crooks who work the flesh palaces along lower Broadway. Those "Silicone Alley" nightclubs, made famous by Carol Doda in the late sixties, also share responsibility: they added a smutty leer to the gaiety of North Beach, turned the heart of it into a ghetto.

Parts of the neighborhood, particularly those up around Coit Tower where Gianna Fornessi lived, are still prime city real estate, and the area around Washington Square Park, *il giardino* to the original immigrants, is where the city's literati now congregates. Here and there, too, you can still get a sense of what it was like in the old days. But most of the landmarks are gone—Enrico's, Vanessi's, The Bocce Ball where you could hear mustachioed waiters in gondolier costumes singing arias from operas by Verdi and Puccini—and so is most of the flavor. North Beach is oddly tasteless now, like a week-old mostaccioli made without good spices or garlic. And that is another thing that is all but gone: twenty-five years ago you could not get within a thousand yards of North Beach without picking up the fine, rich fragrance of garlic. Nowadays you're much more likely to smell fried egg roll and the sour stench of somebody's garbage.

Parking in the Beach is the worst in the city; on weekends you can drive around its hilly streets for hours without finding a legal parking space. So today, in the perverse way of things, I found a spot waiting for me when I came down Stockton.

In a public telephone booth near Washington Square Park I discovered a second minor miracle: a directory that had yet to be either stolen or mutilated. The only Bisconte listed was Bisconte Florist Shop, with an address on upper Grant a few blocks away. I took myself off in that direction, through the usual good-weather Sunday crowds of locals and gawking sightseers and drifting homeless.

Upper Grant, like the rest of the area, has changed drastically over the past few decades. Once a rock-ribbed Little Italy, it has become an ethnic mixed bag: Italian markets, trattorias, pizza parlors, bakeries cheek by jowl with Chinese sewing-machine sweat shops, food and herb vendors, and fortune-cookie companies. But most of the faces on the streets are Asian and most of the apartments in the vicinity are occupied by Chinese.

The Bisconte Florist Shop was a hole-in-the-wall near Filbert, sandwiched between an Italian saloon and the Sip Hing Herb Company. It was open for business, not surprisingly on a Sunday in this neighborhood: tourists buy flowers too, given the opportunity.

The front part of the shop was cramped and jungly with cut flowers, ferns, plants in pots and hanging baskets. A small glass-fronted cooler contained a variety of roses and orchids. There was nobody in sight, but a bell had gone off when I entered and a male voice from beyond a rear doorway called, "Be right with you." I shut the door, went up near the counter. Some people like florist shops; I don't. All of them have the same damp, cloyingly sweet smell that reminds me of funeral parlors; of my mother in her casket at the Figlia Brothers Mortuary in Daly City nearly forty years ago. That day, with all its smells, all its painful images, is as clear to me now as if it were yesterday.

I had been waiting about a minute when the voice's owner came out of the back room. Late thirties, dark, on the beefy side; wearing a professional smile and a floral-patterned apron that should have been ludicrous on a man of his size and coloring but wasn't. We had a good look at each other before he said, "Sorry to keep you waiting—I was putting up an arrangement. What can I do for you?"

"Mr. Bisconte? Jack Bisconte?"

"That's me. Something for the wife, maybe?"

"I'm not here for flowers. I'd like to ask you a few questions."

The smile didn't waver. "Oh? What about?"

"Gianna Fornessi."

"Who?"

"You don't know her?"

"Name's not familiar, no."

"She lives up on Chestnut with Ashley Hansen."

"Ashley Hansen . . . I don't know that name either."

"She knows you. Young, blonde, looks Norwegian."

"Well, I know a lot of young blondes," Bisconte said. He winked at me. "I'm a bachelor and I get around pretty good, you know?"

"Uh-huh."

"Lot of bars and clubs in North Beach, lot of women to pick and choose from." He shrugged. "So how come you're asking about these two?"

"Not both of them. Just Gianna Fornessi."

"That so? You a friend of hers?"

"Of her grandfather's. She's had a little trouble."

"What kind of trouble?"

"Manager of her building accused her of stealing some money. But somebody convinced him to drop the charges."

"That so?" Bisconte said again, but not as if he cared.

"Leaned on him to do it. Scared the hell out of him."

"You don't think it was me, do you? I told you, I don't know anybody named Gianna Fornessi."

"So you did."

"What's the big deal anyway?" he said. "I mean, if the guy dropped the charges, then this Gianna is off the hook, right?"

"Right."

"Then why all the questions?"

"Curiosity," I said. "Mine and her grandfather's."

Another shrug. "I'd like to help you, pal, but like I said, I don't know the lady. Sorry."

"Sure."

"Come back any time you need flowers," Bisconte said. He gave me a little salute, waited for me to turn, and then did the same himself. He was hidden away again in the back room when I let myself out.

Today was my day for liars. Liars and puzzles.

He hadn't asked me who I was or what I did for a living; that was because he already knew. And the way he knew, I thought, was that Ashley Hansen had gotten on the horn after I left and told him about me. He knew Gianna Fornessi pretty well too, and exactly where the two women lived.

He was the man in the tan trenchcoat I'd seen earlier, the one who wouldn't hold the door for me at 7250 Chestnut.

5

I treated myself to a plate of linguine and fresh clams at a ristorante off Washington Square and then drove back over to Aquatic Park. Now, in mid-afternoon, with fog seeping in through the Gate and the temperature dropping sharply, the number of bocce players and kibitzers had thinned by half. Pietro Lombardi was one of those remaining; Dominick Marra was another. Bocce may be dying easy in the city but not in men like them. They cling to it and to the other old ways as tenaciously as they cling to life itself.

I told Pietro—and Dominick, who wasn't about to let us talk in private—what I'd learned so far. He was relieved that Ferry had dropped his complaint, but just as curious as I was about the Jack Bisconte connection.

"Do you know Bisconte?" I asked him.

"No. I see his shop but I never go inside."

"Know anything about him?"

"*Niente.*"

"How about you, Dominick?"

He shook his head. "He's too old for Gianna, hah? Almost forty, you say—that's too old for girl twenty-three."

"If that's their relationship," I said.

"Men almost forty they go after young woman, they only got one reason. *Fatto 'na bella chiavata.* You remember, eh, Pietro?"

"*Pazzo!* You think I forget *'na bella chiavata?*"

I asked Pietro, "You know anything about Gianna's roommate?"

"Only once I meet her," he said. "Pretty, but not so pretty like my Gianna, *la bellezza delle bellezze.* I don't like her too much."

"Why not?"

"She don't have respect like she should."

"What does she do for a living, do you know?"

"No. She don't say and Gianna don't tell me."

"How long have they been sharing the apartment?"

"Eight, nine months."

"Did they know each other long before they moved in together?"

He shrugged. "Gianna and me, we don't talk much like when she's little girl," he said sadly. "Young people now, they got no time for *la famiglia*." Another shrug, a sigh. "*Ognuno pensa per sè*," he said. Everybody thinks only of himself.

Dominick gripped his shoulder. Then he said to me, "You find out what's happen with Bisconte and Ferry and those girls. Then you see they don't bother them no more. Hah?"

"If I can, Dominick. If I can."

The fog was coming in thickly now and the other players were making noises about ending the day's tournament. Dominick got into an argument with one of them; he wanted to play another game or two. He was outvoted, but he was still pleading his case when I left. Their Sunday was almost over. So was mine.

I went home to my flat in Pacific Heights. And Kerry came over later on and we had dinner and listened to some jazz. I thought maybe Gianna Fornessi might call but she didn't. No one called. Good thing, too. I would not have been pleased to hear the phone ring after eight o'clock; I was busy then.

Men in their late fifties are just as interested in '*na bella chiavata*. Women in their early forties, too.

6

At the office in the morning I called TRW for credit checks on Jack Bisconte, George Ferry, Gianna Fornessi, and Ashley Hansen. I also asked my partner, Eberhardt, who has been off the cops just a few years and who still has plenty of cronies sprinkled throughout the SFPD, to find out what Inspector Cullen and the Robbery Detail had on Ferry's theft complaint, and to have the four names run through R&I for any local arrest record.

The report out of Robbery told me nothing much. Ferry's complaint had been filed on Friday morning; Cullen had gone to investigate, talked to the two principals, and determined that there wasn't enough evidence to take Gianna Fornessi into custody. Thirty hours later Ferry had called in and withdrawn the complaint, giving the same flimsy reason he'd handed me. As far as Cullen and the department were concerned, it was all very minor and routine.

The TRW and R&I checks took a little longer to come

through, but I had the information by noon. It went like this:

Jack Bisconte. Good credit rating. Owner and sole operator, Bisconte Florist Shop, since 1978; lived on upper Greenwich Street, in a rented apartment, same length of time. No listing of previous jobs held or previous local addresses. No felony or misdemeanor arrests.

George Ferry. Excellent credit rating. Owner and principal operator, Ferry Temporary Employment Agency, since 1972. Resident of 7250 Chestnut since 1980. No felony arrests; one DWI arrest and conviction following a minor traffic accident in May 1981, sentenced to ninety days in jail (suspended), driver's license revoked for six months.

Gianna Fornessi. Fair to good credit rating. Employed by Home Draperies, Showplace Square, as a sales representative since 1988. Resident of 7250 Chestnut for eight months; address prior to that, her parents' home in Daly City. No felony or misdemeanor arrests.

Ashley Hansen. No credit rating. No felony or misdemeanor arrests.

There wasn't much in any of that, either, except for the fact that TRW had no listing on Ashley Hansen. Almost everybody uses credit cards these days, establishes some kind of credit—especially a young woman whose income is substantial enough to afford an apartment in one of the city's best neighborhoods. Why not Ashley Hansen?

She was one person who could tell me; another was Gianna Fornessi. I had yet to talk to Pietro's granddaughter and I thought it was high time. I left the office in Eberhardt's care, picked up my car, and drove south of Market to Showplace Square.

The Square is a newish complex of manufacturers' showrooms for the interior decorating trade—carpets, draperies, lighting fixtures, and other types of home furnishings. It's not open to the public, but I showed the photostat of my license to one of the security men at the door and talked him into calling the Home Draperies showroom and asking them to send Gianna Fornessi out to talk to me.

They sent somebody out but it wasn't Gianna Fornessi. It was a fluffy looking little man in his forties named Lundquist, who said, "I'm sorry, Ms. Fornessi is no longer employed by us."

"Oh? When did she leave?"

"Eight months ago."

"Eight months?"

"At the end of September."

"Quit or terminated?"

"Quit. Rather abruptly, too."

"To take another job?"

"I don't know. She gave no adequate reason."

"No one called afterward for a reference?"

"No one," Lundquist said.

"She worked for you two years, is that right?"

"About two years, yes."

"As a sales representative?"

"That's correct."

"May I ask her salary?"

"I really couldn't tell you that."

"Just this, then: Was hers a high-salaried position? In excess of thirty thousand a year, say?"

Lundquist smiled a faint, fluffy smile. "Hardly," he said.

"Were her skills such that she could have taken another, better paying job in the industry?"

Another fluffy smile. And another "Hardly."

So why had she quit Home Draperies so suddenly eight months ago, at just about the same time she moved into the Chestnut Street apartment with Ashley Hansen? And what was she doing to pay her share of the rent?

7

There was an appliance store delivery truck double-parked in front of 7250 Chestnut, and when I went up the stairs I found the entrance door wedged wide open, Nobody was in the vestibule or lobby, but the murmur of voices filtered down from the third floor. If I'd been a burglar I would have rubbed my hands together in glee. As it was, I walked in as if I belonged there and climbed the inside staircase to the second floor.

When I swung off the stairs I came face to face with Jack Bisconte.

He was hurrying toward me from the direction of apartment #4, something small and red and rectangular clutched in the fingers of his left hand. He broke stride when he saw me; and then recognition made him do a jerky double-take and he came to a halt. I stopped, too, with maybe fifteen feet separating us. That was close enough, and the hallway was well-lighted enough, for me to get a good look at his face. It was pinched, sweat-slicked, the eyes wide and shiny—the face of a man on the cutting edge of panic.

Frozen time, maybe five seconds of it, while we stood staring at each other. There was nobody else in the hall; no audible sounds on this floor except for the quick rasp of Bisconte's breathing. Then we both moved at the same time—Bisconte in the same jerky fashion of his double-take, shoving the red object into his coat pocket as he came forward. And then, when we had closed the gap between us by half, we both stopped again as if on cue. It might have been a mildly amusing little pantomime if you'd been a disinterested observer. It wasn't amusing to me. Or to Bisconte, from the look of him.

I said, "Fancy meeting you here. I thought you didn't know Gianna Fornessi or Ashley Hansen."

"Get out of my way."

"What's your hurry?"

"Get out of my way. I mean it." The edge of panic had cut into his voice; it was thick, liquidy, as if it were bleeding.

"What did you put in your pocket, the red thing?"

He said, "Christ!" and tried to lunge past me.

I blocked his way, getting my hands up between us to push him back. He made a noise in his throat and swung at me. It was a clumsy shot; I ducked away from it without much effort, so that his knuckles just grazed my neck. But then the son of a bitch kicked me, hard, on the left shinbone. I yelled and went down. He kicked out again, this time at my head; didn't connect because I was already rolling away. I fetched up tight against the wall and by the time I got myself twisted back around he was pelting toward the stairs.

I shoved up the wall to my feet, almost fell again when I put weight on the leg he'd kicked. Hobbling, wiping pain-wet out of my eyes, I went after him. People were piling down from the third floor; the one in the lead was George Ferry. He called something that I didn't listen to as I started to descend. Bisconte, damn him, had already crossed the lobby and was running out through the open front door.

Hop, hop, hop down the stairs like a contestant in a one-legged race, using the railing for support. By the time I reached the lobby, some of the sting had gone out of my shinbone and I could put more weight on the leg. Out into the vestibule, half running and half hobbling now, looking for him. He was across the street and down a ways, fumbling with a set of keys at the driver's door of a new silver Mercedes.

But he didn't stay there long. He was too wrought up to get the right key into the lock, and when he saw me pounding across the street in his direction, the panic goosed him and he ran again. Around behind the Mercedes, onto the sidewalk, up and over the concrete retaining wall. And gone.

I heard him go sliding or tumbling through the undergrowth below. I staggered up to the wall, leaned over it. The slope down there was steep, covered with trees and brush, strewn with the leavings of semi-humans who had used it for a dumping ground. Bisconte was on his buttocks, digging hands and heels into the ground to slow his momentum. For a few seconds I thought he was going to turn into a one-man avalanche and plummet over the edge where the slope ended in a sheer bluff face. But then he managed to catch hold of one of the tree trunks and swing himself away from the bluff, in among a tangle of bushes where I couldn't see him anymore. I could hear him—and then I couldn't. He'd found purchase, I thought, and was easing himself down to where the backside of another apartment building leaned in against the cliff.

There was no way I was going down there after him. I turned and went to the Mercedes.

It had a vanity plate, the kind that makes you wonder why somebody would pay twenty-five dollars extra to the DMV to put it on his car: BISFLWR. If the Mercedes had had an external hood release, I would have popped it and disabled the engine; but it didn't, and all four doors were locked. All right. Chances were, he wouldn't risk coming back soon—and even if he ran the risk, it would take him a good long while to get here.

I limped back to 7250. Four people were clustered in the vestibule, staring at me—Ferry and a couple of uniformed deliverymen and a fat woman in her forties. Ferry said as I came up the steps, "What happened, what's going on?" I didn't answer him. There was a bad feeling in me now; or maybe it had been there since I'd first seen the look on Bisconte's face. I pushed through the cluster—none of them tried to stop me—and crossed the lobby and went up to the second floor.

Nobody answered the bell at apartment #4. 1 tried the door, and it was unlocked, and I opened it and walked in and shut it again and locked it behind me.

She was lying on the floor in the living room, sprawled and bent on her back near a heavy teak coffee table, peach-colored dressing gown hiked up over her knees; head twisted at an off-angle, blood and a deep triangular puncture wound on her left temple. The blood was still wet and clotting. She hadn't been dead much more than an hour.

In the sunlight that spilled in through the undraped windows, the blood had a kind of shimmery radiance. So did her hair—her long gold-blond hair.

Goodbye Ashley Hansen.

8

I called the Hall of Justice and talked to a Homicide inspector I knew slightly named Craddock. I told him what I'd found, and about my little skirmish with Jack Biscone, and said that yes, I would wait right here and no, I wouldn't touch anything. He didn't tell me not to look around and I didn't say that I wouldn't.

Somebody had started banging on the door. Ferry, probably. I went the other way, into one of the bedrooms. Ashley Hansen's: there was a photograph of her prominently displayed on the dresser, and lots of mirrors to give her a live image of herself. A narcissist, among other things. On one nightstand was a telephone and an answering machine. On the unmade bed, tipped on its side with some of the contents spilled out, was a fancy leather purse. I used the backs of my two index fingers to stir around among the spilled items and the stuff inside. Everything you'd expect to find in a woman's purse and one thing that should have been there and wasn't.

Gianna Fornessi's bedroom was across the hall. She also had a telephone and an answering machine; the number on the telephone dial was different from her roommate's. I hesitated for maybe five seconds, then I went to the answering machine and pushed the button marked "playback calls" and listened to two old messages before I stopped the tape and rewound it. One message would have been enough.

Back into the living room. The knocking was still going on. I started over there; stopped after a few feet and stood sniffing the air. I thought I smelled something—a faint lingering acrid odor. Or maybe I was just imagining it ...

Bang, bang, bang. And Ferry's voice: "What's going on in there?"

I moved ahead to the door, threw the bolt lock, yanked the door open. "Quit making so damned much noise."

Ferry blinked and backed off a step; he didn't know whether to be afraid of me or not. Behind and to one side of him, the two deliverymen and the fat woman looked on with hungry eyes. They would have liked seeing what lay inside; blood attracts some people, the gawkers, the insensitive ones, the same way it attracts flies.

"What's happened?" Ferry asked nervously.

"Come in and see for yourself. Just you."

I opened up a little wider and he came in past me, showing reluctance. I shut and locked the door again behind him. And when I turned he said, "Oh my God," in a sickened voice. He was staring at the body on the floor, one hand pressed up under his breastbone. "Is she . . . ?"

"Very."

"Gianna . . . is she here?"

"No."

"Somebody did that to Ashley? It wasn't an accident?"

"What do you think?"

"Who? Who did it?"

"You know who, Ferry. You saw me chase him out of here."

"I . . . don't know who he is. I never saw him before."

"The hell you never saw him. He's the one put those cuts and bruises on your face."

"No," Ferry said, "that's not true." He looked and sounded even sicker now. "I told you how that happened . . ."

"You told me lies. Bisconte roughed you up so you'd drop your complaint against Gianna. He did it because Gianna and Ashley Hansen have been working as call girls and he's their pimp and he didn't want the cops digging into her background and finding out the truth."

Ferry leaned unsteadily against the wall, facing away from what was left of the Hansen woman. He didn't speak.

"Nice quiet little operation they had," I said, "until you got wind of it. That's how it was, wasn't it? You found out and you wanted some of what Gianna's been selling."

Nothing for ten seconds. Then, softly, "It wasn't like that, not at first. I . . . loved her."

"Sure you did."

"I did. But she wouldn't have anything to do with me."

"So then you offered to pay her."

". . . Yes. Whatever she charged."

"Only you wanted kinky sex and she wouldn't play."

"No! I never asked for anything except a night with her . . . one night. She pretended to be insulted; she denied that she's been selling herself to men. She . . . she said she'd never go to bed with a man as . . . ugly . . ." He moved against the wall—a writhing movement, as if he were in pain.

"That was when you decided to get even with her."

"I wanted to hurt her, the way she'd hurt me. It was stupid, I know that, but I wasn't thinking clearly. I just wanted to hurt her . . ."

"Well, you succeeded," I said. "But the one you really hurt is

Ashley Hansen. If it hadn't been for you, she'd still be alive."

He started to say something but the words were lost in the sudden summons of the doorbell.

"That'll be the police," I said.

"The police? But . . . I thought you were . . ."

"I know you did. I never told you I was, did I?"

I left him holding up the wall and went to buzz them in.

9

I spent more than two hours in the company of the law, alternately answering questions and waiting around. I told Inspector Craddock how I happened to be there. I told him how I'd come to realize that Gianna Fornessi and Ashley Hansen were call girls, and how George Ferry and Jack Bisconte figured into it. I told him about the small red rectangular object I'd seen Bisconte shove into his pocket—an address book, no doubt, with the names of some of Hansen's johns. That was the common item that was missing from her purse.

Craddock seemed satisfied. I wished I was.

When he finally let me go I drove back to the office. But I didn't stay long; it was late afternoon, Eberhardt had already gone for the day, and I felt too restless to tackle the stack of routine paperwork on my desk. I went out to Ocean Beach and walked on the sand, as I sometimes do when an edginess is on me. It helped a little—not much.

I ate an early dinner out, and when I got home I put in a call to the Hall of Justice to ask if Jack Bisconte had been picked up yet. But Craddock was off duty and the inspector I spoke to wouldn't tell me anything.

The edginess stayed with me all evening, and kept me awake past midnight. I knew what was causing it, all right; and I knew what to do to get rid of it. Only I wasn't ready to do it yet.

In the morning, after eight, I called the Hall again. Craddock came on duty at eight, I'd been told. He was there and willing to talk, but what he had to tell me was not what I wanted to hear. Bisconte was in custody but not because he'd been apprehended. At eight-thirty Monday night he'd walked into the North Beach precinct station with his lawyer in tow and given himself up. He'd confessed to being a pimp for the two women; he'd confessed to working over George Ferry; he'd confessed to being in the women's apartment just prior to his tussle with me. But he swore up and down that he hadn't killed

Ashley Hansen. He'd never had any trouble with her, he said; in fact he'd been half in love with her. The cops had Gianna Fornessi in custody too by this time, and she'd confirmed that there had never been any rough stuff or bad feelings between her roommate and Bisconte.

Hansen had been dead when he got to the apartment, Bisconte said. Fear that he'd be blamed had pushed him into a panic. He'd taken the address book out of her purse—he hadn't thought about the answering machine tapes or he'd have erased the messages left by eager johns—and when he'd encountered me in the hallway he'd lost his head completely. Later, after he'd had time to calm down, he'd gone to the lawyer, who had advised him to turn himself in.

Craddock wasn't so sure Bisconte was telling the truth, but I was. I knew who had been responsible for Ashley Hansen's death; I'd known it a few minutes after I found her body. I just hadn't wanted it to be that way.

I didn't tell Craddock any of this. When he heard the truth it would not be over the phone. And it would not be from me.

10

It did not take me long to track him down. He wasn't home but a woman in his building said that in nice weather he liked to sit in Washington Square Park with his cronies. That was where I found him, in the park. Not in the company of anyone; just sitting alone on a bench across from the Saints Peter and Paul Catholic Church, in the same slumped, bowed-head posture as when I'd first seen him on Sunday—the posture of *la miseria*.

I sat down beside him. He didn't look at me, not even when I said, "*Buon giorno*, Pietro."

He took out one of his twisted black cigars and lit it carefully with a kitchen match. Its odor was acrid on the warm morning air—the same odor that had been in his granddaughter's apartment, that I'd pretended to myself I was imagining. Nothing smells like a Toscana; nothing. And only old men like Pietro smoke Toscanas these days. They don't even have to smoke one in a closed room for the smell to linger after them; it gets into and comes off the heavy user's clothing.

"It's time for us to talk," I said.

"*Che sopra?*"

"Ashley Hansen. How she died."

A little silence. Then he sighed and said, "You already know, hah, good detective like you? How you find out?"

"Does it matter?"

"It don't matter. You tell police yet?"

"It'll be better if you tell them."

More silence, while he smoked his little cigar.

I said, "But first tell me. Exactly what happened."

He shut his eyes; he didn't want to relive what had happened.

"It was me telling you about Bisconte that started it," I said to prod him. "After you got home Sunday night you called Gianna and asked her about him. Or she called you."

". . . I call her," he said. "She's angry, she tell me mind my own business. Never before she talks to her goombah this way."

"Because of me. Because she was afraid of what I'd find out about her and Ashley Hansen and Bisconte."

"Bisconte." He spat the name, as if ridding his mouth of something foul.

"So this morning you asked around the neighborhood about him. And somebody told you he wasn't just a florist, about his little sideline. Then you got on a bus and went to see your granddaughter."

"I don't believe it, not about Gianna. I want her tell me it's not true. But she's not there. Only the other one, the *bionda*."

"And then?"

"She don't want to let me in, that one. I go in anyway. I ask if she and Gianna are . . . if they sell themselves for money. She laugh. In my face she laugh, this girl what have no respect. She says what difference it make? She says I am old man—dinosaur, she says. But she pat my cheek like I am little boy or big joke. Then she . . . ah, *Cristo*, she come up close to me and she say you want some, old man, I give you some. To me she says this. Me." Pietro shook his head; there were tears in his eyes now. "I push her away. I feel . . . *feroce*, like when I am young man and somebody he make trouble with me. I push her too hard and she fall, her head hit the table and I see blood and she don't move . . . ah, *mio Dio!* She was wicked, that one, but I don't mean to hurt her . . ."

"I know you didn't, Pietro."

"I think, call doctor quick. But she is dead. And I hurt here, inside"—he tapped his chest—"and I think, what if Gianna she come home? I don't want to see Gianna. You understand? Never again I want to see her."

"I understand," I said. And I thought: Funny—I've never laid eyes on her, not even a photograph of her. I don't know what she looks like; now I don't want to know. I never want to see her.

Pietro finished his cigar. Then he straightened on the bench, seemed to compose himself. His eyes had dried; they were clear and sad. He looked past me, across at the looming Romanesque pile of the church. "I make confession to priest," he said, "little while before you come. Now we go to police and I make confession to them."

"Yes."

"You think they put me in gas chamber?"

"I doubt they'll put you in prison at all. It was an accident. Just a bad accident."

Another silence. On Pietro's face was an expression of the deepest pain. "This thing, this accident, she shouldn't have happen. Once . . . ah, once . . ." Pause. "*Morto*," he said.

He didn't mean the death of Ashley Hansen. He meant the death of the old days, the days when families were tightly knit and there was respect for elders, the days when bocce was king of his world and that world was a far simpler and better place. The bitterest of woes is to remember old happy days.

We sat there in the pale sun. And pretty soon he said, in a voice so low I barely heard the words, "*La bellezza delle bellezze*." Twice before he had used that phrase in my presence and both times he had been referring to his granddaughter. This time I knew he was not.

"*Si, 'paesano*," I said. "*La bellezza delle bellezze.*"

HOME IS THE PLACE WHERE

It was one of those little crossroads places you still find occasionally in the California backcountry. Relics of another era; old dying things, with precious little time left before they crumble into dust. Weathered wooden store building, gas pumps, a detached service garage that also housed restrooms, some warped little tourist cabins clustered close behind; a couple of junk-car husks and a stand of dusty shade trees. This one was down in the central part of the state, southeast of San Juan Bautista, on the way to the Pinnacles National Monument. The name on the pocked metal sign on the store roof was *Benson's Oasis*. There were four cabins and the shade trees were cottonwoods.

No other cars sat on the apron in front when I pulled in at a few minutes past two. Nor were there any vehicles back by the cabins. The only spot to hide one was in the detached garage—and it was shut up tight. Maybe something in that, maybe not.

Heat hammered at me when I got out, thick and deep-summer dry. In the distance, haze blurred the shapes of the brown hills of the Diablo Range. It was flat here, and dust-blown, and quiet. The feeling you had was of isolation, emptiness, and displacement in time. For me, it was a pleasant feeling, not at all unsettling. I like the past; I like it a hell of a lot better than I like the present or the prospects for the future.

It was even hotter inside the store. No air-conditioning, just an old-fashioned ceiling fan that stirred the air in a way that made me think of a ladle stirring bouillon. Under the fan flies floated in random lethargic circles, as if they'd been drugged. The old man behind the counter at the rear had the same drugged, listless aspect. He was perched on a stool, studying a book of some kind that was open on the countertop. A bell had tinkled to announce my arrival but at first he didn't look up. He turned a page as I crossed the room; it made a dry rustling sound. The page was black, with what looked to be photographs and paper items affixed to it. A scrapbook.

When I reached him he shut the book. It had a brown simulated leather cover, the word *Memories* embossed on it in gilt. The gilt had flaked and faded and the ersatz leather was cracked: the book was almost as old as he was. Over seventy, I judged. Thin, stoop-shouldered, white hair as fine as rabbit fur. Heavily seamed face. Bent left arm that was also knobbed and crooked at the wrist, as if it had been badly broken once and hadn't healed well.

"What can I do for you?" he asked.

"You're the owner? Everett Benson?"

"I am."

"I'm looking for your son, Mr. Benson."

No reaction.

"Have you seen him, heard from him, in the past two days?"

Still nothing for several seconds. Then, "I have no son."

"Stephen," I said. "Stephen Arthur Benson."

"No."

"He's in trouble. Serious trouble."

Face like a chunk of eroded limestone, eyes like cloudy agates imbedded in it. "I have no son," he said again.

I took out one of my business cards, tried to give it to him. He wouldn't take it. Finally I laid it on the counter in front of him. "Stephen was in jail in San Francisco," I said, "on a charge of selling amphetamines and crack cocaine. Did you know that?"

Silence.

"He talked the woman he was living with into going to a bondsman and bailing him out. The bail was low and she had just enough collateral to swing it. His trial date was yesterday. Two nights ago he stole a hundred dollars from the woman, and her car, and jumped bail."

More silence.

"The bondsman hired me to find him and bring him back," I said. "I think he came here. You're his only living relative, and he needs more money than he's got to keep on running. He could steal it but it would be easier and safer to get it from you."

Benson pushed off his stool, picked up the scrapbook, laid it on a shelf behind him. Several regular hardback books lined the rest of the shelf, all of them old and well-read; in the weak light I couldn't make out any of the titles.

"Aiding and abetting a fugitive is a felony," I said to his back, "even if the fugitive is your own son. You don't want to get yourself in trouble with the law, do you?"

He said again, without turning, "I have no son."

For the moment I'd taken the argument as far as it would go. I left him and went out into the midday glare. And straight over to the closed-up service garage.

There were two windows along the near side, both dusty and speckled with ground-in dirt, but I could see clearly enough through the first. Sufficient daylight penetrated the gloom so I could identify the two vehicles parked in there. One was a dented, rusted, thirty-year-old Ford pickup that no doubt belonged to the old man. The other was a newish red Mitsubishi. I didn't have to see the license plate to know that the Mitsubishi belonged to Stephen Arthur Benson's girlfriend.

Cars drifted past on the highway; they made the only sound in the stillness. Behind the store, where the cabins were, nothing moved except for shimmers of heat. I went to my car, sleeving away sweat, and unclipped the short-barrelled .38 revolver from under the dash and slid it into the pocket of my suit jacket. Maybe I'd need the gun and maybe I wouldn't, but I felt better armed. Stephen Benson was a convicted felon and something of a hardcase, and for all I knew he was armed himself. He hadn't had a weapon two nights ago, according to the girlfriend, but he might have picked one up somewhere in the interim. From his father, for instance.

The stand of cottonwoods grew along the far side of the parking area. I moved over into them, made my way behind the two cabins on the south side. Both had blank rear walls and uncurtained side windows; I took my time approaching each. Their interiors were sparsely furnished, and empty of people and personal belongings.

The direct route to the other two cabins was across open ground. I didn't like the idea of that, so I went the long way—back through the trees, across in front of the store, around on the far side of the garage. It was an unnecessary precaution, as it turned out. The farthest of the northside cabins was also empty; the near one showed plenty of signs of occupancy—clothing, books, photographs, a hotplate, a small refrigerator — but there wasn't anybody in it. This was where the old man lived, I thought. The clothing was the type he would wear and the books were similar to the ones in the store.

Nothing to do now but to go back inside and brace him again. When I entered the store he was on his stool, eating a Milky Way in little nibbling bites. He had loose false teeth and on each bite they clicked like beads on a string.

"Where is he, Mr. Benson?"

No response. The cloudy agate eyes regarded me with the same lack of expression as before.

"I saw the car in the garage," I said. "It's the one Stephen stole from the woman in San Francisco, no mistake. Either he's still in this area or you gave him money and another car and he's on the road again. Which is it?"

He clicked and chewed; he didn't speak.

"All right then. You don't want to do this the easy way, we'll have to do it the hard way. I'll call the county police and have them come out here and look at the stolen car; then they'll charge you with aiding and abetting and with harboring stolen property. And your son will still get picked up and sent back to San Francisco to stand trial. It's only a matter of time."

Benson finished the candy bar; I couldn't tell if he was thinking over what I'd said, but I decided I'd give him a few more minutes in case he was. In the stillness, a refrigeration unit made a broken chattery hum. The heat-drugged flies droned and circled. A car drew up out front and a grumpy-looking citizen came in and bought two cans of soda pop and a bag of potato chips. "Hot as Hades out there," he said. Neither Benson nor I answered him.

When he was gone I said to the old man, "Last chance. Where's Stephen?" He didn't respond, so I said, "I've got a car phone. I'll use that to call the sheriff," and turned and started out.

He let me get halfway to the door before he said, "You win, mister," in a dull, empty voice. "Not much point in keeping quiet about it. Like you said, it's only a matter of time."

I came back to the counter. "Now you're being smart. Where is he?"

"I'll take you to him."

"Just tell me where I can find him."

"No. I'll take you there."

Might be better at that, I thought, if Stephen's close by. Easier, less chance for trouble, with the old man along. I nodded, and Benson came out from behind the counter and crossed to where a sign hung in the window; he reversed the sign so that the word *Closed* faced outward. Then we went out and he locked up.

I asked him, "How far do we have to go?"

"Not far."

"I'll drive, you tell me where."

We got into the car. He directed me east on the county road that intersected the main highway. We rode in silence for about a mile. Benson sat stiff-backed, his hands gripping his knees, eyes straight ahead. In the hard daylight the knobbed bone on his left wrist looked as big as a plum.

Abruptly he said, "'Home is the place where.'"

". . . How's that again?"

"'Home is the place where, when you have to go there, they have to take you in.'"

I shrugged because the words didn't mean anything to me.

"Lines from a poem by Robert Frost," he said. "'The Death of the Hired Man,' I think. You read Frost?"

"No."

"I like him. Makes sense to me, more than a lot of them."

I remembered the well-read books on the store shelf and in the cabin. A rural storekeeper who read poetry and admired Robert Frost. Well, why not? People don't fit into easy little stereotypes. In my profession, you learn not to lose sight of that fact.

Home is the place where, when you have to go there, they have to take you in. The words ran around inside my head like song lyrics. No, like a chant or an invocation—all subtle rhythm and gathering power. They made sense to me, too, on more than one level. Now I knew something more about Everett Benson, and something more about the nature of his relationship with his son.

Another couple of silent miles through sun-struck farmland. Alfalfa and wine grapes, mostly. A private farm road came up on the right; Benson told me to turn there. It had once been a good road, unpaved but well graded, but that had been a long time ago. Now there were deep grooves in it, and weeds and tall brown grass between the ruts. Not used much these days. It led along the shoulder of a sere hill, then up to the crest; from there I could see where it ended.

Benson's Oasis was a dying place, with not much time left. The farm down below was already dead—years dead. It had been built alongside a shallow creek where willows and cottonwoods grew, in the tuck where two hillocks came together: farmhouse, barn, two chicken coops, a shedlike outbuilding. Skeletons now, all of them, broken and half-hidden by high grass and shrubs and tangles of wild berry vines. Climbing primroses covered part of the house from foundation to roof, bright pink in the sunlight, like a gaudy fungus.

"Your property?" I asked him.

"Built it all with my own hands," he said. "After the war—Second World War—when land was cheap hereabouts. Raised chickens, alfalfa, apples. You can see there's still part of the orchard left."

There were a dozen or so apple trees, stretching away behind the barn. Gnarled, bent, twisted, but still producing fruit. Rotting fruit now.

"Moved out eight years ago, when my wife died," Benson said. "Couldn't bear to live here any more without Betty.

Couldn't bear to sell the place, either." He paused, drew a heavy breath, let it out slowly. "Don't come out here much anymore. Just a couple of times a year to visit her grave."

There were no other cars in sight, but I could make out where one had angled off the roadway and mashed down an irregular swath of the summer-dead grass, not long ago. I followed the same route when we reached the farmyard. The swath stopped ten yards from what was left of the farmhouse's front porch. So did I.

I had my window rolled down but there was nothing to hear except birds and insects. The air was swollen with the smells of heat and dry grass and decaying apples.

I said, "Is he inside the house?"

"Around back."

"Where around back?"

"There's a beat-down path. Just follow that."

"You don't want to come along?"

"No need. I'll stay here."

I gave him a long look. There was no tension in him, no guile; not much emotion of any kind, it seemed. He just sat there, hands on knees, eyes front—the same posture he'd held throughout the short trip from the crossroads.

I thought about insisting he come with me, but something kept me from doing it. I got out, taking the keys from the ignition. Before I shut the door I drew the .38; then I leaned back in to look at Benson, holding the gun down low so he couldn't see it.

"You won't blow the horn or anything like that, will you?"

"No," he said, "I won't."

"Just wait quiet."

"Yes."

The beaten-down path was off to the right. I walked it slowly through the tangled vegetation, listening, watching my backtrail. Nothing made noise and nothing happened. The fermenting-apples smell grew stronger as I came around the house to the rear; bees swarmed back there, making a muted sawmill sound. Near where the orchard began, the path veered off toward the creek, toward a big weeping willow that grew on the bank.

And under the willow was where it ended: at the grave of Benson's wife, marked by a marble headstone etched with the words *Beloved Elizabeth—Rest in Eternal Peace.*

But hers was not the only grave there. Next to it was a second one, a new one, the earth so freshly turned some of the clods on top were still moist. That one bore no marker of any kind.

I went back to the car, not quite running. Benson was out of it now, standing a few feet away looking at the house and the climbing primroses. He turned when he heard me coming, faced me squarely as I neared him.

"Now you know," he said without emotion and without irony. "I didn't lie to you, mister. I have no son."

"Why didn't you tell me he was dead?"

"Wanted you to see it for yourself. His grave."

"How did he die?"

"I shot him," the old man said. "Last night, about ten o'clock."

"You shot him?"

"With my old Iver Johnson. Two rounds through the heart."

"Why? What happened?"

"He brought me trouble, just like before."

"You can state it plainer than that."

A little silence. Then, "He was bad, Stephen was. Mean and bad clear through. Always was, even as a boy. Stealing things, breaking up property, hurting other boys. Hurting his mother." Benson held up his crooked left arm. "Hurting me too."

"Stephen did that to you?"

"When he was eighteen. Broke my arm in three places. Two operations and it still wouldn't heal right."

"What made him do it?"

"I wouldn't give him the money he wanted. So he beat up on me to get it. I told him before he ran off, don't ever come back, you're not welcome in my house anymore. And he didn't come back, not in more than a dozen years. Not until last night, at the Oasis."

"He wanted money again, is that it? Tried to hurt you again when you wouldn't give it to him?"

"Punched me in the belly," Benson said. "Still hurts when I move sudden. So I went and got the Iver Johnson. He laughed when I pointed it at him and told him to get out. 'Won't shoot me, old man,' he said. 'Your own son. You won't shoot me.'"

"What did he do? Try to take the gun away from you?"

Benson nodded. "Didn't leave me any choice but to shoot him. Twice through the heart. Then I brought him out here and buried him next to his mother."

"Why did you do that?"

"I told you before. 'Home is the place where.' I had to take him in, didn't I? For the last time?"

The smell of the rotting apples seemed stronger now. And the heat was intense and the skeletal buildings and fungoid primroses were ugly. I didn't want to be here any longer—not another minute in this place.

"Get back in the car, Mr. Benson."

"Where we going?"

"Just get back in the car. Please."

He did what I told him. I backed the car around and drove up the hill and over it without glancing in the rear view mirror. Neither of us said anything until I swung off the county road, onto the apron in front of Benson's Oasis, and braked to a stop.

Then he asked, "You going to call the sheriff now?" Matter-of-factly; not as if he cared.

"No," I said.

"How come?"

"Stephen's dead and buried. I don't see any reason not to leave him right where he is."

"But I killed him. Shot him down like a dog."

Old and dying like his crossroads store, with precious little time left. Where was the sense—or the justice—in forcing him to die somewhere else? But all I said was, "You did what you had to do. I'll be going now. I've got another long drive ahead of me."

He put his hand on the door latch, paused with it there. "What'll you say to the man who hired you, the bail bondsman?"

What would I say to Abe Melikian? The truth—some of it, at least. Stephen Arthur Benson is dead and in the ground and what's left of his family is poor; the bail money's gone, Abe, and there's no way you can get any of it back; write it off your taxes and forget about it. He trusted me and my judgment and he wouldn't press for details, particularly not when I waived the balance of my fee.

"You let me worry about that," I said, and Benson shrugged and lifted himself out of the car. He seemed to want to say something else; instead he turned, walked to the store. There was nothing more to say. Neither thank-yous nor goodbyes were appropriate and we both knew it.

I watched him unlock the door, switch the window sign from *Closed* to *Open* before he disappeared into the dimness within. Then I drove out onto the highway and headed north. To San Francisco. To my office and my flat and Kerry.

Home is the place where.

THE BIG BITE

I laid a red queen on a black king, glanced up at Jay Cohalan through the open door of his office. He was pacing again, back and forth in front of his desk, his hands in constant restless motion at his sides. The office was carpeted: his footfalls made no sound. There was no discernible sound anywhere except for the faint snap and slap when I turned over a card and put it down. An office building at night is one of the quietest places there is. Eerily so, if you spend enough time listening to the silence.

Trey. Nine of diamonds. Deuce. Jack of spades. I was marrying the jack to the red queen when Cohalan quit pacing and came over to stand in the doorway. He watched me for a time, his hands still doing scoop-shovel maneuvers—a big man in his late thirties, handsome except for a weak chin, a little sweaty and disheveled now.

"How can you just sit there playing cards?" he said.

There were several answers to that. Years of stakeouts and dull routine. We'd been waiting only about two hours. The money, fifty thousand in fifties and hundreds, didn't belong to me. I wasn't worried, upset, or afraid that something might go wrong. I passed on all of those and settled instead for a neutral response: "Solitaire's good for waiting. Keeps your mind off the clock."

"It's after seven. Why the hell doesn't he call?"

"You know the answer to that. He wants you to sweat."

"Sadistic bastard."

"Blackmail's that kind of game," I said. "Torture the victim, bend his will to yours."

"Game. My God." Cohalan came out into the anteroom and began to pace in front of his secretary's desk, where I was sitting. "It's driving me crazy, trying to figure out who he is, how he found out about my past. Not a hint, any of the times I talked to him. But he knows everything, every damn detail."

"You'll have the answers before long."

"Yeah." He stopped abruptly, leaned toward me. "Listen, this has to be the end of it. You've got to stay with him, see to it he's arrested. I can't take any more."

"I'll do my job. Mr. Cohalan, don't worry."

"Fifty thousand dollars. I almost had a heart attack when he told me that was how much he wanted this time. The last payment, he said. What a crock. He'll come back for more someday. I know it, Carolyn knows it, you know it." Pacing again. "Poor Carolyn. Highstrung, emotional . . . it's been even harder on her. She wanted me to go to the police this time, did I tell you that?"

"You told me."

"I should have, I guess. Now I've got to pay a middleman for what I could've had for nothing . . . no offense."

"None taken."

"I just couldn't bring myself to do it, walk into the Hall of Justice and confess everything to a cop. It was hard enough letting Carolyn talk me into hiring a private detective. That trouble when I was a kid . . . it's a criminal offense, I could still be prosecuted for it. And it's liable to cost me my job if it comes out. I went through hell telling Carolyn in the beginning, and I didn't go into all the sordid details. With you, either. The police . . . no. I know that bastard will probably spill the whole story when he's arrested, try to drag me down with him, but still . . . I keep hoping he won't. You understand?"

"I understand," I said.

"I shouldn't've paid him when he crawled out of the woodwork eight months ago. I know that now. But back then it seemed like the only way to keep from ruining my life. Carolyn thought so, too. If I hadn't started paying him, half of her inheritance wouldn't already be gone . . ." He let the rest of it trail off, paced in bitter silence for a time, and started up again. "I hated taking money from her—hated it, no matter how much she insisted it belongs to both of us. And I hate myself for doing it, almost as much as I hate him. Blackmail's the worst goddamn crime there is short of murder."

"Not the worst," I said, "but bad enough."

"This has to be the end of it. The fifty thousand in there . . . it's the last of her inheritance, our savings. If that son of a bitch gets away with it, we'll be wiped out. You can't let that happen."

I didn't say anything. We'd been through all this before, more than once.

Cohalan let the silence resettle. Then, as I shuffled the cards for a new hand, "This job of mine, you'd think it pays pretty well, wouldn't you? My own office, secretary, executive title, expense account . . . looks good and sounds good, but it's a frigging dead end. Junior account executive stuck in corporate middle management—that's all I am or ever will be. Sixty thousand a year gross. And Carolyn makes twenty-five teaching. Eighty-five thousand for two people, no kids, that seems like plenty but it's not, not these days. Taxes, high cost of living, you have to scrimp to put anything away. And then some stupid mistake you made when you were a kid comes back to haunt you, drains your future along with your bank account, preys on your mind so you can't sleep, can barely do your work . . . you see what I mean? But I didn't think I had a choice at first, I was afraid of losing this crappy job, going to prison. Caught between a rock and a hard place. I still feel that way, but now I don't care, I just want that scum to get what's coming to him . . ."

Repetitious babbling caused by his anxiety. His mouth had a wet look and his eyes kept jumping from me to other points in the room.

I said, "Why don't you sit down?"

"I can't sit. My nerves are shot."

"Take a few deep breaths before you start to hyperventilate."

"Listen, don't tell me what—"

The telephone on his desk went off.

The sudden clamor jerked him half around, as if with an electric shock. In the quiet that followed the first ring I could hear the harsh rasp of his breathing. He looked back at me as the bell sounded again. I was on my feet, too, by then.

I said, "Go ahead, answer it. Keep your head."

He went into his office, picked up just after the third ring. I timed the lifting of the extension to coincide so there wouldn't be a second click on the open line.

"Yes," he said, "Cohalan."

"You know who this is." The voice was harsh, muffled, indistinctively male. "You got the fifty thousand?"

"I told you I would. The last payment, you promised me."

"Yeah, the last one."

"Where this time?"

"Golden Gate Park. Kennedy Drive, in front of the buffalo pen. Put it in the trash barrel beside the bench there."

Cohalan was watching me through the open doorway. I shook my head at him. He said into the phone, "Can't we make it someplace else? There might be people around . . ."

"Not at nine p.m."

"Nine? But it's only a little after seven now—"

"Nine sharp. Be there with the cash."

The line went dead.

I cradled the extension. Cohalan was still standing alongside his desk, hanging onto the receiver the way a drowning man might hang onto a lifeline, when I went into his office. I said,

"Put it down, Mr. Cohalan."

"What? Oh, yes." He lowered the receiver. "Christ," he said then.

"You all right?"

His head bobbed up and down a couple of times. He ran a hand over his face and then swung away to where his briefcase lay. The fifty thousand was in there; he'd shown it to me when I first arrived. He picked the case up, set it down again. Rubbed his face another time.

"Maybe I shouldn't risk the money," he said.

He wasn't talking to me so I didn't answer.

"I could leave it right here where it'll be safe. Put a phone book or something in for weight." He sank into his desk chair, popped up again like a jack-in-the-box. He was wired so tight I could almost hear him humming. "No, what's the matter with me? That won't work. I'm not thinking straight. He might open the case in the park. There's no telling what he'd do if the money's not there. And he's got to have it in his possession when the police come."

"That's why I insisted we mark some of the bills."

"Yes, right, I remember. Proof of extortion. All right, but for God's sake don't let him get away with it."

"He won't get away with it."

Another jerky nod. "When're you leaving?"

"Right now. You stay put until at least eight-thirty. It won't take you more than twenty minutes to get out to the park."

"I'm not sure I can get through another hour of waiting around here."

"Keep telling yourself it'll be over soon. Calm down. The state you're in now, you shouldn't even be behind the wheel."

"I'll be okay."

"Come straight back here after you make the drop. You'll hear from me as soon as I have anything to report."

"Just don't make me wait too long," Cohalan said. And then, again and to himself, "I'll be okay."

Cohalan's office building was on Kearney, not far from where Kerry works at the Bates and Carpenter ad agency on lower Geary. She was on my mind as I drove down to Geary and turned west toward the park: my thoughts prompted me to lift the car phone and call the condo. No answer. Like me, she puts in a lot of overtime night work. A wonder we manage to spend as much time together as we do.

I tried her private number at B & C and got her voice mail.

In transit probably, the same as I was. Headlights crossing the dark city. Urban night riders. Except that she was going home and I was on my way to nail a shakedown artist for a paying client.

That started me thinking about the kind of work I do. One of the downsides of urban night riding is that it gives vent to sometimes broody self-analysis. Skip traces, insurance claim investigations, employee background checks—they're the meat of my business. There used to be some challenge to jobs like that, some creative maneuvering required, but nowadays it's little more than routine legwork (mine) and a lot of computer time (Tamara Corbin, my techno-whiz assistant). I don't get to use my head as much as I once did. My problem, in Tamara's Generation X opinion, was that I was a "retro dick" pining away for the old days and old ways. True enough; I never have adapted well to change. The detective racket just isn't as satisfying or stimulating after thirty-plus years and with a new set of rules.

Every now and then, though, a case comes along that stirs the juices—one with some spark and sizzle and a much higher satisfaction level than the run-of-the-mill stuff. I live for cases like that; they're what keep me from packing it in, taking an early retirement. They usually involve a felony of some sort, and sometimes a whisper if not a shout of danger, and allow me to use my full complement of functional brain cells. This Cohalan case, for instance. This one I liked, because shakedown artists are high on my list of worthless lowlifes and I enjoy hell out of taking one down.

Yeah, this one I liked a whole lot.

Golden Gate Park has plenty of daytime attractions—museums, tiny lakes, rolling lawns, windmills, an arboretum—but on a foggy November night it's a mostly empty dark place to pass through on your way to somewhere else. Mostly empty because it does have its night denizens: homeless squatters, not all of whom are harmless or drug-free, and predators on the prowl in its sprawling acres of shadows and nightshapes. On a night like this it also has an atmosphere of lonely isolation, the fog hiding the city lights and turning street lamps and passing headlights into surreal blurs.

The buffalo enclosure is at the westward end, less than a mile from the ocean—the least-traveled section of the park at night. There were no cars in the vicinity, moving or parked, when I came down Kennedy Drive. My lights picked out the fence on the north side, the rolling pastureland beyond; the trash barrel and bench were about halfway along, at the edge of the bicycle path that parallels the road. I drove past there, looking for a place to park and wait. I didn't want to sit on Kennedy; a lone car close to the drop point would be too conspicuous. I had to do this right. If anything did not seem kosher, the whole thing might fail to go off the way it was supposed to.

The perfect spot came up fifty yards or so from the trash barrel, opposite the buffalo feeding corral—a narrow road that leads to Anglers Lodge, where the city maintains casting pools for fly fishermen to practice on. Nobody was likely to go up there at night, and trees and shrubbery bordered one side, the shadows in close to them thick and clotted. Kennedy Drive was still empty in both directions; I cut in past the Anglers Lodge sign and drove up the road until I found a place where I could turn around. Then I shut off my lights, made the U-turn, and coasted back down into the heavy shadows. From there I could see the drop point clearly enough, even with the low-riding fog. I shut off the engine, slumped down on the seat with my back against the door.

No detective, public or private, likes stakeouts. Dull, boring, dead time that can be a literal pain in the ass if it goes on long enough. This one wasn't too bad because it was short, only about an hour, but time lagged and crawled just the same. Now and then a car drifted by, its lights reflecting off rather than boring through the wall of mist. The ones heading west might have been able to see my car briefly in dark silhouette as they passed, but none of them happened to be a police patrol and nobody else was curious enough or venal enough to stop and investigate.

The luminous dial on my watch showed five minutes to nine when Cohalan arrived. Predictably early because he was so anxious to get it over with. He came down Kennedy too fast for the conditions; I heard the squeal of brakes as he swung over and rocked to a stop near the trash barrel. I watched the shape of him get out and run across the path to make the drop and then run back. Ten seconds later his car hissed past where I was hidden, again going too fast, and was gone.

Nine o'clock.
Nine oh five.
Nine oh eight.
Headlights probed past, this set heading east, the car low-slung and smallish. It rolled along slowly until it was opposite

the barrel, then veered sharply across the road and slid to a crooked stop with its brake lights flashing blood red. I sat up straighter, put my hand on the ignition key. The door opened without a light coming on inside, and the driver jumped out in a hurry, bulky and indistinct in a heavy coat and some kind of head covering; ran to the barrel, scooped out the briefcase, raced back and hurled it inside; hopped in after it and took off. Fast, even faster than Cohalan had been driving, the car's rear end fishtailing a little as the tires fought for traction on the slick pavement.

I was out on Kennedy and in pursuit within seconds. No way I could drive in the fog-laden darkness without putting on my lights, and in the far reach of the beams I could see the other car a hundred yards or so ahead. But even when I accelerated I couldn't get close enough to read the license plate.

Where the drive forks on the east end of the buffalo enclosure, the sports job made a tight-angle left turn, brake lights flashing again, headlights yawing as the driver fought for control. Looping around Spreckels Lake to quit the park on Thirty-Sixth Avenue. I took the turn at about half the speed, but I still had it in sight when it made a sliding right through a red light on Fulton, narrowly missing an oncoming car, and disappeared to the east. I wasn't even trying to keep up any longer. If I continued pursuit, somebody—an innocent party— was liable to get hurt or killed. That was the last thing I wanted to happen. High-speed car chases are for damn fools and the makers of trite Hollywood films.

I pulled over near the Fulton intersection, still inside the park, and used the car phone to call my client.

Cohalan threw a fit when I told him what had happened. He called me all kinds of names, the least offensive of which was "incompetent idiot." I just let him rant. There were no excuses to be made and no point in wasting my own breath.

He ran out of abuse finally and segued into lament. "What am I going to do now? What am I going to tell Carolyn? All our savings gone and I still don't have any idea who that blackmailing bastard is. What if he comes back for more? We couldn't even sell the house, there's hardly any equity . . ."

Pretty soon he ran down there, too. I waited through about five seconds of dead air. Then, "All right," followed by a heavy sigh. "But don't expect me to pay your bill. You can damn well sue me and you can't get blood out of a turnip." And he banged the receiver in my ear.

Some Cohalan. Some piece of work.

The apartment building was on Locust Street a half block off California, close to the Presidio. Built in the twenties, judging by its ornate facade, once somebody's modestly affluent private home, long ago cut up into three floors of studios and one-bedroom apartments. It had no garage, forcing its tenants—like most of those in the neighborhood buildings—into street parking. There wasn't a legal space to be had on that block, or in the next, or anywhere in the vicinity. Back on California, I slotted my car into a bus zone. If I got a ticket I got a ticket.

Not much chance I'd need a weapon for the rest of it, but sometimes trouble comes when you least expect it. So I unclipped the .38 Colt Bodyguard from under the dash, slipped it into my coat pocket before I got out for the walk down Locust.

The building had a tiny foyer with the usual bank of mailboxes. I found the button for 2-C, leaned on it. This was the ticklish part; I was banking on the fact that one voice sounds pretty much like another over an intercom. Turned out not to be an issue at all: the squawk box stayed silent and the door release buzzed instead, almost immediately. Confident. Arrogant. Or just plain stupid.

I pushed inside, smiling a little, cynically, and climbed the stairs to the second floor. The first apartment on the right was 2-C. The door opened just as I got to it, and Annette Byers put her head out and said with excitement in her voice, "You made really good—"

The rest of it snapped off when she got a look at me; the excitement gave way to confusion, froze her in the half-open doorway. I had time to move up on her, wedge my shoulder against the door before she could decide to jump back and slam it in my face. She let out a little bleat and tried to kick me as I crowded her inside. I caught her arms, gave her a shove to get clear of her. Then I nudged the door closed with my heel.

"I'll start screaming," she said. Shaky bravado, the kind without anything to back it up. Her eyes were frightened now. "These walls are paper thin, and I've got a neighbor who's a cop."

That last part was a lie. I said, "Go ahead. Be my guest."

"Who the hell do you think you are—"

"We both know who I am, Ms. Byers. And why I'm here. The reason's on the table over there."

In spite of herself she glanced to her left. The apartment was a studio, and the kitchenette and dining area were over that way. The briefcase sat on the dinette table, its lid raised. I couldn't see inside from where I was, but then I didn't need to.

"I don't know what you're talking about," she said.

She hadn't been back long; she still wore the heavy coat and the head covering, a wool stocking cap that completely hid her blond hair. Her cheeks were flushed—the cold night, money lust, now fear. She was attractive enough in a too-ripe way, intelligent enough to hold down a job with a downtown travel service, and immoral enough to have been in trouble with the San Francisco police before this. She was twenty-three, divorced, and evidently a crankhead: she'd been arrested once for possession and once for trying to sell a small quantity of methamphetamine to an undercover cop.

"Counting the cash, right?" I said.

". . . What?"

"What you were doing when I rang the bell. Fifty thousand in fifties and hundreds. It's all there, according to plan."

"I don't know what you're talking about."

"You said that already."

I moved a little to get a better scan of the studio. Her phone was on a breakfast bar that separated the kitchenette from the living room, one of those cordless types with a built-in answering machine. The gadget beside it was clearly a portable cassette player. She hadn't bothered to put it away before she went out; there'd been no reason to, or so she'd have thought then. The tape would still be inside.

I looked at her again. "I've got to admit, you're a pretty good driver. Reckless as hell, though, the way you went flying out of the park on a red light. You came close to a collision with another car."

"I don't know what—" She broke off and backed away a couple of paces, her hand rubbing the side of her face, her tongue making little flicks between her lips. It was sinking in now, how it had all gone wrong, how much trouble she was in. "You couldn't have followed me. I *know* you didn't."

"That's right, I couldn't and I didn't."

"Then how—?"

"Think about it. You'll figure it out."

A little silence. And, "Oh God, you knew about me all along."

"About you, the plan, everything."

"How? How could you? I don't—"

The downstairs bell made a sudden racket.

Her gaze jerked past me toward the intercom unit next to the door. She sucked in her lower lip, began to gnaw on it.

"You know who it is," I said. "Don't use the intercom, just the door release."

She did what I told her, moving slowly. I went the other way, first to the breakfast bar, where I popped the tape out of the cassette player and slipped it into my pocket, then to the dinette table. I lowered the lid on the briefcase, snapped the catches. I had the case in my hand when she turned to face me again.

She said, "What're you going to do with the money?"

"Give it back to its rightful owner."

"Jay. It belongs to him."

I didn't say anything to that.

"You better not try to keep it for yourself," she said. "You don't have any right to that money . . ."

"You dumb kid," I said disgustedly, "neither do you."

She quit looking at me. When she started to open the door I told her no, wait for his knock. She stood with her back to me, shoulders hunched. She was no longer afraid; dull resignation had taken over. For her, I thought, the money was the only thing that had ever mattered.

Knuckles rapped on the door. She opened it without any hesitation, and he blew in, talking fast the way he did when he was keyed up. "Oh, baby, baby, we did it, we pulled it off," and he grabbed her and started to pull her against him. That was when he saw me.

"Hello, Cohalan," I said.

He went rigid for three or four seconds, his eyes popped wide, then disentangled himself from the woman and stood gaping at me. His mouth worked but nothing came out. Manic as hell in his office, all nerves and talking a blue streak, but now he was speechless. Lies were easy for him; the truth would have to be dragged out.

I told him to close the door. He did it, automatically, and turned snarling on Annette Byers. "You let him follow you home!"

"I didn't," she said. "He already knew about me. He knows everything."

"No, you're lying . . ."

"You were so goddamn smart, you had it all figured out. You didn't fool him for a minute."

"Shut up." His eyes shifted to me. "Don't listen to her. She's the one who's been blackmailing me—"

"Knock it off, Cohalan," I said. "Nobody's been blackmailing you. You're the shakedown artist here, you and Annette—a fancy little scheme to get your wife's money. You couldn't just grab the whole bundle from her, and you couldn't get any of it by divorcing her—a spouse's inheritance isn't community property in this state. So you cooked up the phony blackmail scam. What were the two of you planning to do with the full hundred thousand? Run off somewhere together? Buy a load of crank for resale, try for an even bigger score?"

"You see?" Annette Byers said bitterly. "You see, smart guy? He knows everything."

Cohalan shook his head. He'd gotten over his initial shock; now he looked stricken, and his nerves were acting up again. His hands had begun repeating that scoop-shovel trick at his sides. "You believed me, I know you did."

"Wrong," I said. "I didn't believe you. I'm a better actor than you, is all. Your story didn't sound right from the first. Too elaborate, full of improbabilities. Fifty thousand is too big a blackmail bite for any crime short of homicide, and you swore to me—your wife, too—you weren't guilty of a major felony. Blackmailers seldom work in big bites anyway. They bleed their victims slow and steady, in small bites, to keep them from throwing the hook. We just didn't believe it, either of us."

"We? Jesus, you mean . . . you and Carolyn . . . ?"

"That's right. Your wife's my client, Cohalan, not you—that's why I never asked you for a retainer. She showed up at my office right after you did the first time; if she hadn't, I'd probably have gone to her. She'd been suspicious all along, but she gave you the benefit of the doubt until you hit her with the fifty-thousand-dollar bite. She figured you might be having an affair, too, and it didn't take me long to find out about Annette. You never had any idea you were being followed, did you? Once I knew about her, it was easy enough to put the rest of it together, including the funny business with the money drop tonight. And here we are."

"Damn you," he said, but there was no heat in the words. "You and that frigid bitch both."

He wasn't talking about Annette Byers, but she took the opportunity to dig into him again. "Smart guy. Big genius. I told you to just take the money and we'd run with it, didn't I?"

"Shut up."

"Don't tell me to shut up, you son of—"

"Don't say it. I'll slap you silly if you say it."

"You won't slap anybody," I said. "Not as long as I'm around."

He wiped his mouth on the sleeve of his jacket. "What're you going to do?"

"What do you think I'm going to do?"

"You can't go to the police. You don't have any proof. It's your word against ours."

"Wrong again." I showed him the voice-activated recorder I'd had hidden in my pocket all evening. High-tech, state-of-the-art equipment, courtesy of George Agonistes, fellow P.I. and electronics expert. "Everything that was said in your office and in this room tonight is on here. I've also got the cassette tape Annette played when she called earlier. Voice prints will prove the muffled voice on it is yours, that you were talking to yourself on the phone, giving yourself orders and directions. If your wife wants to press charges, she'll have more than enough evidence to put the two of you away."

"She won't press charges," he said. "Not Carolyn."

"Maybe not, if you return the rest of her money. What you and baby here haven't already blown."

He sleeved his mouth again. "I suppose you intend to take the briefcase straight to her."

"You suppose right."

"I could stop you," he said, as if he were trying to convince himself. "I'm as big as you, younger—I could take it away from you."

I repocketed the recorder. I could have showed him the .38, but I grinned at him instead. "Go ahead and try. Or else move away from the door. You've got five seconds to make up your mind."

He moved in three, as I started toward him. Sideways, clear of both me and the door. Annette Byers let out a sharp, scornful laugh, and he whirled on her—somebody his own size to face off against. "Shut your stupid mouth!" he yelled at her.

"Shut yours, big man. You and your brilliant ideas."

"Goddamn you . . ."

I went out and closed the door against their vicious, whining voices.

Outside, the fog had thickened to a near drizzle, slicking the pavement and turning the lines of parked cars along both curbs into two-dimensional black shapes. Parking was at such a premium in this neighborhood, there was now a car, dark and silent, double-parked across the street. I walked quickly to California. Nobody, police included, had bothered my wheels in the bus zone. I locked the briefcase in the trunk, let myself inside. A quick call to Carolyn Cohalan to let her know I was coming, a short ride out to her house by the zoo to deliver the fifty thousand, and I'd be finished for the night.

Only she didn't answer her phone.

Funny, when I'd called her earlier from the park, she'd said she would wait for my next call. No reason for her to leave the house in the interim. Unless—

Christ!

I heaved out of the car and ran back down Locust Street. The darkened vehicle was still double-parked across from Annette Byers' building. I swung into the foyer, jammed my finger against the bell button for 2-C and left it there. No response. I rattled the door—latched tight—and then began jabbing buttons on all the other mailboxes. The intercom crackled; somebody's voice said, "Who the hell is that?" I said, "Police emergency, buzz me in." Nothing, nothing, and then finally the door release sounded; I hit the door hard and lunged into the lobby.

I was at the foot of the stairs when the first shot echoed from above. Two more in swift succession, a fourth as I was pounding up to the second-floor landing.

Querulous voices, the sound of a door banging open somewhere . . . and I was at 2-C. The door there was shut but not latched; I kicked it open, hanging back with the .38 in my hand for self-protection. But there was no need. It was over by then. Too late and all over.

All three of them were on the floor. Cohalan on his back next to the couch, blood obscuring his face, not moving. Annette Byers sprawled bloody and moaning by the dinette table. And Carolyn Cohalan sitting with her back against a wall, a long-barreled .22 on the carpet nearby, weeping in deep, broken sobs.

I leaned hard on the doorjamb, the stink of cordite in my nostrils, my throat full of bile. Telling myself it was not my fault, there was no way I could have known it wasn't the money but paying them back that mattered to her—the big payoff, the biggest bite there is. Telling myself I could've done nothing to prevent this, and remembering what I'd been thinking in the car earlier about how I lived for cases like this, how I liked this one a whole lot . . .

WHO YOU BEEN GRAPPLIN' WITH?

He was sitting on one of the anteroom chairs when I came into the agency that morning. A rather shabbily dressed black man well up in his seventies, thin and on the frail side, with a mostly hairless, liver-spotted scalp, rheumy eyes, a long, ridged upper lip, and the kind of slumped posture and pain-etched features that indicate failing health. At first glance you might have taken him for one of San Francisco's legion of homeless street people, but only at first glance. His jacket and slacks were frayed and threadbare, but clean, he wore a tie over a patterned shirt, and his seamed cheeks looked freshly shaven. On his lap were an old brown hat with a faded red band that might once have had a feather stuck in it, and a battered case the size and shape of a trumpet. I had never seen him before.

The door to Tamara's office was open and I could hear her rattling around in the back alcove where we kept a hotplate. Getting coffee for herself and the visitor, I thought.

"Morning," I said to him.

"Mornin'." His voice had traces of a Southern accent and was stronger than the rest of him looked, with a gravelly quality that made me think of Louis Armstrong. "You Miz Corbin's partner?"

"That's me." I added my name to confirm it.

He said his name was Charles Anthony Brown, and we shook hands. His palm was so dry it had the feel of fine-grain sandpaper. "Heard of you," he said then, "what you and Miz Corbin willin' to do for poor folks. That's why I come here. Times, they sure do change."

I didn't need to ask him what he meant by the first and last statements. The first referred to the advertised fact that we took on pro bono cases now and then, mainly for minorities who otherwise couldn't afford detective services—an estimable idea of Tamara's when the agency began to prosper under her direction. The second referred to our partnership—computer-savvy, street-savvy black woman in her late twenties, old-school white guy with forty-plus of his sixty-five years in law enforcement and detective work. It was the kind of alliance that would not have been possible back when Charles Anthony Brown was young, particularly if he was originally from south of the Mason-Dixon line.

There were footsteps and Tamara appeared in the doorway. "I thought I heard your voice," she said to me.

"Just getting acquainted with Mr. Brown."

"He'd like us to locate his niece for him."

"Robin Louise," Brown said, nodding.

She smiled at him. "Coffee's ready in my office. Be more comfortable talking in there."

He nodded and got up slowly, the hat in one hand and the trumpet case in the other. Tamara's glance in my direction was an invitation to join the interview. Brown followed her into the office, moving in a shuffling gait that had everything to do with age and infirmity and nothing to do with the old racial stereotype, and I followed him. She indicated the client's chair nearest her desk, the one within easy reach of the steaming coffee mug she'd set there.

"Milk and three teaspoons of sugar, right?"

"Always did like it sweet," Brown said.

While he was lowering himself into the chair, I went into the alcove and poured myself some coffee and then came back and sat down in the client chair's mate. Tamara was tapping away on her computer keyboard, getting a case file started. Brown sipped from his mug with one hand; the other continued to grip the trumpet case.

He saw me looking at the case. "My horn," he said. "Never go anywheres without it."

"Are you a professional musician?" I asked.

"Most of my life." He tugged at his ridged upper lip as if offering proof, then his mouth stretched in a small, mirthless smile that revealed missing and neglected teeth. "Too old and broke-down to play in a band. Outdoors now, when the weather's good."

Street musician. There are a lot of them, men and some women of all ages, spotted around the city: Embarcadero Center Plaza, Pier 39, Ghirardelli Square, Civic Center, the entrances to BART stations, on random corners—anywhere there is heavy foot traffic and the likelihood of somebody willing to part with dollar bills or coins for a few minutes' entertainment. It may be a form of panhandling, but it's considerably more honest than the direct, too-often aggressive solicitation. Those who possess a reasonable degree of talent can make enough to get by, if they don't spend it all on alcohol or drugs. Brown didn't seem to have any of the telltale signs of either addiction.

"But I don't sleep outdoors," he said, "I ain't homeless. Got me a room and a job cleanin' up at the Blue Moon Cafe on Howard Street. Got a little money saved up to give my niece when you find her."

"There's no need to explain—"

"Just wanted you to know."

Tamara said, "What's your niece's full name, Mr. Brown?"

"Robin Louise—" slight pause "—Arceneaux."

"How do you spell the last name?"

He spelled it for her and she typed it into the computer file.

"When did you last have any contact with her?"

"Long time ago. Way too long."

"How long, approximately?"

"Fifty-one years," he said. "Summer, nineteen sixty-three."

Tamara and I exchanged glances.

"How old was your niece at that time?" I asked him.

"Seven years old. Born in fifty-six, April eighteen."

"Have you had any contact with her since then? Phone conversations, letters?"

"No."

"Tried to locate her before now?"

"No."

"Mind if we ask why?"

Brown didn't care for the question; it showed in his rheumy eyes. But he said, "Just lost touch, that's all. Lot of reasons. Travelin' around the country, workin', playin' my music."

"You realize she might not still be living?"

He didn't like that one either. A muscle jumped in his cheek. "She's alive," he said emphatically. "Got to be."

Tamara asked, "Who was she living with in nineteen sixty-three? Father, mother, both?"

He sat for a few seconds without answering. Then his face suddenly bunched up and he was seized by a fit of coughing. He fumbled a handkerchief out of his pocket to cover his mouth until the spell passed. It left him wheezing and with a sickly gray undertone to his dark features.

Tamara asked if he was all right. He said, "For the time bein'. Comes and goes. What'd you ask me before?"

"If your niece was living with her father, mother, or both in nineteen sixty-three."

"With her mama's sister Jolene and her man. Jolene and Bobby Franklin."

Tamara's computer keys clicked again. "Where was this?"

"N'Orleans."

"The city itself or a suburb?"

"French Quarter. Dauphine Street."

"Do you remember the number?"

Headshake. "My memory ain't so good anymore."

"What about the girl's parents? Something happen to them?"

"They both died."

"How and when?"

Another headshake. He didn't seem to want to answer the question.

"Last name Arceneaux. What were their given names?"

Or that one. It took him three or four seconds to say, "Don't matter. Robin Louise, she with Jolene and Bobby Franklin, like I said. They raised her up."

"All right. What did the Franklins do for a living?"

"Jolene worked in one of the clubs, don't remember which. Bobby, he was a drummer. Good one, too. Real good chops."

"Play with a particular band?"

"Don't remember." Brown seemed agitated now. "Listen, ain't I already told you enough so you can find Robin Louise?"

"The more information we have—"

A second bout of coughing struck him, not as intense as the first. He covered his mouth with the handkerchief again, and this time I could see flecks of blood on the fabric.

When the fit passed and he had his breath back, he said, "Already told you all I remember. Find her from that, can't you?"

"I think so. Do our best."

"Got to be soon," he said. "I ain't got much time left. You can see the kind of shape I'm in."

"Are you under a doctor's care?" I asked.

"Can't afford no doctor."

"There are free clinics—"

"Charity. No, sir. Wouldn't do no good anyway. Man gets to be my age, he knows when his time's near up. Be playin' a duet with Gabriel pretty soon now." The wry little mouth-stretch again. "Or maybe Old Scratch, if I end up down below."

What can you say to that? Tamara and I were both silent.

Brown finished his coffee. "I got to be goin' now," he said, and used the corner of the desk to shove up onto his feet.

I walked out with him. On the way he stumbled once and I caught hold of his arm, but he shrugged my hand off more or less gently. Didn't want to be helped. Pride.

At the door he clamped the battered old hat on his head. "Don't know where I'll be rest of today," he said then. "But tonight, any night after six o'clock, I'll be at the Blue Moon Café. All right?" He waited for my nod, and then he was gone.

Tamara had other, pressing business to attend to and had

only just started on the Robin Louise Arceneaux trace when I left for the day. Now that I'm semi-retired, my time at the agency is generally limited to two nonconsecutive days a week. But I had some leftover work on an insurance-fraud case to finish up, so I went in again the following morning.

My partner is a workaholic and as usual she was already at her computer. What wasn't usual this morning was that she was humming as she worked, something I had never heard her do before. The tune had an old-fashioned bluesy rhythm. Jazz is my favorite type of music and I'm fairly knowledgeable, but this was one I didn't recognize.

"What's that you're humming?"

She hadn't heard me come in, hadn't realized I was standing behind her. She broke off and swung around in her chair to look up at me. There are several different mood-driven personas occupying her plump young body, most but not all of them pleasant; you're never sure quite which one you're going to face on a given day. The one I was looking at this morning was Glum Tamara. Curious. As bluesy as the tune had been, it had also had a lively beat that didn't fit with the Glum Tamara persona.

"Old jazz song," she said.

"I gathered as much. What's it called?"

"'Who You Been Grapplin' With?'"

"Catchy title."

"Yeah."

"I don't think I've heard it before. Sounds Dixieland."

"It is. New Orleans club band called The Sweetmeat Five cut a record of it in 'fifty-nine, but it didn't get much play until the early sixties, after . . ." She let the rest of the sentence trail off and said instead, "Pretty much been forgotten since."

"Where'd you come across it?"

"Internet," she said. "And a dude I know collects old jazz records."

She surprised me again, then—twice. First by closing her eyes and starting to sing softly, something else she'd never before done in my presence, and second by the low, smoky, Billie Holiday quality of her voice.

> "Who you been grapplin' with, ba-by?
> "While I been away.
> "Who you been grapplin' with, hon-ey?
> "Every night and day.

> "Who you gonna grapple with, ba-by?
> "Now I'm home to stay.
> "Who you gonna grapple with, hon-ey?
> "Every night and day.
>
> "Well, I'll tell you, sweet dad-dy,
> "The way it's gonna be.
> "Yeah, I'll tell you, sweet dad-dy,
> "You better grapple with me.
> "Every night and day—nobody but me."

Tamara let out a long, sighing breath. "There're more verses, but those are the only three I remember."

"I didn't know you could sing."

"Yeah, well, mostly in the shower."

"You ought to do it more often—you have a nice voice."

The compliment didn't seem to cheer her much. Her smile was fleeting. "Wish I could get the damn song out of my head."

"Why? It has a good beat."

"You think so? Bet the man who wrote it doesn't anymore."

"No? Who would he be?"

"Moses Arceneaux."

"Arceneaux. Related to Charles Brown's niece?"

"Robin Louise isn't his niece, she's his daughter. Charles Anthony Brown's real name is Moses Arceneaux."

"Oh," I said, "so that's it."

"That's it."

"So why did he lie to us? Why the false name?"

"Man's a fugitive, that's why," Tamara said. "Been a fugitive ever since nineteen sixty-three."

Well, that explained the glumness. "What's he wanted for?"

"Double homicide. Murdered his wife and her lover, another musician named Dupres."

She handed me a couple of pages of printout. Her computer skills are exceptional; if there is information on any topic available anywhere online, she'll find it. What she'd pulled up here were a copy of the fugitive warrant issued by the New Orleans Police Department in August of 1963, and a brief newspaper account of the crimes. The gist of both was that Moses Arceneaux, jazz trumpeter, songwriter, and member of The Sweetmeat Five, had in cold blood and with malice aforethought shot to death his wife, Lily, the band's lead singer, and a jazz pianist with another group named Marcus Dupres. He'd done this, it was alleged, in a jealous rage after finding out that the two were having an affair. Two neighbors of Dupres' who'd heard the shots had arrived on the scene in time to witness Arceneaux standing over his wife's body with the murder weapon, a .38 revolver registered to him, in his hand. Arceneaux had immediately dropped the weapon and taken flight. After which he had evidently stopped at his own apartment long enough to gather some cash and a few personal belongings, then fled the city and disappeared without a trace.

The fact that he had continued to evade capture for more than half a century was not as amazing as it might seem. There were other such cases on record—men and women who had changed their identities, maintained a low profile, and done nothing to attract police attention, and either were never caught or for one reason or another had been finally found and brought to justice. Still, half a century is a lot of years to be on the run. Moses Arceneaux had beaten long odds. Very long odds.

"Damn," I said when I returned the printout. "I liked that man."

"So did I. So what do we do now?"

"You know the answer to that. What we're bound to do by law—turn him in. There's no statute of limitations on homicide."

"Even though he's old and sick?"

"The two people he shot never had a chance to grow old."

"Yeah. But maybe they had it coming to them."

"Nobody has murder coming to them."

Tamara knew that as well as I did; she didn't put up any more argument. "But not with a phone call, okay? He came to us on his own, he's a client no matter what he did fifty years ago, and he's dying . . . can't treat the man cold that way"

"No, we can't and we won't. I'll take him in."

"Right away?"

"Tonight," I said. "I don't want to have to go looking for him on the streets, make a public thing out of it."

"I could go along—"

"What for? Wouldn't make it any easier."

". . . I guess not."

"What about Robin Louise?" I asked. "You locate her?"

"No problem with that. She was raised by Jolene and Bobby Franklin, all right—the murdered wife's sister and her husband. They adopted her, had her last name legally changed to Franklin."

"Is she still living?"

"In Shreveport. Trained and now working as a physical therapist. Married once to a man named Davis. Two children, both grown. Old Moses doesn't even know he's a grandpop." Tamara's mouth took on a lemony twist. "Sometimes I hate this damn business."

"Yeah," I said. "So do I."

The Blue Moon Cafe was on the fringe of skid row, in that section below Market Street that used to be called South of the Slot. Much of the old warehouse district farther south had undergone urban renewal, was now home to nightclubs and expensive condos and loft apartments, and known locally as SoMa. But the skid row pocket remained mostly unchanged, as filled as ever with drunks and drug addicts and hookers and scruffy bars and cheap lodging places, like an ugly piece of the city caught in a time warp. You walked carefully in that neighborhood after dark. I walked carefully even though it was only seven o'clock and just dusk when I got there.

The cafe was not quite a greasy spoon, though grease was one of the dominant odors along with beer and human effluvium. One long, wide room with a counter along the right-hand wall, booths along another, and several tables in two rows down the middle. The kitchen was at the rear and wrapped partway around behind the counter. An open corridor yawned on its other side.

Business was good at this hour: More than half of the spaces were occupied by a mixed-race and mostly poverty-level clientele. There was the low buzz of conversation, but none of the punctuations of laughter you heard in better restaurants. Eating was serious business here. And not a particularly enjoyable one, judging from the samples of the fare I saw in passing and the expressions worn by the diners.

I found an open spot at the counter, and when a tired-looking Latina waitress got around to me, I said I was there to see Charles Anthony Brown. Her expression of surprise indicated he had few if any callers, but she didn't ask questions. "Down past the johns," she said, gesturing. "Last door on the left."

Kitchen and bathroom smells were strong in the dimly lit corridor. The two doors on the left were unmarked. I stopped at the last one, knocked, and pretty soon it opened and he peered out at me. Recognition put a look of hope in the rheumy eyes— and I took it away quick, because there was no other, more merciful way to do it.

"Hello, Moses," I said.

He stood frozen for half a dozen beats. Other emotions flickered briefly in his eyes and on his deeply seamed face; the one that remained, I thought, was resignation.

"So you found out," he said.

"Did you really believe we wouldn't?"

"Figured you might. It don't matter much anymore. You gonna take me to the po-lice now?"

"Let's talk a little first."

He backed up slowly into the room. I stepped inside, closed the door against the dish-rattle and voice murmurs out front. The room was a windowless, fourteen-by-fourteen box, dimly lit by a low-wattage ceiling bulb, that had once been used for storage; still was, to an extent, judging by the cartons stacked along one wall. In the remaining space were a cot covered with an old army blanket, a rickety chair, a small table, and a kind of open, makeshift closet that contained Moses Arceneaux's meager belongings. I wondered if he realized how much the room looked and felt like what he'd spent fifty-one years avoiding—a prison cell.

His trumpet lay on the cot. He caught it up when he sat down, held it on his lap. It was old and a little dinged here and there, but the brass surfaces still shone from myriad polishings. The one thing he owned that he cared about, I thought.

He said, "You find Robin Louise?"

"Yes, we found her. She lives in Shreveport."

"Knew she was still alive. Knew it for sure."

"She may not want to have anything to do with you," I said. "You must know that too."

"I believe she will. Got some money saved for her, like I told you yesterday. Got to talk to her one last time before I die. Tell her I'm sorry. Tell her I never stopped loving her. Tell her the truth."

"What truth?"

"About what happened to her mama and Marcus Dupres that night in 'sixty-three." Arceneaux ran his long, gnarled fingers around the rim of the trumpet's bell. "Tell you the truth, too, you want to hear it."

"Go ahead."

"I didn't kill Lily or that piano man," he said, "neither of 'em."

I said nothing. The number of men and women charged with capital crimes who profess their innocence to the bitter end is countless. Nearly all such claims are self-serving obfuscations or outright lies. Ninety-five percent, at a reasonable guess. But it's the five percent that make a cry of innocence worth listening to.

"Swear it on a Bible," Arceneaux said. "I never done it."

I stayed mute.

He put the wrong interpretation on my silence. "You like everybody down in N'Orleans," he said, "you don't believe it." Surprisingly, there was no discernible bitterness in the words.

"Suppose you tell me the way it was."

"I loved that woman, that's the way it was. Even after I found out she was cheatin' on me with that piano man. I might've whipped her ass some if I'd had the chance, but kill her dead? No, sir. Never."

"She was shot with your pistol. Both of them were."

"Not by me. Didn't happen the way it looked."

"All right. How did it happen?"

"Kind of hard to remember exactly, after so many years." A bunch of seconds went by while he either worked his memory or built a framework of lies.

"Horn man in Dupres' band told me about her and him. Drunk, and he let it slip out. Man, it cut me deep. I was half outa my head, I admit that, when I went harin' over to Dupres' place that night."

"With your pistol in your pocket."

"No, sir. Lily was the one brought the gun. Dupres been stringin' her along, told her they was gonna run off together. She believed him, must've wanted him bad, more'n she ever wanted me, but then she found out he had him another woman besides her, stringin' that one along too. She had a bad temper, Lily did. Didn't go to Dupres' place for screwin' that night, went there for a showdown—make him choose between her and his other woman. That's why she took the pistol with her."

"How do you know all this?"

"They was yellin' it at each other when I got there," Arceneaux said. "Bastard must've hit her 'cause I heard a sound like a slap, and she screamed, and next thing I heard was that gun goin' off. Door wasn't locked. I got it open and run inside, and Dupres was on the floor with blood all over his face and Lily standin' there with her eyes crazy wild. She swung around on me wavin' the pistol like she was gonna shoot me too. I tried to take it away from her, we grappled some, and ... Lord, it went off again and she fell down dead as Dupres. Somebody come runnin' in then, must've been one of the neighbors, and somebody else outside was hollering for the cops, and there I was holding the pistol that killed 'em both. . . ."

"So you panicked and ran."

"Yeah, that's what I done. I threw the gun down and hauled ass outa there. I didn't have no other choice."

"Sure you did. You could've stayed and told the police what you just told me."

He laughed, a hollow sound that morphed suddenly into one of his coughing fits. It took a little while, once the spell subsided, before he was able to go on talking.

"Man, you don't know what it was like down south in them Jim Crow days. Black man in a room with his dead wife and her dead lover and his own pistol smokin' in his hand. You think they'd of believed me? No way. They'd of thrown me in jail, likely beat on me, then put me in prison and the 'lectric chair. I wouldn't of stood a chance in hell. Sure, I ran. Ain't been closer to N'Orleans than five hundred miles since."

"Fifty years of running and hiding," I said. "What'd you do all that time?"

"Stayed out of trouble. Swear that on a Bible too—I ain't never once broke the law, nor even been tempted to. Mr. Good Citizen everywhere I went, one end of the country to the other. Never stayed too long in one place until I come out here to San Fran, been here seven years now. Worked to put food in my belly and clothes on my back, any kind of job I could get where I didn't have to show identification. Pickin' crops. Washin' dishes. Diggin' ditches. Janitor work, handyman work." He ran his hands over the trumpet again, fingered the buttons. "Played and sang on the streets. In back-street bars now and then, when I could get a gig and I was sure wouldn't nobody recognize me or my style. Guess I been lucky."

Yeah, I thought. Lucky.

I said, "And you have no regrets?"

"About runnin' off the way I done? No. My music . . . yeah, some there, but the band I played with in N'Orleans wasn't goin' nowhere and neither was I. Only wrote one song that was any good. Leavin' and losin' my daughter, that's my only regret. But I knew she'd be all right, I knew her auntie'd take care of her."

"You could have at least tried to find out."

"Did once, year or so after. Man I knew, only one I figured I could trust, I got in touch with him and he told me Jolene and Bobby adopted Robin Louise. Asked him to keep an eye on her and he said he would, but went and got himself killed in an accident."

"And you never tried to contact her until now?"

"Thought about it plenty. Come close a dozen times, but I never could nerve myself up to it. Too scared of the po-lice, dyin' in prison for something I never done. Never stopped bein' scared until just a little while ago, when I come to know for sure my time was almost up. Funny thing. Now I ain't scared anymore."

I had been watching him closely as he laid out his story. When you've been lied to as often as I have over the years, by all sorts of people, good and bad, you develop ways to separate the truths from the untruths, a kind of homespun lie detector. Body language: nervous gestures, facial tics, shifty looks or too-direct eye contact. Statements too glib or overly earnest, points glossed over or omitted or contradictory, voice inflections that don't ring true. I'd neither seen nor heard any of those telltale indicators in Moses Arceneaux or his account of what had happened that August night in 1963.

He'd told me the truth, the whole truth. I would have staked my reputation on it.

The man was not a murderer, not a criminal. Just the opposite, in fact—a victim of circumstance, and racial prejudice, and the kind of crippling fear that overrides all other human emotions.

He sat slumped now, as if the conversation had exhausted him. His dark face was beaded with sweat; that and the glow from the pale ceiling bulb gave it an oddly burnished quality, like a casting in bronze.

"We goin' to the po-lice now?" he said.

I'd already made up my mind. Sometimes you have to go with your gut instincts and to hell with rules and regulations and strict adherence to the letter of the law. There is more than one kind of justice in this world, even if it's too little and too late.

"No," I said. "No reason to, Mr. Brown."

". . . Brown?"

"Our client is Charles Anthony Brown. As far as we know, nobody by that name is wanted by the authorities."

I handed him Tamara's printout containing the personal and contact information for Robin Louise Franklin Davis. He looked at it, looked up at me with emotions playing over his face again—gratitude, renewed hope, something that might have been shame.

"Goodbye, Mr. Brown," I said. "Good luck with Robin Louise."

I went to the door. I had my hand on the knob when the trumpet notes sounded behind me, tentative at first, then clear and sharp and now familiar. When I turned back toward him, he lowered the instrument and said, "I ain't played nor sung 'Who You Been Grapplin' With?' in fifty years. Lily's song, wrote it special for her, but it's mine now. Been mine ever since I left N'Orleans."

I didn't say anything. There was nothing left to say.

In a low, age-cracked voice, he began to sing. The melody was the same but the beat was slower, the lyrics slightly different and with different meaning than the ones Tamara had sung for me—a mournful elegy for a tragically broken life that stayed with me long after I left him.

"Who you been grapplin' with, Mo-ses?
"Since back in sixty-three.
"Who you been grapplin' with, Mo-ses?
"I been grapplin' with me.
"Lord, Lard, I been grapplin' with me."

THE END

BILL PRONZINI BIBLIOGRAPHY
(1943–)

Crime Fiction:
The Stalker (Random House, 1971)
Panic! (Random House, 1972)
Snowbound (Putnam's, 1974)
Games (Putnam's, 1976)
Masques (Arbor House, 1981)
The Cambodia File (with Jack Anderson; Doubleday, 1981; mainstream)
Day of the Moon (with Jeffrey Wallmann; Robert Hale, 1983)
The Eye (with John Lutz; Mysterious Press, 1984)
The Lighthouse (with Marcia Muller; St. Martin's, 1987)
With an Extreme Burning (Carroll & Graf, 1994; reprinted as *The Tormentor*, Leisure, 2000)
Blue Lonesome (Walker, 1995)
A Wasteland of Strangers (Walker, 1997)
Nothing But the Night (Walker, 1999)
In an Evil Time (Walker, 2001)
Step to the Graveyard Easy (Walker, 2002)
The Alias Man (Walker, 2004)
The Crimes of Jordan Wise (Walker, 2006)
The Other Side of Silence (Walker, 2008)
The Hidden (Walker, 2010)
The Violated (Bloomsbury, 2017)
The Peaceful Valley Crime Wave (Tor/Forge, 2019; western mystery)

"Nameless Detective" Series:
The Snatch (Random House, 1972)
The Vanished (Random House, 1973)
Undercurrent (Random House, 1973)
Blowback (Random House, 1977)
Twospot (with Colin Wilcox; Putnam's, 1978)
Labyrinth (St. Martin's, 1980)
Hoodwink (St. Martin's, 1981)
Scattershot (St. Martin's, 1982)
Dragonfire (St. Martin's, 1982)
Casefile: The Best of the "Nameless Detective" Stories (St. Martin's, 1983; stories)
Bindlestiff (St. Martin's, 1983)
Quicksilver (St. Martin's, 1984)
Double (with Marcia Muller; St. Martin's, 1984)
Nighshades (St. Martin's, 1984)
Bones (St. Martin's, 1985)
Deadfall (St. Martin's, 1986)
Shackles (St. Martin's, 1988)
Jackpot (Delacorte, 1990)
Breakdown (Delacorte, 1991)
Quarry (Delacorte, 1992)
Epitaphs (Delacorte, 1992)
Demons (Delacorte, 1993)
Hardcase (Delacorte, 1995)
Sentinels (Carroll & Graf, 1996)
Spadework: "Nameless Detective" Stories (Crippen & Landru, 1996; stories)
Illusions (Carroll & Graf, 1997)
Boobytrap (Carroll & Graf, 1998)
Crazybone (Carroll & Graf, 2000)
Bleeders (Carroll & Graf, 2002)
Spook (Carroll & Graf, 2003)
Scenarios: A "Nameless Detective" Casebook (Five-Star, 2003; stories)
Nightcrawlers (Tor/Forge, 2005)
Mourners (Tor/Forge, 2006)
Savages (Tor/Forge, 2007)
Fever (Tor/Forge, 2008)
Schemers (Tor/Forge, 2009)
Betrayers (Tor/Forge, 2010)
Camouflage (Tor/Forge, 2011)
Hellbox (Tor/Forge, 2012)
Kinsmen (Cemetery Dance, 2012; novella)
Femme (Cemetery Dance, 2012; novella)
Nemesis (Tor/Forge, 2013)
Strangers (Tor/Forge, 2014)
Vixen (Tor/Forge, 2015)
Zigzag (Tor/Forge, 2016; stories)
Endgame (Tor/Forge, 2017)

Carpenter and Quincannon Series:

Quincannon (Walker, 1985)
Beyond the Grave (with Marcia Muller; Walker, 1986)
Carpenter and Quincannon (Crippen & Landru, 1998; stories)
Burgade's Crossing (Five-Star, 2003)
Quincannon's Game (Five-Star,

2005)
The Bughouse Affair (with Marcia Muller; Tor/Forge, 2013)
The Spook Lights Affair (with Marcia Muller; Tor/Forge, 2013)
The Body Snatchers Affair (with Marcia Muller; Tor/Forge, 2015)
The Plague of Thieves Affair (with Marcia Muller; Tor/Forge, 2016)
The Dangerous Ladies Affair (with Marcia Muller; Tor/Forge, 2017)
The Bags of Tricks Affair (Tor/Forge, 2018)
The Flimflam Affair (Tor/Forge, 2019)
The Stolen Gold Affair (Tor/Forge, 2020)
The Paradise Affair (Tor/Forge, 2021)

As by Robert Hart Davis
The Pillars of Salt Affair (*The Man from U.N.C.L.E. Magazine*, 1967; novella)
Charlie Chan in The Pawns of Death (with Jeffrey Wallmann; *Charlie Chan's Mystery Magazine*, 1974; reprinted as by Bill Pronzini & Jeffrey Wallman, Wildside Press, 2002)

As by Jack Foxx
The Jade Figurine (Bobbs-Merrill, 1972)
Dead Run (Bobbs-Merrill, 1975)
Freebooty (Bobbs-Merrill, 1976)
Wildfire (Bobbs-Merrill, 1978)

As by Alex Saxon
A Run in Diamonds (Pocket, 1973)

In Collaboration with Barry N. Malzberg
The Running of Beasts (Putnam's, 1976)
Acts of Mercy (Putnam's, 1977)
Night Screams (Playboy Press, 1979)
Prose Bowl (St. Martin's, 1980)
Problems Solved (Crippen & Landru, 2003; stories)
On Account of Darkness and Other SF Stories (2004; stories)

Mystery Short-Story Collections:

Graveyard Plots (St. Martin's, 1985)
Small Felonies (St. Martin's, 1988)
Stacked Deck (Pulphouse, 1991)
Carmody's Run (Dark Harvest, 1992)
Duo (with Marcia Muller; Five-Star, 1998)
Sleuths (Five-Star, 1999)
Night Freight (Leisure, 2000)
Oddments (Five-Star, 2000)
More Oddments (Five-Star, 2001)
Dago Red (Ramble House, 2010)
The Cemetery Man (Perfect Crime, 2014)
A Little Red Book of Murder Stories (Borderlands Press, 2016)
Small Felonies 2 (Stark House Press, 2022)

Western Novels:

The Gallows Land (Walker, 1983)
Starvation Camp (Doubleday, 1984)
The Last Days of Horse-Shy Halloran (M. Evans, 1987)
The Hangings (Walker, 1989)
Firewind (M. Evans, 1989)
Give-A-Damn Jones (Tor/Forge, 2018)

As by William Jeffrey
Duel at Gold Buttes (with Jeffrey Wallmann; Tower, 1981)
Border Fever (with Jeffrey Wallmann; Leisure, 1983)

Western Short-Story Collections:

The Best Western Stories of Bill Pronzini (Ohio University Press, 1990)
All the Long Years: Western Stories (Five-Star, 2001)
Coyote and Quarter-Moon (Five-Star, 2006)
Crucifixion River (with Marcia Muller; Five-Star, 2007)

Non-Fiction Books:

Gun in Cheek (Coward McCann, 1982)
1001 Midnights: The Aficionado's Guide to Mystery and Detective Fiction (with Marcia Muller; Arbor House, 1986)
Son of a Gun in Cheek (Mysterious Press, 1987)
Sixgun in Cheek (Crossover Press, 1997)

www.ingramcontent.com/pod-product-compliance
Lightning Source LLC
LaVergne TN
LVHW021757060526
838201LV00058B/3137